MISTRESS
OF
MY FATE

www.transworldbooks.co.uk

For more information on Hallie Rubenhold and her books, see her
website at www.hallierubenhold.com

MISTRESS
OF
MY FATE

THE CONFESSIONS OF
Henrietta Lightfoot

HALLIE
RUBENHOLD

Doubleday
LONDON · TORONTO · SYDNEY · AUCKLAND · JOHANNESBURG

TRANSWORLD PUBLISHERS
61–63 Uxbridge Road, London W5 5SA
A Random House Group Company
www.rbooks.co.uk

First published in Great Britain
in 2011 by Doubleday
an imprint of Transworld Publishers

A CIP catalogue record for this book
is available from the British Library.

ISBNs 9780385618854 (hb)
9780385618861 (tpb)

Addresses for Random House Group Ltd companies outside the UK
can be found at: www.randomhouse.co.uk
The Random House Group Ltd Reg. No. 954009

The Random House Group Ltd supports the Forest Stewardship
Council® (FSC®), the leading international forest certification organization.
All our titles that are printed on Greenpeace-approved FSC® certified paper
carry the FSC® logo. Our paper procurement policy can be found at
www.rbooks.co.uk/environment

Typeset in 11/15pt Minion by
Falcon Oast Graphic Art Ltd.
Printed and bound in Great Britain by
CPI Mackays, Chatham, ME5 8TD

2 4 6 8 10 9 7 5 3

For my mother, Marsha,
and the many other women in my life
who encouraged me to write fiction.

Chapter 1

My dear reader, how pleased I am that you have purchased this volume! It warms my heart that you have requested it from your bookseller; that he has wrapped it carefully in brown paper and string and handed it to you. How happy I am that you have taken it home with you to read in the quiet of your sitting room or library. Now you may know the truth, and nothing gives me greater relief than this.

I have no doubt that many of you have come to this work out of curiosity. You have heard so much about me, most of which is pure fabrication. Now that you have torn off the packaging and cut the pages, you can begin to read my story and to know who I am. You see, for some time a relation of mine has been attempting to discredit me in the most reprehensible manner. I have no doubt that he too sent a servant to his local bookseller to collect a copy of this work. As you read this, so does he. His eyes are scanning every word, searching every syllable. He is among you, taking in my story alongside you.

To him I say, Lord Dennington, do not think I have written these memoirs because of you. Do not flatter yourself. You are only part of the reason. There is much I need to say on the matter of my life and I have grown weary of your slander. Whomever you have hired to do your disgraceful deeds, whether it is those shameless scribes who will print anything for a crust of bread, or that unscrupulous little spy you planted among my loyal staff, they are not capable of telling the truth.

7

You pay them and so they will say anything. Certainly, a man who has seen as much of the world as you should know this.

Now it is my turn to pick up my pen, to clear my name, to scrub away the lies with which you have stained it. I must commend you for the amusement you have provided for me and my friends. We laughed heartily at your accusations – that I had been a circus performer, that I worked as a charlatan attempting to revive the dead and, worse still, that I murdered a ship of sailors. Really, this is quite absurd.

No, sir, as you will come to realize, these memoirs are not written solely because of you. I write because it is time for the public to hear my story, because for as long as I have been called Mrs Lightfoot, great men and women have asked for it. The world wants my confession yet, until this moment, I refused to honour that request. I wished to keep my life and my adventures quiet. Like you, my lord, discretion was one of the virtues I was taught as a child.

As for my other readers, whose sensibilities I wish to protect, I feel the need to issue a warning. In these pages I set out to tell the absolute truth. If you take offence easily, if you are faint of heart or of a delicate nature, there is much here that you are likely to find objectionable. It is necessary for you to understand why I have, in the past, refused to discuss these private matters. My story is not an easy one to relay, nor is it likely to be short.

I shall begin by telling you what I remember most vividly: an early morning in late October. I was but seventeen and so unprepared for the world that I hardly knew how to dress myself, let alone judge character or transact the business of ordinary life. I sat on the floor of my bed-chamber in the darkness, entirely unaware of the hour. There was no fire in my grate, nor would there be anyone coming to light it. I shivered, from both the cold and a complete terror of that which I knew I must do.

For most of the night I had sobbed. I had lain outstretched on the floor, like a condemned prisoner, unable to move or think, able only to ache. My life as I had known it was now about to end. But, as any good Christian will tell you, with death there also comes resurrection and the possibility of a better existence elsewhere. I knew this in my heart, and that rebirth was the sole path open to me. I had only to muster the courage to grab for it and, in doing so, let go of all that tied me to the girl I had been.

So I did this, while the moon threw its dim cast across my window sill. I worked without so much as a candle to guide me, rummaging through the most essential of my belongings: linens, stockings, skirts, a petticoat and, most importantly, the few small items of value that I as a young lady owned. Of all a woman's possessions, jewels will get her the furthest and mine, on several occasions, have saved me from experiencing the grossest of depredations. At the time, I had but two trinkets: a gold and pearl cross, which I always wore upon my person; and a pair of simple pearl eardrops. I was too young for diamonds. Those are for married women, and in any case, owing to my precarious position within their family, Lord and Lady Stavourley saw no need to adorn me so lavishly.

I wrapped my bundle as a servant would, in a sheet. I had never before carried my own belongings and I did not even know how to tie them up securely. However, I found that soft packet offered me some comfort as I clutched it to my breast. It calmed my trembling.

I dressed for the road, but not without some struggle, sliding on my sturdiest shoes and fumbling with the buttons of my grey riding habit. Around my shoulders I threw my blue cape, the hood of which rested atop my black hat. I hoped to look respectable for my journey without drawing attention to myself. In truth, I knew that most people would be able to guess my circumstances. It is not usual to see a well-dressed young lady with spotless white gloves and a quivering expression travelling unchaperoned.

It was not until after I had attired myself and gathered my belongings that my mind, like a lamp, flickered out. My lungs and heart and legs took over. My breathing was so harsh that I feared all of Melmouth could hear my gasps as I carefully navigated the treacherous steps of the back stairs. The chill within the stony walls turned my breath to steam. I was like an animal, clambering through the darkness. I stole through the narrow corridor near the kitchens, passing by the doors of servants, still sunk deeply into their warm straw mattresses. In an hour, the first light of morning would wake them and, with so many pairs of eyes on guard, my flight would have been impossible. You must understand that, by then, they hated me. They would have set upon me like a pack of slavering dogs.

Aware of this, I picked my way carefully along the row of doors. To my ear, the gentle clack of my heels reverberated like cannon fire. How I wished to bolt when I saw that window above the entryway, illuminating the porthole to my release! Instead, I continued to creep nearer and nearer, until my hands rested on the entry door. At last, with a firm push, I passed out of one life and into the next.

I can understand why infants scream when they come into our world. The strain of birth is enormous. The cold that greets them foretells what awaits them in life. It is as if they know from their very first breath that the warmth of the womb and all of its comforts have been lost for ever.

When I stepped over the threshold of Melmouth House and into the sprawl of parkland, I bawled as if my heart would break. The sobs came with such force that I feared they would echo through the park and wake the entire household. I had to stop my mouth with my fist. As I ran, scrambling, tripping across the frost-crusted grass, I howled, unable to contain my anguish. I have never known such heart-tearing pain as I did that morning, when I cut the cord that held me to my only true parent.

My legs knew where they carried me: to the perimeter wall. I would not risk passing the gatehouses, or scaling the heights to my freedom. There was one break, filled in loosely with stones, where an old door had been. Poachers were known to slip through it, their sacks dripping with Lord Stavourley's grouse and rabbits. I had seen the spot several months earlier, but finding it in the dark was to prove difficult.

I tumbled through the park, startling sleepy deer, dislodging bats and rousing a variety of creatures that squealed and scampered off at my approach. I tore through the copse with an urgency that they alone might have understood. Although I knew every path and trail, every pool and corner of Melmouth, I was not so familiar with it while it lay beneath the curtain of night. With my eyes ablaze with tears, I travelled in a state of near blindness, sinking in mud to my shins, my cape hemmed with filth and fallen leaves, my stockings already sodden and stained beyond laundering. It took some scrambling for me to find the precise point in the wall. By then the sky was softening into the deep blue of dawn. I pushed and kicked with all my might. Eventually, three of the stones fell away and I was able to squeeze myself, mouse-like, through the opening.

I emerged upon the road to Norwich and stood there, blinking into the stillness. I had no way of knowing which direction I should turn. I cannot say whether it was fortune or instinct that led me, but the route I chose was the correct one. Although I had given up running, my pace remained steady and brisk. My heart continued to thump like a battalion's drummer. It was nearly three miles to the White Hart Inn, where the mail coach called. I had not an inkling when it arrived, but knew I had to try my luck.

Ah, was that a sigh of relief I heard from you? You think I have made a successful escape? Let me remind you, my friends, before you become certain that the worst was behind me, that any obstacle might have thwarted my progress. I might have been discovered by the steward or his men; I might have met with an accident. By mid-morning my absence would have been discovered and the entire house would have been thrown into turmoil. I realize now that I must have caused Lord Stavourley a great deal of anguish. The images that entered his mind would have been dreadful. I am certain he thought I had taken my own life, that his men were likely to find me at the bottom of the lake or hanging from a tree in the park. For this, I am truly sorry.

The possibility that I would be found out and marched back to Melmouth was ever-present. I had no idea what I might find on my arrival at the inn, or how long I might have to wait for my transport-ation. I knew only that the longer I remained in one place, the more likely I was to be found. Until I boarded the coach, there would also be the possibility I would lose my nerve. At any time, the same legs that had carried me from Melmouth in a thoughtless panic might suddenly decide to turn me around and take me home. I do sometimes marvel that I had the courage to continue onward to the White Hart through the empty, half-lit woods.

Although my childhood had been a sheltered one, I had been fortunate enough to have seen some of the scenery beyond Melmouth's walls. On the occasions I had been taken to London or to Bath, or to visit Lady Stavourley's relations, our coach had set out upon the road on which I presently walked. As a girl, the sign of the White Hart had impressed me greatly. A large picture of a downy-coloured creature bearing a wide rack of antlers swung above the road. I had spent many journeys imagining what it would be like to tame and ride such a splendid animal. In my daydreams I would approach him with soft, beckoning words. He would bend his head and permit me to stroke his coat and to tie red silk ribbons on to his antlers.

As I came round the final bend in the road, the buck on the inn's signboard roused my tears. My mind swirled with memories and confusion. I wept for myself, for the innocent girl whom I would never see again.

As it was mid-morning by the time I arrived, the White Hart bustled with activity. Its yard clattered with the sound of beasts and wheels. Outside, chickens clucked and pecked, scattering at the approach of each pair of boots or wooden clogs. I saw no evidence of the mail coach or any indication of when it might arrive. My mind was a complete muddle. What was I to do? It was only then that I realized how little I knew about my proposed method of escape. I did not even know how much a fare would cost me, or if there was a direct route to my destination.

I held back from this hive of activity, attempting to gather my wits. I paced this way and that like a stray dog, and stanched my streaming nose and eyes against my sleeve.

You must understand, it all seemed desperately overwhelming. The tavern itself terrified me. I had never been alone in such a place. Even in daylight, these establishments could be loud and rough, filled with mud and men in heavy boots, raucous shouts and lewd behaviour. In the past, when I had travelled with Lord or Lady Stavourley, a private room upstairs would always be taken, so that our sensibilities would not be offended. Now, without a protector, without a footman or a servant, what would I do in such a place? I wished more than anything to avoid going inside, but my feet were so sore from the road and the damp had seeped through my skirts and given me a terrible chill. I looked longingly at the warm light of the fire through dusty, bevelled windows. Eventually, I steadied my nerve and approached the entry.

Inside, the dark taproom with its low ceiling seemed less threatening than I had predicted. Its patrons sat contentedly around the hearths murmuring to each other, sucking on pipes and mugs of stout. Each pair of eyes was raised as I slipped through the door. I kept my hood over my head and lowered my gaze. I am not certain which posed a greater danger to me at the time: that I should be accosted by some malevolent stranger or that I should be recognized by a well-intentioned acquaintance.

Like a skulking thief, I took myself to the furthest corner. It did not matter to me that it was beyond the cast of the fire. I wished only to remain hidden from view as I rested my throbbing feet. My large left toe and heel were beginning to blister. The state of my skirts, crusted with mud, was nothing short of disgraceful.

I ordered some small beer from the pot-boy in his leather apron, and consumed it so greedily that he stared in disbelief. I doubt he had ever seen a young lady choke down her drink. He refilled my tankard and brought me some bread, which I tore into like a beggar. This meagre meal cost me a penny ha'penny. It was frightening to me how quickly money could be spent. I had only a few coins in my purse, which was all the means I possessed in the world.

Until that moment, I had never before considered the cost of ordinary items. All my earthly needs had always been seen to. There was never any question of expense. I had not imagined that small beer would cost me a ha'penny and a loaf, double that amount. As I fingered my remaining coins, I worried that I might not have enough to complete my journey. My fare would cost a sum, as would any meals. My heart began to pick up pace again. I felt the tiny pearl cross around my neck and thought about the other trinkets in my bundle. What were they worth? One question led to another and, once more, I began to quiver with anxiety.

I had in total £6 2s. 9d. It was not an inconsiderable sum. Of course,

I only discovered this by laying out each of the coins and counting them several times. Imagine that! I can scarcely believe my own stupidity. I am only grateful that country folk are an honest sort. In London or Paris or Rome, I might have been wrestled to the ground and divested of my entire life's savings. Where would that have left me, I wonder.

It seemed an eternity before the arrival of the mail coach was announced. At the sound of the coach horn my stomach and heart lurched. I sprang to my feet. This was to be it, the chariot that would spirit me away.

'To Cambridge and all stops to London,' cried the innkeeper through his taproom. Just then, the thunder and rattle of the charging team with its heavy wagon shook the walls as it pulled to a halt.

I walked briskly to the yard, where the lumbering black-and-red-painted carriage sat, burdened with boxes and human cargo. Inside the compartment, a woman and two neat but plainly dressed men peered at me through the windows. When I saw that I was to be the sole passenger joining at the White Hart, I grew quite uneasy and crept awkwardly around the horses. The guard, who had jumped from his box atop the carriage, held his watch in one hand while bellowing commands to the inn's staff. They scurried around him with buckets and tankards, sacks and harnesses. He looked at me sternly and I cowered.

'Please, sir,' I whispered meekly, 'I am for Gloucestershire. What is the fare?'

'Gloucestershire? Gloucestershire?' he boomed. 'Miss, this coach will take you as far west as Royston and then, at the Bull Inn, you must board a stage for points beyond.'

I stared at him, as if struck dumb.

'The fare for Royston is five pounds and three shillings,' said he, reaching for the ledger in his waistcoat pocket. Like a simpleton, I held out my purse to him. He must have thought me an idiot. In truth, I was little more capable than one. He took £5 3s. 2d. from me, smiling as he did it. I may have been a blockhead, but he was a rogue!

Hugging my bundle to me, I mounted the step into the sprung carriage. One of the gentlemen inside offered his assistance by tugging my hand. I was hardly seated for more than a moment in the close, box-like compartment when the coach jerked forward and began its hurried progress.

I knew I would begin to weep if I looked through the back window. I resisted the urge at first, and then, as foolishly as Lot's wife, I turned my gaze over my shoulder. In the wake of our departure, the sign of the White Hart rocked back and forth, its sleek stag waving to me in a final salute. I pursed my face tightly and forced back the tears. The cabin in which we travelled was exceptionally snug and I had convinced myself that sobbing before this audience would only have drawn attention to my plight. In truth, it was folly of me to think I might escape inspection in such an enclosed space. I was no better than a jarred specimen, and as soon as I had assumed my seat, I felt the questioning eyes of my fellow passengers upon me. You see, everything about my person looked most suspicious.

Although it is no longer the case in the current age, there once was a time when there were only two reasons why a politely attired young lady would be travelling unaccompanied and in an obvious state of distress. The first of these was that she was a lady's maid who had run off, perhaps with some of her mistress's possessions. The second was that she was a girl of a good family who had eloped on a promise of marriage. I could tell from the curious looks of those surrounding me that they were deciding in which category I belonged. In truth, I belonged in neither and my circumstances were beyond any that those in the rattling coach could imagine.

I had not prepared myself to be the subject of such scrutiny, nor was I in a fit state to contend with enquiries or even idle conversation. Ashamed of my bedraggled appearance, I wished for nothing more than to make my passage in silence. I therefore kept my head down and my frightened features hidden beneath the shade of my hat. As you might imagine, my unwillingness to engage with any of those within the cabin only excited their interest further. This held especially true for the smirking lady sitting directly opposite me. I could tell from the manner in which she craned her neck and peered beneath the brim of my hat that she was determined to have my story from me. She would prise me open like an oyster. I would not meet her gaze, but this did not deter her. Her dark eyes fixed on me, glowing like two pieces of jet beneath her enormous, beribboned hat. For some time, she attempted to draw my notice, fidgeting, dropping her embroidery and harrumphing in great, proud breaths. Unable to bear it any longer, she finally exclaimed, 'My, how bad the road is! I do not recall it being so full of rocks and potholes, do you not agree, miss?'

I looked up, surprised by her address.

'La, but it is not as bad as the stagecoach . . .' she continued, directing her comments to her husband, who slumbered beside her. 'No, the stage is not for those who value manners'.

Oh, this woman was a clever one. She knew precisely how to heighten my sense of alarm; after all, I was to board the stage for the next leg of my journey.

'Please, madam,' I said timorously, 'why is this so? I am to join the stage at Royston.'

'My dear miss, I take it that you have not before travelled upon the stage?' she asked, arching an eyebrow and leaning towards me the better to examine my features. I turned from her quickly but her eyes clung to me like burrs.

'No, I have not.'

'Do avoid it if you can. Find some other means of travelling to your destination. If it is possible, hire a post chaise. The stage is filled with none but ruffians and thieves. The coachman will almost certainly be drunk. You are sure to be robbed or to have your pocket picked.'

'Oh,' I uttered, a look of dread overcoming my expression. The threat of yet more danger seemed almost too much to bear. I felt my throat tighten.

Until that moment the gentleman sitting beside my interrogator had been entirely engrossed in a book, and had seemed the least curious among the passengers. But he must have sensed my discomfort, for now he too was staring at my wide-eyed face.

'Poppycock,' he stated firmly. 'It is true, the mail provides a better service, but you are as likely to meet with ruffians in this coach as you are upon the stage.'

He then looked at me. 'I take it that your friends will protect you from such dangers, miss.'

I knew not how to respond to this.

The gentleman placed his book upon his lap and looked at me sternly. 'You do not mean to tell us, miss, that you travel unaccompanied?'

It was the one question the entire cabin had wished to ask me from the outset. All eyes were upon me, even those of my interrogator's sleepy husband.

What a child I was! In all of that time, as I had walked the route to the White Hart, as I had waited for the arrival of the coach, as I had sat bouncing against its leather seat, it had never occurred to me to concoct a plausible story to explain my position. I was not, nor have I ever been, a natural liar.

'No . . .' I stuttered, 'I am to meet a friend . . . of my family . . .'

'At Royston?' enquired the woman opposite.

'In Gloucestershire.'

'And Gloucestershire is your destination?' asked the bookish gentleman.

A knowing smile began to creep across my female interrogator's mouth. 'How curious that you should be all alone, that your friends should send you off on such a journey unaccompanied. And what of your family?'

'I have none.' I spoke boldly. That was the truth, in part.

'And so you are very much alone in the world,' said the gentleman, with a softness in his tone.

'I am, sir.'

Neither could formulate a satisfactory response to that.

'Well then,' began the gentleman, 'I shall see to it that you arrive safely at Royston and that you are not troubled by ruffians and pickpockets along the way. My name is Fortune,' said he, holding out his hand for me to shake it.

I must say that I was relieved, however temporarily, to have the protection of Mr Fortune, who appeared to me an honest, sensible man. Close in age to Lord Stavourley, he was a solicitor to some families in

Norfolk and was en route to London to attend to business on their behalf. Although he resumed reading his copy of *Tristram Shandy* and said little more to me, there seemed something avuncular in his manner. Every so often he looked up from his book and gave me a genteel nod.

The journey by mail coach was swift and Cambridge seemed not as far as I had believed. Comforted by my new friend's presence, I occupied myself with a view of the East Anglian landscape and watched the Gothic tops of the colleges rising from the flat, marshy horizon. Our pace began to slacken as we drew nearer and joined with an eddying flow of freight, cattle and carts, steadily pushing their way through the network of narrow cobbled streets. Eventually we came to a stop under the sign of the Eagle Inn. Here, my fashionably adorned inquisitor and her husband disembarked. Before she flounced from the vehicle, she permitted herself a last lingering look at me. 'I shan't tell your secret, Miss Runaway,' she leaned in and whispered, her face aglow with furtive pleasure. I recoiled, ashamed that I should have been the cause of such entertainment and speculation. To her I must have seemed like a character from a romantic novel, though I felt anything but that.

As the mail was running to a timetable, we had only a brief spell at the Eagle, enough time to change horses and gather a further sack of post. I had believed that my protector, Mr Fortune, and I would be the only two in the carriage, until the final moments before departure when a boisterous party of young men clambered aboard. There were three in total and they heaved themselves on to the seats with laughter and groans. They smelled powerfully of drink, and I dare say that it took them hardly the blink of an eye to notice my presence. The door was slammed shut on the tightly packed compartment. Three foxes could not have felt more at home in a hen house.

I did not venture raising my eyes to them. As they were in high spirits, I wished more than anything not to draw their attention. However, I soon found that to be unavoidable.

'Good day, miss,' said the young man next to me with an exaggerated, unsteady motion. 'I am Thomas Masham, and these are my friends. I shall not trouble you with their names.' The cabin erupted into laughter.

'And whom do I have the pleasure of addressing?' he continued.

I spoke quietly: 'I am Miss Ingerton.'

'How do you do, miss?'

'Please, sir, I am not well and do not care much for conversation at present,' I replied, shrinking away from him.

'Perhaps you would like a drink to ease you,' said the fattest of the three, offering me a flask he had stowed in his coat pocket.

'No, thank you, sir.' My audience was disappointed that I would not engage with them.

'You claim to be unwell, miss, but how could that be so when you have such a healthy blush upon your cheek. Your face is so round and pretty and your eyes so bright. I would say you are in fine health,' teased Thomas Masham.

I looked away.

'Or perhaps it is my presence that makes you blush . . .'

His friends chuckled once more.

'I do think she is in love, Tom!' declared the auburn-haired gentleman across from me.

'Ah, Dick,' he sighed theatrically, 'I fear the longer I sit beside Miss Ingerton the more attached to her I become. Madam, I have no doubt that by the time we arrive in London you will have agreed to be my wife, or else offer to perform the services of one.'

'That, sir, is quite enough!' barked Mr Fortune, springing to my rescue.

The young men reacted sharply. Tom bowed his head. 'My apologies to you, sir, I did not think that she was—'

'No, sir, you did not think at all and you have greatly offended Miss Ingerton.'

'My apologies to you, madam,' said my assailant, 'for my baseness.' He then locked his gaze on me in a hot, predatory manner. 'You see, Miss Ingerton, I am very much in drink, and am no better than a beast. My passions have been raised and I mean to slake them in London.' He finished his sentence with a loud belch.

'Sir!' exclaimed Mr Fortune, before pulling down the window. 'Guard!' he called out. 'Stop the coach at once!'

The galloping horses were immediately reined in and the flying vehicle pulled to a halt. Mr Fortune shouted from the window, 'There is a gentleman here unfit to ride inside and I beg you to take him on top with you. He is in need of air.' With that, the odious Thomas Masham was ushered on to the roof to sit alongside the guard and his sobering blunderbuss.

With their ringleader removed, Tom Masham's fellows held their tongues and stared at their shoes. Pleased to have played the role of a knight errant, Mr Fortune sat erect and smug the rest of the way to Royston. I was truly grateful for his assistance, but the reassurance I had felt in his company would be temporary. From the moment I stepped out of the coach, I would be left open to all sorts of approaches and possible indignities. I began to fret about what I might find upon the stagecoach and the difficult characters I might encounter.

The day was now disappearing. Along the final stretch of road the sun had faded into deep, rich shadows. I had not progressed as far as I had naively hoped and night would bring a further round of difficulties and pitfalls. Mr Fortune must have noticed my worried expression as I caught my first sight of the sign of the Bull. The coach pulled through the arch and into the inn yard but I could only look at the light-filled windows with trepidation.

'Royston!' announced the guard. I could not move. Something held me back. Perhaps it was the thought of entering yet another tavern alone, or the dizzying realization that, beyond this point, I had no further instructions. I did not know which stage to take or when it would arrive. I might have to spend the night here, amidst the noise and fray and the strangers sodden in drink.

'Oh . . .' I spoke to myself, clutching my bundle, tears welling in my eyes.

'Miss Ingerton, this is Royston. You are due to disembark,' said Mr Fortune, stepping out of the coach to assist me. 'But your face, it is entirely white!' he exclaimed with genuine concern, taking my hand. 'No. No. This will not do,' and with that, Mr Fortune ordered his box to be taken off the carriage. 'I cannot leave you here in such a condition.'

I regarded him with gratitude.

As he escorted me away, I could hear Tom Masham muttering something rude to his associates about my protector. I was pleased I could not make out his precise words, though it might have served me well to listen.

The relief I felt at hearing their vehicle depart was great, nearly as great as my reassurance at being offered Mr Fortune's arm.

Oh reader, I know what you are thinking. You are wondering how I could possibly have entered an inn at night with an unknown gentleman. Yes, here too I must pause and marvel at my youthful innocence. I am also reminded of that saying: that one goes out of the frying pan and into the fire. Did I not think myself in some danger? To be truthful, I suppose the possibility of danger did briefly fly through my feather head, but Mr Fortune seemed to be such an honourable, Christian man. He was genteel and sensible. He seemed no different from any other gentleman I had ever known while living at Melmouth. (You, Lord Dennington, I discount.)

Mr Fortune was a paragon of chivalry. He immediately ordered me a set of rooms where I could dine in private and later sleep undisturbed. He made all the necessary arrangements for my journey on the stage to Oxford the following day. He ordered that a roaring fire be lit in the hearths of both rooms. 'I would not have you take ill from the cold,' he said to me with a kind look. I watched as the wood was piled into the fireplace, Mr Fortune tipping the boy for each additional log he laid on to the growing pyre. By the time I sat down to dine the room was radiant with heat. It was then that my gallant protector made a motion to leave, claiming that he would take his meal downstairs in the public room.

'Oh, but you must join me here,' I said innocently to him, and to his credit, he offered several false protests before taking a seat at my table.

We dined well. In fact, I had not eaten so richly in days, perhaps weeks. He ordered the finest fare that the Bull's kitchens could provide: quails with plum sauce, soused hare, roast capon, suet pudding, fritters and syllabub. Mr Fortune was a convivial man, who seemed most at home behind a plate heaped with food. The more wine he drank, the ruddier his cheeks glowed. His conversation, which revolved around

London gossip and the races at Newmarket, was so entertaining that he succeeded in making me forget for a short while the pain that weighted down my heart. I was so charmed by his good company and manners that I was entirely unprepared for what transpired next.

It had grown late and the large meal, wine and heated surroundings had caused me to become sleepy. I expressed my wish to retire, whereupon Mr Fortune rose to his feet and graciously assisted me from my chair. I was not yet standing upright when I was grabbed fiercely, spun around and pinned to his chest. I screamed and struggled. 'Release me!' I demanded.

Retaining his hold on my wrist, he glared at me, panting. 'Whatever do you mean by this?' he snapped, obviously confused. 'You have accepted my hospitality, even encouraged my advances, and yet you refuse me?'

'No, sir, I did not mean . . .'

'What, madam? You travel alone and have no protector. What would you have me think? You are an innocent miss?' he leered. Then his eyes hardened on me. 'Now you may give up this game and we shall get on with the deed.'

I shook my head furiously in utter disbelief. The shock of his sudden transformation bewildered me. I was speechless at his suggestion and terrified of what he might try. I began to panic. Twisting with all my might, I managed to pull free from his grasp and tear through the doorway into the adjoining room. How grateful I was for the bolt upon the door! It does not bear imagining what would have happened had there not been one. So many poor wretches have seen their ruin in such rooms, all on account of an innkeeper who would not pay the extra expense for a small bar of metal.

Dear Mr Fortune. The man who had once been my saviour and my only friend was now my persecutor. He pounded upon the door, demanding that I open it at once. Inside the Bull's most costly bedchamber, I trembled. The door bounced on its hinges with each angry impact of his fists. Frightened that it might not hold against his battery, I dragged a tallboy with all my might until it rested against the entryway. Mr Fortune continued to hammer away, determined to claim his prize.

I backed myself towards the canopied bed and sat frozen upon it. This had been but my first day from Melmouth. What else might I have to endure? I lived on the faintest hope of what I might find when I arrived in Gloucestershire. But at that very moment I had nothing; no family, no home, no love, no prospects, not even a protector. The bleakness of my situation broke over me like a wave and I collapsed under it in a torrent of miserable sobs.

Chapter 2

Now, dear reader, you have followed me this far but I sense your confusion. I suspect you are wondering how a young lady of good breeding came to find herself in such desperate circumstances. I do not simply mean my precarious position at the Bull, but the entire sequence of events that led up to this moment. Forgive me. There is much still that requires explanation. As you will understand, my past is most difficult to unravel.

I must confess, for much of the early part of my life, I had no real knowledge of my history. It was never made clear to me how precisely I came to live with Edwin Ingerton, the 4th Earl of Stavourley, and his family at Melmouth House. Each of the nursemaids who reared me delighted in relaying their own version of events.

'You had been deposited at the Foundling Hospital before his lordship rescued you,' said one.

'You arrived on the steps like Moses in a basket,' said another.

I might well have appeared on a mountaintop. No one could agree on any one story. However, for those who knew about the Earl's younger brother, the reasons why his lordship had taken me in were self-evident.

As it was later explained to me, I was the daughter of the Honourable William Ingerton, a wastrel who had eloped with my mother, Miss Ridgemount, a child-bride of fifteen. The young Mrs Ingerton lasted no more than nine months. Having borne me, she promptly expired of puerperal fever. My father, inconsolable at the loss of his wife, took a packet to France, which went down in a storm. It was a small stroke of fortune that William Ingerton did not have an appetite for fatherhood and had left me behind in the care of a wet nurse. However, it was less fortunate that long before my birth he had squandered his entire fortune at the gaming tables of his London club. When my uncle Stavourley brought me into his care, I was just two years old and without so much as a halfpenny to my name.

'As blood, his lordship had a family obligation to maintain you,' explained my governess, 'but it was uncertain whether you would benefit more under his roof or that of another. Being a man of learning, he spent much time cogitating on the benefits that might be had by either option.' You see, he already had one daughter, Lady Catherine Ingerton, who was no more than a year and a half my senior.

'The matter was decided quite suddenly. The Earl had gone for a brisk ride one morning and upon his return, without so much as removing his boots, came stamping up the stairs, through the long gallery and into his library. He pulled from his shelves various works by Monsieur Rousseau on the education of girls. He ordered a dish of chocolate to be brought to him and was not seen again until dinner was announced.'

'What did he do in all that time?' I asked in my little voice.

'My dear,' said my governess, 'he was concerning himself with you!'

I did not then make the connection between a pile of books by a Frenchman and my own fate, but it seemed Lord Stavourley wished to turn the opportunity of my arrival into a philosophical experiment.

It was decided that I was to be raised alongside my cousins, not only Lady Catherine, but later the two younger boys: his lordship's heir, Robert, the future Marquess of Dennington, and his brother, Master Edwin. They were to be my upstanding examples. Their noble conduct would guide my actions. I was to receive an education no different from theirs and to be schooled by the same tutors and governesses. Along with Lady Catherine I would learn French, some Latin, mathematics, geography, a bit of history, music, painting, dancing and how to write in a good hand. My uncle wished us to enjoy all the freedoms of the 'noble savage'; we would be at liberty to run and tumble. The servants would assist us in maintaining a small kitchen garden of our own in which we might sow herbs, lettuces and legumes. We would be taught to fish and tend the cows in the dairy. The country air would embolden our health and make us robust. As much as it was possible, we would be kept at Melmouth, far from the diseases of London.

Under these ideal conditions, Lady Catherine would take me to her heart. Our lives would grow together, twining like two vines. We would be as sisters: a pair of straw-haired girls with eyes the colour of blue porcelain. Each night we were laid in our shared bed, and to look at us, slumbering beneath our nightcaps, curled against one another, we seemed the perfect portrait of affection. This was how his lordship intended it to be, so that in later life, I would continue to be looked after.

From the very outset, I was designed to be Lady Catherine's companion, that uncomfortable role assumed by a penniless female relation; the grateful toad-eater, the quietly tolerated impoverished cousin, part lady's maid, part genteel guest, who without a fortune of her own would be unlikely to marry. It was not that this was such a poor path: after all, what else might a lady of polite upbringing and no income do? She cannot have a profession, she cannot go to sea; perhaps she might live by her pen, but that never offers any real reward. No, the problem did not lie in the scheme itself, but rather in his lordship's failure to consider the part his wife would play in it.

With all due respect, my aunt, Susannah, Lady Stavourley, was no better than a child herself. She had been an heiress and indulged extravagantly throughout her youth. I have heard it said that before she was brought to bed of Lady Catherine, she was merry and impish in her ways. Her cheeks bore a bright flush, and she ate with an appetite so hearty that her bosom swelled against the top of her bodice. But this was not the lady I knew as my aunt. For as long as I remember, Lady Stavourley appeared as if she had been wrung of life. Her eyes were hollow and her face always bereft of its glow. While most women applied powders and creams to achieve such a wan look, my aunt wore it naturally. Her once round frame withered into an assembly of spindles. It was as if in bearing her daughter she had pushed out all of her passion.

Where once her wealth had provided her with a sense of entitlement, now her delicate constitution justified the gratification of her every whim. She went wherever she could find a warm room and a sofa. She did not ride or exert herself and her pleasures became quiet ones. My uncle commanded that whatever his wife desired be brought to her without question. While he imagined this to be porcelain and hats, it was in fact something far dearer. Chief among her amusements was Lady Catherine, who became as much a fixture at her mother's side as her two Pekinese. Every morning, her little girl was brought down to her apartments to pass most of the day in her company. While it is no bad thing for a child to be so adored by its mother, the Countess indulged her daughter above her other children. As my aunt entertained guests, Lady Catherine sat upon her lap, making impertinent remarks and tipping over teacups. Her mother laughed and clapped her hands, but her acquaintances smiled weakly. They knew better than to scold. I had heard that one well-meaning friend, who had seen quite enough of Lady Catherine's behaviour, had written a letter to Lady Stavourley, warning her that if she did not see fit to correct the deficits in her daughter's character, she would ruin her entirely! Needless to say, Lady Catherine's mamma terminated that association.

Not a word could be said to contradict either mother or daughter. My cousin was free to do as she pleased, and sought only to please herself and her mamma. Her lessons were almost entirely neglected. Lady Stavourley taught her to read and figure, and how to write letters in a pretty hand. She had no mind for French, but for the odd phrase, and mostly where it related to dancing. She did not attend lessons with me and her two younger brothers in our schoolroom; instead my aunt had the music tutor come especially to her drawing room and instruct Lady Catherine there, upon a specially fashioned white and gold fortepiano. There was nothing my cousin loved more than to play and sing and to be adored.

As you might imagine, this sort of upbringing did not make for an agreeable young lady. This is not to say that my cousin was never gentle and sweet, but rather that she viewed herself as superior to the others in the nursery. She snapped and shouted and could be capable of great mischief. While my uncle had envisaged us joining hands and frolicking like fairies in the wooded glades of Melmouth Park, a truer scene would be of Lady Catherine with a horsewhip, her eyes glinting like two shards of glass as she hunted down her victims, who sobbed and cowered under their beds. Her moods were treacherous: at one moment she might rage with a red face, clawing and biting anyone who dared approach her, and then at the next ignore us altogether. No one could account for the irregularity of her temper. As a child, the nurses believed she had suffered terribly from colic, but as this did not subside when she matured, Lord and Lady Stavourley began to grow concerned. A physician was called to examine her. He came into the nursery, studied her plates of food and the contents of her chamber pot, and looked into her eyes.

'He says it is an imbalance of the humours,' repeated Sally Pickering, the most junior of the nurses, who had a great fondness for Lady Catherine.

'Imbalance of the humours?' snorted Miss Jones, who tended the boys. 'Does he not know she's as spoilt as an old pail of milk? That child should be thrashed, not petted like the Countess's dogs.'

For all the trouble they cause, there is no one in a household who sees a situation more clearly than its servants. Those at Melmouth knew precisely what, or rather who, had made the Earl's daughter as she was. But Lady Stavourley would have none of it.

It must be said that my cousin's difficult disposition and her mother's favouritism made my existence at Melmouth notably awkward. Our household was very much a divided one. My uncle's life revolved almost exclusively around politics and his dedication to the causes of the Whig party. My aunt's life was devoted to social engagements and to petting her daughter. I was excluded from both worlds equally. In truth, I felt very much like a shoe without a mate. I rattled about Melmouth, no one knowing precisely what was to be done with me. When not under the guidance of a tutor, I was left to run free with the unruly, tousle-haired Lord Dennington and gentle, pretty-faced Master Edwin. We swung sticks and barrelled through the fields like Mohawks, until my governess began to correct my unbridled behaviour and the boys were dispatched to Eton.

I learned when very young how to make my own entertainment. I pulled books from the shelves of my uncle's library, that long, light-filled gallery of brown volumes, and sat at the round table at its centre, languorously turning pages, admiring engravings of the Forum ruins or the temples at Paestum. When slightly older, I began to render my own scenes under the direction of a drawing master, Mr Dance, whom my uncle had brought from London. This I enjoyed more than any other activity. Indeed, as my tutor observed, I seemed to take naturally to chalk and later to watercolour. I had what he called 'an exceptional talent', not usually seen in girls my age. There was much crowing about this; Mr Dance praising me effusively before my uncle, displaying to him some sketches I had taken of Melmouth House and a few pastel drawings of the landscape. 'Her trees, my lord, I think you will agree have the light touch of Mr Gainsborough.' My uncle examined the pictures while I, a knot of nerves and modesty, stared at my feet.

'Henrietta, my dear, you show great promise,' he congratulated me. His words were proud ones. I was not often the recipient of either approval or even attention, and to have deserved this acclaim felt to me like a remarkable achievement. If anything, that odd occasion of praise, that unusual incident when my uncle came upon me drawing in the library and took an interest in my work, encouraged me to take an interest in him.

I cannot recall a time when I did not occupy myself by tiptoeing through the halls and chambers of Melmouth, chasing a mouse down a corridor, or frightening myself by staring into the blank eyes of marble statues. Like any child with a curious nature, I listened at doorways to the conversation of adults and then scurried away at the approach of footsteps. My uncle's masculine world had always appeared to me quite strange and alien. The deep boom of gentlemen's voices that echoed from the drawing rooms and study, which burst forth from the dining room in great huzzahs – 'To His Highness, the Prince of Wales!', 'To the Buff and Blue!' – had once alarmed me. I found the volume and violence of their conversation rattling, but after Lord Stavourley's acknowledgement of me, I grew less frightened. I lingered nearer to his study, I listened more intently to the discussions, and though I failed to understand a word of what they spoke, eventually found myself enchanted by their vigorous tone and the passion of their convictions.

Little did I know that the gentlemen to whom I curtseyed and who stopped to pat my head were some of the greatest orators of their day, Charles James Fox, Edmund Burke and Richard Brinsley Sheridan, whose life was later to intersect with mine under less pleasant circumstances.

But in spite of the fascination that my uncle's life inspired in me, I was still a young girl and desired the company of my own sex more than anything. For years, I watched with a tug of sadness as Lady Catherine disappeared into her mother's apartments. Before the door was shut fast, I would often glimpse a scene in which I longed to be included: a flurry of pastel silks and giggling lady visitors, the smell of tea and the clatter of silver upon china. On the rare occasion when I was permitted entrance, it was seen as an act of benevolence. Too frightened to breathe, I would take my seat silently and fold my hands upon my lap.

'Who is the quiet little thing?' I once overheard one matron whisper to a younger, beribboned guest.

'Lady Stavourley's niece,' she replied, before mouthing the word 'orphan'.

Then Lady Stavourley's accomplished young protégée would play a piece upon her fortepiano or chirp out a song to the delight of all present. The guests applauded and cooed, and exclaimed over her pretty golden curls and creamy complexion. She had the voice of a nightingale and, when aiming to please, possessed the charm of an angel.

In truth, reader, there was no one whom I adored more than my cousin. In spite of her cruelties and inconsistencies, I was utterly devoted to her. She seemed to me to radiate with feminine perfection, with all of the qualities I most admired. She stood half a head taller than me, her back as straight as the strings of a bow. Her chin was held upward, her toes turned out, and when she strode into a room, she did so with the grace and presence of a dancer. Even as she wavered upon the threshold of womanhood, she possessed a confidence well beyond her innocent years and conversed easily with her mother's companions. I, on the other hand, barely knew how to open my mouth.

In short, I lived in awe of her, for she represented to me everything I wished I might be, but knew, owing to my circumstances, to be an impossibility.

One would think that two girls who were reared in the same nursery, who laid their heads upon the same pillows, would have shared a mutual affection. Here lies the great injustice: although I loved her with all my heart, she hardly saw fit to speak to me. My cousin was entirely indifferent.

I would have done anything to secure her notice, to have some acknowledgement of my fondness for her. I followed her about like a page boy. If she lost her cap or dropped a toy, I would retrieve it and return it to her with eagerness. She would say nothing, before abandoning me for the comforts of her mamma's rooms.

I would bring her posies of wildflowers, carefully tied in my own ribbons.

'See what your dutiful cousin has brought to you,' would comment our governess.

Lady Catherine would grimace and lay the bundle aside to rot.

I brought her an elegant violet-winged butterfly, which I had cradled in my hand, but she screamed and slapped me for frightening her with the creature.

I did all that was required of me. I was good, so very good. I performed every task with a smile; I applied myself to my studies; I rarely complained; I never shouted. I had no desires but to be obedient, to be modest, to be virtuous, clean and honest. I possessed no wishes of my own but to please Lady Catherine, and to be a dutiful niece to my uncle and aunt. For this reason, I could not comprehend why my cousin refused my friendship, when I had acted always with charity, love and grace.

It was shortly after the incident with the butterfly that I began to pray. Of course, I had always said my prayers, parroting the words I had been instructed to utter, but my heart had never formulated its own prayer. As I kneeled one Sunday, in St Mary's Melmouth, that cold

Norman church on my uncle's estate, I felt a strange passion rise from within me. I shut my eyes as tightly as I could and clasped my hands together firmly.

'Dear Lord,' my heart cried, 'make Lady Catherine my bosom friend, please cause her to love me and share with me all her secrets and delights. Please, Lord, for I have been so good, and done all you asked of me.'

I was not quite nine years old.

From that day, I never ceased to imagine a time when we would sit together and gossip, laughing as freely as two sisters, as two dear companions. I repeated that prayer, that fervent wish, for years, until one day, quite to my surprise, it came true.

Chapter 3

This miracle occurred at a time when, it has been claimed by Lord Dennington, all our troubles commenced. I beg to differ, for these 'troubles' were only such for Lord and Lady Stavourley. Lady Catherine was not disturbed in the least bit. On the contrary, she was enjoying herself immensely.

It was in 1787 that my cousin made her first appearance in society. I recall that night most vividly and how my aunt fluttered and fretted, while her daughter, attired in a gooseberry-green gown, remained composed and proud. I was but fourteen at the time and observed the scene through dreamy eyes, wondering all the while with whom she might dance. I understood well enough that I would never embark upon such an adventure as this: I was not destined for the marriage market in such a grand fashion, if at all. But in truth, the knowledge of this did not concern me, for I was pleased to remain a spectator and to pursue the quiet, humble existence for which I was intended. I did not think for a moment that Lady Catherine's entrance into the world would disrupt the pattern of life by which we all had lived for so long. I do not expect any of us did, least of all Lady Stavourley.

It should not have come as a surprise to the Countess that her daughter would thrive when set loose in the social arena, but this it did. Indeed, it somewhat startled my aunt to see her fledgling take flight with such confidence. That is what comes of rearing a young lady like a dancing bear, of placing her always before an adoring audience. My cousin wore not a stitch of modesty on her person, but, like an actress, courted the gaze of every pair of eyes in a room. She took to dancing with the surety of the famous Giovanna Baccelli, and received compliments on her singing with a complete absence of grace. 'Mamma reckons I have the finest voice in England,' she would reply with a haughty smile.

It was true, Lady Catherine did possess an exceptional voice, but accomplishments without humility detract greatly from a young lady's character; a girl can be thought to be too showy, too precocious and affected. This became the case with my cousin.

The situation was only to worsen with time, as one uncorrected habit gave rise to another. In fact, the gentlemen to whom she was introduced were most bemused by her forward manner. She did not behave in the usual quivering way of most young ingénues, and was not in the least bit timid. Instead, she was prone to casting long, lingering stares across a supper table. How she acquired the art of manipulating her fan is anyone's guess, but soon she had mastered the flirtatious skills of a bored wife, languorously opening and folding the object in her hand. This teasing sport amused her vastly, as did turning her dancing partners into rivals for her attention. At first, her mother observed these developments with no more than a vague uneasiness, until one evening when the word 'coquette' was breathed from a crowd of ladies.

'Pert! Insolent! Immodest! A coquette, Catherine!' Lady Stavourley sobbed as they returned home in his lordship's coach. 'Your behaviour is most unbecoming.' My aunt was utterly beside herself.

Lady Catherine regarded her mamma as if it were a jest. She tossed her head and laughed.

'This is no lark, miss,' Lady Stavourley cried. 'If you carry on in such a way you will have no reputation.'

'Goodness, I have never seen her in such a rage,' my cousin shrieked as she stood in our dressing room, relating the details of the incident. Indeed, I was equally dismayed, for until that moment Lady Catherine had never before confided in me. I sat, fairly frozen, not knowing how to respond to this sudden outpouring.

'It is intolerable,' she huffed. 'She is forever observing me, forever pulling a cross face when I speak. She taps upon my arm if she believes me too gay with a gentleman. *You have been too free with him, Catherine, whatever will he make of you?* She mimicked her mother's high-pitched tones.

My cousin paced and kneaded her hands, ranting at the inequity of the situation, how her mother saw fit to curtail all her pleasures. I listened with wide eyes, nodding at each of her impassioned statements, hardly able to take in that which I was witnessing: Lady Catherine conversing with me!

To be sure, it all occurred quite suddenly. One moment it seemed our lives were fixed as firmly in stone as the foundations of Melmouth, and then, quite without warning, this pattern of being was entirely over-turned. At first, I did not appreciate the grave implications of it, but with hindsight I can say that the entire balance of our household shifted that night. It was as if some supernatural force had intervened and broken the spell that bound Lady Catherine to her mother.

The morning following her outburst, she did not disappear down-stairs into Lady Stavourley's rooms, as was her usual routine. Instead, she moved very gently to the sofa where I sat reading. She approached me in silence, her eyes lowered like those of a supplicant. Carefully, she sat down beside me and smoothed the white muslin of her gown. I remained still, motionless, not knowing how to respond. Then, quite unexpectedly, she laid her head upon my shoulder.

'Hetty,' she breathed, taking my hand in hers. 'Dear cousin.'

At first I knew not how to contend with her attention. Although I had passed so many years in hopeful prayer, begging that we should become friends when God or Fortune or whoever looks down upon us saw fit to grant my wish, I was consumed by disbelief. It was with great hesitation that I accepted my cousin's change of sentiment. Suddenly she desired my opinion on every subject, and requested my presence as she pre-pared for any ball or gathering of importance. Now it was my advice she sought rather than Lady Stavourley's when the friseur worked upon her froth of fashionable curls. No matter what instruction my aunt gave to the hairdresser, her daughter saw fit to contradict it as soon as her mother's back was turned.

'Do not mind what Mamma says,' she whispered to the giddy,

thin-wristed Frenchman. 'I shall have the false curls and the rats at either side. Hetty, what think you of this? Is it not *à la mode*?'

'Yes, yes.' I nodded excitedly.

'Come!' She beckoned me with a smile and, taking a pink ribbon from her dressing table, she bid me lean into the looking glass while she wove it through my linen cap.

'There,' she said with a small giggle, 'now you are as splendidly attired as I.'

I could hardly fathom how it came to pass, how my once indifferent cousin had become my devoted bosom friend.

At about the time Lady Catherine had made her appearance in society, she requested her own apartments, both at Melmouth and at her father's townhouse in Berkeley Square. Not wishing to object to any of their daughter's desires, Lord and Lady Stavourley provided her with a tidy set of rooms in both places. I was at first abandoned in the attic nursery, until Lady Catherine demanded otherwise.

'Papa has agreed to it and we shall be together!' she squealed. And so at Melmouth, the small closet room opposite what was to be our shared drawing room was allocated to me. Although it was but an intimate space, the luxury of sleeping in a bed of my own and enjoying the use of an oak clothes press, a compact dressing table and an escritoire was almost more than I could believe. I had never dared dream of such an honour: to be granted a place in my cousin's very rooms. It was if, after so many years of darkness, the sun had quite suddenly burst forth.

As you might imagine, this new arrangement led to a good deal of girlish conspiring. Lady Catherine was at liberty to lock the doors behind us as we gossiped and mused. She was not much one for embroidery, nor did she enjoy painting, drawing or any of the diversions in which I indulged. I soon learned that she found my choice of reading 'desperately, desperately dull'. She loathed Virgil and Homer and the tales of the ancient world that had occupied me in my loneliness. She had no mind for serious study, for works of moral advice, or for the long, melancholy verses of Donne or Milton.

'I far prefer novels,' she announced one afternoon, flouncing into a chair. 'Have you never read *The Castle of Otranto*, Hetty?'

'I cannot say I have,' I apologized.

'Mamma read it to me and it frightened me vastly.' She smiled broadly. 'Oh, we must read it together, Hetty! We simply must!'

With that, she jumped to her feet and took hold of my arm. We fairly ran through the corridors of Melmouth to the library, laughing and singing as we went.

And so the seeds of what would become our greatest shared joy were sown. In the privacy of our rooms, we would shutter the windows and draw the drapery, so that even in the brightness of day no light seeped through. We lit our candles and sat very close upon a sofa or a bed and began our dramatic readings of what we came to call 'dark tales'.

By the cast of the candle we would work ourselves up into a terror. My cousin read in a breathy, suspenseful tone of apparitions, disembodied limbs and giant swords. We shivered and screamed and laughed, acting out the various scenes, until, utterly consumed with fear, I would dash to the window to throw open the shutters.

'No!' my cousin would shout, pulling me back. And then, with a mischievous giggle, she would extinguish all the candles until I cried out in alarm.

I cannot say why, but I do believe she enjoyed this sport, for there was more than a hint of cruelty in her trickery, especially the occasion when I awoke to find her standing at the foot of my bed, her face covered in white powder, the cast of the full moon illuminating her nightdress. My goodness, how I howled with terror, while she could scarcely breathe for laughing!

The Castle of Otranto was followed by every ghostly, Gothic book to be found. Together we devoured *The Old English Baron*, *The Recess*, *Hamlet*, *Macbeth*, even *Ossian*. Mind you, this was in the days before Mrs Radcliffe wrote her novels. I cannot bear think how my cousin would have horrified me with *The Mysteries of Udolpho*.

Our mutual indulgence in these gloomy delights somehow served to draw us into an even closer union, so that soon Lady Catherine was sharing all her most intimate thoughts with me. The grand events, which I was not permitted to attend, would be recounted to me in minute detail, often in the earliest hours of the morning.

'Hetty, Hetty . . . Henrietta!' She would shake me awake, and then slide beneath the bed coverings as she launched upon her stories of the Marquess of Worcester, who would not let her dance with anyone else, of Lady Bessborough's petticoat with a fashionable new furbelow, or how she drank two glasses of rum punch without her mother noticing.

Then, of course, there were the letters. As any well-bred young lady is taught, it is appropriate and expected that she show her correspondence from gentlemen to her mamma, but my cousin was now well beyond the domain of my aunt. Instead, she read her letters aloud to me, squealing and squawking with delight.

' "My daaah-liiing angel," ' she purred, mocking the heartfelt devotions of Sir Philip Digby, ' "I shall die if I fail to spy you on your constitutional tomorrow. Love will cause my heart to explode with the frustrated fury of Vesuvius . . ." '

'Well, I should like to bear witness to such a spectacle as that!' she cried. 'What a blockhead he is, Hetty.'

It all meant very little to her.

In Lady Catherine's mind, this endless round of assemblies, gatherings, routs and public promenades served no purpose other than to amuse her. The young men who pursued her – Sir Charles Coote, Sir Philip Digby and Mr John Wentworth – came and went. She accepted their offers to dance, their billets-doux and their gifts of kid gloves, but refused their professions of love. After a time, even I began to sense that this attitude of careless abandon could not endure. One day, there would come an abrupt and unpleasant end to the levity. Of this, I was certain.

My cousin's behaviour caused my aunt no end of grief. The despair was graven upon her features, held in her drooping eyes and downturned mouth. She did not have it within her to pull in Lady Catherine's reins and act the tyrant. She was weak, and now her daughter ruled her, just as she had been warned would happen so many years earlier. Daily, she fretted and wept, her frail constitution growing ever more fragile. 'I know not what to do, I know not what to do . . .' she could be heard wailing from behind the doors of her apartments, the now lonely rooms that had once been the scene of her daughter's sprightly antics. The sound of her distress was so charged with unhappiness that it caused my heart to jolt. These were not merely the moans of one who had lost all authority over her charge, but the plaintive cries of a soul who mourned the loss of love. A cold shiver shook me. Had I not prayed for this, to be the recipient of my cousin's affection? Had my violent wishing not caused this to come true? Had my years of imagining and hoping not played some role in transferring my cousin's devotion from her mother to me? I had achieved my aim, but never had I considered that it might come at a cost.

Lady Catherine never appreciated her mother's sufferings, which had begun on the evening she jilted Lady Stavourley in favour of me, and carried on for the better part of two years, until the early spring of 1789. By then, so many words had been whispered about the fecklessness of the mother and the character of the daughter as to call for drastic measures. At the age of eighteen, it was time my cousin married.

My uncle, being a generous and enlightened soul, had always expressed a wish that his daughter enter into a union of her own choosing. Of course, Lord Stavourley also desired her choice to be a suitable one and accordingly had settled an adequate but not immoderate portion of £15,000 upon her to ensure that men of title, rather than fortune hunters stepped forward. However, as Lady Catherine seemed to have no intention of ever making a choice, the Earl and Countess decided that the time had arrived for them to choose for her.

With the assistance of the Duchess of Devonshire, who enjoyed nothing better than making matches, my aunt conspired to introduce her daughter to the young Duke of Bedford. After a great toing and froing of letters, this meeting came about at Devonshire House during a musical party, where Lady Catherine simpered and flicked her fan while Bedford gazed at her longingly. She recounted the entire scene to me later that evening.

'He was a good deal anxious of me at first, and stammered and made excuses,' she explained, 'but then I paid him so many compliments as to make him positively fall in love with me!' she announced. 'La, but he is so ugly. He has a fat, brutish face.'

Brutish face or no, the Duke was not bashful about his intentions and on the following day he began a campaign of courtship. First came the gifts: the patch box and the fan, and eventually a goldfinch. The latter was returned. My cousin was not fond of birds. Then came the letters: first tepid in tone, referring to her as 'dearest Lady Catherine', and then 'the mistress of my heart' when he was more certain of himself. My cousin roared with laughter at his missives, reading them to me with a sneer before dropping them into the fire. She had tired of Bedford by then and refused to respond, but the poor lovesick swain was too far gone to see it. At Ranelagh Gardens she turned her back on him, and then at the Pantheon attempted to ignore him altogether.

After all my aunt had endured, she could hardly bear to witness yet another scene of her daughter's ill-mannered indifference. Upon their return that evening, she fell into a fit of inconsolable sobbing.

'What makes you think you have the right to refuse the attentions of a gentleman like the Duke of Bedford?' she cried.

Her daughter bit her cheek and looked away shamefacedly.

'Oh Mamma,' she peeped, 'I mean no harm. It is just a lark . . .'

'The Duke of Bedford!' Lady Stavourley cried, her face now glowing red with distress. 'No, no, Catherine, it is too much to bear! It is too much.' She gasped for breath and pressed her handkerchief to her face. 'All the Quality believe you to be a coquette, and now this. They will talk of nothing else. Child, do you know what a marriage to the Duke of Bedford would mean for this family, for your father's ambitions? Stavourley and Bedford united in marriage – why, you as a pair would trump the Duke and Duchess of Devonshire for your influence! But no, you think nothing of this. You would dismiss him as if he were some ballad singer wishing to serenade you!'

My cousin stood in silence, observing her mother's tear-drenched cheeks with as much pity as an executioner.

'Pray then, Mamma, what would you have me do?'

Lady Stavourley raised her eyes, her face a picture of disbelief.

'Oh, you silly, silly girl.' She shook her head ruefully.

At that moment, my cousin knew precisely what her mother wished her to do. Her tightly pursed lips began to tremble.

'No, I will not!' she cried defiantly. 'I will never marry him, Mamma.'

Then she too began to sob. 'How could you force my hand, my own dear Mamma and Papa? I do not love him! He is beastly ugly! Oh, what cruelty is this! What horror! I shall be a slave; you would put me in shackles!' She shrieked and fled from the room, like the heroine of one of our Gothic novels.

Oh, my dear friends, I am afraid things became very bitter after this. It was as if the ice of winter, which had all but disappeared from the streets, had retreated indoors and chilled our home. While my cousin took to her bed and wept for a day or so, my aunt suffered greatly. This turn of events proved more than her frayed nerves could withstand. The following morning she succumbed to 'a plague of infernal headaches' and 'a weakness of the lungs and limbs'. She confined herself to her bed-chamber and lay all day with the shutters and drapery pulled across her windows. After a pint of blood was removed from her arm, her physician gently suggested to my uncle that he might consider removing her to Bath for a spell, as ladies with her sort of complaint benefited greatly by a change of air.

My uncle understood precisely his meaning.

And so this was how we came to Bath in April 1789. Contrary to what you may have read elsewhere, there was no fiendish design at work, no devious plan involved. Not one among us could have guessed what would transpire there, or how that innocent sojourn was destined to alter all of our lives entirely.

Chapter 4

Until this moment, dear reader, nothing has been said of George William Allenham, 2nd Baron Allenham of Herberton Park. My good friends, had you been alive during the early months of 1789, you would know what an omission this name has been from my story.

At that time, there were only two Georges of whom society spoke. The first of these was the King, who had recently reacquired the use of his senses. All the country was rapt in celebration at the return of his health. There were fireworks and balls and dinners where His Majesty King George was toasted loudly, even by my uncle and his Whig brothers, who had made no secret of their wish to see the Prince of Wales on his father's throne.

The second George was the gentleman whom I have just introduced. To say he caused a stir among *haute* society would be too mild a phrase to use. I would say he caused a flutter or a flush, for these two things generally accompanied the hushed mention of his name. Ladies looked at one another earnestly when they spoke. 'He is all they say . . . truly, I have never seen a gentleman's face so . . . beautiful.'

It was at a celebratory gathering, a supper party at my uncle's town-house, where candles had been placed in all the windows and a great banner crying 'God Save the King' was strung over the door, that I had first heard some of my aunt's associates conversing about George, Lord Allenham. Respectable dowagers made themselves giddy as they described him. 'He has the appearance of a Grecian athlete – such fine features and so tall!' They seemed almost conspiratorial when they mentioned his name, looking over their shoulders to ensure that the unmarried girls could not hear them.

'He has altered greatly since his return from Grand Tour. He was a mere child when I saw him last. And now . . . well, I doubt there is a heart he will be incapable of conquering!' exclaimed another.

'I hear that Lady Powis has him in mind for her daughter.'

'No, I'm certain that is untrue, as Mrs Howe has written to me to say her niece Miss Featherstonehaugh is about to be engaged to him . . .'

It was then that my aunt had noticed me lingering at the drawing-room door and shooed me away with her eyes.

It was not as if I had been genuinely listening to their prattle; such gossip is the constant background noise to any gathering, and I had no reason to turn my ear to such nonsense. However, it is fair to say that I had heard enough to recall the name when it was next mentioned at Bath.

In the entire two-year period in which my cousin had been 'out', never had a visit been undertaken anywhere which was not with the sole intention of displaying her charms in public. On several previous occasions, my aunt had taken Lady Catherine around the various assembly rooms and drawing rooms of Bath, hosted card parties and excursions, but to no avail. It was therefore not surprising that, in this instance, she seemed incapable of demonstrating any interest in these sociable pursuits. Lady Stavourley wished only to be quiet, to have glasses of spa water brought to her daily, and physicians at her call to take her pulse and examine her tongue on command.

My uncle had taken a comfortable but modest house for us in the Circus expressly for this purpose. Had he intended us to give lavish entertainments and receive many guests, I have no doubt he would have sought out more commodious lodgings. As it was, we were pushed into close quarters, which greatly unnerved my cousin. Our shared bed-chamber was joined by a thin wall to Lady Stavourley's dressing room, which, after placing her ear to the wood panels, Lady Catherine declared to be 'Intolerable! I swear it, she will hear every word we speak!'

You see, by then, she was certain Lord and Lady Stavourley had determined to marry her off to Bedford, perhaps at some secret ceremony.

'Oh cousin,' she sighed, 'you will save me from him, you will save me from Pug Face, oh, please say you will . . .'

I swore my allegiance to her; I swore that if my aunt and uncle attempted to bundle her into a sealed carriage bound for Gretna Green, we should both run off together, though to where precisely, we had not yet determined.

But as the days passed, there seemed to be little sign that her mother had any desire either to eavesdrop upon our ridiculous chatter, or to sacrifice her daughter to Pug Face Bedford. In fact, it was only upon the instruction of her physicians that Lady Stavourley was encouraged to do anything at all. Slowly she begin receiving social calls and bathing in the bubbling sulphur springs, and eventually, once her spirits appeared slightly more fortified, my uncle suggested a visit to the Assembly Rooms.

While Lady Stavourley was not averse to this in principle, it equally failed to hold much appeal. I have no doubt that she feared the possibility of further humiliation and a crushing public defeat at the hands of her daughter.

Truthfully, none of the ladies of Lord Stavourley's household cared much for this idea. And here, dear reader, I include myself among them.

Having passed my sixteenth birthday in the previous year, it was deemed appropriate that I be invited to attend certain less formal gatherings and parties, and to make appearances at public assemblies. You see, my aunt and uncle never wished me to be excluded from society, yet in order to avoid disappointments, they made it well known that I had no marriage portion. There was no need for sumptuous clothing or jewels. That would only mislead. However, while I remained visible, there existed the slim hope that some gentleman of fortune might fall in love with me and take me off their hands – but I must not rely on this, my aunt had cautioned, for 'it was more often the case in novels than in life'. In any eventuality, I knew that my destiny lay in a long spinsterhood, as a companion to my cousin, and I accepted this prospect with cheerful good grace.

There was no sense of urgency to our preparations that evening. In fact, my cousin nearly prevented us from going at all, moaning that she was vapourish and that her monthly courses were about to begin.

'Nonsense,' chided her mother, her face pinched with annoyance. 'You claim always to be indisposed with that. I do not believe it for a moment.' She then had some spa water brought to Lady Catherine as her hair was being curled. My cousin sighed and frowned, never once sipping from the glass on her dressing table.

We were all in low spirits, our sojourn in Bath becoming duller and more tedious by the day. Without my aunt to order our activities, we had sunk into a sort of listlessness since our arrival. So, rather than deliberating over our dress and style of hair, we simply changed from our day gowns into our evening attire. I wore my gown of pale blue silk, my neck and ears adorned by the only jewels I owned: my modest pearl cross and eardrops. My cousin was attired in a simple pink taffeta. Feathers were placed in our carelessly arranged coiffures. Lady Catherine was so laissez-faire that she managed to lose her sash before we left the house. With hindsight, perhaps it was not such a terrible thing that we approached the ball with an air of *sans souci*; after all, there is nothing so becoming as a girl with a candid, effortless look about her.

Just now, I have paused my pen mid air, between the ink pot and the page.

I was about to describe my cousin's physical appearance, but I hesitate. Lord Dennington is likely to accuse me of maligning his sister if I do not choose my words carefully. I believe it is fair to say that Lady Catherine was no great beauty, but neither was she plain. Her hair was that pleasing golden colour, so often praised in fairy tales, and her eyes, though close set, gleamed like two blue gems. Between this pair of sapphires rested a rather high-arched, prominent nose, which she shared with her mother.

Reader, if you are fortunate enough to one day make a tour of Melmouth House, enquire of the housekeeper to be shown the portrait by George Romney. There you will see a likeness of Lady Catherine created at the time she was first launched in society. You will also see a tree beside her where I once sat. That was before Lord Dennington, many years later, had me painted out of the scene. You see, he remembered all too well what occurred when we went to view the picture at the summer exhibition at Somerset House.

Lady Stanhope, whom my aunt always despised, was standing with a friend before our portrait. She failed to notice that we, the Earl, the Countess, their three children and niece, were directly behind them. After a long inspection of the work, Lady Stanhope muttered to her companion, 'That Miss Ingerton is by far the most beautiful of Lord Stavourley's tribe. I do so pity his daughter. She is not half so fair.'

Now, I fear you will think me vain. Please, do indulge me, and allow an old woman the pleasure of remembering the fleeting gifts of her youth. Perhaps you will have some sympathy for me when I reveal to you that for much of my girlhood I was entirely ignorant of the effects of my beauty.

Imagine now the sketch I have just drawn of my cousin's face, but with several distinct alterations. I possessed the same honey-coloured hair and dark blue eyes, which have long been an Ingerton inheritance. However, where my cousin's nose was long and pronounced, mine was tiny and narrow, and where her eyes were small and placed near together, mine were wide and round as two delftware plates. Indeed, my face bore such a soft, childlike appearance that, when taken together with my diminutive stature, many found it difficult to believe that I had not escaped the nursery prematurely, even into the later years of my life. But in my girlhood, my guardians made no reference to the merits of my beauty, and for good reason: as the penniless relation, they feared I would become a distraction. They worried that their daughter would not shine half so brightly beside me. I had not appreciated that the Earl and Countess had been approached by gentlemen because of me, because young men believed, and hoped, that the girl with the delicate features and bowed mouth was Lord Stavourley's daughter. Indeed, it was not entirely unknown for the two of us to be confused altogether, and by far the most awkward instance of this occurred during our very visit to Bath.

I doubt that most of you knew the Lower Assembly Rooms as I did, before they burned down. Bath was in her glory then, like a young lady in the flush of her youth. Now, sadly, she has become a tawdry old madam. Paste buckles and brooches have replaced the diamonds that used to be seen in earlier years, while the streets are jammed with anonymous post chaises, rather than the carriages of the great families.

In my day, this place offered the spectacle of a magician's tent, especially to the wondering eyes of a young lady who was not an attendee at many lavish occasions. Chandeliers and wall sconces glimmered with hundreds of tiny flames, while music and the rhythmic clatter of dancing heels could be heard throughout. From all around came the dim murmur of conversation, and that scent which never fails to rise from a dense crowd: part Hungary water, eau de Cologne and pomade, part sour, oniony stink.

On that night, we had arrived at seven o'clock, precisely an hour after the dancing began. Already the rooms were heaving with guests. The tea room, the card room, all the antechambers and, needless to say, the ballroom were full. As Lord and Lady Stavourley bowed and smiled at their acquaintances, Lady Catherine and I marvelled at the crowd, surveying the sea of feather-topped heads, false hair, wigs and frilled caps.

There is nothing so amusing as observing the circus of humanity with all of its curious specimens of men and women: the bulbous noses, the crooked backs, the portly figures squeezed into waistcoats too small. Indeed, passing comment on the faces and fashions in such places was my cousin's preferred sport.

'Good gracious,' began Lady Catherine, prudently raising her fan so she might whisper to me. 'I did not think anyone so ignorant of fashion as to still wear a sacque-back mantua!' she declared, rolling her eyes in the direction of a plump woman in a gold-coloured gown.

'Oh yes, it is *très outré*, to be sure,' I agreed, using one of my cousin's favourite turns of phrase.

'And that hideous petticoat . . .' She began to giggle while inspecting another poorly attired creature. 'One would think her maid blind, or that she dressed Madam by the light of a single candle.'

As I took in her cutting remarks, my eyes began to rove the room, running over trains of shimmering silk and ensembles of stripes and sprigs, until quite abruptly my attention stuck fast upon a gentleman in a green coat.

Until that day, I had never stared at anyone, least of all a member of the opposite sex. I could not have contemplated such a bold gesture. Unlike my self-assured cousin, I was a quivering mouse, demure and reserved to a fault. Therefore I surprised even myself when I found my gaze consumed by the man I have just mentioned.

I cannot rightly say what it was about him that held my notice. I felt for some time utterly fascinated, like a child beholding a colourful spinning top. He was quite unlike anything, unlike any one person I had known.

He was, it must be said, exceptionally . . . no, profoundly handsome. I saw him first in profile and he seemed so statuesque, his stance so square and firm, his back tall and straight, yet he stood with such comfortable elegance, like a swordsman or a dancer. His face, even at a distance, was remarkable for its perfection. His cheeks and chin were flawlessly hewn, as if from marble; his nose was long yet well pro-portioned, and finished in a perfect, slightly upward point. At first, I could not see either the startling hue of his eyes or the true richness of his dark hair. The light was not good, and he dipped his face in and out of shadow as he conversed, nodding every so often and smiling generously. He was most certainly a gentleman of breeding, which was plain not only in the finely tailored fit of his coat, but in his self-assured comportment. By this, I do not mean he wore that disagreeable air of self-importance, but rather that he appeared polished, while still having about him all the ease and honesty of a country man.

It was not until he turned his head that I realized I had lost myself and all sense of propriety. Oh reader, our stares collided in one mortifying instant! I cannot relay to you the horror I experienced; it was as if my heart had dropped into the pit of my stomach. He would think me forward and impertinent. He would take offence. Shame swept over me like a fever, washing my face in colour.

'Hetty!' My cousin spoke sharply. 'Your face is quite red. '

All at once, my aunt, who had been conversing with her relation, Mrs Villiers, broke off her chat and examined me with a furrowed brow.

'Are you well, child?' she asked with some concern.

'I . . . it is the heat,' I stammered, hardly knowing myself what had come over me. I touched my fan lightly and then, as they studied me, slowly unfurled it.

I fear the humiliation was so great that I could not take my eyes off my shoes for some time. While the company continued with their gossip, I fanned myself dreamily, catching my breath and calming my racing pulse. When curiosity drove me to hazard a fleeting glance in the direction where he had stood, I was relieved to see he had gone.

'My Lord Allenham,' exclaimed my uncle, quite suddenly.

I drew in my breath. I knew what I was to find. Reader, you know it too! There, standing to my right, was the gentleman in the green coat.

Oh Jupiter! I wished the roof might fall in and bury me! I could hardly think.

To this day, I could not tell you which sensation had more command of my senses: the horror of embarrassment or the ecstasy of being so near to him. My face was as hot as a smelting furnace. You would think I had never before stood beside a man.

I could scarcely look at him. What little I had learned of his divine features from a distance was magnified at closer range. His eyes were truly like nothing I had seen: they were so full of blue! Like buckets of clear well water – no, like the well itself, rimmed with deep green moss and shade. I shall always recall their effect on me, how I shivered when his gaze encompassed me. Lady Jersey once described him as an Adonis. Although it is a word much overused, I do believe it fitted Lord Allenham perfectly in his youth.

'I had a letter from Mr Fox today, claiming you to be with him at St Ann's Hill,' commented Lord Stavourley.

'Alas, I was, but am no longer,' he responded with a wry smile and a courtly bow. 'My visit to our friend was regrettably short, though long enough to settle some matters concerning the candidacy.'

'My lord,' interrupted my aunt, wishing to avoid a political conversation and eager to make use of the situation, 'I believe you have not yet been introduced to my daughter, Lady Catherine, or to her cousin, Miss Ingerton.'

We both bowed our heads. '. . . Or indeed to my cousin, Mrs Villiers.'

'And what a misfortune that has been, to have been so long an acquaintance of Lord Stavourley and not to have had an opportunity for an introduction.' He regarded both of us with a warm look. 'If I may beg leave of your lord and ladyship, as the next dance is beginning, I shall have to make amends immediately.' Then, entirely unexpectedly, he turned to me. 'Madam, would you do me the honour of accompanying me to the ballroom?'

I am not certain who among us was the most aghast. He hardly waited for an answer before offering me his arm. Before any of my party could utter a protestation, Lord Allenham, the most handsome man I had ever beheld, the subject of my transfixed stares just moments before, led me away. As he did, I noticed Lady Catherine's lips part in disbelief.

Dear reader, I was a trembling wreck! My head whirled with the most terrible confusion. I had done nothing to invite this. Surely Lord Allenham meant to dance with my cousin, not with me. I could not decide if there had been some mistake or indeed whether this had been calculated. My heart thumped inside my chest. What fired it more, my terror that I should upset Lady Catherine or the sensation of Allenham's sturdy arm beneath my fingertips, I could not say.

As we passed through the entrance to the ballroom, I felt as if I had been turned upside down. Everything spun; the light from the chandeliers intensified; the crowd swelled wider; the odour of the rooms grew more cloying and nauseating. It seemed that the gaze of the entire assembly followed me. I could hardly breathe and my fingers tightened around his forearm like the claws of a hawk.

We stood amid the other couples poised to begin a cotillion. I knew I would have to concentrate with all my might on the steps, counting them out just as our dancing master had warned us not to. I held my focus, avoiding his gaze where possible, though this was of little use. It was his nearness that distracted me. As we circled round one another, first left and then right, I sensed a great blush begin to spread from my throat on to my cheeks. His lordship could not help but notice the throbbing pinkness of my face, and attempted to put me at ease by making polite conversation.

'Have you been long at Bath?'

'No, my lord, less than a fortnight,' I stuttered.

'And how have you been diverting yourself in that time?' he asked.

'I fear that Lady Stavourley's health has kept us confined, my lord, but she has improved greatly since our arrival here.'

'I do not doubt that to be the case, for she has you to amuse her.' He spoke with a teasing glimmer in his eye. I was far too inexperienced to recognize flirtation when I encountered it, and began to panic.

'Oh no,' I spluttered, 'I think you mean my cousin . . . she is the one who plays and sings . . .'

'And you? What of your accomplishments?' He raised an intrigued eyebrow, choosing to ignore my awkward response. 'I cannot imagine that a gentleman of Lord Stavourley's learning would countenance a child reared in his nursery to be turned out unfinished.'

'Painting.' I swallowed. 'But I cannot pretend to talent . . .'

'You hide behind your modesty, madam.'

His rapid parry flustered me.

'I . . . I . . . have received compliments on my watercolours . . . landscapes . . . my tutor thinks them accomplished, but really, my lord, I merely apply myself to my studies and then practise with my brushes what I have learned . . .' I replied as we crossed one another.

This comment appeared to pique Lord Allenham, who threw me an amused look. 'Your tutor has prescribed you texts?'

'Only Sir Joshua Reynolds' *Discourses*,' I answered, which drew a crooked smile from him.

'I dare say you will not learn much about painting nature from that!' He laughed lightly. 'Have you not read Mr Burke's *Philosophical Enquiry* on the subjects of beauty and the sublime? Mr Burke is, I believe, an acquaintance of Lord Stavourley.'

Goodness, thought I, his lordship must think me a philosopher! I grew bashful and lowered my eyes, regretting that I did not have my cousin's talent for conversation.

'When I was a child, Mr Burke came to Melmouth and petted me upon the head . . .' I smiled awkwardly, realizing what a dunce I sounded. 'But I cannot say that I have read his treatise.'

At that instant his arm rubbed against my silk sleeve, the side of his

51

coat against my gown. His touch caused me to draw in breath, and then exhale with shame. I felt so gauche, so mortified by my quivering and utterly convinced that the entire room of dancers and spectators knew that my being there was some dreadful mistake.

'Ah, but you must!' he exclaimed as he moved towards me, his face glowing with the fire of his ideas. He pursed his lips, patiently waiting as the dance drew us apart and then back together again before he could relay his thoughts. My gaze was fixed upon his expression, for I found myself captivated by its intensity, eager to know what sentiments so animated his features. At last, he reached for my hand, taking it into his firm, warm one, and then turned his bright eyes on to mine.

'Beauty,' he began, 'is born out of the passion of love. An artist cannot make sense of a landscape without an understanding of this.' He smiled and then gave a deferential nod. 'So says Mr Burke.'

So entirely distracted was I that I missed a step.

Allenham paid no mind and continued.

'And the sublime, the sublime is greater than beauty. It overwhelms the senses. It consumes us. It is the pure fury and power of nature. It must be felt to be known. An artist must feel in order to paint, and of that, madam, you will never learn from reading Sir Joshua's dry *Discourses*.'

Well, reader, I simply could not fathom how I might respond to that. What might a girl who knows nothing of society, of worldly behaviour, of nature or passion make of such a statement? I stared at him, so spellbound by his vitality, his light, his perfect assembly of features, as to be awed into silence. Why, he was the most remarkable person I had ever encountered. As I joined hands and circled with the other ladies in our square, I picked over his comments. If only I had the wit and vivacity of my cousin, I lamented. I was so simple, so frightened, such a milksop!

'Perhaps I should improve myself by reading Mr Burke,' was all I could think of to say.

As we danced, I prayed he could not read the pain of embarrassment on my face. Beside Allenham I felt graceless and clumsy, while he seemed utterly unshakeable, as if he hardly needed to think, as if everything he did, every comment and step, came as naturally as breathing.

Surely, I told myself, he wished to dance with my cousin, not with me. The more I contemplated this, the greater my discomfort grew. A picture settled in my mind of Lady Catherine bursting with fury at this error, the humiliation I would cause Lord Allenham, the scandal that would explode before me. Panic began to rise within me as the dance wound to its conclusion, and before I had so much as recovered myself, I found my partner leading me across the room to where our party stood. There I spied my aunt, her brows arched in an expression of disapproval, and my cousin beside her with a face hard and indignant. My heart lurched.

'My lord,' I said with urgency as we approached the group, 'I fear . . . I fear there has been some error . . .'

He regarded me with a playful glance.

As we stood before my cousin, I explained, 'I believe you had wished to dance with Lady Catherine but . . . there was some confusion. I . . . I am Miss Ingerton.' My mouth trembled as I forced a smile.

Allenham bowed his head at Lady Catherine and then at me, his face never once wavering from its polite cast. He made no remark upon my comment, but turned to my cousin and requested the next dance.

One comment that is often made about Lord Allenham is that he had a genius for discretion. That much was apparent from our first meeting. What could have been perceived as a *faux pas* was instantly smoothed away by the attention he lavished upon my cousin. For the one cotillion he danced with me, he partnered Lady Catherine in both a minuet and a reel. I cannot express to you the contentment I felt at seeing them, hands joined, step and bounce together in careful formation. Honestly, I enjoyed this sight more than I did my own dance with the Baron. After all, the scene was meant to have played out in this way. My heart swelled for Lady Catherine. It also sighed with relief. Had the situation not been put right, I dread to think how she might have taken against me. I had been embraced as her dearest, most treasured friend, but knew all too well the power of her wrath and how easily I might be cast down.

Happily, the night was remembered as a triumph. Allenham remained affixed to our group for the duration of the ball, offering us his arms and escorting our party between the tea room and the card tables. At his side, my cousin burst into life, giggling and casting looks with as much accomplishment as an actress. To be sure, she was perhaps on occasion too loud and too ebullient in her conversation, but, as I was to observe, the Baron had this effect on most ladies. They either quaked with nerves or fell into a silent stupefaction in his presence. Indeed, I have known only one other gentleman to possess such a hold over the female sex, and that was Lord Byron, who with his clubbed foot could not even dance!

You can imagine our delight when, at the conclusion of the evening, Lord Allenham turned to my aunt and uncle with a reverential bow and requested permission to call upon us the following day. As he put his question, a hint of boyish uncertainty darted across his confident expression. His bright smile quivered endearingly, as if he feared for an instant we would refuse him. As if that were at all possible.

Needless to say, neither I nor my cousin had more than a wink of sleep that night. We lay huddled together in the bed we shared, just as we had done as children. Lady Catherine squeezed my hand as she recounted every sentence he had spoken, every compliment he had paid her, every dance they had enjoyed. Indeed, I had never heard her gush with such heartfelt enthusiasm for any previous admirer.

'I shall die of love, I think I shall die of love,' she panted. 'Do you not think him the most handsome man in the world, Hetty?' she asked for what must have been the seventh or eighth time.

'Oh yes,' I agreed.

'Do you think he is in love with me?'

'How could he not be, cousin? You are so pretty and accomplished.'

Then she gasped quite suddenly, as if startled by a realization.

'I do believe I shall marry him!' she squealed.

I held her hand tightly and shut my eyes fast.

'Yes, I do believe you will.'

Chapter 5

It could be said that the courtship of Lady Catherine Ingerton and George, Lord Allenham, began in earnest when they appeared beside one another in the Baron's box at the Theatre Royal. I was fortunate enough to have accompanied them, as was Mrs Villiers, my uncle and my triumphant aunt, who was eager for all of Bath to observe her. Especially eager, I might add, after she received confirmation from a friend that Lord Allenham was not, as she had heard, engaged to either Miss Featherstonehaugh or to Miss Powis. In the wake of this news, it was remarkable how rapidly she recovered her health. Why, to look upon her that evening at the theatre, one would never have thought she had suffered a moment's pain. She sat alongside her daughter, her colour heightened, her head held high, as proud as a goose upon her eggs.

Needless to say, this turn of events altered the tempo of our stay quite markedly. In fact, following my uncle's departure for London that week, our little band of ladies was thrown into a positive fit of giddiness. My aunt's lethargy was replaced by a constant, nervous bustle. A fuss was required for every occasion, every possible meeting with Lord Allenham was strategized as if Lady Stavourley were preparing her daughter for battle. New feathers and shoe buckles were purchased, and two further boxes of Lady Catherine's apparel were sent for from Berkeley Square. Sally Pickering, one of our childhood nurses who now served as our lady's maid, was set to work brushing down and making repairs to all of my cousin's gowns. An entire day was devoted to this task, to sewing a new silver edging on a bodice, applying a lace trim to a set of sleeves, reshaping several pairs of satin shoes. Sally stitched love into her mistress's attire, smiling as she moved her needle. Indeed, to this day I have never seen a maid so devoted to her lady. She tended Lady Catherine with the adoration of a mother, but saw to me grudgingly, angrily combing the tangles from my hair or viciously pulling at my laces. She despised me, to be sure, that much was plain.

As I have explained, there was never a time when I was not mindful of my place within my uncle's household. Like Sally, I too recognized that I was no more than a minor player within this larger drama. By the time Lord Allenham made his entrance into our lives, I had acquired a great deal of practice in performing my part. I knew precisely what would be required of me: I would be called upon to participate in most small social occasions, though not expected to contribute much by way of conversation. I had grown accustomed to providing a fourth pair of hands in a game of cards, to quietly turning sheets of music for Lady Catherine, and accompanying her on walks with her suitors. Where a party set out for a ride or a visit to the theatre or some public exhibition, I was always among them, simpering demurely with lowered eyes. I never once expected any mind to be paid to me; I never wished for any notice. It was Lady Catherine's place to radiate, like a diamond set among garnets.

In the daily visits that Lord Allenham began paying to our lodgings, when he joined us for dinner, or came for an evening of entertainment, I never once courted his attention. I was adept at sliding from a room, or retreating into a sunlit corner with a book or some piece of embroidery. It therefore surprised me, or shall I say caused me embarrassment, that no matter where I hid or how silent I kept myself he seemed always able to locate me. On one occasion, I had been so entirely engrossed in my book that I had not even been aware of his entrance into the small parlour.

'*The Vicar of Wakefield*,' he had announced, startling me terribly. 'Dear Miss Ingerton!' he apologized, 'I did not mean to frighten you.' He stood quite still, afraid perhaps that I should faint from fear, until he noticed the appearance of my bashful smile. This caused him to laugh, and I soon joined him, my cheeks growing ever hotter and ruddier under his gaze.

'You find Mr Goldsmith to your liking?' he questioned me, when at last we caught our breath.

'Very much so,' I answered, before Allenham took a seat beside me. I could hardly bring myself to look upon him, knowing that if I did, I should begin to tremble. Why he took an interest in my thoughts, I could not comprehend, but he soon drew me into a discussion on the merits of the book and its characters.

Incidents such as this occurred on several occasions. They lasted but a few moments, before Allenham, realizing he would be missed, or that my cousin had thrown me a jealous look from across the room, made his excuses and rejoined the others. I must admit I thought nothing of these friendly exchanges at the time, though I cannot say the same for my aunt, who monitored them with some interest.

'It is rare to see a young man so generally concerned with all members of a party,' she had stated to Lady Jervas, a relation of Lord Allenham's who had joined us for a game of whist one evening. The Baron was at the fortepiano with my cousin and well beyond earshot. 'His manners are so cordial. He has the air of a courtier.'

Lady Jervas smiled archly. 'He learned it from his father, who was Minister Resident at Turin for a good many years. Such is to be expected in a family of diplomats. His lordship spent his boyhood learning to tip-toe across marble palace floors.' Then, thoughtfully, she pressed her cards to her chest, and leaned towards Lady Stavourley's ear. 'There are many benefits to a foreign education. He rides and fences as well as a French chevalier – and speaks the language as well as one. Of course, he has also mastered Italian.' She looked at him across the room. 'He will be a catch indeed.'

My aunt gazed over the top of her cards towards her daughter with an expression that spoke of both pleasure and concern.

I understood what preoccupied her thoughts: she did not trust Lady Catherine. My cousin bore that familiar mischievous look when she stood near Allenham; her narrowed eyes and mild smile gave her a feline air, as if she were preparing to splay her claws.

'Yes,' Lady Stavourley replied, 'and someone need catch him quickly.'

But as the days folded over into one another, my cousin failed to bare her teeth. She did not resort to her usual trickery. There were no cutting remarks and no turned backs; on the contrary, her habitual ebullience seemed muted, she seemed contained, calm, tamed by Allenham's influence. She hung upon his every utterance, as did we all.

He had that particular gift, you see. He possessed a unique ability to compel and captivate with his words and, when this gift was coupled with his startlingly handsome features, there was no one whom he had not the power to persuade. It was for this reason that gentlemen such as my uncle, Mr Fox and Mr Sheridan saw a great future for him in politics. He was by all regards a natural statesman. Why, to this very day you may go to Brooks's Club in St James's and there speak with half a dozen or more fellows of an august age who will vouch for his talent at telling a good tale. Everyone around the table, or riding with him in a carriage, would fall silent as he painted scenes all about us. Of course, in his youth, he spoke a great deal of the places he had seen as a boy: the Forum ruins in Rome, the carnival at Venice, Pompeii and Herculaneum. For ladies who had seen very little of the world, this was greatly diverting. We listened with fascination, not knowing which was more enchanting, the stories or the animated, tenor-voiced storyteller.

I remember distinctly our visit to Spring Gardens and how he regaled us with talk of the luxurious palace gardens at Caserta. Allenham insisted on taking us to view the rows of pink-blossomed trees, which had recently burst into colour. It looked like a fairy landscape, with the breeze sending rose-coloured petals in swirls around us, but I was hardly aware of this picturesque scene, so lost was I in his words.

'The park spreads for almost as far as the eye can see, and at the end of it there is a cascade which tumbles down what looks to be a row of steps into Venus's Grotto,' he told us as we strolled, my cousin and I with our arms resting upon his.

'I have read of this,' said I. Lady Catherine looked at me with a cold expression. 'There are several fountains within the cascade. There is one dedicated to Diana and Actaeon. All around the cascade are placed statues representing the winds and zephyrs. I should like to see it one day.'

'I cannot imagine such a thing,' said my cousin. 'I should have to see it to know you had not invented, Hetty.'

'No, I have seen it and it is quite real. Miss Ingerton is correct; it is decorated with all manner of fantastic things. There is another cascade just like it at Vienna and at the Palace of Versailles.'

Lady Catherine did not enjoy being proven incorrect. She replaced her merry face with a downcast one and fell conspicuously silent. Noting this, Allenham stopped, placed his hand upon hers and addressed her in a gentle tone.

'There is a book I would like to show you. You may see a print of the cascade in there and many of the other sites I visited as a boy. Tomorrow we shall go to Pratt and Marshall's Library.'

As he gazed at her, she raised her eyes to him adoringly.

You have heard of bee charmers and snake charmers, lion tamers and those who have a calming way with wild dogs? Allenham was a person such as this. He had an instinct for sadness or disappointment, and an understanding of how to lift it. On that day, he must have sensed it in me. In fact, I believe he had seen it in me all along, even before I myself understood what I felt.

There had been a moment, as we advanced towards the carriage, when Allenham and I found ourselves separated from the others by several paces. We had walked for some time without speaking, listening to the breeze and to the calls of a noisy flock of blackbirds. It was then that he turned to me, his handsome face candid.

'It is difficult to be always in the shadows,' he stated.

When I looked at him quizzically, not comprehending his meaning, he continued. 'Most do not know that I had an elder brother. I was not intended to be my father's heir.' He glanced at me, the wind teasing a strand of his dark hair. 'He died of scarlet fever when I was but fourteen.'

'I did not know this,' said I, apologetically.

'It is no matter.' He shook his head. 'He was far better formed for this role than I. He excelled in all things. In strength . . . as a scholar – he was barely nine years old and reading Pliny!' Allenham exclaimed with a sniff of laughter. 'I, by contrast, was always awkward.'

'I cannot believe that, my lord,' I spoke up, chiding him slightly.

'No, it is true. As a boy, I was very shy. Naturally, my father favoured my brother . . .' The Baron looked wistfully at me. 'Miss Ingerton, I know what it is to be considered the lesser of two. Sometimes it is the cause of genuine pain.'

I listened to these words with a sense of unease, but chose to say nothing in response. My first thought was to deny what he was claiming, to state that I had no such experience of this pain that he described. But it was not true, and it surprised me greatly to hear someone depict so plainly that which I held privately inside me.

After he disclosed this, I realized why he had been so intent on never excluding me and on always paying my cousin and me equal attention. Although my position was no more than that of a chaperone, I was aware of a warm friendship taking root between us. We had many similar interests, more, it must be said, than his lordship and my cousin. Although Lady Catherine entertained him with her merry wit, filling our suppers with droll remarks about Bath's swaggering or gouty visitors, it was to me that Allenham turned when he wished to discuss opinions and ideas. He spoke of the sublime beauty of the Alps, he mused on the subject of painting, on architecture and on Rome, but nothing animated him as vividly as did mention of Jean-Jacques Rousseau. To see him, you would understand, dear reader, how the writings of this great philosopher burned within his mind, for his very eyes flickered with admiration.

Unfortunately, talk of such lofty subjects did not amuse my cousin. As we stood around the long library table at Pratt & Marshall, examining an illustrated volume of palace gardens, she wearily wandered off.

She left Allenham and me to pore over the detailed engravings, each diagram more intricate than the last. I opened a page to reveal images of all the statues in the gardens of Versailles. The Baron and I bent our heads to study these mythical figures more closely. At times, his cheek would pass so near to mine that I could feel its warmth upon my own. His fingers crept across the page as he spoke, brushing once or twice against my hand or wrist.

'Daphne and Apollo,' I announced. My voice was higher and more nervous than usual. 'That is my favourite.'

'But it is such a sad tale,' said he. 'You surprise me. It is about a broken heart, a god who loves, who will never be loved in return.'

'But Daphne's virtue is admirable, do you not think?'

'What I think, Miss Ingerton,' said he, lowering his voice, 'is that you have read but a few of these ancient tales, and only those selected by your governess.'

'Perhaps that is so . . .' said I, recalling all too well how my tutor attached a moral lesson to each of these readings, carefully prescribing which pages among the many volumes we were to examine.

'One day you must read all these stories, with all their brutality and beauty . . .' He paused thoughtfully. '. . . And not merely the mythology of the ancients, but truthful accounts of the human heart . . . Monsieur Rousseau, his *Confessions*. There are few pictures so well painted of life . . . of the joys of love . . .'

My mouth grew suddenly dry when he spoke that phrase. My heart began to beat quite rapidly. Unknowingly, I moved away from him.

'Perhaps, once you are married,' he corrected himself with a hopeful note in his voice. But Allenham knew as well as I how limited were my prospects of that.

I recalled that episode in my mind many, many times. It stayed with me, spinning round and round like a globe, returning with each revolution to the same point: the word 'love'. From the moment I had met Allenham, I did what was expected of me and smothered at birth those feelings to which I felt my heart succumbing. The thought that my pulse should leap at the mention of his name sickened me. Throughout my young life I had become very good at learning to want nothing, joining my wishes and dreams with those of my cousin's. Allenham was not and would never be for me, and, my dear reader, I swear to you I adhered to this belief with every particle of my being. Whenever I felt the forbidden spark begin to smoulder in my heart, I stamped upon it. I turned my every attention to making him love Lady Catherine.

By then, you see, an engagement was inevitable. A young man cannot pay so much attention to a young lady without it leading somewhere. In fact, my aunt and cousin and Mrs Villiers had talked of nothing else since the evening he accompanied us to the theatre.

At the end of our second week at Bath, my cousin had begun to sulk. For days she had swung from giddiness to weepiness. Patience was not one of her greatest virtues. She was unaccustomed to waiting for anything. 'But certainly he must be in love with me by now!' she exclaimed in exasperation, after another night of dancing with Allenham at the Assembly Rooms failed to produce a proposal of marriage.

'Love is only the half of it,' sighed her mother. 'The rest is a matter of business between men.'

'He must put his affairs in order first,' comforted Mrs Villiers, who, as a widow, claimed to know more about the inner thoughts of men than most. Lady Catherine listened, but never seemed entirely satisfied. Her disbelieving scowl was only softened, not erased.

Strange as it may sound to you, her temper did not change until she received word of Allenham's departure. It came in the form of a letter, accompanied by two parcels wrapped loosely in brown paper. These items were delivered into the hands of a housemaid who brought them up to us. My cousin cooed and clapped like a child at the sight of her round, thin box.

'There is one for Miss Ingerton as well,' said the servant, gesturing to the flat object upon the card table. Bemused, I rose to examine my package as my aunt read the letter.

'These are from Lord Allenham. He regrets to say that he will be quitting Bath this afternoon . . .'

'Oh!' exclaimed Lady Catherine, who had failed to note her mother's announcement. She gently removed one of Allenham's gifts from its box and raised it up to be admired. Four opalescent pearls set into a comb of gold swirled with light. This was a genuine lover's gift, a confirmation of her suitor's affections. My cousin squealed with delight as my aunt leaned in to admire the tokens.

So distracted were they that my gift slipped their notice altogether. I slid the paper off to reveal the rich leather binding of a small thin book. I opened the cover. *A Philosophical Enquiry into the Origin of our Ideas of the Sublime and Beautiful, by E. Burke,* read the title page. On the inside of the volume, I then noticed he had written an inscription: 'To Miss Ingerton, so she might know beauty when it appears before her'. I was astonished at this, that he had recalled our conversation that night in the Lower Assembly Rooms. I could not conceal my smile, or my blush. I was only pleased the others were too preoccupied to see it upon my face!

That afternoon, Lady Catherine's admirer appeared in person to make his farewells. He was shown into the drawing room, which he had come to know so intimately over the fortnight. There he found my cousin, with her set of pearl combs arranged in her hair, sitting at the edge of her chair, more uncomfortably than usual. The Baron's gifts had made her more convinced than ever that a proposal was imminent.

Allenham explained that he had business with his solicitor in London, and at the mention of this, I watched a sly smile creep across my cousin's lips, and then across my aunt's. There was a long, heavy pause. Whether it was this that prompted him to leave or the need to make haste for London, I know not, but Allenham then rose to his feet.

'I shall miss you all very much. You have been exceptional company and I have enjoyed myself greatly.'

'And we shall miss you terribly, my lord,' answered Lady Catherine in her softest, most kitten-like voice. She stared at him with pleading eyes.

He swallowed hard. For a fleeting moment he glanced at me, and then back at my cousin. 'I would be especially honoured, Lady Catherine, if you would permit me to correspond with you.'

My cousin beamed. My aunt attempted to suppress her elation. 'I should like that very much,' said Lady Catherine.

And what more need I say, reader?

As there was no reason for us to continue at Bath without Lord Allenham, we too took our leave and returned to Melmouth, where Lady Catherine prepared to receive her suitor's written professions of love.

Chapter 6

Of course, there was no question of Allenham not writing. The dance of courtship had begun in earnest and everyone expected it to be taken to its natural conclusion.

We had been at Melmouth for a little under a week before a small packet arrived with a London postmark for Lady Catherine. The letter was laid before her at breakfast. With deliberate slowness, she placed down the roll she was buttering, wiped her fingers and smiled nervously.

'It is from Lord Allenham.'

My aunt and I paused as she broke the seal and began to read its contents. Her hands trembled.

'Might you read us some of it, my dear?' asked her mother.

'Oh, there is nothing in it, really,' my cousin answered with a hint of disappointment. 'He has gone to some masquerade at Almack's and talks of politics a good deal . . .' Then she let out a satisfied titter. 'He thinks of me often and of our time in Bath . . .'

Lady Stavourley corrected her posture. 'As he rightly should.' Her eyes lingered on her daughter for a good deal longer than they ought. My aunt was never completely certain of what trick Lady Catherine might play, whether she would awaken one morning and decide she had had enough of Allenham, and that it might indeed be more fun to tease him, like a cat with a string. But from what I could see of her, this was unlikely to happen. My cousin had been truly smitten. In fact, since we had returned from Bath, I had never known her to be so serene. She was less prone to sulk, and enjoyed long periods of stillness, sitting at her piano or simply staring out of a window, with the mild, fixed expression of a Madonna. In these respects, her character had been altered, but underneath still remained the capricious creature with whom I had always been acquainted. I was reminded of this that very day, after we had left the breakfast table.

There were few games my cousin and I enjoyed more than sharing the flowery outpourings of affection she received from her suitors and I had expected to be entertained by Lord Allenham's letters just as I had been with Bedford's, Digby's, Coote's and Wentworth's.

'Oh, do tell me, Cathy, what he writes!' I had begged her. I knew she would never have revealed its complete contents to Lady Stavourley, but I was privy to her dearest secrets; my position was sacred. On most occasions, she would have grabbed my arm and pulled us into some shielded corner, but instead she looked at me and nibbled at her lower lip.

'He writes of personal matters, cousin. I would not wish to betray his thoughts publicly.'

I felt as if my heart had been thrown upon the floor.

'But you have always read to me . . .'

'That was different,' she scolded. Her words came as sharply as a slap.

I stared at her, the injury plain upon my face.

'What?' she demanded.

I could not bring myself to say any more, and seeing this, she turned on her heel in a huff, as if I had paid her some insult.

Allenham's first letter was soon followed by others. There were two more directly after this one; and a total of five in nine days. From what I could observe, some were very short, taking up only one side of one sheet, while others filled three pages in neat, tiny script. The arrival of another letter would always send Lady Catherine into a spin. She would snatch it up from wherever it had been laid and then run into a corner or to a chair where she would devour it like a hungry dog. As soon as she had consumed it, she would leap to her feet and dash to her escritoire. I would often see her, her head bent over her writing desk, grinning at the sport of what she wrote, her hand flying rapidly over the page. Sometimes, if she was especially excited by her correspondent's words, she would press the letter to her heart and cry aloud, 'Oh, my dear, dear Allenham,' as if she were Mrs Siddons or some other artful lady of the stage.

I hope you do not think me too contemptuous in my remarks? It is not my desire to appear scornful, for I was not in the least. In spite of my cousin's coolness towards me, I remained elated for her. But, you see, those were difficult weeks, filled with anticipation. There was little more we could do than wait for a sign: a word from either my uncle or Lord Allenham that they had met and that some discussion or negotiation had been opened. All the time we forced ourselves not to think about what may (or may not) have been transpiring in London. We walked, we embroidered, read, played music, rode, painted and paid visits to local friends and to the shops in Bury St Edmunds, pretending our thoughts were upon other matters. In truth we thought of nothing else. We paced, fidgeted and stared blankly at our stitching and books. If you have ever trapped a wasp beneath a glass and observed it spin round and round in a frustrated fury, you would know precisely how we felt.

'This really cannot continue for much longer without his lordship declaring his intentions,' my aunt muttered one afternoon as I accompanied her through the garden. She was directing her woman, Betty, to cut some of the newly sprung flowers for her apartments. I assisted her, carrying the basket.

'I cannot imagine why he delays,' she mused. 'The Earl has sent him a letter, inviting him to Melmouth. I can only guess that he is fixing on a date to come.'

'Perhaps it is Parliament that distracts him,' I offered in my small voice. My aunt looked at me as if I had trodden on the hem of her muslin gown. What could I possibly know of such things?

'I do not like to contemplate what occupies him, Hetty,' she said finally. 'Such a delay speaks of hesitation – whatever the reason may be.'

It was after that exchange with my aunt, when the skies began to darken and fill with rain, that we returned to the house. I handed the basket full of lilacs and roses to Betty, slipped out of my garden pattens and returned to my bedchamber, where I hoped to replace my soiled stockings with a clean pair. As I opened the connecting door that led from the dressing room to my bedchamber, I noticed a small sealed letter sitting upon my writing desk. It was rare that I received correspondence, and even more curious that the note had not been brought directly to me by a servant. At first I thought the letter might have been intended for Lady Catherine, but it was addressed in a clear hand to Miss Henrietta Ingerton. As there was no postmark, I realized that it must have been delivered by hand.

Carefully I opened the seal, which was a plain patch of red wax, void of any crest or design. That which lay inside gave me such a shock as to nearly make my knees give way.

Over the years, for many reasons (most of which you will discover as you continue to read my history) I have learned to commit to memory the details of the more significant correspondence, books, documents, etc, that I have read. A very learned gentleman in Italy once taught me that it is possible to fashion the mind into a tablet and lay every essential fact upon it. Age makes this task rather more difficult. Much of the writing stored upon my own tablet has faded with the decades, but there are some things, some letters and conversations, which pertain mainly to matters of the heart, that have remained more or less permanently inscribed. This, reader, was one such letter, and I shall recount it to you the best I can. He began it thus:

> I hope you will forgive me, my dearest Miss Ingerton, for taking this enormous liberty in sending you this letter, but I have meditated a great deal on the predicament which I now face, and have alighted upon no immediate answer to it. I have concluded that there is nothing more I can do but present my dilemma to the one who is the subject of it, in the hope of finding some solution.
>
> I hope I do not presume to say that, at Bath, I believe we came to know one another intimately, though there is much about my current situation of which you are not apprised. As I write this, the Earl of Stavourley will be learning the truth of my income and the mortgages entailed on Herberton, the estate in

Gloucestershire I inherited from my father. Due to some imprudent investments made by my father and my uncle during my childhood, I have found my income greatly reduced. Indeed there are a good many obligations which I must meet, not the least being the improvements begun on Herberton which I have not had the means of completing. This is a disagreeable situation with which I am faced, and one which I hoped to remedy though the usual means of making a good marriage.

It has always been my belief that a marriage should be a union based upon friendship and enduring affection. This I feel for your cousin, Lady Catherine, but that which I had not anticipated were the sensations I felt when in your presence, Miss Ingerton.

You, madam, are all I imagined that my wife might be. In you, I see all the qualities of a dear life companion; your soul is a sympathetic one, your heart is kind, you possess an understanding unrivalled in any young lady I have met. Indeed, your conversation and friendship have been so warm and artless that I have often imagined passing my days beside you in the manner so rarely seen among ladies and gentlemen. This in itself, madam, would have been enough to capture my heart entirely had you not also been blessed with such great beauty, charm and grace. You have in your looks the power to enslave any man in a mere glance!

My dear Miss Ingerton, you have not been out of my thoughts since the evening I first danced with you and I have struggled, nay, I have literally torn my heart to pieces in an attempt to free myself from the love that has overwhelmed me. I cannot for the sake of my duties and obligations marry as my heart dictates, but madam, my heart dictates that I cannot live without you. What then am I to do? I have resolved to write these words to you in the hope that you will put me beyond my misery, that you will confirm to me your shared affection, or else deny me and send me into a life of desperate unhappiness.

I am, madam, your most tormented servant,
Allenham

I stood for a long while staring at the words. I read them several times over. My heart beat so heavily that it jarred my stomach. I believed I might be sick. My skin prickled with heat and then a chill. Oh gracious heaven! I thought to myself, rubbing my wet hand across my brow. I paced the room. I read the letter again, and then I caught sight of myself in my mirror.

There on my pale, frightened face sat a smile. It was to me like glimpsing the moon in the daytime, it was a sight so contradictory – as if my mind said one thing and my heart another. It was my heart that produced the smile, that heart which, like Allenham's, had fought for weeks to deny the sensations pounding within it. Tears came to my eyes.

What was I to do? He is to marry Lady Catherine, he is not for me! my head, the even-tempered philosopher, argued. But the heart, it is a wilful thing. Once the heart acknowledges a truth, it refuses to relinquish it. The mind has the power of reason, it may ignore anything it chooses; but the heart knows no return, once a truth has penetrated its armour it has no ability to recant it. The truth lives within the heart, it ignites passion like a bonfire and the mind is helpless to extinguish it.

Dinner was called, but I was so unwell that I rang for Sally to unlace me and climbed into my bed. 'I believe I have caught a chill in the garden,' I told her, and she relayed the message to my aunt and cousin below. I lay there, my eyes wide open, my heart, that demanding, violent organ, thumping like horses' hoofs in my head. I knew I must write to him, but what? I should remain guarded about my feelings, but remind him of his duty to my cousin. I should promise him a life of friendship.

It was very late when I pulled myself from my bed and sat down at my writing desk.

'My dear Lord Allenham,' I wrote, while listening for any stirrings outside my door. All was silent.

> As you may imagine, the contents of your letter have thrown my own heart into a great deal of turmoil. I know not the proper response to make, only that which is my duty to write. I must begin by declaring that in the time of our acquaintance at Bath,

I did nothing to invite your attentions or to encourage the feelings that have taken root within you. You have indicated that you know the whole truth of my circumstances, that my position here is a precarious one. I have no fortune of which to speak, I have not even a hundred pounds entailed upon me and am dependent entirely on the goodness of my uncle and his family to maintain me throughout my life. Sir, in this condition, it is unlikely that I should marry. You know as well as I that few gentlemen would have for their wife a young lady of no means, however decent her character or winning her charms. Therefore, you cannot fault yourself for maintaining your familial duty and considering first the obligations you retain to Herberton.

I, for my part, have been prepared since childhood for a life of dependency. My expectations were always for a single state and my failure to marry should therefore prove no hardship to me. In light of this, my aunt has impressed upon me the importance of seeing Lady Catherine make a good marriage, so that my future comfort might be secured within her household, or in the households of either of her two brothers, as a lady's companion.

In these circumstances I must do what is incumbent upon me and beg that you do what is honourable. For the sake of my cousin, who is most powerfully in love with you, make an offer of marriage. In spite of your reduced fortune, I am certain it will not be refused. Their lord- and ladyships have always indulged their daughter and wish her to be married according to her desires, provided she has attached her affections to a suitable candidate of upstanding character and family name, of which you have both. Do not delay, sir. I beg you.

As for my own feelings, I hesitate to write of them. Suffice to say, your letter has granted me the greatest happiness my heart has ever known. I will say no more on the subject. A pledge of everlasting friendship, the truest devotion and sisterly affection is what I shall always offer you, as your most adoring,

Henrietta Ingerton

I read my missive several times over and, satisfied that I had acquitted myself in the appropriate manner, sealed the letter.

Allenham had left no address to which I might send a reply, but had given instructions that I write my response addressed simply to Lord A – and that I 'leave the letter behind the stone urn to the left side of Melmouth's north gate, whence it shall be collected'. I can only imagine the lengths he had gone to in hiring a messenger to ride between London and Suffolk.

The following morning, after a night of little rest, I stole away to the north gate and placed the letter in the agreed position.

You may wonder: did I not feel myself to be dishonest in entering into this correspondence? Yes, it is true, the matter played upon my mind a great deal, but I felt as if I had committed no crime in responding as I did, imploring him to marry Lady Catherine. There was no error in this. I did not lead him astray, reader. And what can be said to a man overcome with love? And, worse still, what can be said to a man overcome with love when a love for him lives and breathes in one's own breast? No, when the entire predicament is considered, you will agree that my actions were noble ones.

In dispatching that answer, I believed there was an end to the matter, as sorrowful as it made me feel. And so you might imagine my surprise when, not two days later, there was another letter sitting in the same position upon my escritoire. I started when I saw it, a mix of dread and thrill rising from my feet into my chest. I carefully shut the door to my bedchamber and snapped the seal.

> You have, my beloved angel, confirmed all that I wished to know by your response; that it is true, you do share the passions which I have attempted to suppress. You cannot make me believe otherwise, my darling creature. Your honour and modesty are only two of the becoming qualities which adorn your perfect character. As for me, I am lost. All that I am has crumbled under this terrible torment. I am not the man I felt I was, but some wretched beast who can neither sleep nor eat, but, dear, dear, madam, your letter has offered me hope, it has provided me with a possible solution to the predicament which I face.
>
> You have stated in your letter that your future depends upon your cousin's marrying, so that you might then be taken into the

household of her husband or the households of her brothers. In this there is great hope for our shared happiness, as upon making Lady Catherine my wife, I shall offer you a place in my home as well. Your cousin would not feel the loneliness to which ladies are often prone directly after marriage, and I, madam, should always have the pleasure of your companionship and sisterly affection, as you suggest.

I am most grateful to you, my dear Henrietta, as your letter has convinced me of the correctness of my next step. You will therefore not blame me, but congratulate me for the action I have taken in order to secure this end. Just this night, I have supped with Lord Stavourley and officially applied to him for the hand of his daughter. After learning of my reduced means, he was, I admit, hesitant at first, but he has since been persuaded that with his daughter's portion and the addition of an income secured through a position in government, we may live comfortably.

The matter is all but agreed and depends only upon your cousin's concurrence. This, I believe, will be made final when I accompany the Earl to Melmouth in three days' time. I have written to Lady Catherine to inform her of my visit.

Oh, my dear Henrietta, should it come to pass, I would be made the happiest man alive. I cannot fail to see how the situation would not be agreeable to all concerned. I am until then your most contented and loving,

Allenham

Burn this.

By the time my eyes had taken in his final paragraph, I had fallen upon my knees and clapped my hand to my mouth. The letter trembled in my grasp. The deed had been done! The wheels had been set in motion at my direction – yet something seemed terribly wrong! I had to read his words three or four times before I was certain of his meanings. He had declared his love for me – oh joy! How my heart radiated with heat, how my head spun, yet my soul was filled with such a discord, such dismay and misery! Was this an honourable course upon which to embark? Oh! I did not know! The mind of a girl not yet seventeen is a clouded thing in the best of times, but when in love there is no clarity of judgement, no sense of direction. And what should such a young lady do without the counsel of even one friend or guardian? Have some pity upon me, reader. I was naive and confused. I had no one to whom I could turn. I could not decide what to do. I panted. I held my chest and lay down to think. I read the letter again, this time attempting to calm myself. It seemed different when I did not panic, when I permitted reason to guide me.

When I caught my breath and considered it, there was nothing in his suggestion at all improper. Was it not the very design my uncle had intended for me all along? Did Allenham not propose we live as brother and sister? The more I reasoned, the more I could see that Allenham's plan was in no way a dishonourable one. He would never have suggested such a deception. Indeed, all parties stood to benefit: Lady Catherine would have Allenham as her husband (which was what she desired); he might have the benefit of a marriage to a suitable wife; I might then be assured of the protection of a man who cared for my well-being, while he and my cousin might also prosper through my companionship. I reasoned and quieted my fears, but in truth I felt no better than a bird caught in a net, not knowing what to do to dis-entangle myself.

'Hetty!' I heard my cousin call from outside my door. I had hardly recovered myself and pushed Allenham's letter into the pocket of my gown before she threw open the door. She too was in possession of a letter. I looked with a flush of shame at the pages she held.

'He is coming and he says he has a question of great importance he wishes to ask me!' she exclaimed in a shriek, her cheeks as pink as roses. 'Oh Hetty!' she squealed, grabbing me by the hands and twirling me about my room. 'I shall be Lady Catherine Allenham! I think I shall die of happiness!'

'Oh cousin!' I exclaimed as she pulled me into an embrace. 'What a joyful day this is!' I tried to muster as much enthusiasm as I could. Looking at her features dancing with delight, her broad smile and high arched eyebrows, knowing that she enjoyed a genuine contentment at this, was, I suppose, all the confirmation I required that Allenham's plan was a noble one, and that I had nothing to fear from the matter. It would all be for the best.

Yet still, knowing the Baron was on his way, comprehending what was about to transpire, I could not entirely suppress a feeling of dread. I was too young to recognize the sensations of anxiety, for this was what it was. I had not seen him since our time in Bath and I yearned, positively hungered to have him stand before me; but, at the same time, my desire repulsed me: it seemed sinful, deceptive, dishonest. I wondered how I might feel in his presence, now that I knew his emotions and he had guessed at mine. What occurs when love is not spoken of or acknowledged? I had only the foolish plots of the novels my cousin and I had read to inform me, where knights and heroines donned disguises and met by moonlight in fragrant gardens. I could not imagine myself engaged in such shameful subterfuge.

I worried what might happen when Allenham and I met. Would my aunt and uncle be able to read my heart in my expression? Would Lady Catherine guess? Perhaps I should take to my bed and feign illness, I thought. But that would not do. It might force Allenham to seek me out. I could not imagine a way out of this conundrum. I must bear it with strength and courage, as I would have to for the rest of my life.

In the few days before Allenham's arrival, my behaviour must have appeared strange to my cousin. While she crackled with high spirits, rushing between rooms in a fit of constant giggles, or breaking into song at every turn, I, by contrast, grew more quiet than usual.

One afternoon, as I lay upon the sofa with a volume of Mr Pope's poetry, Lady Catherine threw herself down beside me. She crunched her nose and made a silly face, 'Oh serious, serious Hetty,' she teased, attempting to shut my book. 'Why so downcast, cousin?'

'But I am not downcast,' I objected.

'You are! And I am so happy, and you are so glum . . .' said she, nuzzling against me like a playful puppy. Her expression was one of mock sympathy. She was accomplished at that look. 'Are you sad that I am to be wed and you are not?'

'No, quite the contrary, I am most happy for you,' I said. She inspected my face, not convinced.

'This is the reason, I think. You are sad that I am to be wed and you shall be a spinster.'

I sighed and shut my book.

'You cannot deny it. I see the look of melancholy in your eyes, Hetty. I do. But you must not despair. Not when the Reverend Pease has been paying you such notice.'

This, reader, was a most cutting remark, one that was intended to provoke rather than to soothe. Now, I must tell you something of the Reverend John Pease, to whom she referred.

I dare say that there are some men put upon this earth who will never appear in the least bit attractive to young, unmarried ladies, no matter how rich or well connected they are. The Reverend John Pease was one such man, but to worsen matters he was neither rich nor from a tolerable family. He was the rector at St Margaret's in the neighbouring parish, which was unfortunately a very poor living, but one which came under the Earl of Stavourley's patronage. Pease had been appointed the previous year, and since then had been a guest at Melmouth Park, though not a frequent one, I am pleased to say.

While there was nothing unpleasant in Reverend Pease's character, he was not the sort whom ladies found entertaining. I doubt gentlemen would find his conversation engrossing either, as he talked of little beyond sermons and fishing and often nodded off to sleep in his chair just when the company became lively. I expect from my description you would imagine him to be an old man, perhaps one who took snuff which he dropped all over his cravat, a miserly septuagenarian whose nose was misshapen and red. But no, in 1789 Reverend Pease was all of twenty-eight! One might never have guessed it. His hair was thin, of a white-blond colour, almost grey. It would have been suitably in vogue had powdering still been *à la mode*, but now that young gentlemen had begun to wear their hair *au naturel*, it made him appear not only unfashionable but ancient as well. He was not a man of complicated manners or dress. His suits were of a plain puritanical wool and shaped to hold his enormous girth, while his jaw had a habit of hanging slack when his attention was fixed on something.

Pease had made his first appearance among us at the annual New

Year ball at Melmouth and no doubt his presence would have gone completely unnoticed had he not made such a spectacle of himself. It was not that he made any outrageous *faux pas*, or fell upon his face in a reel, or drank himself into a slumber, as many are inclined to do. No, Pease was more amusing than that. He caught Lady Catherine's notice by attaching himself firmly to my side. In fact, I found it near impossible to shake free of him the entire night. Wherever I walked, he followed, wherever I sat, he joined me. He spoke of nothing, but stared at me, like an infant child beside its mother. He drove off nearly every dancing partner with cross looks and guarded me with the fierceness of a sultana's eunuch. I had not the courage to jilt him and sent pleading looks to my cousin, who spent most of the occasion laughing cruelly behind her fan. Thereafter he became our favourite object of ridicule. For several weeks Lady Catherine's sharp-witted comments would throw me into fits of laughter and bring a hesitant smile to my aunt's face, but all of this came to an end after Lord Stavourley received a letter from Pease, in which he expressed his 'great affection' for me. From then onward, Lady Stavourley forbade her daughter from speaking so unkindly.

My aunt told me little of what was in his letter, only that the Earl had put him off because he possessed an income of no more than two hundred pounds a year. This news might have provided me with some comfort, had my aunt not delivered it to me with a pinch of spite. 'He was disappointed to learn you had nothing entailed upon you,' said she, her face blank of expression. 'I believe he thought you were worth more.'

After this, I could never quite fathom what plans she had for me and Pease. Although my uncle had discouraged him, I suppose she had not quite dismissed the possibility that he might take me off their hands. This, I am certain, is the reason why she invited him to dine with us on the evening when Lord Allenham and my uncle were due from London. She wished him to think the door had not completely shut on his ambitions, regardless of what my uncle had led him to conclude. At the time, I was surprised by her actions. It would be a few months still before I would come to understand her motives and to view her in an altogether different light.

The thought that Allenham was on his way to Melmouth was enough to unnerve me, without the promise of Pease's company as well. I tried all I could not to appear perturbed. I had not slept much the night prior to his arrival and I rose very early that morning. I dressed and went for a lengthy walk through the park. When I returned it was past midday and my absence had worried my aunt. I had been out for so long that I had lost any sense of time.

'Hetty, my dear,' she addressed me with a stern look, 'you cannot avoid seeing Mr Pease or paying him the basic politeness to which he is entitled. You must remain at all times civil while he is our guest.' I bowed my head, dutifully acknowledging my aunt's concerns. She knew nothing of what genuinely troubled me.

Pease, it turned out, had arrived and was in the library, writing his sermon for Sunday with the assistance of the Earl's large collection of texts. I managed to avoid this room for the better part of the afternoon. After all, he was not my immediate concern.

It was Lady Catherine and her nervous state that consumed me. She fluttered and flapped much as she had during our stay in Bath. Such was always the way with my cousin; she lived forever in extremes, fits of tears, passions of hatred or the dizziness of ecstasy. Her dressing room was a scene of chaos: a broken porcelain box lay on the floor along with a spilt jar of pomade. While she paced and babbled like a madwoman, Sally crawled around her, attempting to tidy the mess. I recoiled from this, shutting myself into the modest sanctity of the only space I felt to be truly mine: my bedchamber. There I waited.

An announcement came in the late afternoon, shortly before dinner, that the Earl and Lord Allenham had arrived. Lady Catherine was beside herself, like a gun dog whipped into a lather of excitement. She threw herself at me as I emerged from my room.

'Hetty,' she pleaded breathlessly, 'you must assist me down the stairs. You must escort me. Take my arm, cousin, or I shall have a fit. I fear I cannot support myself.'

'Hush,' I said, stroking her. 'If Lord Allenham inspires this in you now, how might you be when you are his wife? When you have to pass every day in his company? He will think you terribly silly and frivolous.'

At this, she exhaled deeply and attempted a serene, if not haughty smile. I took hold of her arm as she desired. In fact, I was shaking nearly as much as she. The words I had used to soothe her were the very ones I had repeated to myself not a moment earlier.

They awaited us in the blue drawing room. As we neared it, I could hear my uncle's voice, his discourse on the state of the turnpikes carrying through the enfilade of rooms, as if he were addressing the House of Lords. My cousin and I progressed in fraught silence. Lady Catherine was so consumed by her own nerves that she failed to notice mine. I remained quiet and composed as the door was opened for us.

As a rule, dear reader, I have found it good policy never to look directly at the object of one's affections upon the moment of reunion. The meeting of two lovers is always a slightly awkward affair, particularly following a first declaration of attachment. And if the attachment is an illicit one, the strain of concealing the electricity of one's feelings can be too intense to bear, even for the most practised flirt or hardened *roué*. No, it is always best to look away. Of course, at the time of this incident, I had not the experience or wherewithal to have invented such a plan. It happened quite by accident. I simply could not bring myself to look at Allenham. His mere presence in the room made me gasp for breath. Instead I fixed my attention on Lady Catherine, who quivered and blushed, before dropping a curtsey that was far too deep for the occasion.

Unlike the two of us, the Baron seemed perfectly self-possessed. Gentlemen are so accomplished at this, at tucking their true emotions behind their expressions. They stand tall, their hands folded behind them, their backs so straight that the tails of their coats lie evenly against their breeches. Allenham held his head high; his posture and manners were flawless. He greeted us both graciously.

That evening was an odd one. A spring thunderstorm had risen up from nowhere and let loose like a cannonade over Melmouth. The candles were lit at early evening, as they might have been in winter. As we sat around the table there seemed to be a heaviness present. I cannot say what it was precisely. It did not seem ominous, more expectant, like the sensation that fills a theatre before the commencement of a performance. All who had sat down to dinner knew the reason for their being there. We were the audience and our attention was set on the hero and heroine, who were positioned directly opposite one another.

Conversation did not flow gently. I have not mentioned that Pease was beside me, and across from him, the parish rector Reverend Hammersley and his wife, who had been invited to swell the company and cut the dullness of Pease's presence. The portly reverend chewed his food with loud relish and turned to address me at any opportunity.

'I am pleased we are no longer upon the road,' said my uncle just as the windows received a lashing of hail.

'I dare say so, my lord,' responded Pease. 'The horses would be terribly frightened by such a cacophony. Do you not agree, Miss Ingerton?'

I nodded.

'Horses are such stupid creatures. I declare my own mare, Maisie, bolts at the slightest commotion, though I have no doubt she is in good hands while in Melmouth's stables, Miss Ingerton.'

Allenham allowed Pease to prattle on in this fashion, permitting him to interrupt his discussion on several occasions; '... *The Recruiting Sergeant*? Oh yes, a capital play, don't you think, Miss Ingerton?' and '... Mr Walton says the same about trout fishing in the *Compleat Angler*. Certainly you have read it, Miss Ingerton?' But by the end of the meal, I could see from the way in which Allenham smiled and inhaled that Pease, his constant interjections and attention to me had become unpleasant to witness.

The Baron and I endeavoured not to let our eyes meet. With the exception of one instant, when I turned and from behind the glare of the candles beheld his soft, longing expression, we behaved with the utmost formality. I have since learned that this is the worst tactic to adopt. When wishing to disguise an unspoken passion, no two people will make a greater attempt to ignore one another than those who fear their love may be discovered. But we were not expert at these things and did only what we thought correct in the circumstances.

The night was only to grow more tiresome. The pelting rain prevented a post-prandial stroll, which would have freed the party from its sense of confinement, and from the discomfort of knowing that we were there not to enjoy one another's company, but merely to fill the hours until the following day, when Allenham might be alone with Lady Catherine and ask for her hand. There seemed to be an endless amount of waiting in all of this, which no one appreciated. We went first to the library and then back to the blue drawing room, where we had tea. Although the fires were unlit, the rooms felt close and hot, as if the grates were blazing. My cousin, who had passed so many hours in anticipation of this reunion, seemed on the verge of combusting. She was breathy and fidgety; I had never before seen her so agitated when in the company of a suitor. As I listened indifferently to Pease's chatter, I studied her, sitting beside Allenham. She looked to me strangely vulnerable and tremulous. At that instant my heart ached. Something pulled inside it. It was pity, pity for all of us.

I have mentioned that I did my best not to meet Allenham's gaze, and indeed, he endeavoured to avoid mine by occupying himself entirely with my cousin. When we moved into the library, that minx Mrs Hammersley suggested that Lord Allenham 'read to us some of the love sonnets from Shakespeare'. He turned away and smiled to himself.

'I do believe a tragedy may be better for the digestion, madam,' he stated, and reached for *Julius Caesar* instead. It was only when he looked up from reading that he would hazard a glance at me.

I did not suspect that he was attempting to communicate something until slightly later, once we had moved back into the drawing room for cards and tea. By then, I could sense in him a growing tension. There was a Boulle clock in that room, a fine object of gilt work and polished wood that struck down each quarter of an hour. Its face seemed to peer over Allenham's shoulder, and almost as regularly as the clock pinged, he would raise his eyes to me, each glance appearing more urgent than the last. This began to unnerve me, and then to frighten me. I could not make out what the matter might be, or how to respond.

At eleven, supper was served, and the assembled guests rose from their conversations and games of whist. Allenham laid down his hand and with great determination shot me a look of such seriousness that it caused me to start. As the party departed through the doors to the adjoining dining room, I took the opportunity to search out the commode. I discreetly slipped through the jib door and into the corridor. There, in that private moment, I was able to gather my wits. I had been greatly shaken and confused by Allenham's sudden alteration.

When I emerged back through the drawing room, I was surprised to see him standing before me in the semi-darkness of the quiet room. He had dropped his mask of pretence, and beneath it lay the expression which he now revealed to me: one of anxiety and pain.

'My dear . . .' he whispered, advancing towards me. 'Forgive me,' he said, reaching out for my hands. He shook his head and seemed unable to find his words. His distress, his candour were so unlike that of the composed gentleman he had been earlier that it made my heart surge with love.

'Please,' he begged of me, 'I cannot do what I have come to do . . .' He fell to his knees and held my tiny frame to him.

Oh Eros! Oh sweet Venus! To be embraced by him! I had never known such a feeling, as if every particle of me might come apart in his arms. He pressed his face to my breast and I, not knowing where to place my shameful hands, rested them upon his shoulders. Although my head was spinning with a sickening mix of forbidden love, desire (which I could not properly put a name to just yet), guilt and unworthiness, I knew I must instruct him – I knew I must instruct myself.

At first I could do little more than inhale but, in doing that, I only drew him closer to me, taking in the aroma of woodsmoke and lavender upon his clothes. I shut my eyes and steadied my thoughts.

'You must,' I managed to whisper. 'It is for the best . . . the best for all concerned.' I felt the strength of his grip, the tightness of his arms around me. 'There is no other way. You yourself have written that to me,' I urged him.

His heaving body continued to press into mine, as he held me for what seemed like an age. It is true what they say, that there is no time in a lover's arms. There are no minutes or hours, no measures, only sensations, heartbeats and breaths.

Very gradually, he released his embrace. He disengaged himself, backing away slightly as he rose to his full height, continuing all the while to hold my gaze.

'It is . . . I believe, not wrong . . .' he stated, now in a more assured tone, 'so long as we resolve to live as brother and sister . . . as friends.' He took another step back, though he looked at me with such intensity that I felt as if I might lose the strength of my legs.

Until that moment, I had never known the true force of love. It is like nothing else on earth. It contains in it all the fierceness of a hurricane, a snowstorm, a volcano. It is the very essence of the sublime, that overwhelming of the emotions which Allenham had attempted to describe. We are helpless in its wake, like ants in a flood.

He stood there, composed and honourable, studying me. 'Because of you, I will do what is correct.' He then took my shaking hand in his. 'You have granted me the conviction to do it.' In saying that, he slowly raised my palm to his cheek, that gentle, defined place above his jaw, and drew it down along the strong line of his chin. A wave of dizziness passed over me. Were he not holding fast to my hand, I would certainly have lost my footing. He closed his eyes. 'Sister,' he breathed. 'Friend. That you shall be.' Then he guided my fingers to that place beneath his shoulder, in the middle of his chest, where I could feel the steady beat of his heart. 'And for ever mistress of this.'

Chapter 7

And so, on the following day, Lord Allenham put his proposal of marriage to my cousin.

Had I been the scheming little hoyden that Lord Dennington suggests, I would not have hidden myself away that morning. Indeed, sir, if my heart is as black as you attest, why had I not eloped with his lordship on the night before, as he had kneeled before me, prepared to pledge his love? No, as I have described, it was on account of my persuasions that he executed his plans, and my actions were guided by only the most virtuous of intentions. It was my pure heart that instructed me to hide myself away on that morning. I went to the top of the house, where I knew I was unlikely to be found. I brought with me my watercolours and brushes and carried them to our former nursery, now quiet and empty. I resolved to absent myself from their company, so that Allenham might be left alone with Lady Catherine and utter those words it was so necessary for him to deliver.

I knew that my cousin would later recount to me every detail of the transaction.

Apparently, Allenham had asked her to take the air with him after breakfast. 'Hetty, I was so very anxious, for I felt certain he would do it then . . .'

'And did he?' I asked, though I knew the answer perfectly well.

'Oh,' she squeaked, shutting her eyes and clasping her hands to her breast. 'He did!'

'And you accepted?'

'But of course! Of course I accepted!'

'Oh cousin!' I exclaimed. 'You are to be wed!' And at that we embraced as ardently as we had ever done.

As we held each other tightly, Lady Catherine leaned her mouth to my ear: 'And I let him kiss me.'

I paid no mind to that part of her confession.

As you may imagine, that day was one of high spirits at Melmouth. The housemaids gathered in the corners and whispered the news between them. Cook made up Lady Catherine's favourite orange pudding as a dinner-table surprise. My cousin's feet hardly trod upon the ground, while my aunt's face seemed to take on the lightness of springtime itself.

I was by no means immune to the happiness of this event. If nothing else, it provided me with an overwhelming sense of the correctness of my actions, that I had conducted myself with dignity and duty through-out. I pushed to the back of my mind the other thoughts: Allenham's words; the professions of love in his letters; how my physical person had throbbed under his touch. Now I would be as a lump of cold stone. After all, what right had I to entertain, even for a moment, a sensation of love? None, I reproached myself. None whatsoever! I would not permit myself to feel so much as a thimbleful of despair at my cousin's triumph. This was a cause for celebration, for Lady Catherine's nuptials promised all three of us a life of contentment. As I sat in her company that evening, watching her glow as brightly as the candles, I permitted myself to feel nothing but her elation. I swore that I would hollow out my heart till it was empty of everything but her desires. I would bind myself to her more fervently than I had ever before. I would mould myself into her handmaiden and my life would be dedicated to serving her. Her joys would become mine; I would live through her completely.

Oh reader, you know as well as I the impossibility of this. I fear that dear Allenham understood it too, and loathed himself for it.

At dinner, he looked at me not even once. It was as if I were nothing but the leather of the chair upon which I sat. Instead, his gaze rested all night upon the lovesick features of his fiancée. He could hardly tolerate my presence, and immediately withdrew with from any room in which he found me. I was not foolish enough to mistake this for rudeness, but rather some commendable effort on his part to conquer his weakness.

It was accident that brought us together at the end of the night. Upon climbing the stairs on my route to bed, I found him at the top of the landing. We were not entirely alone, as two housemaids were occupied in laying Melmouth to rest, snuffing out candles along the corridor where we met. I stopped awkwardly, and lowered my eyes.

'I have not yet offered you my congratulations, my lord,' said I, with a curtsey.

'I am most grateful for them, madam,' Allenham responded, before a heavy silence began to expand between us.

Slowly, I removed my gaze from the floorboards, and for the first time that day, took in the spectacle of his striking features. The shadows were resting softly along his cheek and chin.

'What would you have me say?' he asked in barely a whisper. He brought his eyes down upon mine, heavily.

I looked away, not on account of shame, but because his stare had been so deeply loaded with longing that I believed it almost indecent.

'I feel as if I have become Werther,' he declared, shutting his eyes and shaking his head. 'And you, you are to me as Lotte was to that poor soul.' He exhaled and regarded me once more. 'But it is done, my angel. This is our fate. And now I shall fulfil my obligations to your family and to mine. My fortune will be repaired. We shall have much to celebrate in future, Miss Ingerton.'

Allenham fixed a smile over his mouth and dipped his head to me graciously before proceeding down the dim corridor to his bed.

I struggled to sleep that night, my mind rolling with thoughts. Among them was the name Werther. I had heard much talk of the book, *The Sorrows of Young Werther*, but had not read it. Lady Stavourley certainly claimed to know enough of it to condemn it outright.

'Was there not a young lady who drowned herself on cause of it? In Brandenburg or Baden, or some such place?'

'A dreadful matter, to be sure,' replied her companion. 'And there have been others too. I have heard the book is prone to make its readers run mad.' She sighed. 'Those with weak natures should not read such violently sentimental novels.'

'Well, I should not like to read it,' declaimed my aunt, before turning the conversation on to paper flowers or some such subject.

Regardless of Lady Stavourley's objections to the work, by the following morning I had thought enough upon the matter to decide that I would like to – no, that I *must* read this book, for in it I believed lay some key to Allenham's thoughts.

As soon as I was able, I went to my uncle's library and there found a translation of Mr Goethe's novel among the shelves. I drew it down and opened the covers of this unassuming text, entirely uncertain of what I should find within it.

I was greatly engaged by the character of Werther, a young German gentleman of some means who desired to discover something of life through his travels. In the course of his wanderings he was introduced to Lotte, with whom he formed a friendship. Werther did not intend to fall in love with Lotte, who was betrothed to another, Albert, but found himself so enthralled by her that he could not do otherwise, and as Werther tumbled further into a vortex of passion, he brought me plummeting with him.

'I can no longer pray except to her; my imagination beholds no figure but hers; and I see the things of the world about me only in relation to her. And as a result I do enjoy many a happy hour – until I have to tear myself away from her again!' Werther cries. And then once more:

> When I have been with her for two or three hours, entranced by her ways and the divine expressiveness of her words, and my senses gradually become excited, my sight grows dim, I can hardly hear a thing, I have difficulty breathing, as if a murderer had me by the throat, and then my heart beats wildly, trying to relieve my tormented senses and only making their confusion worse!

Oh reader, I hung upon Mr Goethe's every word. I positively ate each metaphor and verb from the page, for what struck me was that these were not merely Werther's thoughts, but Allenham's! Here lay a picture of his lordship's sufferings for me! Did he not call me his Lotte? Had he not confessed his similar torments?

I read more and more, my entire person quaking, my eyes barely able to take in this feast of revelations.

Werther leaves Lotte to marry Albert, a cold, selfish man incapable of feeling the warmth of love expressed by his rival. 'How cruel is life!' I found myself exclaiming. Werther then returns, determined to conquer his passions, but fails. Even after befriending Albert, he is powerless to staunch the outflow of love he feels for Lotte and begins his descent into madness. 'I am resolved to die!' poor Werther declares to the object of his passion. 'It is not despair: I am convinced I have endured my fill of sorrows, and I am sacrificing myself for you. Yes, Lotte! Why should I not say it? One of us three must die, so let it be me!'

How I wept at this. Why, I nearly soaked my uncle's book with my tears. My heart begged Werther not to take his own life, but as I read line upon line, I saw how his own destruction neared, until that very instant when he pulled the trigger and extinguished himself. 'What grief! What senseless tragedy!' I mourned. 'And Lotte, stricken by her loss, and Albert made miserable too.' In truth, until I ventured to read *The Sorrows of Young Werther*, I did not think it possible for a human heart to ache and rejoice with such fervour. Dear friends, I was dizzy with this thought, stunned, like one who has been hit upon the head.

The novel was a very short one, and without so much as leaving my chair, I had consumed it whole. Indeed, by the time I shut the book, I was surprised to learn that dinner was to be called. My stomach turned over at the thought of sitting opposite Allenham. After reading so far into his soul, I wondered how I might ever look upon him again. Fortunately, fate intervened and spared me this discomfort.

'My fiancé has taken his leave,' moaned Lady Catherine as Sally assisted her out of her day dress. 'Business has called him to London.' I was at first surprised at this news, but then understood why Allenham had not made his farewell to me: did Werther not ache whenever he quit Lotte's company? No, Allenham could not have remained among us for long while his thoughts spun with such confusion. He required some distance to restore his composure. Indeed, we all required some time to catch our breath.

As you well understand, a wedding creates a fair deal of work for both sexes. My uncle and his solicitors were soon consumed with the business of negotiating the marriage contract. There were stocks to be disposed of and property to be purchased. Documents were to be inspected and disputed before the men could press their hard seals into the soft red wax beside Lady Catherine's name. As for the ladies, there was the matter of the wedding trousseau.

Lord Allenham's coach had hardly passed through Melmouth's gates before talk of this had begun. There were all manner of practical things to be gathered in London; the purchase of gowns appropriate for a married lady of quality was only the half of it. There was the childbed linen to be assembled, nightdresses and nightcaps, sporting attire, and a hoop procured for wear at court. But even if there had not been a reason to set out for the capital, my aunt would have invented one. It was June, and as Parliament was to be in session for several weeks more, many of the families of quality remained in town. Lady Stavourley would not have them depart without all of London hearing her news. She wished to make a very visible show of her daughter upon the arm of Lord Allenham.

Reader, I cannot describe to you my uneasiness at the thought of meeting with the Baron again. I confess that since his feelings had been put so plainly to me by way of Werther, my mind had been thrown into a turmoil. My heart pulled this way and that. While strolling with my cousin or idling beside the fortepiano as she played, my thoughts would stray to Allenham until, horrified by the sensations I felt, I shook my head to rid myself of them. At other times, when I believed myself quite distracted in sketching a landscape or a still life, he would come to me again; his words – Werther's words! Then I would drop my chalk and fly to Mr Goethe's novel, to read some passage or other that would set my heart alight. When alone in my bedchamber, I would unlock my escritoire and feel for the small cache of his letters, hidden at the back of a drawer, and take secret delight in them. What sickness this was that overtook me! How I struggled to free myself from it, and to set myself back upon the correct path!

All the way to London I trembled in the coach as I sat beside my cousin.

'Hetty, are you ill?' she finally enquired.

'No,' I answered, mortified. I immediately corrected my conduct and berated myself for my foolishness, until my heart, like an unbroken horse, attempted to bolt from its restraints once more.

I could not imagine how Allenham fared in the midst of this tempest, though at our next meeting, which occurred in the drawing room of my uncle's house in Berkeley Square, he was all good humour and politeness. In fact, he came upon us by surprise, as we had not expected to see him until that evening. This was truly a blessing, for otherwise the anticipation of meeting with him would have undone me. There he found us, my aunt attending to her morning correspondence and Lady Catherine and I upon the sofa with our embroidery. I blushed as much as my cousin when he entered the room, and averted my gaze when he placed a kiss upon her cheek. It was only then that I noticed the book I had so carelessly left upon the table beside my embroidery: *The Sorrows of Young Werther*. Unable to part with it, I had carried it with me to London. It is with shame I admit that by then it was as indispensable to me as a prayer book. I was forever thumbing through its pages, searching for some reminder of Allenham's love for me. Oh, and as I did it, I despised myself all the more!

As Allenham greeted me, I saw that his eyes briefly landed upon it, and in an instant I felt as if all my vices had been unmasked. I shrank back, ashamed of my conduct, and resolved once more to dispel all my absurd longings, however impossible this task may have seemed.

It was not until the following day, as we took our constitutional in Hyde Park, that he made mention of the novel to me. He had Lady Catherine upon his arm for the entire afternoon, while I hung back, strolling beside my aunt, who had hardly uttered more than three or four words to me. It was not until meeting with Lady Carlisle and her daughters, who distracted my cousin with gossip, that Allenham turned to me.

'You have been reading *The Sorrows of Young Werther*?' he asked, a hint of eagerness in his tone.

'Yes. Yes, my lord,' I confessed, colouring furiously.

'And what think you of it?'

If I had one accomplishment as a young lady which outshone all others, it was my ability to tie my tongue in knots.

'It . . . Well, my lord . . . I . . . It . . . is the most extraordinary book I have ever read . . .'

He smiled at this, seemingly reassured by my response.

'Indeed, I believe it is matchless,' he agreed. '*The Sorrows of Young Werther* has no equal. I have found nothing to rival its true portrayal of anguish.' He looked at me, his features softening. 'Not even Monsieur Rousseau can describe as well the expressions of true passion . . . of love . . . the sufferings . . .'

'Yes,' I exclaimed, my eyes wide with ardour. 'I have never read such a depiction . . .'

'. . . of what it is to burn?'

My steps stopped quite suddenly; Allenham saw my quaking. My face was now bright as a berry. Too much had been spoken for delicacy's sake.

In his azure eyes there lived such desire. I caught my breath and pressed my hand to the gauze of my buffon.

'Lotte,' he muttered, his mouth moving almost in silence. 'You are my Lotte. I am your Werther.'

'My lord,' called Lady Catherine at that moment, at that terrible instant, when I thought I might fall dead in a fit upon the ground. How grateful I was for her intrusion, how wrought with despair I felt upon hearing her voice – my beloved cousin, to whose happiness my heart was sworn.

She wished for her fiancé to catch her up as she and Lady Carlisle sauntered arm in arm. I turned away from Allenham, and nodded for him to leave me to Lady Stavourley and two of Lady Carlisle's daughters who followed closely behind.

How I was to recover from that encounter, I knew not. The effect of it upon me was like the introduction of a venom into my veins. It took hold of my senses, causing me to grow light-headed and distracted. I stared like an idiot into the distance. I was deaf to any conversation but his. This poison, this corruption remained in my body for all that day and into the next. At night, I wept into my bed sheets, so disgusted by my desires, so knotted with confusion that I writhed in pain. Love, I feared, had conquered my rational mind. 'I am lost!' I cried, doomed to live out my years pining for my cousin's husband. Indeed, had Lady Stavourley not intervened when she did, I do believe my situation may have ended rather differently.

As I have explained, the purpose of our visit to London was, as expressed by my aunt, to gather the necessary items for Lady Catherine's trousseau. Greater still was the need to have as many eyes as possible witness these activities. While Lady Stavourley might have arranged for the various tradesmen to call at Berkeley Square, instead she chose for us to pay visits to purveyors of millinery, stockings, gloves and linens in person. 'It will make for a day's amusement,' she suggested, while searching beyond the window of Lord Stavourley's coach in the hope of spotting some acquaintance or other.

Lady Catherine certainly raised no objection to her mother's plan, for how often is it in a woman's life that she may anticipate a succession of gifts and purchases to be made on her behalf? Since her engagement, my aunt and cousin's conversation had turned entirely to gowns and hats, fabrics and trimmings, yellow silks and tabbies, gauze shawls and petticoats. Indeed, these thoughts preoccupied Lady Catherine so greatly that we rarely spoke of anything else. Our shared pleasure of reading aloud 'dark works' had come to an abrupt end. In fact, nothing I said or recommended seemed to capture her attention any longer. I wished more than anything to ignite her interest in *The Sorrows of Young Werther*, but failed on that account as well.

'It is the most possessing love story I have ever read,' I gushed, but my cousin merely turned the book over in her hand and laid it down again.

'I fear I have little time now for novels, Hetty.' She sighed. 'There are far more worthy distractions when one is to be married.'

Instead, she preferred to list the jewels her mamma claimed Allenham would purchase for her. 'All manner of necklaces and eardrops and bracelets . . . why, this in itself is reason enough to marry!'

With so much to be acquired, it did not surprise me in the least when the Baron proposed that we amuse ourselves with a visit to the shops along New Bond Street. Hardly two days had passed since our last encounter in Hyde Park, and I was not at all myself. I seemed to pass each moment in a reverie, my mood swinging like a clock pendulum between joy and despair.

As it was a fine summer's day, we went in Lord Allenham's barouche, his horses proudly pulling us down Piccadilly under the warm sunshine. He sat opposite me, composed, his dark fringed eyes never daring to touch mine. So long as he kept his gaze from me, I could venture to look at him, to study the perfectly straight line of his nose and the light scattering of freckles along it I had not before noticed.

We paid a visit to Randall and Son, the glove-maker, and then called at Wilding and Kent, which in my day was a cavernous hall of billowing colours and oak shelves stuffed with bolts of bombazine and muslin, taffeta and broadcloth. Although I took in this scene, although I heard Lady Stavourley speaking with Mr Wilding, although I watched buttery silks and cards of lace rolled out before me, I seemed to be hardly present at all. My eyes stared vacantly at the drolls in the window of Mrs Humphrey's engraving shop, which sent Lady Catherine into fits of giggles. In truth, I could see little else but Allenham. I could admire nothing beyond the mahogany of his hair, or the strength of his stance. This was until we visited Barnaby's, the fan-maker on Old Bond Street.

Mr Barnaby had his wares arrayed along his dark shelves; they sat spread open, each like beautifully painted butterflies, displaying their scenes. Some bore tableaux of dancing muses, others of floral swags and cameos in pastel hues. There was one, made of white kid leather and set in the window, to which Allenham's attention was drawn. He directed the shopkeeper to fetch it and as he did, the design caught my eye.

Painted on to a background of white and green were three round portraits: one of Werther in his blue coat and buff breeches; another of Lotte, a blue ribbon tied into her hair; and a further image of Albert.

'This is from Frankfurt, my lord. A fine piece of foreign manufacture. You are familiar with the novel by Mr Goethe?'

'I shall have it,' Allenham stated, 'and the pink silk with the punched ivory handle as well.'

He glanced at me and smiled, and then at my cousin.

'I do hope the pink fan is to your liking, my lady?'

I do not believe Allenham saw any harm in buying me a trinket. He was too well versed in the nuances of genteel behaviour to have carelessly committed a *faux pas*. My cousin, who had been lavished with gifts, certainly did not object, but my aunt, that was another matter entirely.

I have no doubt that from the time we arrived in London, Lady Stavourley had fixed her eye upon me. In truth, the symptoms of my condition were most likely evident to her before we had quit Melmouth. My lovesickness was apparent in my demeanour; it was worn upon my face as obviously as a pot of rouge. In such a state, I was a menace to all her well-intentioned designs. Allenham's gift confirmed her concerns and prompted her to take immediate action. I suspect she dashed off a letter to Mrs Villiers as soon as we returned to Berkeley Square – and sent it by express to Bath, for not three days later, I was in Lord Stavourley's town coach, making the lengthy journey along the Great West Road.

As for the fan, I never saw it again.

Chapter 8

I was such an inexperienced child. For the life of me, I could not begin to fathom what I had done to merit this banishment. I was dispatched to spend the summer with Mrs Villiers, in whose care I was to remain until September, when my cousin was due to wed. How I despaired at being torn from Lady Catherine at such a time! I wished so much to share in her excitement, to join in entertainments and outings with Lord Allenham.

Instead, I had been sent to Bath, where I was to act as company to an ageing widow. While Mrs Villiers was not quite infirm enough to be thought dull, neither was she young enough to be considered amusing. To be sure, she had a broad circle of acquaintances, composed of every manner of person from grand dowagers to sea-weathered admirals, but very few among them were agreeable companions for an unmarried girl.

Our days ticked by to a rhythm of visits to the Pump Room, promenades, modest dinners and games of cards. In the evening we attended the theatre and occasionally the Assembly Rooms. My hostess was most generous and kind, but failed to distract me from that which preoccupied my mind. Many hours were spent sitting in the window of her dark, quiet drawing room gazing out on to Gay Street, watching the sedan chairs and horses move to and fro while I revisited the memories of my last visit to Bath. When I first arrived at Mrs Villiers' home, I wrote nearly every day to Lady Catherine, but, during the entire course of my stay, received only a handful of letters from her in return. These were filled with trivial news: talk of two new gowns she had had made up, and of a visit to Mr Boydell's gallery of Shakespeare paintings. She hardly made mention of Allenham at all, except to announce in July that they were to go to Gloucestershire, where she would inspect Herberton, the house of which she was to become mistress. There they would be joined by a number of the Baron's relations and neighbours, and together, she anticipated, 'they would make a merry party'. I confess, upon reading this, my heart sank very low indeed.

Oh Allenham. There was scarcely an hour when my thoughts were free of him. I failed to purge him from my heart; the flame I bore for him did not, as my aunt must have hoped, burn out at a distance. I kept *The Sorrows of Young Werther* at my side. If it was not lying upon the table nearest to my bed, then I had it in my pocket, or in my hand. By now certain pages had begun to display wear, for I had read my favourite passages so regularly that I had almost committed them to heart.

My lonely sojourn with Mrs Villiers provided me with much time for reflection, and as an unfortunate result of this, I descended far deeper into Werther's world than I had before. As I lay in my bed, I contemplated any number of alternative endings for the hero and heroine. I was even compelled to write my own, where Albert, seeing that his fiancée was so smitten with Werther, and Werther so in love with her, stood aside, and permitted the couple to marry instead. However, what haunted me most was Werther's love-addled decision to take his own life. Why? *Why?* I asked myself again and again, when happiness was so near to his grasp?

> One of us three must die, so let it be me! Oh my dearest one! This broken heart of mine has often harboured furious thoughts of – killing your husband!

What if Werther had done that instead? It was an unconscionable thought, but the heart is not a reasonable organ.

With time, it is possible that my passion for Mr Goethe's novel may have boiled away of its own accord. Like any young miss of just seventeen, some other book or object would have taken hold of my attention and enthralled me. But this was not the case. The fires that permitted my fascination to simmer were stoked continually by Allenham's equal enthusiasm for the story. I had not expected to receive proof of this during my stay in Bath, and was therefore taken entirely by surprise when I received a letter from him. He had been brave indeed to write. His message found me as it had at Melmouth, by way of hand delivery. There was no postmark. One of Mrs Villiers' maids handed the small packet to me while her mistress dozed in her dressing room.

'My dearest heart,' I recall he began it:

> I have struggled a good deal to learn of your whereabouts, and as you must appreciate, it is most dangerous for me to write. By now, I have no doubt you will have heard of the momentous events in Paris, that the Bastille prison has been taken, and with it, an entire nation has embarked upon the infant steps of revolution! It is a time of great excitement – would that Monsieur Rousseau had lived to see it, for they cry the words of his Social Contract in the streets! Indeed, the French are making a fine show of throwing off their chains – your uncle, Mr Fox and Mr Burke speak of nothing else. At Herberton, the gentle-men raise toasts every night to the end of tyranny. Oh my darling, sweet Henrietta, I dream every day of seeing you here, of having you here to rejoice with me. Knowing that you are less than a half-day's ride from where I reside is a constant distraction to my thoughts. There is much I long to show you: our avenue of ancient oaks, the paintings and treasures brought here by my father and grandfather – my dearest, you will vastly admire the beauty of Herberton, of that I am certain. Not two days ago, I enquired of Lady Catherine if she favoured the notion of your coming to live here after we are wed, and she did not oppose it. I fear the furnishings, which she claims are both *outré et passé*, are of more concern to her at present. So it is to be, my angel! You are to come and live among us, and we may delight in one another's company every day of our lives.

> Until that time, my Cherished One, I fear that hazarding a response to this letter would prove unwise. While Herberton is occupied with guests, there are more pairs of eyes about than

usual. But I beg you, do carry in your heart my undying flame,
dear Lotte, as I am for ever your devoted Werther.

And here, reader, I found myself lost once more, pitched back into a
stultifying reverie of love. I pressed my copy of *The Sorrows of Young
Werther* to my breast and shed tears of bliss and heartache.

There was no cure to be found for my afflicted heart at Bath. I regret
to say that my aunt's plan to rid me of my attachment to Lord Allenham
had come to nothing. In truth, by the time I returned to Melmouth in
late August, my thoughts were as possessed by him as they had ever
been – perhaps more so, for now I counted the days until my cousin's
nuptials, when I was certain the happiness of we three would be sealed.

Hardly a fortnight stood between Lady Catherine and her wedding
day and I was most eager to be reunited with her: my bosom friend, my
dearest companion. I had missed her company, her constant chatter and
witty remarks, almost as much as I had longed for Allenham's. I was
never so pleased to travel up the long, straight drive to Melmouth as I
was upon the occasion of that homecoming. How delighted I was to
survey the familiar fields and paddocks, the hedges and chestnut trees
tipped with yellows and browns. What contentment it gave me to
mount the steps of my uncle's house, to pass through the portico and
into the echoing, marble-lined great hall. But my joy was short
lived.

My relations seemed almost indifferent to my reappearance. It was if
I had never been away. My aunt was far more grateful to see Mrs Villiers,
who had been my companion upon our journey, than to receive me. My
uncle I did not have chance to greet until supper, and even then his
attention was distracted with some urgent matter of correspondence or
other. Lord Dennington and his brother, whom I had not seen for
nearly a year owing to their being at school, were as cool and formal
with me as they might have been with their tutors. Worse still, my dear
Lady Catherine, my *chère amie*, to whose life I was devoted, seemed
entirely unmoved at our reunion. When I appeared in our apartments,
she behaved as if we had only been parted since breakfast.

'Oh,' said she, 'you are returned.' She rose from the writing desk where she sat and, with her attention still fixed upon the letter in her hand, beckoned me to her. 'Come kiss me, Hetty.'

'Oh cousin,' I exclaimed, vibrating with the excitement of seeing my most cherished friend once more, 'do tell me all your news.'

'I am afraid there is not much to tell.' She mustered a vague smile and then sat down with a sigh. 'Herberton is not at all what I expected. It requires much improvement. There is an entire wing left unfinished, not even the rooms plastered. His lordship will have to order new furnishings . . .' She drifted off, her mind clearly preoccupied with some other matter.

'And what of Lord Allenham?' I enquired, my pulse quickening.

'Oh, there were a great number of relations and friends at Herberton to whom I was introduced,' she stated, her expression unmoved by the mention of his name. 'Did I not write to you of this?'

I shook my head.

'I met his cousin Mrs Ayres, who is only just wed. We became fast friends,' she pronounced, her expression suddenly brightening. 'Mr Ayres has a phaeton and we raced about in it through the villages, causing such a scene! What fun it was! I dare say she has the most fashionable hats and gowns I ever did see. I shall see her mantua-maker after I am married and spend all my pin money upon having gowns made up like hers!'

'But what of your wedding trousseau?'

She laughed haughtily.

'Hetty dear, you know so little of the fashionable world.'

'Oh, but you must instruct me . . . I should like to know everything. I should love to know what you do and what you see. Your stories are vastly entertaining . . .'

'Mr and Mrs Ayres have a house not ten miles from Herberton, and a house in town as well. We shall be constant companions! She pledged as much to me before we departed. I have received a letter from her nearly every day and she tells me all I should like to know of married life. She informs me of all the gossip and the intrigue . . . such things Mamma would never disclose!' She giggled.

The longer I regarded her, the more my smile began to sink.

'I was replying to her last letter when you arrived.' She looked over at her escritoire. 'I should return to it. She will be anticipating my response.' Lady Catherine began to rise from where she sat, and then, recalling something of importance, turned to me. 'Mamma spoke to me about the arrangements for you.'

'Arrangements?'

'Yes, after I am wed. Lord Allenham has offered you a home at Herberton.'

My expression brightened once more.

'But Mamma opposes it. She says you are too young by far to make your home with us, especially so soon after we are married. You are to remain at Melmouth for some time longer.'

So startled was I by her words, that I continued to stare in disbelief.

'But . . . what shall I do . . . without you . . . ?' I managed to say.

She snorted. 'Occupy yourself, dear cousin. You are accomplished at that. And I shall visit and see you . . . on occasion.'

My wounded gaze followed her across the room.

'Now, this letter must be closed before it is too late to send it.'

I confess, this unanticipated turn of events rattled me so greatly that my eyes began to fill with tears. I sprang from where I sat and ran directly to my little bedchamber. There I lay, gently weeping for the loss of all that I held dear. I dare say Lady Catherine could hear every sniffle of my sufferings, but chose to ignore them entirely.

Until that time, I had not experienced anything like the true despondency, the aching sense of desperation that poor Werther had endured. More than ever, I felt myself in a hopeless situation. I had no means of communicating with Allenham, no channel through which I might plead my case. For so long I had dreamed of the promised scenario, I had passed so many hours musing on our contented life, I had wished and wished and now it would amount to nothing. For several days I hung my head, speaking very little, observing the preparations and the merriment through moist eyes. 'Dear child,' my aunt eventually remarked, 'it would do you well to appear pleased at your cousin's good fortune.' At her prompting, I attempted a smile, but it quivered and soon dropped. Dear reader, such a fit of melancholy consumed me that I took to wandering my uncle's estate, searching out the most secluded groves and desolate spots. There I would throw myself upon the hard ground and give in entirely to my despair.

I confess that emulating Werther's fate did enter my mind.

One of us three must die!

I thought on how I might do it. Perhaps I should sew stones into my skirts and drown myself like lovelorn Ophelia? I should not like to hang myself, nor resort to a pistol, as Werther did. I knew not where to procure poison.

After an hour or so of mourning my fate, I would then brush the leaves from my gown and lumber back to the house.

It was following one such fit of misery that I returned to a terrible shock.

I thought myself alone when I pushed open the door to our drawing room. The sun streamed in through the window, still full of the golden hues of summer. My cousin had thrown a book upon a chair and left some writing paper spread across her open escritoire. I wondered why Sally or one of the housemaids had not tidied it away. It was then that I heard a strange noise.

At first I was uncertain what it was, or whence it came. I stopped and listened to what sounded like wheezing and sniffling. It was then I heard my cousin's strained voice and noticed that my bedchamber door had been left ajar. Cautiously, I approached it.

The scene that greeted me is one that has remained imprinted on my memory. To this day, I can still recall each detail, even the pinks and greens of my cousin's gown and the browns and blues worn by Sally, who sat upon my bed, cradling her mistress's head in her lap.

The drawer of my escritoire lay upon the floor, its contents scattered across the room. At the clawed feet of the desk, an overturned jar of black ink spread like tar. But this damage could be undone. The ink could be blotted away, the pieces collected, the drawer put back into place. That which could not be undone was clutched in my cousin's left hand.

By my own admission, I had been exceptionally foolish to keep the letters Allenham had instructed me to burn. I had tried on several occasions, but simply could not bring myself to do it. I had wept at the prospect of destroying the only gentle words that had ever been written to me. Instead of doing what I ought, I had stuffed them into the drawer of my escritoire, just behind a jar of ink, and locked them away. I had not even the wherewithal to hide the key, but rather let it sit in its treacherous little lock for anyone to turn. Eventually, Lady Catherine opened the drawer. As I understand it, she had emptied her pot of ink and, knowing I kept some in my writing desk, came in search of it. Then, like Pandora lifting the lid of her box, all manner of horrors came flying out.

It was Sally who first noticed me in the doorway, and, sensing her alarm, my cousin then lifted her head. Her face, swollen and pink, appeared battered. Indeed, her cheeks had been so puffed by grief that her eyes had all but disappeared. I watched her eyebrows slowly arch and her mouth part, before it drew back into a snarl. Cautiously, I began to move away, like one retreating from a vicious animal, but before I managed to take two or three steps, she sprang from Sally's embrace.

'You . . . Jade! Judas!' she howled with fury as she grabbed for me.

'Cathy!' I cried as she raised her hand and slapped me in a rage. Horrified, I pulled away and collapsed into a shamed, frightened heap at her feet. 'Please no, cousin, please . . .' I begged, raising my arm to shield myself from her blows, but it was of no use. She began to kick me, softly at first to see what damage her foot might incur, and then harder and harder still, until I shrieked with pain. I rolled away from her and attempted to rise, but all at once she was upon me, her face contorted with wrath. With her fingers curled into claws, she continued with her frantic attack, each strike of her hand cutting into my cheeks. Believing I might be murdered, I begged for mercy, calling to Sally to rescue me from the talons of this harpy, but rather than pulling us apart, the vicious little demon ran for the door and locked it fast!

In true fear for my life, I struggled to free myself, twisting, kicking and pushing with all my might. I heard some part of my gown rend as the taste of blood and tears dripped into my mouth. It was only when Lady Catherine got hold of my throat and began to squeeze that Sally saw fit to intervene. Until then, she had been content to stand over us like a judge at a bare-knuckle boxing match, grinning at the spectacle with a type of stupid pleasure. Having decided I had taken beating enough, the maid got hold of my cousin's waist and pulled her on to my bed. There Lady Catherine sat, restrained like a beast, panting and growling until Sally took her into her arms and began to hush her. She smoothed her ruffled hair and rocked her gently, until her mistress's howls subsided into whimpers, and eventually into silence.

I remained upon the floor, winded and sobbing. My face had been raked with scratches, my lower lip bled on to my chin. The seam that held my bodice to my skirt had been ripped open. My head ached, as did my shoulders and back. I coughed and wept, almost uncontrollably, though more from fright and shock than from pain. In all the years I had been victim to my cousin's rages, I had never known her to attack with such viciousness.

For some time, I sat where I had fallen, too terrified so much as to wipe the blood from my face. I dared not raise my head, even when Lady Catherine began to address me.

'If my father learns of these letters, there will be no wedding.' She spoke in a cold and measured voice. 'You must understand, cousin, I will marry Lord Allenham. But I shall also see to it that he will never have you. You will never look upon one another again. You will be dead to him.'

At that, the tears flooded into my eyes.

'Oh, you may weep, you treacherous, ungrateful vixen . . . scheming little harlot,' she hissed at me. 'You may weep for your loss, for these will be the last days I ever call you cousin!'

She turned her head away, but Sally's defiant eyes continued to press into me. It was a look that ordinarily might lose a maid her place, but as her triumph over me was now complete, she felt entitled to display it.

With her she-wolf's gaze firmly fixed upon me, Sally assisted her mistress from my bed and, with a great show of tenderness, led her through the door. It was only when she turned to shut it behind her that I noted my letters, wet with tears, still in her hand.

Chapter 9

Now, my friends, I lived in true fear, for I understood too well my cousin's temper. I knew this incident had been merely the spark that lit it, and that once ire had been ignited in her heart, it would continue to smoulder there, long after the initial injury had burned out. Worse still was the firm alliance she had forged with Sally. With the two united against me, there was no cruelty they were incapable of inflicting. Oh, how I trembled at the prospect of this.

To be sure, my heart had been deeply injured by her attack; the violence of it had left me terrified and shaken, but remorse, too, crippled me. If I could have unpicked the events of the past, if we had never gone to Bath, if I had refused to dance with Lord Allenham, I would have done it. I contemplated this unfortunate chain of events over and over, as I sat, alone and terrified, in my bedchamber.

It would be unfair to call me a coward; I had not yet developed that strength of character necessary to be resilient, so I remained in hiding, too distraught and frightened to show my face that evening. I lay curled upon my bed like an injured cat, listening with wide, fearful eyes to the conversation that transpired in the drawing room.

It at first appeared that Lady Catherine had recovered with remarkable speed from her shock. As Sally dressed her for dinner, she chatted with surprising good cheer about the night ahead, prattling about their neighbours, Lord and Lady Bristol: how her mamma disliked the Earl, and how disgusting she found his wife's teeth. Then she sighed.

'What might we tell Mamma about Hetty?' she mused to Sally. At the mention of my name, my stomach bunched into a knot. 'I do not suppose she will emerge this evening,' she snorted.

'Miss Ingerton has taken ill, my lady,' Sally suggested.

'But I dare say her face will be scratched mightily and I must account for that somehow. If I do not invent some tale to explain it, the little fibbing minx may confess it to someone.'

Indeed, to hear my cousin plotting in such a manner chilled my blood.

'Perhaps she took a fall, madam,' offered Sally, enjoying this sport far more than she ought.

My cousin thought upon this for a moment. 'I shall say she took a tumble while out walking. She tripped upon the hem of her skirt and went face first through the shrubbery.' She laughed merrily. 'My stars, Sally, what ingenuity have I for telling a tale.'

'I shall have cook send her up a tray. Some boiled chicken perhaps. Food for an invalid?' They both cackled at this.

My eyes began to smart with tears. Dear Lord, I knew not how I was to endure the trials that lay in store. I was certain this was only the prelude. I laid my head upon my pillow that evening, unable to fathom how I was to face the days ahead of me.

It is often said that for every predicted outcome, Fate invents one more, which could not have been foreseen. I had imagined a torturous string of days leading to my cousin's wedding, where I would be made to suffer torments both to the body as well as to the heart – but this was not Fortune's plan.

I confess, I had thought it queer how rapidly Lady Catherine had recovered her good humour following the discovery of my letters. Outwardly she seemed entirely mended, but inwardly the venom of her anger had only just begun its ruinous course.

She awoke the following morning with a fever upon her and insisted on remaining in bed. I listened at my door as Sally described her mistress's symptoms to her concerned mamma. 'Her throat is mightily sore and her voice nearly gone. She shivers a good deal too.'

'Then for heaven's sake, girl, have the fire lit in her chamber!' snapped Lady Stavourley as she hurried to her daughter's side,

'And fetch some of Dr James's fever powder, you stupid hussy.'

Unfortunately, the powders did not succeed in suppressing her temperature and by that evening, she was shaking furiously. Lady Stavourley became greatly unnerved by this. She ordered a glass of sack whey to be brought up, but her daughter felt too unwell to take any nourishment. 'I insist upon it, Catherine,' I heard my aunt protest, her voice high and anxious. 'You are to be wed in scarcely a week, my dear – *a week!*' she pleaded, as if she believed her daughter's illness to be another of Lady Catherine's tricks, designed to vex her. 'I will not countenance a postponement,' my aunt scolded.

But my cousin's affliction could not be commanded away, least of all by her mother. It proved as stubborn as she had ever been. It wrapped itself around her chest and filled it with a racking cough. Higher still burned the fever, until, by the second evening, she could do little more than moan and wheeze. Sally had sat with her through the night, mopping her wet brow and speaking to her in gentle tones.

On the third day of her illness, when it appeared that she would not repair herself, my uncle sent for the physician. Dr Stirling came directly from Bury St Edmunds that afternoon, escorted to Melmouth in Lord Stavourley's coach. He arrived in a flurry, his apprentice carrying a box of potions and instruments necessary to cure her. They and my aunt disappeared into my cousin's chamber and within the hour, Sally emerged ferrying a bowl of her mistress's blood through our drawing room. She coughed violently as she did so, her face now plainly pallid and drawn.

Several moments later, Dr Stirling and my aunt withdrew from the invalid's room, discussing the sedative that he had administered.

'It will enable her to recover,' he assured Lady Stavourley, before putting his hand into the pocket of his frock coat. 'Then, once she awakens, you must give her this powder,' he said, gesturing to a packet in his hand. 'Foxglove is much recommended for respiratory ailments.' At that moment, Sally returned, rubbing the inside of the empty bleeding bowl with a cloth.

'Miss,' the physician began, preparing to instruct her in the administration of the medicine, but stopped as Sally fell into a fit of coughing. He examined her with a frown, and then turned to my aunt.

'My lady, your daughter's woman is too ill to wait upon her,' he pronounced. 'As it is necessary that Lady Catherine be kept from further contagion, is there not another among your number who may tend her?'

I had been sitting in the far corner of the drawing room, attempting as much as possible to remain invisible behind my book, but my aunt's desperate eyes soon fell upon me.

'Henrietta,' she called harshly, as one might summon a wayward lap dog. I crossed the floor obediently, my gaze lowered.

'My niece is a most capable substitute.'

I watched his eyes take in the scratches upon my face. He pursed his lips, but did not venture to ask as to their cause.

'This medicine is to be given twice daily,' said he sternly, 'once upon rising in the morning, then again in the late evening.' He unfolded the packet of gritty powder. 'Each measure should be no more than a pinch. Observe . . .' Then he dug his fat thumb and forefinger into the substance and held out what looked to me like an amount far greater than any pinch my little fingers could produce. 'Like so.'

I nodded.

'It is to be brewed as a tea, or diluted in some form of drink, such as watered wine or small beer. Do you hear me, miss?'

I nodded again. 'Yes, sir.'

'In large doses, it is a strong medicine . . .' said he, glancing at my aunt, 'but be assured, my lady, it is a good one. I do believe your daughter will shortly be returned to health,' he concluded, offering a brief bow.

I recall those words most clearly, Lord Dennington. I have listened to them in my mind for these many years now, echoing without end. 'In large doses, it is a strong medicine,' he had said. A strong medicine, but perhaps not a good one, my lord. Not at all a good one.

You have seen the treatises written recently by Dr Josiah Kipp at the medical school in Edinburgh? Digitalis, or foxglove, is now no longer employed in the cure of respiratory illness, it being (to quote that learned gentleman) 'in some cases more harmful to the patient than beneficial'. You cannot suppose I knew that, my lord. To suggest so is pure lunacy.

Upon Dr Stirling's direction, Sally was relieved of her duties and sent to bed. Her place at Lady Catherine's bedside was then assumed by my aunt and her maid, and when Lady Stavourley wished to retire, I was called upon to fill her position.

Speaking in hushed tones, she instructed me that a kettle of water and a teapot had been ordered in which to brew the foxglove. 'Do make certain she takes the full dose, Hetty,' she commanded me.

It would be somewhat dishonest if I did not confess that the prospect of entering my cousin's bedchamber filled me with the greatest apprehension. We had neither spoken nor laid eyes upon one another since our terrible altercation. Although I knew her to be greatly weakened by her illness and incapable of causing me harm, I still trembled at the thought of an encounter.

Hesitantly, I pushed open the door and stepped into the still, thick air of the sickroom. On either side of the bed sat two candles, while a low fire guttered in the grate. Although Lady Catherine lay in what appeared to be a deep sleep, each breath came with a wheeze as she struggled to draw it.

Frightened of disturbing her, I crept near to the large bed hung with fashionable Indian chintz, and assumed my place in a nearby chair. At first I was too shy, too ashamed to look upon her, and then, gradually, I permitted myself to glance at her still features. In spite of our unfortunate circumstances, my heart heaved nonetheless to see her so unwell. Unbeknownst to myself, I emitted a short sigh.

'Hetty,' she said suddenly, but in a subdued and raspy voice. 'Where is Sally?'

'Sally is taken ill.'

Just then, one of the housemaids came through the door with the kettle and teapot.

'Why cannot another of the maids tend to me? Where is my mother's woman?'

'Dorothy is here,' said I cheerfully, gesturing to the girl, not much older than me, who was now pouring hot water into the teapot. 'Dr

Stirling and Lady Stavourley have both directed me to wait upon you.'

She rumpled her face at this. I could sense her indignation and it disquieted me. The packet of foxglove sat next to a candle by the bed; I took hold of both of these items, my hands trembling.

'Well,' pronounced my cousin, 'I do not wish you here.'

By the low cast of the candle, my fingers worked quickly, and I measured out what I believed to be the precise dosage shown to me by Dr Stirling. I weighed that pinch of snuff-like powder between my fingers before releasing it into the water, where it fell to the bottom of the teapot and began to dissolve.

'At your request, I shall leave you, cousin, but not before the directions of your mother and your physician are carried out,' and with that, I poured the brew into a dish.

She began to draw herself upright, but was too gravely ill to manage it unassisted. I reached over to lend my hand, but she batted me away and instead motioned to Dorothy. I then offered her the dish of foxglove tea. As she took it from me, her gaze danced over the marks upon my cheeks. A hint of a smirk passed along her mouth.

'I have made pretty work of your face,' she commented before taking a draught of her medicine and wincing at its bitterness. 'I am only sorry I did not manage to gouge out your eyes.' She regarded me with an unmoving stare. 'But there is time still for that, I think.'

I moved away from her, my skin prickling with cold fear.

'Leave me,' she commanded in her strained tone. This I did, without any further hesitation.

This, dear reader, is my true and honest account of events. I have recalled every movement, every word and every action. What occurred between the late hours of the night and the early morning was no doing of mine. I have always made it known to my persecutors that I would swear an affidavit to this, but, as you see, they have found no means of supporting their accusations against me. There is no evidence, because there was no crime.

Where this matter is concerned, I will confess to you but one thing: it will forever torment me that my cousin's last words were spoken in malice. Whatever cruelty she inflicted upon me has long since been forgotten. I bear no ill will, nor would I ever have wished such a fate upon my own kinswoman.

At her insistence, it was little Dorothy who remained with Lady Catherine that night, dozing in the chair at her bedside. In the morning, it was she who found her; her fingers like ice, her lips blue as periwinkles.

I awoke to frenzied noises, to the sounds that follow on from the discovery of an accident: quick feet, gasps and shouts. Upon opening the door to the drawing room, I found the servants flying about like frightened wasps and Dorothy doubled over with sobs. Lewis, the butler, saw my terrified expression.

'Miss,' said he with disbelief, 'your cousin . . . Lady Catherine, she has died.'

At first I could hardly take it in. 'That cannot be,' said I, but no one heard, nor were they listening. In a daze I stumbled, still in a state of undress, across to her chamber.

But for an awkwardly outstretched arm, she lay much in the way I had last seen her. I approached the bed incredulously. I had only ever seen death from afar – the bodies of beggars by the road, criminals hanging by the neck from the gallows – but never, never the empty vessel of a loved one, one whose warm hand I had once felt in my own. What drew me near to her, I cannot say; perhaps it was a desire to know that I did not dream this in some nightmare, that I was indeed awake and alive. I moved my fingers to her motionless mouth, but felt no heat, no air. I half expected my cousin to unfurl her lips and bite me, but the sure recognition of death did that instead.

Chapter 10

What came over me at that instant, I cannot describe. Horror, like some dark vapour, rose up from within me. It filled my mouth, until I began to low like a beast in distress. As I did, I sensed the tips of my fingers, that part of me which had touched death, throb along my hand. I began to rub them vigorously against my night shift, before crying out in revulsion and then fleeing from that most terrible of sights.

Dear Lord, to this day I still recall it.

I shut myself behind the door of my bedchamber and wailed, gripping on to the bolster for fear that death might swoop in and spirit me away too. 'Oh my beloved cousin,' I sobbed, 'oh my dearest companion, my only true friend.'

As I cried, so I heard the echoes of my sorrow in the rooms beyond, the dismayed whispers and weeping of the household. The shock of this dreadful tragedy plunged all of Melmouth into the deepest of mourning.

As you might imagine, no one person suffered more greatly than did my aunt. Upon hearing the news, she collapsed into a fit of hysterics from which she never recovered. She was carried into her apartments where she lay for several weeks lifeless upon her bed, much like her daughter.

Save one unfortunate encounter, we never again spoke. It was a terrible incident. I came upon her at the foot of the dining table, a weary skeletal figure shrouded in black, so gaunt and wasted that she required assistance even to sit. Grief had ploughed furrows into her now limp face. I thought her unearthly appearance overwhelming, but she seemed to find my presence more alarming by far. Upon locking her eyes on to me, she froze and then, beginning to shake with fury or madness, cried out like a lunatic, until she was taken from the room and dosed with laudanum.

My uncle bore the tragedy with greater fortitude. In the midst of these distressing circumstances, he assumed the role of a ship's captain in a storm, a stoic who lifted his head towards adversity and who tightened his hands upon the wheel. The day following his daughter's death, he appeared, perfectly turned out in mourning, marching through the corridors of Melmouth, with the steward at his heels.

Arrangements for Lady Catherine's funeral were made and executed without the knowledge of any of the female members of the family. This was the manner in which these things were performed in my day. My poor, sweet cousin was conveyed from Melmouth and laid to rest in the very church in which she had been due to wed. I knew not even when they removed her from the house, or who, beyond Lord Stavourley and his sons, was present to witness her interment in the family vault.

To be sure, my uncle was masterful at placing a lid of silence over the entire matter. How precisely he managed to contain the gossip, I do not know. He is certain to have paid the London newspapermen each a hefty purse for never laying in type one word of the affair. His friends and relations would have held their tongues likewise. It remains a marvel to me how few in society heard the full story of Lady Catherine's death, and then only a great while after the event.

As for Lord Allenham, I cannot say for certain what came to pass in the days and weeks that followed the death of his fiancée. I overheard two servants recounting that his lordship had been notified the day before he was due to set out for Melmouth. Whether this is true, I cannot say. All correspondence between us had, quite wisely, ceased. Indeed, I do not even know if he was present at Lady Catherine's funeral. It is possible that he may have been, but refused Lord Stavourley's hospitality through a sense of shame. He would never have dared stay at Melmouth, for fear of meeting with me.

Dear reader, if you knew what distress descended upon me in that period. I not only bore the loss of my adored relation, but the painful knowledge that I was unlikely ever again to lay eyes upon Lord Allenham. How bitterly I wept, how remorseful I felt at all that had come to pass.

I dare say that grief can cause one to view matters in a mistaken light. So may have been the case with me. I do believe I was left too long to mourn unaccompanied. I saw my uncle only at meals. Lord Dennington and his brother had returned to school, and so Melmouth, without either Lady Catherine or the active presence of her mother, wallowed in silence. I remained for long spells in our apartments, attempting, as I had always done, to amuse myself. Gradually, I took up my paints, my sketching and embroidery. When my heart began to yearn for company, for the sound of Lady Catherine's familiar voice, I took myself to the library or out into the grounds of Melmouth, where I contemplated the browning flora and the rows of winter vegetables newly laid down in the kitchen garden. Yet no matter where I roamed, or how I attempted to distract my thoughts, I could not entirely calm my mind. More than anything, it was *The Sorrows of Young Werther* that haunted me. I thought of how I had dreamed of Allenham. In entertaining these fantasies, had I called down the hand of Fate to intercede?

One of us three must die!

Oh dear Lord! I paced and wrung my hands; I cried and gripped my head. My mind could not release this notion. I recalled that other occasion when my prayers had been answered, when as a child I had begged so fervently for the friendship of my cousin. This indeed had come to pass. The more I contemplated the possibility that somehow my desperate wishing may have inadvertently been to blame, the more I trembled. I feared it would drive me to madness! Whenever my eyes alighted upon the spine of Mr Goethe's book, I was thrown into a panic, and reminded of my anxieties.

Soon it was too much for my young, foolish mind to bear. I decided the only thing to be done was to part with the book, to bury it in my uncle's library where I should never look upon it again. In doing this, so too would I bury my shame, and the misguided belief that my will had played some part in this disaster.

I stole away to the library and there tucked it behind some other volumes. Upon turning my back to the shelves, I issued a great sigh. 'I shall never again permit that thought to enter my brain,' I swore to myself. 'I am a creature of reason. I am made of rational thought.' I shook my head, and then, fearing the idea might steal up behind me, I fled the room. From that moment, I resolved quite firmly to banish such absurd notions and, remarkably, I remained untroubled by them for some time.

It must be said that while I am entirely blameless for the misfortune which befell our house, there have always been others who believed – and still believe – to the contrary. That, at the tender age of sixteen, I had fallen in love with Lord Allenham, and he in love with me, I cannot deny. That dear Lady Catherine came upon a trove of letters which broke her heart is a matter of terrible sadness to me. But neither of these regretful circumstances renders me a murderess. All that you have heard from Lord Dennington and his friends are lies, drawn from the poison well of Sally Pickering.

I knew not what Sally intended when she carried away my handful of treasured letters. I own that the matter consumed my thoughts entirely until my cousin fell ill. Following her death, I assumed they had been thrown upon the fire. But this was not what happened.

Reader, you have seen the monstrous behaviour of which Sally Pickering was capable. A more vicious and untrustworthy slut I have never met. Indeed, when she had recovered from the illness that stole her beloved mistress's life, she returned to tend me, but chose for herself how she might perform her duties. The role she had played in my beating had emboldened her. She now wore insolence upon her face when I called for her, and was slow to come when I rang.

I had waited for nearly an hour for her one morning. She came through the jib door carrying Lady Catherine's mourning attire, the skirts of which had been shortened and the bodice altered to fit me. She regarded me disdainfully as she entered, as if I had paid her an insult.

'You did not come when I rang,' I scolded. 'I have waited almost an hour.'

She answered with nothing more than a sneer.

I might have checked her for her impertinence, but I was far too cowed to raise my voice. With her big hands and broad shoulders, she frightened me terribly.

She began to tug at the strings of my wrapper and then pull off my night clothes and cap. Once I was in my chemise and stockings, she took to tightening the laces of my stays, though with such violence that I cried out.

'Sally!' I exclaimed. 'You mean to kill me!'

Again, she offered no response, but haughtily continued to dress me, tying on my underskirts and Lady Catherine's hemmed black petticoat. I regarded myself in the looking glass, wearing her mourning apparel, the clothing that had been designed for her to wear should death come unexpectedly to one among our family. The sight of this caused me to sigh with sadness. I smoothed the skirts and adjusted myself within the bodice.

'Poor, dear Cathy,' I said wistfully, 'she has no need of these now.'

'As she has no need for Lord Allenham, eh, miss?' came a wicked voice from behind me.

I was so taken aback by this comment that I spun around and glared at her.

'How dare you?' I shot. 'How . . . How dare you speak in such a way!' I was shaking a good deal, and Sally could see this.

She smirked, unmoved by my outburst, her lip curled in amusement.

'I read the letters, miss,' she announced with pride. Slowly she slid her hand into her pocket and drew out the three wretched packets. In places, my cousin's tears had smeared away Allenham's handwriting. My expression fell.

'I wonder', she taunted, 'what would Lord Stavourley make of these? Or her ladyship?'

'How dare you?'

'How dare *you*, you murderous bitch?' she roared. 'I reckon there be enough in these to have you hanged!'

114

I opened my mouth, horrified at her suggestion. What if she was correct? Tears came flooding into my eyes.

'My silence demands a price.' She folded her arms over her round chest. 'What have you to pay me with?'

So shocked was I by her proposal that I did not react, unable to move or speak.

She studied me for a moment, before deciding that she would take matters into her own hands. She felt at her waist for the keys to my clothes press and then began to unlock it. She opened each of the drawers and cabinets until she came upon a roll of French lace my uncle had given to me. She swiftly slipped this into her thief's pocket, and then, quick as lightning, locked the drawers and cupboard once more.

'Now see here, little jade, I shall take from you what I will, when I will it, or you shall know my wrath,' she announced in a hiss.

The tears rolled freely down my face.

'Murderess!' she spat at me, before disappearing down the back stairs.

The matter did not conclude there. No indeed, Sally's game had only just commenced. In the weeks that followed the funeral, I lived in a constant state of fear. Each night I locked myself into my bedchamber, dreading that she might find me in my sleep and seek to avenge her mistress's death. In my nightmares she held a knife to my throat, or smothered me with her wide, flat hands. I slept poorly or not at all, and I awakened each morning to find that the daylight offered no more comfort than the darkness.

I began to seek out my uncle's company, lingering near to where I heard him, much as I had when a child. Sally would never dare torment me in his presence, and so this provided me with respite. However, she took my absence from my rooms as licence to pillage my belongings. I would often return to find that items had gone missing. She took from me, on various occasions, a lacquered sewing box, a fox fur muff and collar, two pair of gloves and a pair of paste shoe buckles; enough to have had her hanged at the assizes. Fortunately, she failed to locate the little net purse I possessed. Embroidered round with flowers, it had been the first article I had sewn as a girl. More importantly, it contained what small monies I owned: a sixpence from a Twelfth Night cake, and enough coin to permit me to pay for a letter, or pass into the hand of a servant or beggar. This I had stowed in a compartment of my escritoire, to which I alone now held the key. I had learned my bitter lesson.

As I lived in mortal terror of Sally, I never dared summon her. At first I relied on Dorothy's kind assistance, but then she too failed to come when I rang. You see, Sally had a much greater scheme in mind for my harassment. It was at about this time that I believe she began her campaign to turn all of Melmouth against me, and her false words brought many recruits to her cause. I soon found that my linens were not laundered. My chemises, stockings and sheets were not removed. But this was not the worst of it. I was left entirely alone, made to struggle into my own clothing each morning. Each day, I roused myself from bed. There was no voice to beckon me, no fire lit to warm the air. I pulled back the bed curtains and discarded my night shift and cap, only to replace these articles with a soiled chemise. I learned to loosely twist on my stays and then fasten myself with an unsteady hand into my dark clothing. I was even left to empty my own chamber pot.

So anxious was I to escape the emptiness of my apartments that I could not trouble myself with trifling matters of appearance. I cannot think what my uncle made of me in my unstarched cap and drooping gown. I must admit it was with great difficulty that I held my tongue and told him nothing of the trials I endured. I suffered so terribly; not only was I beset by sorrow for my loss, but burdened with a broken heart, pricked constantly by a remorseful conscience, and fearful for my life. I existed as a prisoner, as a character in my own 'dark tale', surrounded by scheming villains, by those who wished my ruin, protected only by the presence of my uncle, a noble lord. Never could I have imagined such a terrible fate for myself, never would I have believed it possible! It was as if the pages of *The Recess* or *The Castle of Otranto* had unfolded and drawn me down into their Gothic terrors.

The worst of it, the climax of my nightmare, occurred one evening in mid-October, in that time of shortening days and widening shadows. By then, I had come to see a foe in every corner. Every footman who passed through the rooms, every housemaid I spied, even Lewis the butler, I saw as one who might pounce upon me. I searched their expressions for traces of malice; I jumped when I heard their footsteps. With the passing of each day came the growing sensation that I was being encircled by a pack of baying wolves. By then, I imagined that Sally had displayed my letters to the entire staff, and in unison, like a chorus, they sang their condemnation of me.

I had been with my uncle that night. We had sat beside the fire in the blue drawing room, as I read to him from Virgil's *Eclogues*. As I did so, I could not prevent myself recalling happier times. I reminisced about the evening I had passed in that same chair, listening to Allenham's rich voice entertain us with *Julius Caesar*. I remembered Lady Catherine's warm, lively cheeks and how they had turned pink in the Baron's presence. The thought brought tears to my eyes and I rubbed them away quickly, hoping Lord Stavourley had not noticed. He had begun to doze in his chair and, at my pause, announced he would retire to bed.

'I shall order you some supper, Hetty, for mourning has turned you thin indeed,' he stated as he rose from his seat and rang for the footman.

It was with great trepidation that I approached the dim dining room alone. I walked unguarded through the empty, half-lit chambers. The windows were shuttered, closed fast like a tomb against the outside. I took my seat where a place had been laid. But for the lit torchères shining against the mirrors, the room was entirely still. I waited for a long while, but no one came to serve me. Now that I was accustomed to such treatment, I rose and was about to creep away when I heard a noise.

From down the darkened corridor came a small figure: Joseph, the hall boy, who under normal circumstances would never have been seen above stairs. Indeed, the sight of him, his untrained gait and his heavy steps, disquieted me.

Unaccustomed to serving, the boy came around to my side and lumped a covered dish in front of me. This was most irregular. The lid was removed and I could see, in spite of the gloom, a plate of fricasséed mushrooms.

Then, feeling around in his waistcoat pocket, he pulled from it a note. His face was most agitated, almost grey in colour.

'Pray, miss,' said he in an uncertain voice, handing me the note. I held it for a moment, not knowing what I should do.

Joseph gazed anxiously about the room.

'Do not eat it . . .' he whispered.

I regarded him with alarm, my shaking fingers picking open the note. There, scrawled upon the paper, was a clumsy phrase: 'An aye for an aye. Murtheress.'

I looked once more at the plate before me, heaped with buttery toadstools, and then, all at once, clapped my hands to my mouth. I leaped so quickly from the table that my chair fell, clattering to the ground. I did not stop to look behind me. I did not wish to see who peered through the darkened doorway, or how many of them sniggered at my fright. Instead I ran, I fled, howling, through the rooms until I reached the safety of my bedchamber and there locked myself away.

Chapter 11

I cannot describe to you the sort of night I passed. No Gothic tale, no ancient castle or dank dungeon held nightmares as real as mine. I sat awake, fully dressed upon my bed, listening for a shuffle of footsteps or the creak of floorboards. Although I had secured both doors from the inside, I anxiously moved my eyes from one to the other. I awaited the rattle of the handle; a sound I was certain would foretell the approach of my assassin. Eventually, as daylight began soften the dark sky, I drifted off into a shallow rest.

I do not know what time I awoke; it was late in the morning. I did not change my dress. I could not even wash my face, for there had been no water brought to me for some time. As I had done every morning, I rushed from my forsaken rooms to the company of my uncle. He was not in his apartments and so I proceeded through the long library to his study. I was relieved to find him there, though unusually, on that morning, the door was shut fast. I stood for a moment beside it, listening for reassuring noises from within: the shuffle of paper or the clearing of a throat. Only once I had heard those sounds could I settle comfortably upon a chair by the fire. I must have drifted into a sleep, for I found myself awakened some time later by his valet. I must say, the menacing sight of a servant standing over me nearly caused me to leap from my skin! The valet jumped too.

'Miss Ingerton,' he said after collecting himself, 'his lordship requires you.'

I smoothed my skirts and rubbed my sore eyes, still dry from the absence of sleep.

It was with some shyness that I entered my uncle's study. With its glass-covered bookcases and gilt-edged furnishings, it had always seemed to me a rather sombre and masculine place. My uncle did nothing to put me at ease, for he stood flanked by the busts of Homer and Virgil, wearing an expression as solemn as theirs.

'Dear child.' He sighed, attempting a twitch of a smile. 'There is a matter upon which I wish to speak to you,' he began, before advancing to his desk. I watched with a mounting sense of concern as his fingers fumbled with the lock on the drawer. 'These were brought to me this morning by Lewis, who had had them from Sally Pickering,' he stated as he drew forth that which I most dreaded seeing in his possession.

At that instant, I believe the blood drained entirely from my face. I stared at the bundle, too shamefaced to meet his gaze, my eyes pooling with tears.

How brutal was Fate! thought I, for I had endured Sally's torments so I might have been spared this end. Oh, how my heart heaved to stand under the glare of this disgrace. My cheeks began to burn as the tears started down them.

As I had not the strength to raise my head, I knew not what expression Lord Stavourley wore, if it was one of bitter condemnation or pity.

'Forgive me, child,' he uttered after a long spell of heavy silence, 'for there is much you do not know.'

Oddly, there was no censure in his voice as he spoke, but rather an unexpected note of anguish. I cautiously lifted my gaze and found that he had turned from me, having chosen instead to fix his eyes upon the view from his windows.

'You see, my dear, the fault, the blame for this . . . terrible misfortune, lies with me,' he announced, 'and I fear it will not please you to hear what I must say.'

I waited for him to turn towards me, to proffer me a look of reassurance, but he did not.

'I was a man much like Lord Allenham,' he began, twisting his hands behind his back. 'Young men are . . . by nature passionate, and as a result flawed. It may sadden you to know it, but none of us are the gallant heroes that your novels would have us be. Most men are of a type, generally unbridled in our desires and terribly foolish, and I, dear girl, I was no different.'

He paused and studied the landscape for a beat. Turning to the side, I saw in his blue-grey eyes a muted sparkle, not mirrored elsewhere in his expression.

'There is much you are too young, too innocent to know about the world, Henrietta. Indeed, I should not expect you to know of what I am about to speak.' He shut his eyes quite suddenly, as if struggling to find his words. 'You must understand, not every woman is an honest one . . . which is to say, there are some who go out into the world to make their living, not by a respectable trade, but rather by pursuing a life of debauchery.' He sighed. 'Love, you see, love is not always to be found in the matrimonial bond. Ladies may find it there, but gentlemen often seek it elsewhere. I did just this.' His words were now coming in a rapid, uneasy stream. 'There was one . . . woman whom I loved, much in the way that Lord Allenham loved you, with as much ardour . . . but it was not in my power to marry her, nor would it have been appropriate, given her position, and it is she, Henrietta, she who gave birth to you.' There he stopped, and turned his pallid face to me. 'I, dear girl, am your rightful father.'

We stood, our gazes held together for a moment or so; his tired eyes a picture of remorse, and mine wide and unflinching in disbelief.

'Do forgive me,' he murmured, shutting them once again. 'I should have informed you many years ago . . . indeed I am surprised you did not hear of my indiscretion through some other source.' He wagged his head. 'Your father is no better than a coward.'

'No,' said I. It was the only word I could think to say, perhaps the only sound I could pronounce, for now I wept great, bitter tears. Seeing my distress, my father, for that is what he was, came to me and placed a gentle hand beneath my elbow.

'Sit . . .' he ordered, guiding me into a chair, but the feel of his kind touch only heightened my sense of grief.

'Dear little sparrow.' He spoke softly, taking a seat beside me. Awkwardly, he reached for my hand; the firmness of his enveloped my small one. I marvelled at the touch of it, that my father – my papa! – comforted me.

'Your mother . . . your mother was called Kitty Kennedy. So now you know it.' He nodded. 'She had you in her care for near two years, dear Hetty, and it was not her design to give you up. You see, there was a gentleman who wished to marry her, and to do right by her, but he would not have the child of another man under his roof. So she wrote to me and begged that I should take you in. Your aunt . . . Lady Stavourley was not pleased by this, not at all. She objected to your coming here – greatly. In the end, I believe my insistence upon it destroyed her health.' My father lowered his gaze and his tone. 'She consented, but with reluctance – and there were to be conditions. She would not have you here on the footing of a fine lady, by which she meant you should have none of the fortune entailed upon her lawful daughter . . . your . . . sister, or any of my heirs. As she had been an heiress in her own right, her trustees, when hearing of this matter, took recourse to law and insisted that I swear an oath to this effect,' said he, drawing a long, sorrowful breath, and pressing my hand in his. 'You must know I wished only the best for you, dear Henrietta. I insisted that you were raised with Catherine, to be her companion, so you might benefit by proxy from whatever fortune passed to her upon marriage. But I see now how misguided was this plan.' Gradually, my father moved his sorrowful eyes from where they rested upon our joined hands, and slowly, silently, studied my face. It struck me then how many of his fine features I possessed: the round visage, the small chin, the arch of his brows. My eyes were a lighter shade than his, though they bore a similar shape. For a moment, I observed his, moving, dancing along my countenance. He shifted in his seat and then, reaching into his waistcoat pocket, removed a white silk handkerchief, which I believe he intended to use. Instead, he gently passed it to me and gestured that I should rub my nose with it, before continuing with a sigh, 'These are not your sins, my dear. The failure is entirely mine.'

As I sat beside my father, quietly sobbing, I could not decide which element of this story struck me most, or how my head should absorb it. I knew not if I should feel pity or horror or sadness or joy upon learning this. My heart was gripped with all four sensations at once: the thrill of learning that here was my papa, my own true flesh and blood, which was then countered by a jolt of sickening remorse for the young lady who had been my sister. My bosom friend, my dearest companion, my beloved *sister*. For so many years I had dreamed her to be just this. Oh, the regret was intolerable. I wept harder still and pressed the handkerchief against my aching eyes.

It was at that point my father rose from my side. I believe my anguish was more than he could bear. Instead he moved to his desk and recovered the bundle of letters from where he had laid them. I watched as he turned them over in his hands, examining their worn corners and tear-stained script. Then, quite suddenly, he reached over and dropped them into the flaming grate before him. Taking the poker, he made certain that each of the little packets caught light and curled and twisted into blackness. So came to an end the only proof of Allenham's love I had ever possessed.

'I shall not tolerate the rumours that have been put about below stairs that you brought about your sister's demise,' he commented as he stoked the coals. 'But Lady Stavourley is of a different mind. You know her disposition, that she is not given to reason.' He gave a slight shake of his head. 'My fear is that she will persist with this notion and divide my household. I cannot have that. Nor could I bear it if she were to inflict further damage to her health.' My father then laid down the poker and wiped his hands together, before turning from me and directing his gaze once more out of the window.

'As you know, or perhaps suspected, the Reverend John Pease has made an offer for your hand. In the past I have put him off, thereby allowing you the opportunity, however slim, of making a match more agreeable to you. He knows that you have no fortune, but your beauty and charms have captivated him, and he is willing to accept you notwithstanding. For my part, I have offered him the promise of a larger living at a parish within my gift in the north of Ireland. The marriage' – my father inhaled and then sighed – 'is to be settled very soon and the banns to be published immediately. It pains me a great deal to force your hand in this affair, Henrietta, but I have taken the liberty of writing to Mr Pease that you will agree to these terms.'

This, when added to my woes, my miseries and confusions, was more than I could bear.

My father waited for my response to this news, but I could bring myself to say nothing, for my sobs had silenced me entirely.

'Dearest little one,' he whispered, 'I grieve for your distress ... I wished it differently, but it will be for the best.'

'But I do not love him ...' I managed to gasp. I thought instantly of Lady Catherine, who had once bleated this same lament. 'I do not believe I could ever love him ...'

It was then that *my father*, my cherished and adored father, approached me. I shall remember for as long as I live how he took my girlish hands into his and offered me comfort.

'Dear Hetty.' He spoke softly. 'Love is but a luxury. We may taste it briefly in our lives but cannot expect to sustain ourselves on it.' He then placed one finger under my chin and raised it. 'Remember its delights, but do not pine for it.'

His words I did not wish to embrace, but his gesture of affection was one of the sweetest gifts I have ever received.

'Go now,' he directed me. 'Do not trouble yourself by thinking on the matter further. It is done, dear daughter.'

In times of extreme distress, I believe it is possible to commune with the soul. The soul knows all the answers, even when the heart and the head cannot find a path through the darkness. Before I had so much as quit my father's study, my soul understood what lay ahead for me. It knew it as I ran through the library and into the corridor. I recognized it as I fell to my knees upon the floor of my apartments and convulsed in wailing agonies.

My heart and head were full of fear and injury. My father had sold me. I was no better than a slave. My happiness was no more considered than that of a sultan's dancing girl, thrown weeping into a Constantinople market. Lady Stavourley would have me banished from my home, the only place of refuge I had ever known, have me torn from my only parent. She had despised me from the day I had arrived: the wretched bastard of her husband. Melmouth hated me. The servants wished me dead. They had tried to murder me and might yet succeed, long before the odious Pease carried me off.

Pease. The thought of his girth, his slack jaw, his idiot's stare, the dullness of his company, made me recoil with disgust. Oh reader, it struck me then that I was not the devoted child I had believed myself to be! Were I truly dutiful, such thoughts would have never entered my head. I would have never questioned my destiny, but gone to it with the open heart of a martyr, wishing to sacrifice myself for the good of my father's name, for the contentment of Lady Stavourley, she who had no fondness for me. For this, this would be a true surrender, and a noble act. But my soul, that lively, kicking thing inside me, would not accept this as my fate.

Had I not had the misfortune of tasting love, as my father had suggested, I believe I would have agreed to a life spent in a distant country rectory as the drudge of a disagreeable man, filling his austere house with children. Too poor to repair the leaking roof or to lay more than a meagre table, there would be little by way of gaiety and less by way of interesting conversation. There would be no genteel company. I would never again see Melmouth, or London. I would never again know love. So it would be until the day I was laid in earth.

I lay all evening upon the floor of my untended chamber, staring into the cold and contemplating my future course.

My soul whispered to my heart. Its urgings became stronger and louder, till the pleas could no longer be dismissed. Once convinced, my heart then began to persuade my head. My soul begged me to let it live, but in doing so, there would be a price: I would leave behind all that I was.

For it had occurred to me that I had but one friend in the world now, one person upon whom I might call. There existed no guarantee that he would assist me, for a good many months had elapsed since I had been assured of his affection. In that time, I supposed he might have purged himself of my memory. If only I had been so thorough in ridding myself of his!

No, I fear that Allenham haunted me, as did the passions I held for him. No ghost was ever more real to me than he, for I saw him everywhere. I shared every thought with him; he was present in every quiet moment, with every book I read or natural wonder I spotted. The rich tones of his voice vibrated inside me, his luminescent blue eyes glittered behind my own. While my soul moved within me and fired heart and head, I could not permit myself to believe that his love for me had been extinguished, when once it had flared like a star. Did Werther's love for Lotte not increase with separation?

All that I possessed was a hope, a butterfly at the bottom of this box of horrors. That, dear readers, was enough for my soul. And so I listened to its calling and I did its bidding.

Chapter 12

My friends, we have now returned to where I began my narrative, to that moment when I sat trembling behind a bolted door at the Bull in Royston. I suspect that you see the irony of my situation: that I had fled from one perilous bedchamber only to find myself trapped in another!

My assailant, Mr Fortune, continued to hammer upon the door for a good half-hour or more, all the while bellowing curses and oaths. I had never before heard such terms of abuse. He was a brute, to be sure. After some time his thumps subsided into taps and scratches and then into silence. I suppose it was then that I fell into a sleep.

My next memory is of being roughly shaken awake by a maid, who had slipped into my chamber through the jib door. She stood over me in a dirty cap and apron, marvelling that she should find me dressed and lying upon the coverlet.

A breakfast of coarse bread and ale was put upon the table, and she warned me to eat quickly as the stage to Oxford was shortly to call. Anxiously, I enquired after my attacker, fearing that I should meet him upon the stairs or, worse still, inside the stage.

'Ah, him,' stated the maid, 'what a racket he did make last night. He went at dawn in a post chaise to London.' Then she squinted at me. 'Did you jilt him, miss?' she enquired in a conspiratorial tone.

'Jilt him?' I asked.

'You know . . .' said she with a wink.

I stared at her blankly. 'You did not think we were engaged to be wed . . . ?'

'No,' she moaned, rolling her eyes, finding my simplicity rather trying. 'You know . . . did you throw him from your bed? Had you enough of him?' She smiled wryly.

My eyes spread wide with indignation. 'I did no such thing! He was merely . . .' Scarcely had I launched into the defence of my character, before the arrival of the stage was announced.

'No time for that, miss,' said the maid, fairly pushing me through the door and down the stairs. And in hardly more than a handful of minutes, I found myself once more in a carriage, surrounded by perfect strangers.

If I had learned anything in that short period, it was not to make conversation with anyone, no matter how kind their countenance. The stage was a lesser breed of transport, to be sure, though not as dreadful or bandit-ridden as I had been led to believe. I sat alongside an assortment of passengers: petty clerks, farmers, men with chafed hands and women in woollen skirts, one of whom who smoked a pipe for most of our journey. I had never before passed so much time in the close company of ordinary folk, and it was plain from their looks that they regarded me with a good deal of suspicion.

We travelled all day to Oxford, calling at several inns along the route. The scenery was most unfamiliar and I possessed no knowledge of my whereabouts. Indeed, the names that were called out as we stopped seemed as foreign to me as those of Aleppo or Alexandria. How much further was Gloucestershire? Amid this wilderness, I did not know. How many more days of travel were required to arrive at the town of Lechlade and then Herberton, near to it? Once again, I began to fret that my small purse would not take me so far, and that I would certainly drop from hunger before I arrived there.

By the time the stage came to a stop at the King's Head in Oxford, it was dark and I had eaten nothing since that morning. The prospect of another night in such a place filled me with dread. The lamps glowed alluringly within the windows, and inside there was the usual scene of clatter and commotion to which I had already grown accustomed. With my hood over my head, I picked my way to a hidden place, carefully shunning the glances of curious men. I was prepared to sit quietly, attempting with all my might to shun the tempting scents of beef dripping, pork and boiled cabbage which swirled about the tavern. I lowered my head and slumped against the wall.

'Miss?' came a woman's voice, rolling with the burr of the countryside.

I glanced up at a stout figure standing over me.

'Miss?' she asked again. 'Poor lamb, are you ailing?'

I wagged my head slowly. 'Thank you for your kindness, madam. I am merely fatigued.'

My well-spoken words caused her to study me carefully. She lowered her voice and then leaned into me. 'See here, miss, I know not what trouble you find yourself in, but you look poorly and it would not be Christian of me were I not to offer you something from our table.'

Having learned only too recently what comes of accepting the kindness of strangers, I hesitated.

'Come now,' said she in a merry voice, 'there is no need to be fearful. I am Mrs Harper, and that is Mr Harper and my son.' She gestured to a nearby table, where sat a square-built man and a boy of no more than thirteen. 'We are honest folk. Just sold a bullock and cow at market today, so we have rabbit pie and parsnip pudding to spare.'

In truth, friends, I was too racked with hunger to refuse her offer and accepted, with many apologies, a place at their table. With hindsight, I am only pleased that she did not prove to be a bawd, for it is well known that such women haunt inns and taverns, hoping to ensnare unfortunate young creatures with just such a ploy as this. But the Harpers wished me no ill and were pleased to have my company, however poor a conversationalist I showed myself to be.

No sooner had I been revived than sense, as well, returned to my head, and I recognized that I would now need to offer my hosts some recompense for their generosity. This, I feared, would cost me the last of my coins, but much to my surprise, they refused to take so much as a ha'penny from me.

'Oh no, miss,' Mr Harper protested loudly, 'we shall take no money for common kindness.'

Indeed, my heart was greatly warmed by their show of common

kindness. Had it not been for their charity, I cannot imagine what ills may have befallen me.

That night I was not only fed, but offered a share of their bed; and in the morning, they invited me to accompany them in their cart as far as Lechlade. I thanked heaven for this blessing, for such occurrences had been so rare of late.

It seemed to me odd, as the cart passed through the hillocks and vales of Oxfordshire, that the Harpers had enquired so little of me. Beyond the most basic of queries, as to my name and family, no more was asked. They were of a plain sort and, unlike others, did not seem concerned about my circumstances. For more than twenty miles, I sat in the cart beside their son, listening only to the wheels in the ruts of the road and the plod of the horses. At moments, I could not believe it was I, there, upon a cart with three strangers, when only days before I was at Melmouth. I hardly knew myself. My skin did not even feel as if it were my own.

Thus I had a great span of time to consider the adventure upon which I had embarked. It was perhaps too much time, for my mind, in its idleness, began to knit all manner of probable outcomes.

I feared that I would arrive at Herberton only to find Allenham else-where. Although I had been led to believe that, in the wake of his tragedy, he had shunned London for the quiet of his estate, I could not be certain of this. Worse still, I was plagued by fear that his love for me had grown cold, that he would refuse me. Remorse perched on my shoulder. What mistake might I have made in doing this, in fleeing from my father's home? My character would be for ever stained. Sorrow and confusion twisted about inside me, knotting themselves together in a tangle of worries and uneasiness.

After several hours, Mr Harper pointed to a steeple rising upon the horizon. 'That there is Lechlade, miss. Not far to go now.'

I could not turn back. Whatever I had intended when I slipped from Melmouth must now be carried though to its conclusion.

We parted at the crossroads of Lechlade, where Mr Harper assisted me from the wagon and directed me towards the town. I lifted my chin and gripped my mean bundle of possessions as I set off on this final part of my journey. Once there, I enquired of an egg-seller in the mar-ketplace how I might make my way to Herberton. She in turn pointed me towards the west road, upon which I should proceed another three miles by foot.

The rain had now begun, falling lightly and then in heavier, leaden drops. Like a persistent foe, it matched its pace to mine; the quicker my stride, the greater its force against me, and in no time at all I was soaked through.

It must be said that the state of my attire was, by the third day of my journey, unspeakably soiled. I looked not much cleaner than a beggar. Indeed the full hem of my cape was splashed brown, and the filth extended entirely up my ruined stockings, into my linens and skirts. My shoes were like two potatoes for the muck upon them. My hair had been untended for weeks, while my figure was so misshapen by hunger that my stays hung loosely from my torso. I could hardly bear that Allenham should lay eyes upon me in this condition, and I feared he would find me much altered, with no looks whatsoever to recommend me.

I trod the road as if in a dream, as if in a delirium. I took in nothing, as if my eyes were made of glass beads and stared out blankly into the world. Allenham had spoken often of the beauty of his county, its velvet hills and mossy brooks, but I was aware of none of this as I strode.

Eventually I reached what seemed to be the wall of Herberton, and then further down a gate. It was not the principal avenue to the house, and so I was forced on to a smaller path through the tall, wet grass. Then, as I came over the crest of the hill, I saw it, and it drew my breath from me.

Mind you, it was not the beauty or splendour of Herberton that caused me to gasp. No, for as Lady Catherine had complained, the house had neither. In the rain, its stone appeared yellow and drab, as if it were stained with grime. The two wings on either side had little more than a roof upon them, and seemed as if they had lain untouched by masons' hands for some many years.

The sight of Herberton did not in itself surprise me, but rather that I should be there to see it. It was the enormity of what I had done, my boldness in coming uninvited to this place that shook me, for it was not the action of the person I had believed myself to be. In fleeing, I had forfeited any good character I might have possessed, and it was in that instant that I fully recognized the truth of the matter. It stunned me; it stopped me quite dead. And I would be dishonest if I did not confess it caused me some great measure of sadness. But surely, reader, by now you understand how few were my options. To this day, it seems a marvel to me that, at seventeen, I had courage enough to embark upon the path I chose. Perhaps it was not so much courage as naivety, for had I known what I was to encounter, I might never have taken such a step.

So, having resolved that I should proceed, that I could do nothing else, I pushed onwards, towards the house in front of me.

Chapter 13

I was cautious in my approach to Herberton, for I knew that Allenham's servants were likely to stare. All servants stare if the opportunity presents itself. With my soiled attire I did not feel myself fit to enter the house by way of the portico. Certainly that would have raised questions and presented such a spectacle for the staff that I did not care to hazard it. Instead I found the door to the servants' entrance and slipped inside. I was indeed beside myself with nerves, flushed red and entirely sodden. I asked to see the housekeeper, and soon she appeared, her jangling bundle of keys announcing her approach from down the corridor.

'I should like to speak with Lord Allenham,' I uttered in hardly more than a whisper.

The housekeeper regarded me with a wary eye.

'And may I beg the favour of your name, miss?'

I hesitated.

'I have come with an urgent message for his lordship. It is necessary that I see him immediately. Is he at home?'

I fear the state of my appearance did not aid my case. Instead, I believe it was my well-bred air that led her to see I was no lovesick country doxy. She said nothing but disappeared for a spell and then returned with a footman who examined me head to toe before escorting me above stairs.

My heart began to pound. Allenham was indeed here in *this* house, *his* house, the place of which he had so fondly spoken. He had known the rooms through which we passed since he was a boy. He had run across these very floors with his wooden toys, shouting and tumbling with his brother. This gold damask-lined room was where he sat and thought; the green painted one, where he ate; everywhere was Allenham, every page of his life, past or present, was laid out for inspection. To see inside his world was a wonder to me.

The footman showed me to a drawing room furnished in the heavy baroque style of his lordship's grandfather, where the silk had faded upon the chairs and where a fire crackled in the hearth.

Once alone I began to shiver, though I realized it was not from the cold. I knew that when the door opened for a second time, it would be he who stepped through it. I paced. I attempted to regain some of my composure, but found it near impossible. All my bravery seemed in danger of capsizing.

I cannot say who was more surprised to see whom, for although I had prepared myself for the sight of him, I had quite forgotten the effect his person had upon me; his strong bearing, the lapis lazuli of his eyes, the perfect symmetry of his features, the sharp point of his nose.

'Miss Ingerton!' he exclaimed, his face betraying true shock. Immediately, he shut the door fast behind him and took in my haggard and slovenly appearance. 'My God! How came you here?'

In the course of my journey, I had contemplated just what I might say to him. I had written a missive in my mind, containing all the details of my flight and the reasons for it, but when I began to speak, I found I could say nothing. At last, I had arrived at my destination. I was alive, I was at Herberton and Allenham, whom my heart recognized instantly, was but several yards from me.

I began to sob.

His lordship came to me and, resting his hand upon my shoulder, directed me to a chair.

'Oh dear, dear angel,' he cried. 'The state of you! What must you have suffered? I cannot imagine.'

I nodded, the tears spilling all about, on to my cloak, on to his sleeve. When I had somewhat settled my emotions, he leaned before me and stroked the damp hair from my face.

'You have come alone?' he enquired in a soft voice.

I nodded again.

'By what means?'

I looked up at him with red eyes. 'I have fled. They would have me dead,' I sniffled.

'They? Pray, who is they?'

And so I recounted my trials with Sally, how she had turned the staff against me, and how the conspirators had served me a plate of poison mushrooms.

He stared at me incredulously. 'Did you not inform Lord Stavourley?'

At that I began to weep again, and related to him what my father had revealed to me, and his plans to marry me to Pease. His lordship's face froze quite solid, his brow set in a deep crease. He stood in silence for several heavy moments, cogitating upon this news.

'Does anyone know you have fled here?' he asked at last.

'No. I have told no one.'

'Have you given your name to any person along your route?'

'None but a gentleman, a solicitor gone to London; and a farmer and his wife from near Circencester.'

Allenham's face bore some concern.

'You cannot stay at Herberton,' he stated firmly, but then noting my look of astonishment, quickly added, 'but I shall keep you safe, and as near to me as is possible.'

He placed his hand upon mine, pressing his soft warmth against the backs of my fingers before swiftly releasing it and moving away. There was a strange air of formality about him. I believe I had taken him so much by surprise that he knew not how he should respond, nor what behaviour was appropriate in the circumstances. He continued his progress around the room, his arms folded, his head lowered as he thought.

'Do you have any reason to believe that his lordship may think you have fled to me?'

'Yes,' said I, 'I fear so.'

At that time, I had not yet informed Lord Allenham that my father had read his correspondence. I did not know how I might approach the subject, for certainly, I reasoned, it would cause him some pain to hear it, and me some shame to say it. Oh, I would that I had not been such a milksop and spoken it aloud right then! I might have spared myself the misery of it much later.

'Then it is necessary that I write to him immediately. I shall tell him you came here and that I returned you post-haste to Melmouth.'

My eyes widened. 'But . . .'

'Henrietta,' he began with a softer, pleading tone, 'it troubles me a great deal to lie, and I do not doubt you think less of me for it, but these are circumstances for which there is no other remedy. You know I should risk injury to myself before I turned you out.' The Baron offered a timid smile. 'When you fail to return to Melmouth, he will believe you have gone elsewhere. To London. Then he will give up the search.'

I imagined my dear father receiving this news, another tragedy to befall him. My heart sank.

I looked up at Allenham, searching his expression for some hint of reassurance. He stood stoically, possessed, running his finger along his firm lower lip as he thought.

'There is a cottage upon my estate. It has lain empty for some time . . .' He then looked over at me, suddenly inspired by some rush of genius. 'Lightfoot. That was the family. That is who you will become.'

'Become?' I regarded him with a quizzical expression. 'I do not understand . . .'

'There were many generations of them, now gone, I know not where. It would not appear so strange if you were to return . . . a Miss Lightfoot, a grown daughter who had some modest settlement placed upon her, returning to the home she once knew. The story put about need not be more than that.'

I fear I was still unable to follow Allenham's reasoning.

'But why need I become someone else?'

'We cannot very well call you Miss Ingerton after I have claimed that you are not here,' said he with a gentle tease. He then drew a breath and lowered his voice. 'At present, there are guests at Herberton. There are often guests – political associates, gentlemen. You are aware there will soon be a General Election and I am favoured for a seat in the next Parliament?'

I nodded.

'It is imperative that you are not known to be here. It would lead to terrible suspicion if you are discovered. We should both be entirely ruined.' He held my gaze steadily as he spoke. 'The servants, I shall see to. There will be no gossip, but while you reside in the house, you must remain confined to your apartments.'

I was taken aback by the sternness of his tone. 'I shall do whatever you ask of me, my lord,' I answered, turning my eyes to the floor.

'Hetty,' he called softly, and then waited until I turned my attention upward. He gazed back, his features now mild and warm. 'I never dared believe . . . I never thought it possible . . .' Allenham stopped and looked away. 'You must recover from your journey. I shall have a maid prepare a set of rooms for you.' He began pacing once again. 'There is much to be done. I must send away my guests . . . If you will excuse me, I must write to Lord Stavourley at once, and set about preparing Orchard Cottage. It will be some days yet before the house is mended and in an orderly condition.'

I sat for a long while after he left me. As I was no longer beneath my father's roof, no more the person I believed myself to be, as I had shed my past and all that belonged to it, it seemed appropriate enough that I should be christened something else. Miss Henrietta Lightfoot. It felt awkward to bear another identity.

'Lightfoot,' I whispered. The name had an unusual resonance to my ear. 'Lightfoot. Henrietta Lightfoot.'

I shut my eyes and listened as I breathed the syllables again and again.

So it was to be. So I became her, this other Henrietta. From that night, I pulled her character around me; I drew it on like a stranger's cloak and wore it, though awkwardly at first, as my own.

Chapter 14

I was not to see his lordship again that evening. Shortly after he had left me, I was taken through a labyrinth of connecting rooms and up the back stairs to a set of apartments. I was truly so weary and shaken that I recall little of what occurred, only that a meal of cold venison and potted ham was laid out for me and that a shy maid had assisted in preparing me for bed. Her hands were slow and soft. She attended to my tangled hair with care, and then, with a basin of warm perfumed water, washed away the soil of the road from my body. Indeed, her ministrations were so gentle that I struggled to recall the last time I had been tended with such kindness. As you may imagine, I slept quite soundly that night.

When I had arrived at Herberton, the sun had been waning and so most of its rooms were obscured by shadow, but when I awoke, the autumn light streamed through the windows, illuminating the plush interior of my rooms. Much to my delight, I discovered that the bed in which I had passed the night was made of a grand oak frame and hung with gold and burgundy fringed velvet. The dressing room seemed an exotic trove of treasures. Two heavy mirrors set in carved gilt frames drew in the daylight, casting a shine upon the japanned lacquer cabinets. All around was placed an assortment of blue and white Chinese vases and delft tulip stands.

Although I was enchanted by the sumptuous surrounds, by the glittering splendour of it, I saw immediately why Lady Catherine had complained so. While these rich decorations may have been *à la mode* one hundred years earlier, they were far from fashionable in 1789. Their tired brocades and gold-painted fronds spoke of a family whose fortune had degraded with the interior.

I ran my curious fingers along the sculpted marble of the hearth and then at fraying edges of the damask upon the walls. The fabric caught the fullness of the sun and felt warm under my touch. All I saw of Allenham's home pleased me, its worn character charmed me and I yearned to learn its secrets.

I would not be so bold as to explore Herberton's corridors, especially as Allenham had warned me against it, but I ached to know what lay on the other side of the doors. There were three in the dressing room: one that led to the bedchamber where I had slept, a second adjacent to the hearth and a third, on the far wall, which I supposed led into an adjoining room. I approached the door nearest to the hearth and was about to bend forward and peer through the keyhole when I heard footsteps from the corridor beyond.

'Miss Lightfoot,' came a whisper and a scratch. It was Allenham.

I bade him enter and he shut the door very softly behind him.

I stood facing him with anxiously folded hands, and offered a curtsey.

He smiled somewhat bashfully and returned my greeting. A boyish awkwardness now replaced the formality of the day before.

'I trust you slept well?'

'I did, my lord.' I glanced at him, wary of admiring his features too closely and for too long. My heart beat very heavily.

'Is all well?' I ventured uneasily. He knew of what I spoke.

'Yes, the matters which we discussed have been undertaken.' Then his eyes rested on mine for a moment. 'I have brought you a gift.'

He took his hands from behind him, where they had been since he entered, and presented me with a book.

'I had been meaning to give this to you for some time, but knew not quite how.'

Along the spine was the name 'Goethe'. I looked up at him with a gasp.

'Open it,' he insisted. 'Four pages in you will find a list of subscribers.'

I thumbed through the volume and opened it wide.

'My name is there,' he pointed, 'and down here . . .' his finger moved along the lords and ladies, the honourables and the sirs to the very last line '. . . and the assistance of a generous lady who wishes only to be known as Miss H– I—'

I squeaked in surprise and quickly placed a hand to my mouth.

Allenham smirked. 'It is a new English translation of *The Sorrows of Young Werther*, completed and printed but two months ago.'

'But . . .' I began, overwhelmed. 'My lord, this is too kind. I know not what to say.' I flushed with embarrassment.

'Nonsense,' he chided. 'It is yours . . . to keep.'

'I shall treasure it.'

He was now standing quite near to me, and though at a respectable distance, the unease and lengthy pauses between us had grown too conspicuous to ignore.

'Come,' said he, quite abruptly. 'There is something I should like to show you.' With that, he pushed open the door against the far wall.

For a moment, I hesitated. I could not do otherwise, for something had tugged me backward, some prick of pain in my heart. I knew I should not be there, at Herberton. I thought of my dear late sister, my father and Lady Stavourley, who had visited only months before. It was not my right to be here, to tread upon these floors, to have Allenham at my side. 'These were my father's apartments,' he announced. 'Those in which you slept were my mother's, and my grandmother's before her.' He neglected to mention that his father's rooms, those through which we passed, were presently his. An admission such as that would have rendered our being there entirely improper.

He took me through a salon of sorts, a large, square room decorated in faded sea-green. A small rococo clock clicked and chattered upon the mantel. Surrounding it, hanging above it, reaching from the skirting boards up to the architraves, were row upon row of masterworks.

'I had thought so often . . . so often of showing you this room, dear Henrietta,' Allenham began, sounding rather more breathless than I had heard him in the past. 'I would often imagine you here, as you are now, copying the paintings. Learning from Titian and Caravaggio.' He smiled, gesturing to a lute-player and then to a bare-shouldered woman. 'The sun comes in so brightly from the west, I had always thought you could make good use of the morning light to—' Then he stopped himself, recalling what terrible occurrences had prevented his plan from bearing fruit. He bore the shame and discomfort of my presence as much as I, and neither of us knew how to speak of it, or how to avoid it.

'Rosalba Carriera. Do you know of her? The Venetian paintress?' said he, turning my attention to a pastel portrait beside the mantel. 'That is my grandmother, Lady Allenham. She was a Scotswoman, a baroness. The family title came through her line. The gentleman with the mask in his hand, just there, is my grandfather, Sir George Allenham, after whom I am called.'

'This is a marvel,' I announced, roaming my gaze about the walls, for it truly was. 'There are so many treasures here. When you spoke of art and beauty, I did not appreciate you were a connoisseur . . .'

'I fear it was my father, and his father, who were the collectors. There is not the means at present to further decorate the walls. And my tastes differ from theirs . . . I should like to commission Mr Fuseli to create a grand series, or else purchase a fire scene, a view of Vesuvius by Mr Wright. Images of the sublime; fire and snow and the like.' The Baron's face was aglow. 'Mr de Loutherbourg too,' he added.

'You have a taste for the modern, my lord,' I laughed.

'But the ancient amuses me just as well,' he parried. 'I shall show you what I mean . . .' He beckoned me towards another doorway.

The sea-green room gave way to a smaller closet, the sort kept by gentlemen collectors. It was a space not much bigger than an ante-chamber, but filled with an assortment of curiosities. My eyes struggled to take in the profusion and variety of objects. From floor to ceiling were all manner of jewels: miniature paintings, landscapes and devotional scenes, surrounded with elaborate frames, some in gold, others in ebony and silver. There were triptychs, studded with rubies, a diamond-encircled portrait of Elizabeth I, and dancing shepherds and gods in nearly every corner. Were it not for the cabinets, the Roman couch and rosewood table, I might have imagined myself to have stepped into a strong box of valuables.

Allenham permitted me to stare in wonderment as he pulled a drawer from a marquetry cabinet. He then laid it on a small table at the centre of the room.

'Come,' he signalled me.

There, nestling in a row of grooves, were perhaps eighty or more antique gems and cameos. They appeared at first like an assortment of large, colourful buttons, but as I examined them, their exceptional beauty and rarity grew apparent. Each was entirely distinct, no one among them resembled another in shape or hue or design. Some were of dark onyx stone, others green as moss, red like blood or the translucent violet of amethyst.

His lordship held one to the light, so I might see it. There before me was a minutely carved scene of the Three Graces, their hands clasped together. The sight of it made me giggle with pleasure. He took another from the drawer. This one was set within a thin frame of tooled gold and featured a chariot drawn by charging horse.

'These were made by Roman craftsman,' he marvelled, drawing forth a pale oval. 'When I was a boy, my father would permit my brother and me to admire them – to hold the ancient world in our hands.' He then laid the object in my hand, resting his fingers along my palm.

The intimacy of his action caused us both to fall silent. His hand sat in mine, a flat rose-coloured cameo residing between his touch and my flesh. Then, after a moment's hesitation, he slowly moved his thumb against the inside of my wrist. 'Henrietta,' he began, his eyes fixed on our joined hands, 'that you should be here, alone with me is ... inappropriate. I would not wish any harm to come to you.'

As he spoke, a sense of embarrassment came over me, for I recognized the truth of his words.

'You know what the world thinks of a young lady who elopes from her home.'

'I do,' said I solemnly.

'You must understand, my good opinion of you will never alter, but others will not look so favourably upon your action. Your character will not be easily redeemed.'

I swallowed hard and turned my head from him.

'I know what the world thinks.' There was a note of pride in my tone. 'I know what this deed will make me in the eyes of others. But what choice had I? To whom else might I have gone, my lord? I have not a friend in the world, not one person who bears any . . .' I stopped myself from uttering my thoughts and studied my hand in his. It appeared small and pink, like the cameo he pressed into it. 'Do not think I have not considered all of which you warn me. I know what it is that I do.'

Allenham listened to my words closely. Indeed, I had never spoken so plainly in all my life. These were not the sentiments of Henrietta Ingerton, the obedient child, the frightened mouse, the well-bred young lady. My admission was bold and shocking, even to myself.

He continued to stand, composed and still.

'What you intended to say . . . the word you withheld . . .'

I looked up at him.

'. . . was love. You wished to say that I bore more love for you than any one person in the world. But you prevented yourself.' Allenham's clear blue eyes were full of question.

I shook my head. 'I did not . . . I was not . . . certain . . .'

'My Lotte, my Lotte . . .' he breathed, suddenly full of fire. He took my other hand into his. 'That I love you more than any one person in the world is undeniable, and now . . .' He guided me to the small sofa that lay behind us, his face beaming with a sort of feverish joy. 'I had longed to have you here, beside me, but never dared believe it . . . my darling, my own dear love . . .' He stroked my cheek until it positively burned red.

It was when he released my hand from his grasp that I noticed the cameo. There, rather to my surprise, was Venus, lying upon her side, bare but for her sandals, and her paramour Mars leaning in to love her.

My heart sprang into a gallop, but how it maintained its speed, I know not, for I had hardly the means to breathe. Upon that instant I knew what was to become of me, for I held a picture of it in my very palm.

I gathered the courage to look at the smooth contours of his face, the dark, finely shaped brows that framed the cool colours of his eyes. He sat so near to me that I could detect the clean scent of his warm shirt.

'My angel, my Venus,' he whispered.

No sooner had he said it, than his lips were at mine.

What words have not been written about a first kiss? And, my friends, this was the original kiss of all kisses. His mouth was the first I had ever tasted and it was far softer and more intimate than I had imagined. Yes, I, like any other girl, had spent many a day lounging upon the sofa nuzzling the back of my hand, dreaming of what it might be like. But when the moment comes, it is not at all how one could fathom it to be, but much sweeter and stranger.

At the start, his kisses were laid delicately upon my lips, and then, when he saw I did not refuse him, he pushed his mouth against mine more forcefully. There seemed to me to be something of a rhythm about it; in fact, it felt to my innocent mind like a dance, where I moved my lips in time with his, meeting them and mirroring their motions. With his hand upon the back of my neck and the other stroking my cheek, the closeness of him became dizzying; so much so that I began to sway under his touch. I hardly knew my own thoughts; my mind grew dull and blank. Our lips were still locked in kisses as he moved to lie against me upon the Roman couch. His breath came steady across my cheek, intensifying with the tempo of his caresses. Soon his hands were upon my hair, my waist and running at the edge of my bodice. Everywhere he touched seemed to come alive, to glow and to throb. These were over-whelming sensations, so new and strong that they frightened me.

'Oh Henrietta,' he murmured as he rolled his kisses up my neck, 'I have thought of nothing but this. I have thought of nothing but you.' He placed his face directly above mine, so that our noses touched and our mouths and eyes were aligned. 'I have loved no one but you.' His words entered me with the force of lightning, sucking the very air from my lungs.

Of course I had always understood where my actions would lead me. When I fled, I knew for certain that I would be ruined and that Lord Allenham would be the one who undid me, but I had not the faintest notion of what a ruination involved. Tell me, what polite, well-bred girl does? In which of the many Romantic novels or moralizing tracts can be found a complete definition of the term 'to ruin'? None. And so our poor young lady, reader, is left without so much as a hint of what awaits her, or whether indeed the loss of virtue is, as so many have solemnly written, 'the worst of all tragedies'.

In my opinion, it is a great plague upon this nation that its daughters are kept so innocent of their fates. All women must come to it, whether by a husband or a seducer, it matters not. Anatomy and its functions are the same for each and every member of the female sex, whether she be a scullery maid or the future Queen of England. Would it not be better that we arm our daughters with knowledge of what awaits them, than send them to the marriage bed as we might an ignorant lamb to its slaughter?

I address my young readers when I say this: pay heed to the words I write and to the scene I now paint. After all, are you not taught that women of my sort exist only to instruct you? Permit me to spare you the embarrassment from which I suffered. That is, of course, providing that your mamma or governess has not by this point torn my memoirs from your delicate hands and thrown them upon the fire.

Now I return us to the small, low sofa with the scrolling arms against which Allenham and I reclined. We continued there for some time, much in the fashion I have described, overtaken by a fever of kissing and gentle touches. It was not long before Allenham's full, firm lips became bolder in their wanderings, moving from my mouth and neck, down to my throat and gauze-covered bosom. Slowly, he parted the material and buried his face in my décolleté, which made me gasp with astonishment. I felt so flushed that I feared I might have a fit and faint dead away.

It was in the midst of this excitement that I became gradually aware of an unusual sensation, which raised some alarm in me. It was centred in that spot that defines us from the male sex. I could not describe it in any other terms but to say that it ached, and with the discomfort was a feeling of dampness, which caused me even greater concern. Once it had come to my attention, I was drawn from my reverie, so that by the time his lordship's hand crept beneath my skirts and across my stocking-covered knee, I jumped with fright.

Allenham pulled back quickly, sat up and composed himself.

'Forgive me, my love . . .' he began. 'I have offended you.'

I sat to one side of the small couch with my knees pressed tightly together and an expression of fear upon my face.

'No,' I assured him, 'you have not.'

Noticing my unease, he took my hand in his.

'Then tell me, what is it that has distressed you?'

I looked at Allenham, who had been rendered breathless by our activity. His dark hair was strewn about and his waistcoat undone. As he gazed at me in his state of dishabille, I believe he appeared more handsome than I had ever seen him.

I shook my head. 'I do not know . . . I cannot say,' for indeed I could not give a name to what was troubling me. That which did not feel right between my legs had unnerved me in other ways as well. I thought of Lady Catherine, I thought again of what I done in leaving Melmouth, in falling in love with Allenham, of what I was about to do. There seemed to me no truths. When once my life had been so clearly defined, now I had nothing to guide me but my own moral compass, which spun and spun and spun.

'I know not what I do,' I said timidly.

Allenham smiled and touched my face.

'Are you uncertain of my love?' he asked.

'No.' I spoke clearly. 'That I know.'

'What then?'

I shook my head again and squeezed together my knees.

'Are you frightened?'

'Yes.' I lowered my eyes.

He moved an inch or two, so that he now sat directly beside me, his leg against mine. 'Henrietta.' He leaned into my ear and whispered while kissing it: 'Have you much understanding of the act of love? How the parts of male and female fit together?'

I thought for a moment. I had seen beasts rutting, many of them: bullocks climbing atop cows, birds upon one another, rams mounting sheep. This awkward dance, which seemed to me quite undignified, was also what occurred between a husband and a wife, once they were wed. Marriage, I had learned, permitted this act to take place, but this explanation only confused me further, for I knew that it could be done without the blessing of matrimony.

In London, from a very young age I had seen the outlines of whores and their culls. Coupling pairs were to be found everywhere: in the shadows of Vauxhall Gardens, down darkened streets, under bridges as the snow fell. 'Wretched creatures,' Lady Stavourley often sneered, before tugging at the carriage blinds. It was a feeble attempt at moral instruction. I knew what it was that I witnessed, but my innocent mind struggled to connect this animal act with that which occurred within the marital bed.

As for the anatomy of it, I knew that the male and female were intended to hook together, that I had an internal part in which seeds were planted that grew into infants. When there was no child in my womb, I bled, or so Sally had told me when my monthly courses began.

I knew that men had a hanging part, which was called a yard or cock, as I had heard the servants name it. When we were quite young, and Lord Dennington and Master Edwin ran about unclothed, I saw their little things on view, bouncing between their legs. The seed that made children came from there. But beyond that, I had no real understanding of the act at all.

I shrugged with embarrassment. 'I know only little.'

He kissed me full on the mouth and then smiled.

'Then I shall show you all that you need know.'

Chapter 15

Maidenheads are not meant to be taken upon sofas. Neither should they be had in chairs nor in the backs of carriages. When a young lady is undone in such a place, it is less likely to be 'an act of love' than an act of rape. You gentlemen may call it what you will. Seduction is a term too freely used. We protest and you persist, unwilling to believe we will not have you. Would that all men were as conciliatory as Lord Allenham was with me. He removed me to his bedchamber, and I, with no wish to resist, tamely went with him there.

It is true, I had no notion of what it was I went to, and had I been apprised of the pain and embarrassment that awaited me, I might have offered more hesitation. But as you know, I had no female counsel, no mother to instruct me, no married sister to whisper guidance into my ear. I had with me but the shreds of knowledge I possessed, and – for this I was grateful – the compassion of a lover who knew the value of the gift I was to bestow upon him.

I was a good deal anxious, as nervous as any bride. But love is like a liquor and I had drunk so heavily of it that my apprehensions, my confusions seemed to matter little, so long as he touched and kissed me.

This he continued to do as he drew me to the side of his bed and felt for the opening of my gown. Once he had divested me of this and untied my skirts, he began to loosen my stays. I could feel his eager hands trembling at the lacings, anticipating, as all men do, that holy first glimpse of the unmasked female charms.

'My God, you are Venus herself,' he exclaimed, falling to his knees and pressing me against him. At that instant, modesty reared upon me and I blushed brilliantly. Though still in his embrace I struggled with my chemise, wishing to cover myself.

'No, no,' he murmured, pulling it down again, his face an expression of bliss, 'you do not know what beauty you possess, nor what joy the sight of your naked breasts gives to me. I have dreamed of this . . . of you, so much so that I have lost nights of sleep.'

He rose from where he worshipped me and, lifting me on to the bed, began to cover my snowy hillocks with adoring kisses. As he placed his mouth at one of the pink tips, I gasped with surprise and delight. He gazed up at me with a satisfied smile, before returning to his task.

Each caress of his, each passionate gesture was as new to me as it was pleasurable. It seemed that wherever he laid his fingers or lips, some electric current followed. The sensations were beyond any I had ever known, for when I felt his skin brush mine, when he sighed his declarations of love, or explored some previously private place, such as my thighs or my belly, all thoughts fled from my mind, as if I had no other desires in the world but that he should forever continue to kiss and fondle me. He, too, wished for nothing but this and struggled with his own clothing, as it seemed he could not bear to remove his hands or mouth from me long enough to undress himself.

When at last his coat, waistcoat, breeches and stockings lay in a litter upon the floor, he pulled back the coverlet of the bed and took me beneath the warm folds. I was glad of this, for not only did I feel the cold through my thin chemise, but in my innocent, bashful state, I could not bring myself to look on him unclothed. It seemed too wanton and indecent to cast my eyes upon his masculine figure. To be sure, he was shaped like a Grecian athlete, with a broad chest and back, and round shoulders formed as if by a sculptor. Few men can boast of such classical perfection, though I did not come to appreciate this until much later.

He placed himself atop me, and to have so little between us, to feel the heat of him, his strong weight against me, his thighs pressing into mine, seemed to me the closest to paradise I might come. My eyes fluttered and closed as if in a fit. For a brief instant, I wondered if this was what it was to be ruined, to feel as if one might expire from love, for I felt utterly transported, enraptured, enslaved. Surely after tasting such joy, one must thereafter always long for it. But then I knew there was more to the act than this, for he had not yet put his member beside mine.

Our kisses had begun to grow ever longer, fuller, slower. Then, quite unexpectedly, he parted my lips and tickled my tongue with his. I pulled back and offered him a shy smile.

He laughed. 'Does that alarm you? It is what the French do with their mouths.'

He then tried it again. On this occasion, there was some thrill in it, some deeper connection to the kiss, which seemed more gratifying.

As I grew accustomed to this, the gentle rhythm of it, he took my hand and guided it below, where I felt the strange object that had for some time been lying against me. It was stiff and quite long. I jumped in surprise.

'I did not think it was that large!' I cried in horror. 'But how? But where? How does it fit?'

Allenham could not contain his laughter. 'Oh dear Hetty,' he exclaimed, 'you are so perfectly innocent!' He put his forehead to mine as his body shook with mirth. 'It is no larger or smaller than any other man's,' said he modestly, before rolling over to recline upon his elbow. 'The male member stiffens so it may enter you.'

'But surely,' said I with some unease, 'there is nowhere for it to go.'

'Shall I show you where it is to go?' said he, his eyes glittering with lust. Then he gently moved apart my thighs and ran his fingers along the rim of my nether parts. Until that moment, he had not dared touch me in that most secret of spots, knowing perhaps that such an intimate approach would have startled me. But I was now so much a captive to love that there was not an inch of my person I did not wish him to possess. His motions, though soft and teasing, grew increasingly insistent, until I felt myself quite stupefied under his touch.

Then, very slowly, there seemed to be a void, which parted as he pushed his finger into it.

I gasped, for it smarted terribly.

He hushed me. 'The pain is fleeting. The longer I toy with you, the less you will feel it,' said he, continuing his movements.

Allenham carried on with this task for a long time. I cannot say how long, for I had entirely lost my senses, and time seemed an irrelevance. Little by little, he widened the passage with his fingers. Eventually, he suggested that I was ready to be tried.

For all the caressing and rubbing, kissing and loving that is done prior to the act, let it not fool you, innocent ones; the first approach is grievously painful. It is painful the second time and the third as well, but with each attempt the tearing sting is lessened, until by the fourth or fifth try it has miraculously vanished. Your mother or aunt, your elder married sisters may neglect to tell you all of this, but you should know it, for it is to your benefit to have knowledge of such a thing, no matter how indelicate. New brides should insist their husbands proceed slowly, and in the manner I described above, for it is the least hurtful method. Men can be brutes when they are fired by desire, and have no understanding of the violence they do to the tender parts of maids. Many are inclined to plough us as roughly as they would a frozen field, when in truth what we require is patience and warmth. It is that which thaws us into a pliable state.

It required several attempts before his lordship claimed my virgin prize. In truth, it took the better part of the day and evening, for I felt such pain that he refused to proceed, insisting that he could not bear to harm me. Instead we lay together, entwined and resting, until desire drove us into the act once more. With each foray, he made greater progress, until I felt his member entirely engulfed by mine.

How strange it was. Never could I have imagined it should be as this, that my small part could accommodate his larger one, that a man should fit inside a woman as a foot into a shoe. Ah, but to know he was within me, that a part of my beloved's person was melded and blended with my own physical form, was perhaps the greatest joy my mind could comprehend. I was still marvelling at this feat of nature when I became aware that my lover had begun to move inside me. This brought some renewal of the discomfort, but his motions were slow and careful. He watched me all the while to see that I did not recoil with pain. As he saw that I did not, he continued, now with greater urgency, until all at once he gasped and sighed.

For a moment I lay there with my love expired against me, wearing a confused smile. I could not fathom what had occurred, until Allenham looked upon my expression and, amused at my simplicity, let out a roar of laughter.

'My darling,' he exclaimed, half breathless, 'you have made me the happiest man alive!' He covered my face with kisses, before drawing back to examine me.

'I have made you expire,' said I apologetically.

He laughed again, this time with so much vigour that he carried me along in his good humour. I too giggled, though I knew not why.

'How I love you, Henrietta,' he sighed. 'Expire I did, my angel. I expired from pleasure. I spent my seed.'

I studied him with concern. 'Were . . . were you meant to?'

'Yes. That is the aim of it,' he explained. Then he stroked my cheek and regarded me with such adoration that I believed he might weep. 'You must never permit the world to pass censure on you, Hetty, not for committing this deed. There is no evil in love, no sin in it at all.'

I nodded, though uneasily.

'The world will attempt to censure you, you must understand that.'

'I care not for the world.'

'Nor do I,' he exclaimed, kissing me triumphantly. 'I hold no love of the laws of man. Monsieur Rousseau says we should be free of such things, free to pursue our true nature, our true inclinations . . .'

'Free to wander, like Werther . . .' I chirped.

'Yes, like Werther too. I strive for this, and so must you.' Then he placed both hands at either side of my face and penetrated my eyes with his. 'I knew always, from the moment I first looked upon you, that you had a will of your own, Hetty. You did not even recognize it in yourself, but I saw it, which is why I contrived to dance with you that night.'

I gasped in disbelief at his words.

'You cannot mean that?'

'You thought it occurred by chance?' He smirked wickedly.

'But of course.' I was astonished at his admission.

'And I was correct. You are courageous, my love, so courageous. Every day that we were apart my heart yearned for you to come to me. I thought of it every morning; at every private moment, every night before I extinguished the light, I wished it to happen.'

'You willed me to you.' I spoke solemnly.

'We willed it together, and so it has come to pass.' He laid a kiss upon my forehead. 'We are joined eternally, as husband and wife.'

His words and tenderness shot a shiver of delight through my heart. I understood then that this act had been irrevocable. While a ring might be pulled from a finger or a marriage dissolved, this deed could never be undone, nor the memory of it lost.

'And the pain, it will pass,' he said with a knowing look, 'and soon be replaced by an unimaginable bliss.'

I could not think what he meant, and I asked him what greater pleasure there might be than feeling his naked limbs against mine.

'You think it will always be as unpleasant as this?' He raised a playful eyebrow to me. 'No wife would ever stand for it! The human race would come to an end.'

'No,' I agreed, 'it would seem very odd were that the case.'

His languorous blue eyes locked with mine and his mouth began to curl. He enjoyed imparting these carnal lessons to me.

'I shall teach you a thing many ladies do not know, something that a woman herself taught to me.'

Though intrigued by his words, I was also a good deal startled by his frank admission that he had known other ladies before me. Now, to think of my naivety makes me double up with laughter. How else might he have acquired such an understanding of love? Most certainly not from a scientific library!

At no point did I ever enquire about Allenham's previous conquests, though I have since learned that he was once the favourite of a Milanese countess and later a French noblewoman, long before he had reached his age of three and twenty. And I dare say there were more, a good many more. He was far too handsome to have learned his art from those two alone.

'The pleasurable part of your instruction is to follow,' he promised as he pulled me nearer to him and tenderly smoothed my hair. 'The first attempt is but the formality of the business . . . you will see.' There was a wantonness in his voice as he spoke.

His member, now relaxed, fell free from my passage. As it came away, he tucked the sheet between my thighs, so as to stanch the blood and sticky seed which flowed from me.

So there it is written, a truthful account of how I came to be debauched. I have not disguised my ruin behind pretty prose or written of it with sad regret. My heart did not mourn for the loss of my virtue. Though undone, I did not wail and sob like Clarissa Harlowe. I did not find the act ignoble, lewd or sinful. On the contrary, now that I had shared the very inside of my being with my true love, now that our souls had mingled, that every space between our persons had been closed, I felt more alive than I had ever been. I might never have otherwise believed that love could be sensed so deeply. In spite of the soreness between my legs, I wished that I might never move from that bed, and I longed eagerly for the next attempt, and the attempt after that!

Does that disgust you?

No, dear readers, I was blessed. Most blessed. Of all the deeds of my life, the one I have never regretted was giving myself entirely to Allenham.

I cannot recall how many days passed after that momentous one. I was scarcely aware of light or dark or the advance of time. The fires were replenished regularly and burned night and day in the grates. Food was brought to us in his drawing room, as was hot water for washing. The servants tripped by on clouds, like Venus's cherubs, hardly ever making a sound. In truth, we had little use for them, for we never dressed. Allenham stalked about in his chemise, or sometimes in nothing at all, as naked and brazen as a savage. I hid my eyes and he scoffed at my modesty. Though no longer an innocent, I had still a virgin's sensibilities.

It soon became apparent that my lover relished the informality of our conduct. For all of his cultivated manners and politeness, he rejoiced in abandoning them to laugh and love and be at ease with me. He directed his household that he was not to be disturbed but for matters of importance, and with the exception of two or three occasions, we were left entirely to ourselves.

'You must forgive me, dear heart,' my beloved would apologize when summoned from our bed, 'but it is not within my power to keep the cares of the world from my door.' He sighed. 'Nor unexpected visitors.'

'A visitor?' I enquired, somewhat concerned by this. I thought at once of my father, or a messenger from Melmouth. Was it possible that he still searched for me? Allenham saw the anxiety upon my face.

'Fear not,' he reassured me, 'it is merely a matter of business.' He gave me a kiss and then added in a lowered voice, 'Nevertheless, it is of the utmost importance that no one knows you are here.' He kissed me again. 'I shall not be long from you, my angel.'

Only briefly did my mind muse on what matters drew him away from me, before I rolled on to the place where he had lain and felt once more his warmth against me. When he returned, it was often with a freshly shaven face and a handful of neglected letters. These he read aloud from our bed, so we might laugh together at the London gossip and dull affairs of others. He greatly enjoyed the game of tearing up invitations to balls and dinners as I watched in horror.

'I shall say it never arrived,' he smirked, scattering the pieces like a child. 'Come now,' he would then chide, checking me for my priggishness, 'it was from Lady Stafford, who has balls more regularly than she sneezes.' And before I could protest, he would grab me about the waist and with a playful groan lay me on my back. 'Besides, I should not like to go without you. I do not wish to be anywhere you are not.'

'And so we shall go nowhere,' said I, quite merrily, between kisses. Though I spoke in jest, I knew the truth of my words, for in spite of the joy I felt in his arms, I understood what sacrifices I had made for that pleasure. In future, there would be many places where I could not venture. My life would be conducted in his shadow, well hidden from view.

Of course, I had always recognized that I was not to live with him at Herberton. That much had been made clear upon my arrival. Propriety would not permit it. But when after several days his lordship received word that Orchard Cottage was prepared, I nevertheless grew terribly apprehensive. My heart was now so tied to his that I could not bear the prospect of a separation or to be uprooted from the safe surroundings of his apartments. His lordship soothed me with his cheerful re-assurances, and on the following morning insisted that he himself take me to the house on the boundary of his estate.

A grey mare had been saddled and brought round to the front of the house for me to ride. Allenham lifted me on to the beast, and then, taking the reins in his gloved hands, proceeded to guide us through the flat, grassy stretch of parkland and into the outer rolls and folds of his estate.

As the mare plodded a path through the thick earth, his lordship pointed out the various spots of beauty and interest: the ancient oaks, as old as the bones of Queen Elizabeth; and a well spring, which the local people thought enchanted. 'Dear Hetty,' he sighed, 'how long I have spent imagining you here, and me beside you. I wish you to love Herberton as do I. I wish it to be your home as much as it is mine.' He gazed up at me from beside the horse, his sharply handsome cheeks brightened by the cool air. In his blue wool coat and unadorned hat, he appeared a simple country gentleman, a man perfectly content to wander among nature. I laughed at this sight. 'My own Werther,' I remarked with a smile.

It was to the edge of an ancient orchard that Allenham was leading us, and he carefully guided my mount through the rows of twisted skeleton trees. Their load of apples had only recently been deposited and the ground still lay soft with their rotten corpses, the sweet smell of mouldering fruit present in the breeze. Through the branches, down the ridge I spied the whitewashed walls of a long plaster house, upon which a picturesque bowed window had been installed beside the door. Thin blue trails of smoke issued from its chimneys and into the damp air.

I was surprised to find the cottage much larger than I had imagined it to be. Once Allenham had assisted me off the horse and through the door, an inviting, comfortably furnished space spread before me.

The house, for it was more of a house than a cottage, contained three rooms below and three above. The first of these appeared to be the oldest, with dark panelled walls and carvings all around. The floors were of cold flagstone, but the hearth was so grand that it engulfed the entire room with a glow of warmth. Beyond it was a parlour, more recently built, with wooden floors that squeaked beneath my feet, and through that lay a smaller dining room and passage to the kitchen. This floor was joined to the next by a modest stair, which led to the rooms above; the largest was to be my bedchamber, with the two others as a dressing room and a servant's room.

I was, dear reader, overwhelmed by what I saw, and as Allenham escorted me through the rooms of my home by one hand, the other remained firmly pressed to my mouth in disbelief. It was not the grandest of places, but what astonished me was that it was mine. Never before had I a home to call my own, nor had I ever believed in all my years of girlish dreaming that I might possess one. More remarkable still was the care that had been taken in its preparation for me. The walls had been freshly whitewashed, and a variety of furniture transported from Herberton: cabinets, chairs, tables, Turkey carpets and even framed landscapes and engravings; and all had been arranged thoughtfully throughout. The bed too was a grand affair, an old walnut structure, hung with newly purchased Indian chintz, as imposing as the one upon which I had passed my first night in Allenham's care.

He was as thrilled as I at the creation of this cosy haven, designed entirely for our happiness. Once downstairs, he drew me to the spacious hearth, which was indeed so broad that there lay two seats on either side of the fire on which to sit. The flames swelled and turned, their heat reflected by the glazed tiles that lined the interior.

As he stood admiring the high wooden mantel, running his hand along a row of carved acorns, leaves and fat roses, his fingers came to rest upon something. He paused and rumpled his brow.

'How very extraordinary,' he exclaimed.

I moved towards him so as to better view what he regarded.

There at his fingertips was the shape of a heart graven deep into the wood. The letter 'L' sat squarely within it, with a 'G' and an 'H' inscribed below.

'Lightfoot?' I asked.

'The family who inhabited the cottage, yes.'

I then thought he must be playing some trick upon me, that he himself had engraved our initials within the heart, but when he removed his hand I glimpsed the date which lay beneath, '1738'. The marks, which had been worn in with soot and time, had been placed there by some other loving G and H.

'So it was intended, Miss Lightfoot,' he pronounced.

'So it was,' I agreed with a smile.

Chapter 16

I cannot, dear reader, ever recall a time of greater happiness than my days at Orchard Cottage. Nor can I call to mind a place more sacred to my heart than that spot beside the hearth. It was there, with G and H to bear witness, that Allenham swore himself to me. He covered my face with kisses, laying them over my lips and cheeks and upon each of my closed lids.

'Hetty,' he said, taking my face into his hands, 'I choose you for my wife. I pledge myself to you. Though my income is small, I vow to do my best by you and by my children. I shall love you like no other.' He then took one step back and, while holding both of my hands, asked, 'Will you pledge yourself to me?'

I nodded. All the heat from my heart now rose into my face. My eyes began to smart with tears of joy. How I had dreamed of a moment such as this, and yet what came to pass, with my adored Allenham before me, in a home that was to be our own, was more than I had ever imagined possible. Never in my short life had I felt so possessed by bliss and contentment.

'My beloved husband,' I breathed, my chin a-quiver, 'I pledge my devotion to you. I am yours alone . . .' I paused, as weeping overcame me. 'My love for you is eternal . . .' I could say no more, for the strength of my feelings had choked me completely. Allenham studied me. His features, so lit by love, seemed fixed in a dazzled expression. He drew me to him and enfolded me in his arms.

'So it is done. I am sworn to you as you are to me. Our love holds us as no institution of man can. Believe that to be true and our union shall never be broken.'

'I believe it to be true.'

'And believe that I shall never leave you, dear Henrietta.'

At that, I drew back my head from his chest and examined him through a watery gaze.

'I have no wish to reside at Herberton while you are here,' said he.

A great sense of relief washed over me at that pronouncement.

'Of course there will be matters of business – I cannot abandon my duties – but I shall always endeavour to return to Orchard Cottage.' He held me tightly. 'Upon my honour, I promise it.'

Allenham made good on his word and it is fair to say that we lived as might a married pair, though with more affection than I have often seen in most lawful unions.

He lay nearly every night in my bed, under the high-pitched roof, and woke as many mornings beside me. We breakfasted on dishes of chocolate and hot buttered bread, which we toasted on forks before my fire. Eventually we dressed, sometimes assisting one another with our clothing rather than spoiling the blissful scene by inviting in the servants. Admittedly we were especially slow to our feet in that first week, and we tarried amid the bedding as youthful paramours often do, but, as Allenham had cautioned me, he could not put off his duties entirely. There was forever some dispatch awaiting an answer, or a servant come galloping from Herberton to alert him of a visitor. Then, after several hours or half a day, he would return, never failing to fulfil his promise to me.

'This will not do,' he announced one morning, after receiving word that he was required at the house. He rose hastily from the warm delights of our bed. 'Ladies require company and diversion, and in my absence you have neither.'

'I do not want for diversion,' I protested with a smile.

He passed me an incredulous look.

'You cannot be pleased when I am not here,' said he, while searching for his stockings and garters. His chemise hung open along his chest.

'But I amuse myself perfectly well. I take the air and admire

Herberton's beauties, and when you are returned, I have scarcely noticed you were gone.'

'I shall have to remedy this,' he announced, dismissing my comment.

Hardly had he been absent from Orchard Cottage for more than a few hours when the first of his proposed diversions arrived upon the back of a cart. Laid in the straw were two glass-fronted bookcases, which were carried into the drawing room and set carefully in place. They were shortly followed by the arrival of a second cart, this one bearing what seemed to be an entire library of books. The servants soon set to work placing each of the volumes upon the shelves, as I stood by and watched, my lips pursed together in an expression of quiet glee. I counted among the authors Henry Fielding and Laurence Sterne, Oliver Goldsmith, Swift, Dryden, Pope, Shakespeare, Milton and the like. My own volume of *The Sorrows of Young Werther* was placed here too. I would have all manner of words for company, those of Hesiod and Ovid, the poetry of Virgil, the wisdom of Montaigne, John Locke, Diderot and Voltaire, and of course Rousseau, whose entire works lined nearly a full shelf.

Allenham returned to me that afternoon to find me in one of the seats tucked within the hearth. I had taken Jean-Jacques Rousseau's *Confessions*, the book about which he had so often spoken, with me into that comfortable corner. The work was in French, and though I read that language tolerably well, there were passages with which I struggled. When he discovered me there furrowing my brow, he came down upon his knees and, after covering both of my hands with kisses, removed the volume from my lap and laid his head there instead.

'You are perfection,' he sighed. 'You are so free of artifice, so true to your nature. Your father has educated you better than Monsieur Rousseau himself. Your love of beauty, the manner in which you wear your sentiments so freely upon your face, these qualities made me love you. These are exceptional traits. I have found them in no other member of your sex.' He peered up at me from where his head rested amid my skirts. 'And you possess a strong mind.' Then a teasing look came over him. 'Permit me to corrupt it by reading to you from a Swiss man's *Confessions*.' And with that, he assumed the seat opposite and read to me in Rousseau's native tongue. The ease with which the words flowed from him bewitched me, almost as much as the tales themselves.

'What do you make of that?' he paused frequently to enquire. He seemed always ready to know my thoughts, much as he had been when we were at Bath and then again in London, when he wished to discuss the merits of Werther with me. To be sure, there were many shocking and intriguing notions to come from Monsieur Rousseau's writings. When not rapt in the joys of love, as we were often, he read to me from most of them. We passed a good many hours debating a formula for living, which Allenham believed should be 'simple, rustic and contemplative'.

'Mankind should be at liberty to follow the instincts of his heart, and not to be so bound to convention and institutions. The Americans have attempted this experiment with great success, and now the French embark upon it . . .' He glowed when he spoke of such things, and my adoration swelled as I listened to his thoughts. 'Darling Hetty, in the spring we shall go abroad. I should like to show you all the places I enjoyed as a boy. I should like to take you to Spa, and to the Alps – the very image of sublime beauty . . .'

'Geneva? We might visit the place of dear Monsieur Rousseau's birth . . .'

'In the spring . . . yes . . . you shall sketch the Alps! And then to Weimar, perhaps to gain an introduction to Mr Goethe.'

I gasped in delight. 'To see the forests where Werther might have wandered . . .'

'And to France – oh, to Paris, my love!' Allenham's expression broadened, his eyes took on a dreamy cast. 'To live a full life, a soul must wander – he must experience and contemplate all that he sees.'

' "Once more I am a wanderer, a pilgrim, through the world . . ." ' I began.

' ". . . But what else are you?" ' said he, finishing Werther's quote.

I imagined how it would be to sit within the cabin of his coach, all the world taking us for husband and wife.

'There is a different way of living abroad,' Allenham continued. 'The French do not much mind if a man brings his mistress into society.'

The mention of that word instantly quashed my appetite for this adventure. My face fell. It was true: that was what I had become, a mistress. While we played out our days in the sanctuary of Orchard Cottage, I was his wife, but to the world, I would be his whore. I thought of my lover's warning, that society would censure me for my deeds. I conjured a picture in my head, recalling how Lady Stavourley and her associates would scowl behind their fans at certain pretty, well-attired ladies. At the time I had not understood why she and the other ladies used such cruel words, but now it had become plain to me who those fallen creatures were.

'Perhaps we should not go abroad so soon . . .' I said after some consideration. 'I like it here just as well.'

'Nonsense,' declared Allenham, who I suspect had guessed what troubled me. 'I believe you will like it better there. Ladies enjoy far more liberty in France and Italy than in England. Not a word will be said against us – and hang the world for their condemnation of love!'

My beloved and his dreams. I cannot fault him for them. After all, he was not much older than I. We were both extremely young and could not foresee the dark cloud that would soon fall across all of Europe and the events that would upend the lives of so many. However, I dare say there were many among Allenham's acquaintance who could well have foretold the storm to come. By the onset of winter, the Baron was called more frequently up the hill to Herberton for longer periods. There came dispatches at night, too, including one that pulled him from the throes of sleep to reach for pen and paper.

'Is there some trouble?' I enquired.

'None,' he reassured me, 'but I have been asked for an immediate reply.'

He then disappeared into the drawing room and scribbled furiously for more than an hour. Only after the letter had been sealed and sent did he return to me, his thoughts still agitated by the news he had read.

Whenever I attempted to press him as to the contents of his letters, he would sigh. 'It is no matter, Hetty. Politics, forever politics. There is much to be done to secure a seat in Parliament.'

At about this time, another cart, like the one which carried the books, arrived at Orchard Cottage. The clatter of moving furniture drew me downstairs from my dressing room. There, I spied what I recognized immediately to be an artist's table, portered by two servants. Allenham was observing its delivery and looked up to see the surprise upon my face.

'I have instructed it to be placed in the drawing room, where the light is best,' he announced.

I was overwhelmed at this sight, for in spite of recognizing my talent for painting, never had anyone, not even my father, thought of purchasing such a thing for me. I could hardly speak from astonishment. The table was an expensive piece and had had to be ordered from London, as had the items that accompanied it: brushes and watercolours, paper, glass jars of pigments, ink and oils.

'This will not entirely make up for my absences,' my beloved apologized, 'but it will allow you to fill your days with an activity you enjoy.'

'Oh my dear George,' I babbled. I ran my hand against the smooth surface of its top and lifted up the hinge. If he had not made me love him by every other measure, then this kind act alone would have secured my affection entirely.

I put myself into his embrace. 'I am so very grateful,' I whispered.

'It is to you that I am grateful,' he responded, 'for you have made the greatest sacrifice in coming to me.' He stroked my hair lovingly, lost in his thoughts. Then, after a pause, he announced that he was required in London.

'When do you depart?' I asked, my face still hidden in the folds of his waistcoat.

'Tomorrow, I am afraid.'

He felt me give way against him.

'As much as I would wish you to accompany me, it is impossible at present. You understand that?'

'Yes,' I responded glumly.

'It will only be for a very short time, and I shall return within the week,' he promised. 'I wish for the separation no more than you, but there is business which cannot be put off . . . This is not my choice.'

Then he sniffed. 'Where matters of my future are concerned, I am very much in chains.'

I nodded, my head heavy with sadness, for I had always known there would come a time when he would have to travel elsewhere to fulfil his duties.

'I swear to you, I shall return as quickly as I am able. I shall think of nothing but our reunion,' he declared.

And so, the following morning, I stood at the threshold of the door, the December wind whipping around me, with all the misery of a cottager's wife watching her husband set off with the recruiting sergeant.

I tried with all my might to distract myself in Allenham's absence. In the hours after his departure, however, I moved aimlessly through the cottage. I could not settle with a book, or with my paints. I stared at the windows and fretted, though for no good reason. I knew he would return to me, but it took some time for my heart to trust my head.

Of course, I had not been left entirely alone, for I was surrounded by servants, whose songs and scolds echoed from the kitchen, whose cat-like footsteps could be heard on the floorboards overhead. Bess, my maid of all work, the girl who had tended me on the day I arrived at Herberton, was never further than the next room. My home was well heated and meals were prepared for me with regularity, but my bed was empty and I could never sleep with ease until it was filled. As I extinguished the candle each night, I reached out beside me to feel the vacant space and shivered.

He had been away three nights when, in the haze of sleep, I repeated that ritual. I stretched out my hand and there felt something touch it. All at once, my pining heart began to rejoice, until I probed the mass further and found it cold. It was too hard to be the bolster, yet too chilled to be the form of my beloved. Curiosity caused me to reach further into the folds of bedding and draw it to me. As I rolled it into the gleam of moonlight, I caught sight of what I thought to be a lady's nightcap. Several golden tendrils trailed from it. I moved my hand through the gloom to inspect this oddity and in doing so passed it over a nose and mouth. At this, my fingers froze. A sense of dread began to pour into me. I squinted into the darkness, now urgently wishing to know who had made their way into my bed. Then I saw her, her face as grey as I last remembered it, her lips darkened with death. Only her eyes retained that vital spark, and they locked on to mine with such hatred that it sucked the very air from my lungs.

I wished to cry out in terror, but found my mouth sealed shut, and my arms and legs as dead as hers.

'You thought yourself free of me, *sister*?' she hissed, as if she loathed the word. 'You thought yourself free, but you are not. Nor will you ever be. You will see my shadow in all your pleasures. I shall sour your every joy – as you have mine,' she whispered, blowing her curses at my face.

I fought for my breath. Indeed, I was aware of my heart racing so quickly that I thought I might expire from fear. I moved to part my lips and awoke with a start. My horrified cries brought Bess running from the adjoining room. She found me stalking, pacing, staring at the empty bed.

'I had a nightmare, a dreadful, dreadful nightmare,' I rambled.

A candle was lit, and only then could I breathe once more.

'Please.' I looked at Bess, as frightened as a child. 'Will you share my bed until morning?'

The maid obligingly climbed under the coverlet, and made no more of it.

I, on the other hand, lay with my eyes open, too troubled by what I had seen to rest.

Save for a few occasions, I had not permitted Lady Catherine to enter my head since my flight from Melmouth. I bore down heavily on any sensations of remorse, on any guilt at my love for Allenham. Whenever they crept upon me, I dispelled my foolish thoughts. My will was not to blame. Werther was not to blame. I had turned my back on all that had occurred and dared not think of it in the wake of my happy life. Yet she came to me. She came to me in the night, as she had when she had lived. I recalled all too well the prank she had played upon me; how she had menaced me at the foot of my bed, her face covered with pearlescent hair powder.

'It was merely a dream. A foolish dream,' I scolded myself, although I was not entirely convinced that my powers of reason were correct. Her curses carried a heaviness of truth in them that I did not wish to acknowledge. In the light of day, I recovered my senses, but failed to dispel my unease, which continued to linger, floating apparition-like about me for some time.

Chapter 17

Five nights and six days had passed before his homecoming. Each of these was punctuated by the arrival of a letter, bearing news of his movements. He complained of long discussions and tiresome dinners, 'when I wish only to be with you at Orchard Cottage, sitting in our hearth'.

'I have supped with Mr Burke,' he wrote to me, 'whose thoughts upon the revolution in France have altered greatly. I own, I was most surprised to hear him speak so violently against it. His words unsettled me a good deal and have given me much to consider.' Whether it was Edmund Burke's sentiments that dampened Allenham's fire, or some other matter, he returned to me in a quieter, more reflective mood.

Let there be no doubt, our reunion filled me with the greatest joy. He had no sooner strode through the door, his nose bright with winter's chill, than I flew to him. I said nothing of my nightmare, but breathed with relief that I should no longer fear the dimming of day into darkness. I held on to his arm and wept.

'Hetty,' he sighed, moved by my sentiments, 'whatever distresses you? I am here and safe.'

'I know,' I sniffled and smiled, 'and I am most glad of it.'

As we greeted one another, his valet laid out several parcels in the drawing room. My beloved bade me to open each of them as he looked on.

In one there was a burgundy cape for winter, lined with fur; and in another a muff to match. Wrapped in a coarse cloth bundle there was some heavy blue and grey striped silk for a gown and buff silk for its petticoat, both to be made up immediately by a local mantua-maker. In another bundle there was a shawl of black taffeta and, folded into brown paper, a vast gauze neckerchief edged with delicate French lace. Were this not enough, he bought me two pairs of cream-coloured gloves and two pairs of the finest stockings.

'I have never had so many gifts at once!' I laughed, after expressing my gratitude with countless kisses.

'Nonsense, these are merely necessities for winter,' he protested, 'and if we are to travel in the spring, you must be suitably attired. You must have several new gowns and fur to warm you in the Alps.' He then stepped away from my embrace and examined me, shamelessly crawling his eyes along the full swell of my bosom. 'But I do fear you lack embellishment.' With that, he drew a small case from his coat pocket. 'I have no doubt that you will remember this and the pleasure to which it led,' he smirked.

He held out the box to me and I, greatly intrigued by his comment, carefully took it. Beneath the lid lay something that, with all the distraction of the past weeks, I had entirely forgotten. There, upon a bed of white satin, was the shell-pink cameo he had once pressed into my hand. He had taken it to London, to have the image of Venus and Mars set into a circlet of brilliant diamonds. He lifted the brooch and, slipping his fingers through the gauze at my décolleté, gently pinned it to the top of my bodice.

My face flushed with colour. His intimate touch, when combined with the sight of the brooch, called to mind many passionate remembrances.

'I see you have not forgotten . . .' said he, with a note of intrigue in his tone.

I attempted to hide my shy smile. 'I could never,' I murmured, now red-faced as Eve's apple.

'You see, my angel, it was not I who seduced you, but Venus, and Eros's arrow.'

At the mention of those words, I clapped my hand over my hot face, which caused my lover to laugh mightily. He did so love to tease me.

That was the very phrase he had used when, lying beneath him, I first succumbed to what he called *la petite mort.*

Although in the course of my instruction he had cautioned me of the sensations I was likely to encounter, I found myself entirely unprepared for the rapture, the urgency of desire and the ecstasy of release that gripped me so completely. I was left dumbstruck and slightly scandalized, for it seemed to me such an immodest thing, to cry out in passion. Allenham, by contrast, appeared perfectly contented by my performance, enough so to congratulate me and offer reassurance that Eros's arrow had hit its proper mark.

Dare I say that in the wake of his short absence, the sight of that memento *d'amour* was all that was required to ignite our desires once more? We immediately retired to bed and took no supper that night.

When I think back on it, I do often marvel on the depth of our love. Youth carries with it a great capacity for emotion and for dreaming. I have known many paramours who profess themselves in the clutches of a passionate romance, only to find that the flame they once thought eternal has blown out in the first gust of wind. But ours was not like that, and I never once doubted the sincerity of Allenham's affections. The security I knew while in his care meant that I asked few questions and was always satisfied with the answers he provided. I did not concern myself with the details of his affairs, or who were the gentlemen he entertained at Herberton, or what they discussed. I knew nothing of politics, or of government; few ladies do. With hindsight, I have often wondered what might have occurred had I been more curious.

By December he was almost always at the house. He retired very late into the night, and rose quite early in the morning, though he took both supper and breakfast with me. He appeared haggard and troubled after many of these absences. As he picked over his boiled ham or roast chicken, he often rubbed his head and spoke of France. 'Hetty,' he confessed to me late one night, 'I know not with whom to agree. There are many who wish to persuade me that this experiment in liberty will be the ruin of the French nation. The mob is an angry force, not a rational one. They have threatened the King; they have rolled a cannon to Versailles and ransacked the Queen's apartments. They wish to demolish the Church. I know not what to think. Mr Fox favours the revolutionaries, but Mr Burke and others within His Majesty's Government fear what may occur if such forces are successful.' He stared at his plate. 'It will soon come to war. Of this I am certain.'

Following his visit to London, he had grown increasingly anxious and distracted. There was nothing irregular in his conduct, he was as affectionate and devoted as he had ever been, but he seemed more cautious about matters. I recall one incident in particular, shortly before Christmas.

In all my time at Orchard Cottage, never did I feel confined. I was free to wander the estate, to gather herbs and mushrooms with Bess, so I did not think much of venturing out on a cold, clear day shortly before Christmas for some sprigs of mistletoe. I had wrapped myself in my fur-lined cape and tucked my hands inside my fox muff, while Bess set about collecting the clusters of white berry in her apron. It was there that Allenham spotted us as he returned from Herberton on his mount. When he called out, there seemed nothing unusual in his cheerful greeting, but when he drew up his horse, I noted his look of concern. He glanced several times over his shoulder towards the road that led from the house. He then assisted me on to his horse and bid Bess to catch us up. I sat before him, between his arms and the reins, as he rode slowly towards the cottage.

'Have you seen anyone ride past since you have been out?' he asked calmly.

'No, I have not,' I responded, slightly alarmed.

'I do not mind you taking the air, my darling,' said he, 'but sometimes I do fear . . .' He trailed off. 'You have not been gone from Melmouth long and we are not entirely free from prying eyes.'

I understood his meaning and said as much to him.

'One favour I must request is that you not come to Herberton if I am there. Do not call at the house. Never call at the house.'

It was a stern caution, in a tone I had never before heard him use.

'I had not intended to do so,' said I, rather meekly.

'It is not that I do not wish you there, Hetty, for I wish you everywhere I am,' he smiled, 'but it is dangerous. Visitors come and go, sometimes quite unexpectedly. I should not want you to be seen by some person who might know you. The silence of my household has been bought, but I do not wish to tempt Fate. Promise me this, my darling. Promise me you will do as I say and not grow curious.'

I promised him, and he appeared satisfied.

I suspect it was this incident that led to the purchase of my next gift. He wished me to have more indoor diversions and less cause to stray beyond Orchard Cottage. However, it is possible that I am incorrect. He may have simply desired some music during the long winter nights. Whatever the case, there came in time for the New Year a fortepiano.

It was a strange thing, the welcoming of this item into our home. At first I was delighted. I passed the day of its arrival stroking its ivory keys and applying myself to making it sing. I did not know that his lordship also played, 'though not so well', he grumbled each time he struck a hard note. 'I learned music upon a violin.'

With the instrument came a pile of music, most of which had been brought down from Herberton. I laboured my way through the compositions of Mr Handel, Mr Linley and Mr Arne, but my fingers felt slow and leaden. They plodded rather than tripped over the chords. I was not an accomplished musician, and yet when I took my place upon the bench, I was reminded of one who was.

In my mind I heard each note struck perfectly. When I shut my eyes, I could see her dainty wrists above the keys. I watched her head tilt and bob as she tapped out a melody. I could hear her sweet lark's voice trill the words to 'Think Not, My Love' and 'The Bells of Aberdovey'. The memory of Lady Catherine stood over me, as I once stood over her, turning the pages of music.

Allenham could not have foreseen the consequences of this purchase. He could not have known that, along with the harmonious chords, disquieting memories would also rise from the fortepiano. With each passing day they grew louder and more disturbing. Happy remembrances of her cheerful countenance began to twist into pictures of her lifeless face, and from there darken into the images of my nightmare and the dissonant words of her curses. Soon, even the keys felt too cold to touch. They called to mind the iciness of her dead lips, a sensation my fingers will never forget.

After a week, I could no longer sit at it. It stared at me wherever I stood. It glared at me when I entered the room. With its polished surface, it shone like a coffin in our drawing room. A part of me, that dark place within the human mind that conjures demons, began to wonder if she had not orchestrated the arrival of this gift in some manner. 'No, no,' I scolded myself. I would not succumb to such irrational imaginings. My head and heart to-ed and fro-ed, one declaiming reason, the other taunting me with the biting words of her malediction.

At last, unable to bear the sight of the instrument any longer, I asked Bess that it be covered. When at last, on a January evening blown with snow, Allenham asked me if I should like to play, I looked down at my lap in silence.

'I do not play well,' said I, rather limply.

'I believe you play very well,' he encouraged me, 'and how will you improve if you do not apply yourself?'

I sighed. 'I am afraid I have never been musical. Lady Catherine was far more accomplished.'

In all the months I had been there, neither of us had ventured to speak one word of the past, fearing it would taint the present, but after the torment of my nightmare and the unsettling appearance of Allenham's gift, I could hold my tongue no longer. This is not to say that, until this time, neither of us grieved. Oh, what a falsehood I should tell if I did not confess to the burden of remorse we carried. It was cumbersome, to be sure, but to expect us, as young as we were, to live out our days in a state of perpetual mourning was most unreasonable.

'Is it because of her that you do not wish to play?' he asked after a pause.

I nodded. 'It reminds me.'

In truth, the sight of the fortepiano called to mind a number of things I had pushed away, not simply the disturbing images of my nightmare. Many shadows had followed me to Herberton, questions I had been too frightened to consider or to mention. Now, by speaking my sister's name aloud, I had invoked these other fears too.

'George,' I whispered, 'is it wrong that we should love one another?'

'No. The love of a man and a woman is never wrong,' he responded in a clear, certain tone.

'No matter what the circumstances may be?'

He looked at me, as if to question why I doubted it.

'Would my father think it wrong?' I asked. My hands had begun to tremble and I gripped them together tightly.

'Lord Stavourley knew only of our friendship, and that he believes to have ended. I wrote to tell him as much when you arrived here.'

It pained me to hear him say that. My heart contracted, and the sharp deception it contained cut into its walls.

Slowly, I shook my head. My mouth held bitter words.

'No,' I breathed. The tears started down my cheeks. 'He has seen your letters.'

My beloved turned to me slowly, but as he opened his mouth to speak, we were disturbed by a rap upon the door. His valet entered, short of breath.

'My lord, your attendance at the house is required. A messenger awaits.'

Allenham rose carefully to his feet. His face appeared quite void of expression. He idled for a moment behind his chair, his hands resting at the top of it. His sight was directed towards the window where large feathers of snow floated in the darkness.

'And what has become of them, these letters?'

'My father burned them,' I wept.

He inhaled, somewhat relieved at that news, though his face remained troubled.

'I dare not think . . .' he began, and then shifted uneasily. He removed his clear, bright eyes from the distant place where they rested and settled them upon me. 'We shall never be free from worry, Henrietta, or the fear of consequences.'

He said no more than that, but moved towards the door where his valet stood.

I heard it shut and watched him, with his hat pulled over his eyes, pass before the window and disappear into a swirl of snow and night.

Chapter 18

Allenham did not return to me that night. I went to my bed and awaited him. I let the candle burn down to its nub before extinguishing it and then rolled over in the darkness and wetted my pillow with self-pity.

I awoke in the morning to find no sign of him. I enquired of his movements from Bess as she dressed me, but she claimed to know nothing more of them than I. I sighed. He had never before been so long at Herberton.

I passed the morning as I might if he were there alongside me. I sat at my artist's table with my back to the fortepiano, that spiteful, uninvited guest whose presence I now abhorred, and worked upon a still-life painting of winter berries. Beyond the window lay a perfect, untrammelled bed of snow, the sky still rolling with angry grey clouds. There were no telltale footprints, no sign of hoof marks outside the cottage.

By the time the servants had lit the candles, an hour before dinner, I had begun to fret. I put my paints away and took a book beside the fire. I could not even recall which story it was that I read, for none of the words penetrated my heavy thoughts. I listened to the snap of wet wood in the flames, hoping those sounds would soon be the accompaniment to the squeal of moving door hinges, but this did not come to pass.

I ate, my knife and fork scratching against the porcelain in the silence. I looked to the window where the snow had resumed its downward progress. An entire day had passed since my love had set out for Herberton. Surely whatever business this was could not occupy him for so long, I thought. I called to Bess and asked again if she had heard any news of Lord Allenham. 'None,' she replied, for she had spent the entire day with me.

I stood at the window for most of the night, until my eyes wished to close. 'I am certain I shall find his lordship here in the morning,' I cheerfully announced to Bess as she helped me into my nightdress and cap.

'Yes,' she agreed in that way that servants have when they mean to please.

But I went to my bed in another mind, full of dark thoughts, growing ever more anxious that my revelation was the cause of his absence. I twisted amid the sheets and then began once more to weep.

On the second morning, I found myself truly distressed. Indeed I felt so ill with worry that I could eat nothing. Bess brought me a hot dish of chocolate to sip, but it smelled, to me, burnt and rancid.

'I shall send a note to the house,' I stated. My maid removed the chocolate and brought instead some writing paper, pen and ink.

'Pray, my lord, I do not wish to trouble you,' I wrote, deciding it was best to write in a formal manner, now vastly cautious of betraying myself upon paper, knowing what misfortune might come of it, 'but the household desires to know when we might expect your return.' I signed it 'H. Lightfoot'.

I sealed it and passed it to Bess, ordering it to be brought up to Herberton immediately.

My maid set out through the frost-painted orchard in her cape and returned the following hour.

'Did you see him?' I queried anxiously.

'No, madam. The housekeeper took it from me.'

'And what did she say?'

'She examined it, madam, and placed it in her pocket.'

'You directed her to bring it him, did you not?'

'Of course, madam.'

I stalked my sitting room like a cat, moving from one corner to the next, hoping there would come an answer, listening for the sound of shoes in snow. I waited hours; two, three, four, perhaps more. The sun began its downward slant, but no word came.

Another meal was prepared and served. This I devoured, for my nerves had raised my hunger. When I finished, I called for Bess.

'Something is not right,' I said to her, my voice quavering. 'You will take another message to Herberton. I insist that you place it directly in his lordship's hand.'

I drew out another sheet of paper and penned the same words I had committed to ink earlier, and then sent Bess abroad with a lantern.

She returned to me, and when she took down her hood I saw the apprehension in her features.

'Oh madam,' she said, wide-eyed, 'I did as you requested. I asked to see his lordship but Mrs Shirley would not permit it.'

'How so? Why would she not permit it?'

'I do so beg your pardon, madam, but she forbade it and took the letter from me. She said there was no need for urgency and it was not my place to demand an audience with him and whatever message I bore would be brought to him by herself, madam,' Bess rattled.

'But what reason did she give?' I demanded.

'None but that. I do so beg madam's pardon.'

I failed to sleep that night. I could not lie still. My mind tumbled with questions. Had I driven him away? Had some accident befallen him? My dear Allenham would not have left me here with no word from him to explain his absence. He would sense my distress and wish to assuage it. No, no, I told myself, I felt it in my heart, this was not right.

I sat at the edge of my bed and listened to the nothingness of night.

He had received a vow from me that I should never venture to Herberton when I knew him to be there. I had given him my word; I had made a promise. I recalled the sight of his hardened features when he begged me; he feared I should put us both in danger. I gripped my head as it howled with frustration. 'No, he has not deceived me, it would not be possible,' I calmed myself. 'His love is true.' The only deceit had come from me. 'Oh!' I cried out miserably. 'I have wrought this!'

Having convinced myself of my wrongdoing, I determined to rectify it, though I might incur his further displeasure by doing so. I had given my promise and now I must break it. (Where the logic was in this, dear friends, I am sure you cannot fathom, but to a lovelorn girl of seventeen in the middle of a restless night, it had all the reason of Aristotle in it.) I resolved that if his lordship did not appear by morning, I should set out after him.

Sure enough, another morning broke with no further sign of my beloved. I called for Bess, in fact, I shouted for her, which is something I had never before done. In my echoing tones, I heard the shrill cry of my sister; her angered voice rang from my lungs. I clapped my hand to my breast, startled at the force within me.

Bess had brought breakfast, which I turned away. I could not stomach it.

'I am going up the hill, to Herberton,' I panted. My heart was racing. 'Dress me. Quickly.'

I do not know what time of the morning it was when I set off through the frozen rows of sleeping apple trees. The sun sat low and thin on the hazy horizon. I struggled through the snow, my breath coming hard and vaporous in the cold, but even this could not slow my steady climb. I recalled that it was not many months earlier that I had mounted this hill. I thought about from whence I had run and the terror of that flight. Herberton had taken me in and it felt as much to me a home as ever did Melmouth. But, reader, I had grown too comfortable. I had forgotten that I was but a guest, and there upon his lordship's sufferance. While I had become accustomed to ordering my own household at Orchard Cottage, I held no sway at Herberton.

I fairly ran the final lengths to the house, so eager was I to see Allenham and bring to an end this disagreeable episode. I thought I might mount the steps to the entrance, but fearing I should make myself conspicuous to any visitors, thought better of it and went round to the side and through the rustic. It was to this same place that I had come in October and it felt as if I might relive that familiar scene once more. However, on this occasion, I strode through the doors with as much command as his lordship himself. Rather than cowering at the prospect of my encounter with the chatelaine, fear had emboldened me. I asked to speak with Mrs Shirley directly.

She approached me from down the corridor, as she had on the day of my arrival, but when she recognized my face, I noticed her demeanour sharpen.

'What may I do for you, miss?' she enquired in a voice that matched my imperious manner.

'I must see his lordship,' I responded firmly.

'I am afraid that is not possible,' said she, 'for his lordship has gone to London.'

I stared at her blankly. This, I had not expected. My face, along with all my strength, began to tremble.

'When . . . when did he depart?' I asked.

'Three days prior.'

'Three days,' I echoed.

'I am afraid so, miss. You are too late for him.'

'But . . . when shall he return?'

'This I do not know. A dispatch came. He left in the dead of night.'

I did not know what to make of this.

'Has he left no instruction for me, no letter?'

'No, miss, he left none.'

'Oh,' I breathed. I felt suddenly as if I were a child, as if I were alone, and very much all at sea. 'What . . . shall I do?'

Why I asked that dragon of woman this, I cannot say; surprise and my own weakness led me to it.

'I do not know, miss. It is no business of mine to say.'

She folded her arms and regarded me with impatience. At that time, I was still too ignorant of the world to recognize that Mrs Shirley had the measure of me. She knew precisely who I was and what I had become. I was so young, so fresh, and his lordship so powerfully handsome, as to leave her in no doubt. Her shrewd eyes had observed me come to the house in that hurried, flustered way before. Although I had not seen her since that first day, she would have understood well enough what had transpired in his lordship's apartments. She also would have known that I now lived as Allenham's mistress in Orchard Cottage. Indeed, she would have had knowledge of all this long before I made my reappearance, sporting fur and a swagger.

There she left me, paying me a nod and withdrawing with no

more care for my concerns than any other stranger might have.

I lingered for a moment in confusion, looking about me for an answer which I knew I should not find there. I twisted my hands inside my muff, until a clear thought came to me.

I started back down the hill to Orchard Cottage in a fury, my pace matching the speed of my galloping mind. Now I was certain he had quit Herberton in a fit of anger, or else he would have left some instruction, some calming note to explain his absence. Oh friends, what panic came over me! I strode without care through the snow, tripping several times over the hem of my petticoat and upon the fur edge of my cloak. Were I so able, I might have run on all fours like a bolting horse back to the cottage! It is remarkable indeed how simple it is to shed one's dignity in a time of trouble.

I had resolved to write to him, to beg his forgiveness, and by the time I had arrived at Orchard Cottage, I had already composed the letter in my head. I scrambled through the door and called for Bess to bring pen and paper. This she did, but as she conveyed it to me, I was distracted by something far more promising.

I own that at that moment, I was not entirely of a rational mind. I saw, amid the collection of items that my maid carried, a small purse containing coin for household expenses – postage and the like. My eyes fixed on it, the pieces bulging within either end.

'What amount is here?' I asked, reaching for it like a desperate beggar.

'One pound, fifteen shillings and threepence.'

I had no sooner clasped my hand around the knitted pouch and felt the weight of coin in my palm than I understood what peace of mind spending it would bring me. As much as I loathed the idea that I should embark upon another journey, I knew I should never have a night's rest till I had seen Allenham's face and, if necessary, thrown myself at his feet and cleansed them with my tears. This was all I required, this small sum to carry me to my beloved's side.

I asked that Bess prepare us for a journey and collect for me a change of linens and my small things in a bundle, for I had not even a box with which to travel and, in my haste, I cared not for what items I brought. I wished only to set out as soon as I might in order to catch that day's mail coach. I feared even then that I would be too late for it. I had not even paused to consider from where I might board the vehicle, or how to convey myself there.

'Lechlade, madam, at the Crown,' said Bess, who then set about arranging a cart to take me there.

It was near midday when the cart, which regularly ferried the servants into town, arrived for me. Bess watched it roll to a stop and lingered near the door sheepishly.

'I mean no disrespect, madam, but . . . there ain't enough coin in that purse for two fares.'

I had not applied my mind to this, and indeed I felt as dim-witted as I had when I first climbed upon the mail coach at the White Hart.

'I have travelled unaccompanied before, Bess,' I announced, raising my head haughtily as if that admission should be some matter of pride for a genteelly bred young lady. 'And I am to return shortly with his lordship.'

Her expression was unmoved by that pronouncement.

One never knows what servants think, or for that matter the nature of the secrets to which they are privy. As she dropped a curtsey at my departure, I believe she held an altogether different view as to what I might encounter and for how long I might be gone.

Chapter 19

I had been too late for the mail, and therein lay my first misfortune.
To make up the time I had lost, I boarded the stage – when it eventually made its appearance. My intention was to join the next day's mail coach at Oxford, but the snow came so hard that day that the roads became impassable, and we were forced to weather the night at an inn not six miles short of my destination. So disappeared the day, for had I managed to depart from Lechlade upon the mail, I would have found myself in London in ten or twelve hours. So also diminished what little funds I possessed, and I felt again all the discomfort and dread I had known on my previous flight. I ordered refreshment, but could hardly touch it for my nerves. The road, too, caused me no end of sickness.

When at last I stepped into the mail's carriage at Oxford, two days had passed since I had set out. 'What folly was this!' I had now begun to chasten myself. Indeed, had I sent a letter it might have reached London long before me, and at far less expense. Each hour of delay spelled another hour in which my dear love thought ill of me. I could hardly tolerate it!

The mail shook us all night upon the road to London, entering it in the darkness of the morning hours, at that time when the night's lamps had begun to burn out and sun had hardly reared its head. Beggars huddled beneath the bulks of shops, a shadowy, slumbering pile of bodies in the dirty snow. The criers were just emerging on to the streets with ballads and quinces, scissors and fish. Servants wrapped against the chill skittered by in wooden pattens. The wheels of the mail slowly churned us through a paste of slush, straw, animal waste and mud. London had never before seemed a place of menace to me, and yet at this early hour, not quite eight o'clock, it appeared drab, washed with mud and soot. Its sounds were louder, the grins of the urchins wider and more sinister. As I alighted in the yard of the Swan with Two Necks, I could think of nothing but racing to Allenham, to Arlington Street in St James's, where I knew his warm, well-lit townhouse to be.

'Oh my love!' thought I, shivering with cold and anxiety. I imagined that I should find him there, still in his bed, that I should request his butler to rouse him, that I should wait impatiently for him in his drawing room, and that my beloved would appear, swathed in his wrapper, his hair undone. There would be a scene, I understood this. I should beg his forgiveness, throw myself upon my knees. I should weep piteously and declare my love for him, and swear I should do whatever penance he required of me to contradict the evils of my mistake. Then he would lift me from the floor and look upon me with grace. He would take me into his arms and heal my heart with kisses. That was how it would play out, I was certain of it.

For all the visits I had made to London, never before had I seen this strange corner of the city. The great dome of St Paul's rose from behind the inn, which was indeed the only sight I recognized. From where I stood, I had not the slightest inkling of how I might make my way to St James's. I enquired of a groom, who laughed insolently at my request for directions and said he would procure a hackney cab for me, for a sum. In the course of my travels, I had come to learn that a young lady unaccompanied attracted nothing but slights and insults. Her protectors are few, and those who come to her assistance more often than not wish to extract some other sort of fee for their kindness. You see, most understood that which I did not: a young lady who travels without a servant or a chaperone is no lady at all.

I presented the rogue with twopence for his trouble, which was half the contents of my small purse, and he set off in search of a hackney cab. When at last one arrived, I eagerly climbed inside its curtained carriage. We had travelled no more than a few streets before the driver brought us to a stop at the mouth of a mews. I could not imagine what was the matter, until the man dismounted and came round to the window.

'St James's is a great distance from here,' spat the driver, his mouth nearly void of teeth. His gloves were black with filth, his red neckerchief as well. 'I would have some of the fare now, if you please, miss.'

Startled, I felt for my purse. I did not recall such a thing happening when I travelled in a hackney cab with Lord or Lady Stavourley. Indeed, I never once saw coin exchanged at all. That was usually left to servants, but as I had no one to attend upon me, I was forced to partake in this ugly bit of commerce.

I swallowed. 'What is the fare?'

'I should think, miss, that necklace you have about you should pay well enough for the distance covered.'

I reached up and felt the modest gold and pearl cross at my throat. It was but a small thing, the only jewels I ever received from my father.

'The eardrops too, miss,' said my driver, 'for Arlington Street is a long ride from here.'

I was too cowed and inexperienced to do anything but hand them to the thieving swine. I was being robbed and did not even know it!

He climbed back aboard his box with my girlhood tokens in his grime-lined pocket and proceeded down Ludgate Hill, west. Although I was saddened by the loss of these objects, at that moment I would have given up any of my personal effects to arrive safely at Allenham's door. Nothing I owned was of any consequence beside the possession of his good favour and love.

We continued through a knot of carriages and carts, down the Strand, where at last the scenery grew familiar, and then through the Haymarket into St James's Square. The streets offered the comfortable spectacle of home: the drapers, the booksellers, the vintners, the large bowed shop fronts I had known and, indeed, that I had not seen since this summer past. All the while my heart raced at our anticipated reunion.

Although I had never before seen his lordship's London residence, I knew the address from his correspondence. We had hardly rounded the corner from St James's Street when I rose to my feet within the carriage and directed that robbing devil to stop. Gathering my skirts and cloak into one hand and my bundle under the other, I sprang from the cabin, not wishing to waste so much as another moment .

Allenham's broad townhouse, at 5 Arlington Street, stood before me. The lantern outside had only just been extinguished, and the faint, telling glimmer of occupation could be seen through the fanlight above the door. I could hardly breathe as I came up the steps and drew the brass knocker down.

I heard the calm approach of footsteps against the floor. My throat was tight, my hands clenched within Allenham's muff.

'I should like to pay a call on his lordship,' I stated with a quiver in my voice.

The butler, dressed in a green and grey livery, stood before me. His face was as impassive as stone.

'His lordship is not at home.'

'But I know him to be,' I stated with determination. 'I was informed by his housekeeper at Herberton that he is in London.'

The servant looked beyond me into the road.

'I am afraid his lordship is not at home.'

'Please inform him that Miss Lightfoot wishes to call upon him.' I was now shaking a good deal. 'It is a matter . . . of urgency.'

'I am afraid I cannot inform him, miss, for he is not here.'

'But when . . . when will he return?'

'I am not at liberty to reveal that.'

'I pray, sir,' I now began to beg, 'it is of great importance that I should see him. I shall wait until he returns, if you permit me . . . I . . .'

'I am under express orders to admit no one, miss.'

'Whose orders?' I demanded. 'Who ordered that?'

The butler declined to answer. The dramatic tenor of my voice was now beginning to draw the curiosity of the house's other servants. In the corridor behind him, I noticed that a freckle-faced maid had stopped to listen.

I felt as if I might choke. My tone became even more desperate.

'I beg of you, sir, I have travelled a great distance at tremendous expense. If he is not here . . . if you will be so kind as to inform me where he may be found . . . ?'

'This I cannot reveal, miss,' he reiterated. There was no sympathy in his expression. No care whatsoever.

'Is there no note for me here? No instructions addressed to Miss Lightfoot from his lordship?' I trembled.

'None, I am afraid.'

'Dear God!' I exclaimed as my words gave way to sobs. I held my hand to my face in distress. 'I beg of you, sir . . .' I wept. So stunned was I by this turn of events that those were the only words I could utter. I repeated them again and again, yet they and my agony failed to soften this wooden man's resolve.

'My apologies, miss,' said he at last, before he pressed the door shut against me.

I stared at the black door in disbelief. Surely, surely there had been some error? My beloved Allenham, my angel, my protector, the husband who had pledged himself to me, would never have turned me out. I could not grasp it. Or perhaps the situation was truly as the butler described it, and my lover was not at home and nowhere to be found.

At that moment, I turned my back on the door, and fairly fell down the steps. So dismayed and confounded was I that I believed I might collapse. I steadied myself against the railing as my stomach heaved forward, and I spilled what little contents were in it upon the snow-covered street. The violent motion came again and again, as if my soul were purging the last of its hope.

When I had finished, my cheeks felt as cold inside as they were without. My brow was beaded with sweat. I looked up and back at the house. I might have noticed before that the shutters were drawn against the windows, so that it appeared unoccupied. I did not know what to make of this, or of anything. I own that I could hardly form a thought. I had not figured on this setback, nor could I imagine beyond this calamity as to what I should do next, or whom I should call upon for assistance. 'Perhaps I should linger here, near the house, to see if he returns,' I reasoned, but already my feet were moving and carrying me elsewhere. I was in a fog. I stumbled, moving this way and that. I stepped out on to the thoroughfare of Piccadilly and looked with blind eyes at the carriages, chaises, horses, the coloured clothing, the mix of hats. My ears were deaf to the roll of noise, the brays of animals, the calls of vendors. Indeed I was nearly had by a man in a phaeton. His team reared and he shouted at me, but I heard none of his curses.

I walked as if in a dream, I do not know where, towards Berkeley Square at first, until I could see my father's house in the far corner. It too was shut up – and even if it were not, it would be to me, for I could never again repair there. I had fled. I had left my father's protection for that of a clandestine amour: my sister's fiancé, my sister whom the whole of Melmouth believed me to have murdered for love.

Ah yes, Lord Dennington, and here I hear your sniggers, for you think we have arrived at the scene where retribution is meted out. Here, at last, has come my Judgment Day. But, sir, you rejoice too soon. The play is not yet at its end. I would ask you to stay a bit longer, read a bit further. You will see.

I moved on, trembling, my mind in complete disarray. In a panic, I began to search faces, peering into windows as I passed, looking amid the moving carriages for those light-filled eyes, for Allenham's rich dark hair. I spied his ghost everywhere, and yet nowhere. For an instant there was his figure in the reflection of a print shop; and then again over the road, moving within a crowd of gentlemen down Charles Street. 'He is not there!' I told myself, coming to a halt. I was mad. 'This has turned me mad,' thought I, my eyes darting from place to place, my expression a picture of fear. What was I to do? My breath came in short, hard pants, my cheeks now streaked with tears. I swayed upon my feet, like a tree blown in a storm.

'Miss? Miss?' came a voice from beside me. Then a smartly gloved hand was laid upon my forearm. 'Are you well, miss?'

I looked over to see that the arm attached to the glove was dressed in a fashionable forest green redingote, with a dark grey cape above it. Smiling down at me were the full, ruddy features of a genteel young lady, not much older than I. Her mousy hair was frizzed beneath her wide black hat.

'Are you in need of assistance, dear?' asked she with concern.

I nodded and, as I did, began to sob.

'Oh blessed soul!' she exclaimed. 'You must come indoors, out of this chill. Come now, you shall sit by our fire. I live just there.' She gestured over the road to a dwelling on Mount Street, near to the workhouse. 'You are in need of refreshment, dear miss. Oh dear, dear miss . . .' she continued as she escorted me, 'I cannot imagine what trouble has befallen you.'

I could not have been more grateful for this lady's comfort and I clung to her arm as a child does to its nurse's hand.

She brought me to the door of her modest house, where a neatly attired maid greeted us and relieved me of my outer garments.

It seemed a long time since I had been a guest in someone's home, though I had never before ventured into such a humble place as this. To be sure, it was respectable and clean, the house of a tradesman and his family, I concluded. I was directed up the dark wooden stair to the first-floor drawing room, which was furnished discreetly with a sofa and chairs and a few well-made cabinets in an older style. The walls were hung with framed engravings, featuring frolicking cherubs and pictures of girls with baskets and embroidery, entitled such things as *Industry* and *Charity*. Beside the hearth stood a tall walnut clock, which ticked out a calm rhythm.

'I am Miss Bradley,' said the young lady, giving herself a proper introduction and inviting me to sit beside the fire. I rejoined and gave my name as 'Miss Lightfoot'.

'I am very much grateful for your kindness, madam,' I said with a sniffle.

Just then, the drawing-room door opened and another woman, also youthful but soberly attired, entered.

'Ah, sister, I was correct in thinking I heard you come up the stairs,' she remarked, giving me a curtsey.

'This is Miss Lightfoot,' said my hostess.

'And I am Mrs Anderson,' said the lady, nodding at me once more. 'How do ye do?'

'I am afraid Miss Lightfoot is unwell,' Miss Bradley spoke for me, 'for

I found her just at the corner, looking as if she might have a fit, and took her inside directly.'

'As you should have!' exclaimed her sister.

At that very moment, the housemaid clattered her way into the room, bearing a blue and white tea service and a kettle of water, which she placed upon the grate above the fire.

'Are you in need of some hartshorn to revive you, Miss Lightfoot?' asked Mrs Anderson.

'Oh no, thank you,' I claimed, 'for your kindness has already performed that task.' I then attempted a polite smile at my hostesses, but found that it soon gave way to a renewal of weeping.

'Oh sweet creature,' sighed Mrs Anderson, shaking her head and handing me a fresh linen handkerchief from her pocket, 'whatever troubles you?'

I looked up at her, at her pretty brown eyes and button nose. She could not have been more than one and twenty, though the dormeuse cap she wore made her look very much the married matron.

I did not know where to begin in revealing my trials. In all other occasions in my life until then, I had had no cause to tell anything but the truth, for I had never done anything of which I was ashamed. I had never brought disgrace upon myself, and yet, I knew, were I to speak of where I had been and why I had come to London, my kind hostesses, whose generosity I had accepted, in whose protection I resided at that moment, would be mortified. What could I say to explain myself? I struggled with the words, balling the embroidered handkerchief in my palm, until I was passed a dish of tea. I received it into my hand and in gazing into the brown liquid glimpsed my frightened reflection. 'Fib,' it said to me.

Well, what other choice had I, gentle reader? There sat I, in a humble woman's drawing room, and you wished me to assail my hostesses' ears with my moral depravity? With the story of my fall from grace? I would be turned out for certain!

'My fiancé . . .' I began uneasily upon my course of falsehoods, 'requested that I . . . elope . . . that I come to London' – I swallowed – '. . . so we might sail to France and there marry . . . against my father's wishes.'

(Well, this was not so great a lie, I told myself.)

'But I came to where he directed me, to his house on Arlington Street' – my chin had now begun to tremble once more – 'and he was not at home. His man said he did not know when he would return or . . . if he would return . . .' I trailed off, unable to speak further for the sobs.

'And you are alone,' Mrs Anderson finished for me, her head cocked sympathetically.

'Yes, madam,' I squeaked, 'quite alone.'

She and her sister exchanged sad glances.

'Have you thought to write him a letter?' enquired Miss Bradley. 'For perhaps there has been some mistake. Perhaps he has been detained somewhere and not informed his household of his movements.'

'Yes,' added Mrs Anderson cheerfully. 'Why, there may be any number of reasons for his not being at home.'

I sniffled and blotted my nose and eyes with the square of linen.

'I . . . had not thought to try a letter,' I said softly.

'Why, yes, you must, Miss Lightfoot,' said her younger sister, reaching for the bell to summon writing paper, 'for your fiancé may be anxiously awaiting your arrival and in fear for your safety.'

Paper and writing implements were brought to me, and Mrs Anderson and Miss Bradley very kindly offered to withdraw while I wrote my letter to Allenham. It took me some moments to think what I would say and my hand quivered over the page as I wrote it, blotting my otherwise neat script with ink. I scribbled that I had come to call but was mistakenly turned away at his door, that I was in London, and I begged him to forgive me for any wrong I might have committed. I told him that, at present, a message might reach me at the home of Mrs Anderson on Mount Street, where I would await his response. I sealed it and gave it to Mrs Anderson's maid to have delivered. Then, alone in the room, I slumped against a broad wing-backed chair and sighed.

After a short while, I was asked if might like to join my hostesses at their table for dinner. I accepted their invitation graciously and retired downstairs, from where the smell of soup and suet rose up through the house.

This room was as unassuming as their drawing room, though the walls had been painted in a fashionable light green and were decorated with the entire printed series of Mr Hogarth's *A Harlot's Progress*. Their table was modestly laid with plain linens and plate. My hostess bade me sit, and gestured to the chair beside her.

'You have dispatched your letter?' she asked with politeness.

I responded that I had.

'And now we await an answer from your fiancé,' smiled Miss Bradley.

'. . . which I am certain will soon arrive,' added her sister.

Of this I remained unconvinced, but simpered hopefully, nevertheless.

As the meal was served, Mrs Anderson began to tell me something of her life, that she had 'a certain sympathy' for my plight, for she herself had eloped with her husband, Captain Anderson; she hoped that my 'situation' might result in a union as happy as hers.

'Though,' she remarked with a slightly pensive air, 'the lot of a sea captain's wife is often a lonely one. My husband commands the *Amphitrite*, which sails between Southampton and Bombay. Sadly, he is absent for most the year. But I have my Anne for company,' said she, smiling at her sister. The fondness they displayed for one another was the close affection I had often dreamed of sharing with Lady Catherine.

'And we have a good many friends beside,' added Miss Bradley.

I am afraid I was a very poor guest that evening, for I sat anxiously awaiting a response from his lordship.

By the end of our dinner, it was quite dark and my hostesses and I repaired upstairs for tea once more. The clock ticked loudly between us.

'If I may, Miss Lightfoot,' began Mrs Anderson, 'should it happen that you do not hear from your betrothed this evening, you are at liberty to reside with us.'

'Yes,' remarked her sister, 'we had thought of going to the play tonight but have determined against it, as we would rather reside here with you, in case some word should arrive.'

That was very kind, I told them, and unnecessary.

'No, no, it was no trouble,' said the elder of the two ladies, 'for our friends have agreed to go without us, but will call afterwards for cards and refreshment.'

191

'You are most welcome to join us, Miss Lightfoot,' chirped Miss Bradley.

Not wishing to be discourteous, and yet with no desire for society while I laboured under such anxiety, I agreed with some hesitation.

'It will do you no good to fret, Miss Lightfoot,' said Mrs Anderson in a reassuring voice. 'The letter will arrive soon enough, perhaps even tomorrow, or the day after. Until it does, you may reside with us as long as you require.'

I thanked her once more with a deep, grateful bow of my head; but all I wished to do was give in to sorrowful wails.

The drawing-room clock had struck half past eleven when Mrs Anderson's guests were shown up the stairs. They were not as I had expected. In fact, they seemed far too rowdy a set to feel at home in such a polite setting.

There were among them two young gentlemen, and one, slightly older, who appeared more composed. All three were dressed very much in the style of shopkeepers or tradesmen, with polished shoes and tidy well-made waistcoats of English silk. The eldest of their party seemed less inclined to follow fashion, and sported a chestnut-coloured wig in the old bobbed style. They were honest, industrious folk, to be sure, but very much in drink and swaying about in a way I had not before encountered.

'Mrs Anderson,' one cried out, 'what a delight it is to call upon you.' He took his hostess's hand to his lips in a grand gesture. 'And Miss Bradley there, as beautiful as a spring peony.'

Then all eyes turned upon me.

'Gentlemen, may I introduce you to Miss Lightfoot, who is a guest at our home this evening.'

I curtseyed shyly, feeling rather cowed by their boldness.

Soon the maid entered with a tray of liqueur glasses and a decanter of ratafia was served round. It was the first time I had tasted this sweet substance and I sipped it cautiously. Cards, too, were brought out and Mrs Anderson, Miss Bradley and two of the gentleman sat down to a hand, which grew quite raucous. In jest, Mr Timson accused Mr Newland of cheating, grabbing his collar and spitting insults at his face.

This was extraordinary behaviour, thought I, unable to take my eyes from the game. What made it even more so was that my hostesses seemed not at all disturbed by it. Mrs Anderson merely placed her hand upon Mr Timson's sleeve. 'That will be enough, sir, or you will do offence to our guest.'

I sat upon the sofa, where the quieter gentleman of the group also sat, too awkward to make conversation. He looked at me with a long, deep gaze on several occasions. 'You are a true beauty, miss,' was all he could bring himself to say. I kept myself entirely contained, my hands folded upon my lap, my eyes upon the activities of my hostesses and their card game.

Until the arrival of Mrs Anderson's guests, there was nothing at all to give me any discomfort in being in that house. This had seemed to me a polite home, and my new friends most well mannered and charitable. But now something did not seem entirely correct. Why Mrs Anderson and Miss Bradley should tolerate such beastly behaviour or have a collection of such uncouth associates made little sense to me.

It was then that I noticed something which caused me to start: in the course of their game, Mr Newland had placed his hand upon Miss Bradley's lap. She permitted him to do so. I blushed in observing this, but then reasoned that perhaps he was her sweetheart; still, such an intimate gesture was quite a liberty. Next there came a kiss, and then another. My mouth was fairly laid open in shock at the brazenness of this display, but it grew worse still, as Mr Newland drew Miss Bradley upon his lap – while in company!

Mrs Anderson laughed at her sister's folly, while her partner at the table whooped a great huzzah, before himself leaning across to place a long, wanton kiss upon her lips! This shocked me more than anything I had heretofore witnessed, for Mrs Anderson was a married woman!

Swiftly, I rose to my feet. 'I am afraid I am unwell . . .' I announced, 'and will retire now.'

Just then, the quiet gentleman beside me reached out and took my hand. 'Do not go so soon, Miss Lightfoot, for you have not yet allowed me so much as a kiss.'

I regarded him with astonishment and then looked at Mrs Anderson, who I had assumed would race to my defence. But my hostess only smiled prettily.

It was then I understood.

I knew such places existed, and such women as well, but I had not thought they would be so perfectly disguised as this! Why, in dress and manner, Mrs Anderson and Miss Bradley seemed a picture of virtue, but they were not. These creatures were sirens, and they had swept me off my course and taken me upon their rock.

'Mrs Anderson,' I said, my voice quite sharp, 'I wish to be shown to my room at once.' My hostess did not oppose me. On her face I saw what seemed to be some hint of disappointment.

'Very well,' said she, ringing the bell.

I was taken one floor above, to a small room with a French day bed. All the way up the stairs, I wept silently as I followed the maid through the dark corridor. I could hear the group below burst into laughter at various intervals, and then fall silent. I did not wish to know what they did in the space of those quiet pauses.

Once within the sanctuary of the room, I did as I had become accustomed to, and dragged a chest of drawers across the door, to prevent a forced entry.

'Oh God . . .' I fell to my knees and howled. 'Allenham.'

Chapter 20

I slept fully dressed that night, ready for a flight, should I find myself under attack. Fortunately, there came none. I was aware only of the noises, the groans and cries that leaked through the walls from the adjoining bedroom. I pushed the bolster over my ears, not because it disturbed my rest, but because the sounds were like those I had once made, and it mortified me to hear the echoes of my own debauchery in the cries of a whore. I sobbed with shame.

On that night I felt more disgusted with myself than I thought possible, for until I gave myself to Allenham, all that had befallen me was on account of Fate. Now where I had landed was on account of my own choices and errors of judgement. I had stepped off the path of moral rectitude and found myself among harlots! This was what I had become in the eyes of the world. No more the obedient and good Miss Ingerton, these dissolutes saw me as one of their own. It must have been as plain as day to them. I resolved to leave the next morning, as soon as I was able, though where I would go, I knew not.

I cannot say when I drifted into sleep. I lay with my ears covered and my eyes staring into the darkness of the room. I could make out the shape of a dressing table and the shuttered window beyond it. A broad chair stood beside the dead embers in the hearth. I recall shutting my tired eyes and then opening them again. On this occasion, I could see more details of the room. On the wall nearest to the window hung a cluster of miniature portraits or silhouettes, while a gown lay draped over the chair. I did not recall seeing it there when I came to bed.

Certainly, it must have been composed of heavy silk, or wool, perhaps even brocade, for it held its shape remarkably well. Oddly, the more accustomed to the darkness my eyes grew, the larger the gown became. Soon it seemed to be sitting upright in the chair, as if it were being worn. It struck me then that this was no heap of lifeless fabric but a woman. There was a woman in my room! How she had managed to gain entry, I could not fathom, for the chest of drawers stood firm against the door. My heart pounded in my ears. Gracious heaven, I was too terrified to move, fearful that if this marauder knew I was awake, I would find myself at her mercy.

I shut my eyes tight, pretending to lie in the deepest grip of sleep. My heart pounded so loudly within my ears that I feared she would hear it. I lay perfectly still for several moments, my limbs rigid with dread. I expected her advance upon me, but it did not come. Instead she seemed content to linger a distance away, and began, rather curiously, to hum beneath her breath. I listened carefully. The hum grew louder, until whispered words floated upon it.

> 'There were two sisters who lived in a hall,
> Hey with the gay and the grandeur O
> And there came a lord to court them all
> At the bonnie bows o' London town.
>
> 'He courted the eldest with a penknife,
> And he vowed that he would take her life.
>
> 'He courted the youngest with a glove,
> And he said that he'd be her true love.'

The voice lifted again in volume; this time it sounded as if the singer had risen to her feet. By then, I knew who sang it, and the sweet, unmistakable tones of her voice. I knew, as well, the song she had chosen.

> '"O sister, O sister, shall we go and walk,
> And see our father's ships how they float?

'"O lean your foot upon the stone,
And wash your hand in that sea-foam."

'She leaned her foot upon the stone,
But her cruel sister had tumbled her down.'

She took one slow step and then another in her progress towards my bed.

'"O sister, sister, give me your hand,
And I'll make you lady of all my land."

'"O I'll not lend to you my hand,
But I'll be lady of your land."'

Her shuffling movement ceased and then I felt her beside me, the folds of her gown brushing against the bedding. By God, she sounded so much alive that I would have sworn an oath to it.

'"O sister, sister, give me your glove,
And I'll make you lady of my true love."'

'Why do you torment me, Cathy?' my mind begged her. But she did not respond. 'Do I not suffer enough?'

'"O I'll not lend to you my glove,
But I'll be lady of your true love . . ."'

She stopped.

'You will taste suffering, sister – and you will remember well who bestows it upon you!'

I awoke with a cry. No sooner had my eyes opened than the most unbearable dizziness came over me. Frantically, I reached for the chamber pot and retched violently. Believing I had recovered, I sat up to find myself sick for a second time. Only after I had caught my breath did I dare peer over the rim of the porcelain basin. I was alone in a daylight-filled room. Even the gown upon the chair was no longer there. I had dreamed it, just as I had at Orchard Cottage. Nevertheless, I remained greatly disturbed. Lady Catherine's voice still rang in my ears, as if she had stood in the flesh beside me. I was unwell, I told myself, rubbing my cold, wet brow. There were no ghosts. No, I had not seen a ghost. Perhaps I had consumed something at Mrs Anderson's table, or perhaps some poison had been slipped to me in a drink. I lay back down upon the bed, attempting to compose myself.

Hardly had I pushed the disturbing incident from my mind when there came a gentle rapping at the door. 'Miss Lightfoot,' whispered a soft voice. It was Miss Bradley. 'Are you taken ill?'

I did not wish to see my false friend, or anyone among her household.

'No,' said I, 'I am perfectly well.' And I might have convinced her of that, had my words not been interrupted by a sudden return of vomiting.

'Miss Lightfoot . . .' came the voice again. 'I do believe you are unwell. May I enter?'

I considered her request but did not answer.

'Please, Miss Lightfoot. I will not harm you. I wish merely to see if you require a surgeon.'

I wished to leave that house. I wished to quit it as soon as possible, and my intention was to unbar the door and tell Miss Bradley so. I would go as soon as the sickness passed.

'There you are,' said she, standing on the threshold, her face alight with health, her pink complexion offset by her deep blue gown. 'By Jove, you are as white as a sheet!'

Miss Bradley was as sweet-tempered as she had been when I first encountered her. She behaved as if nothing untoward had come to pass the night before. She was a whore. How was it possible for her to behave as a gentlewoman? (Oh reader, I had so much to learn!)

I was a good deal cautious of her as she sat beside me upon the bed. Had I felt stronger I might have gathered my belongings, sprung from her company and down the stairs, quick as a hare.

She looked directly at my face, her lips formed into a thin simper. 'How far gone are you?'

I did not comprehend her meaning.

'How many months are you along?'

'Months?' I asked.

Now she looked at me with disbelief.

'You are breeding, are you not?'

'Breeding?' said I, entirely confused. 'But . . .' It had never occurred to me. In all my fluster, in the shock of his lordship's disappearance, I had not even thought, and how could I? I had no prior experience of pregnancy. I did not know the signs. I did not have a mother to direct me. This was indeed the first moment at which the idea had so much as entered my head.

'Dear girl!' exclaimed Miss Bradley, quite taken aback at my innocence, which she most certainly mistook for dullness. 'Did you not know?'

'Is it possible?' I asked incredulously, placing my hand against my belly, thinking I might feel something, some swelling or quickening.

'It is possible if you lay with your fiancé.'

I cast my gaze downward. How might a whore know my secrets, unless I myself were like her?

I nodded.

'And when did you last bleed?'

I squirmed at this intrusive question, but began to cast my mind back to the last time when I had my monthly courses. Since I began them at fourteen, they had never come regularly, and after Lady Catherine's death they did not come at all for a spell. 'November,' I stated.

'Late or early?'

'Early.'

'Then you are near to two months gone, my dear.'

I did not know how to take this news. I was, quite frankly, a great deal shocked by it. But for the sickness, I felt no differently. I certainly did not look like a woman big with child.

'Will you have it?' asked Miss Bradley.

'Have it?'

'Oh come now, you silly thing, you need not play the innocent with me. You are among friends here,' she said with a laugh and a shake of her head. 'It is not too late to rid yourself of it. Blatchford's elixir works quite a trick. There is a bit of sickness, but it is not as bad as taking a mercury cure, and then it is out of you, as easy as that.'

I must admit, this was all entirely new to me and I could not fathom what to make of it. I had hardly taken in that I was with child and now Miss Bradley was advising me of a way to remove it from myself.

'But why, why should I want to do that?'

My confidante let out a great laugh, and then placed her hand upon my sleeve.

'Miss Lightfoot, I take it you have not been upon the town and that your story is genuine.' She cleared her throat. 'In which case you must forgive my affront to your sensibilities, but there are a few things you must understand.' She stopped, caught my eye and sighed. 'You are an innocent ... of a sort, poor lamb.' Her expression then became quite sober. 'Your fiancé, the father of your child ... I take it he has abandoned you?'

I wished not to weep, and shut my eyes fast. 'I do not know. I do not believe he could. He loves me.'

'All men will say they love you, dear, but most do not mean it.'

'No,' I corrected her. 'No, he meant what he said. He pledged it to me. He called me his wife. We lived as husband and wife. I shall not give up hope. I shall not. I have nothing else, Miss Bradley, but him ... and now' – I began to laugh and cry as I spoke – 'and now there will be a child ... and he swore an oath to me that he would love ...' I could speak no more.

'Then, Miss Lightfoot,' my counsellor began, 'if you are determined to keep this child, should it live and should you not miscarry, you will be in need of a livelihood until you are reunited with your beloved.'

I stopped at her words. They were practical and harsh.

'How do you propose to keep yourself off the street, or the child alive for its father to see it? You will need an income, madam.'

I had never before considered this, for I had lived always under the protection of someone.

'And what thoughts have you on how you might procure one, should you quit our house? Where have you to go?' Her voice had risen in pitch. 'Miss Lightfoot, I do not wish to cajole you but I have known many a girl like yourself end as a common harlot, deep in pox and pints of wine, plying her trade in the by-ways and taverns till she is as worn as an old broom. The babe, should it live to be born, will almost certainly die young or end as footpad or rogue. Why, I have only to look through this window on to the road to show you an example of such a hapless creature. They are all about us, or have you had no cause to notice them before?'

I stared at Miss Bradley, quite shaken by her sermon.

'If you wish it, you may have a home with us. Our life here is quite comfortable. My sister and I concur that you are exceptionally fair and would do well. We pay heed to no bawd, but trade off our own bottoms and my sister has the run of the house, owing to the good favours she had secured from the Captain, her protector . . . not her husband, as you may have gathered,' she explained with a wry smile. 'We are free to choose our own beaux from among the gentlemen who call on us, and take no one but a select few.'

I could not look at her as she posed her offer. I had withdrawn into my mind, which was twisted and tangled with thoughts and terrors. Indeed, my world had shifted shape so quickly that I had hardly come to accept one truth than another was thrust upon me, and another, in rapid succession. What on earth had my life come to? I was not six months earlier a modest young lady with no parentage; I then became the daughter of an earl and his mistress, before becoming a mistress myself. And now I sat upon a whore's bed with a child in my womb. I was numb. I ceased to hear Miss Bradley's words; there came nothing but a dull noise.

At that moment, instinct caused me to fold my hands over my belly, as if to cradle what lay inside. A strange thing happened as I did it; my heart became like a flower unfolding, blooming with a pride and happiness in the midst of this terrible winter. It was as if I could feel Allenham inside me. I shut my eyes against the tears that wished to come.

'Should you like to join us,' continued Miss Bradley, oblivious to the wanderings of my head, 'there is but one condition.' She hesitated. 'I shall tell you now that to keep a child in a house such as this is a folly. As might any wife, you are likely to find yourself breeding often, and were we to maintain all the children of our liaisons, we should have hardly enough bread for our table.' She laughed merrily. 'And ... gentlemen do not like the sound of squawking babes ... as it calls to mind too much of their homes.' She turned to me. 'You should rid yourself of this burden, Miss Lightfoot ... if you wish to be among us.'

'No,' I whispered. 'I shall not be among you, Miss Bradley.'

I admit it was a rather thoughtless thing to say to someone whose hand had been extended in charity. But, as I have made plain, I was, for my part, beyond politeness. I lived merely in hope that I should leave this coven of sirens on Mount Street and go again to Arlington Street and there find Allenham, it all having been a terrible error.

My counsellor shifted uncomfortably, having undoubtedly taken offence at my decision, and the manner in which I put it to her.

'That, madam, is of your choosing.' She sniffed. 'I must ask you then, for your own sake, and because neither I nor my sister are cruel by nature, if you do not have some family to go to? Some family who would not turn you out in your condition?'

I thought to say to her that I did not intend to repair to the house of 'some family', for my beloved was sure to be found and to forgive me for any wrongs when he knew I carried his child, but some molecule of common sense, most rare in the addled brain of a seventeen-year-old girl, prevented me. Perhaps I feared she would laugh at me, or perhaps somewhere within me lay a certain stubborn determination, that same instinct which in my greatest peril had carried me from Melmouth to Herberton.

I hung my head and, in exasperation, moved it from side to side. Suddenly, it seemed as if something had come loose within it. There rattled a thought I had not before considered: my mother.

You cannot blame me for not thinking of her before this time. My entire life prior to October had been spent believing I had none. While

202

knowing this gave me periods of sadness when I was a child, I eventually came to accept the tragedy of my circumstances and pined no more. When at last my father revealed himself and the name of my mother to me, I was in the deepest shock and distress. I hardly had any time to consider the implications of his words. In fact, in the intervening period she and her compromised circumstances in life had entered my preoccupied mind only fleetingly. It was not until that very moment that I had ever considered seeking her. After all, she was, as my hostesses might have put it, 'upon the town', one of those frail creatures to whom men fall prey. I attempted to shake from my head the understanding which then entered it: that gentlemen such as my father visited light girls such as these, such as Miss Bradley and her sister. I could not believe it. The world no longer made sense to me.

'I have a mother . . .' I began. 'I know nothing of her, but that she made her living as you do . . .'

Miss Bradley regarded me, her face now quite intrigued. At that moment, I looked up to see Mrs Anderson at the open door, and a servant bearing a small pot of tea.

'I believe her name is Mrs Kennedy, Mrs Kitty Kennedy.'

'Kitty Kennedy?' Mrs Anderson echoed. She exchanged looks with her sister.

'*The* Mrs Kennedy?' enquired Miss Bradley with a squint.

'I do not know,' I replied, rather surprised at their response. 'My father said only that she was quite well known in her time . . . a beauty.'

'Jerusalem!' exclaimed Miss Bradley. 'Here sits the daughter of Mrs Kennedy—'

'And we might never have known it!' finished her sister. 'Oh my dear, Mrs Kennedy was celebrated in her day, long before we arrived upon the town. It has been some many years since I have heard anything of her. I know only that she retired from the life and made good. Why, I believe she married. She last lived with Mr John St John on Park Street. You might go there and enquire after her.'

The dish of steaming tea, smelling redolent of hot ginger, was handed to me by the maid.

'For your morning sickness,' explained Miss Bradley. Indeed it now seemed that Mrs Anderson was aware of my condition, for she had been listening just beyond the door as her sister invited me to join their household.

I must own, I felt most confused at this. Part of me pulled one way and part another, for the understanding that I had a mother and that she might be so near warmed me at a time when I felt most exposed, but Allenham . . . it was he I wished to see, it was to him I wished to fly, and all else paled beside this urgent need.

'I do not think that will be necessary,' said I, straightening my back, 'for I intend to call at the house of my fiancé once more today and I am certain he will be home to receive me on this occasion.'

Mrs Anderson wore a doubtful expression, as did Miss Bradley.

'Miss Lightfoot,' said the elder of the two, 'do as you will, but pay heed to our advice. Call upon Mr St John on Park Street, and afterwards, if you fail to locate Mrs Kennedy, may I invite you to join our small but happy household of women at any time.'

I nodded to Mrs Anderson, for although that which she proposed offended my sensibilities greatly, it was not intended as an insult. I knew a gesture of kindness when it was laid before me.

And with that, I once more gathered my bundle and set out for Arlington Street.

Chapter 21

My erstwhile hostesses were correct, of course. That which I found at Arlington Street did not lift my spirits. Allenham's butler greeted me in much the same way as he had the time before, and we repeated, almost to the word, the scene that had transpired the previous day. His lordship was not at home and he knew not when he was to return. Oh reader, the tears spilled down my cheeks in rivers at my crushed attempt! So distressed was I that, much to my dishonour and shame, I resorted to begging.

'Pray, sir,' I cried, 'have pity upon me, for I have no means by which to return to my home at Herberton. I am abandoned here with no more than two pennies in my purse. I have no friends. I am certain that if his lordship knew, he should ensure my safe passage back to Orchard Cottage. Pray, sir . . .' I pleaded.

His lordship's servant's face remained as blank as ever, and how could I fault him? London is bursting with fraudsters. Even I had seen my father's butler at the house in Berkeley Square turn away many who offered more compelling stories than that which I brought to Allenham's doorstep.

'Miss, I care not to dally with beggars and should you return I shall be forced to call the magistrate,' he said grandly before fairly slamming the door upon me.

What mortification that caused me! How debased I had become, even in the eyes of servants. Oh, my situation was dire indeed, thought I, as I choked on my sobs. I was coming to believe Allenham's butler;

perhaps he did speak the truth in stating that my beloved had been called away. But why and for what purpose I could not begin to comprehend. Had there been some dreadful occurrence of which I knew nothing? Was there some trouble? Was this to do with Lady Catherine or Lord Stavourley? Whatever the reason, I simply could not believe that my devoted Allenham would leave me thus, with no word of his whereabouts or anticipated return, had these been ordinary circumstances.

My plans now dashed a second time, I recognized that I could not very well wander the streets. It was then that I decided I should do as Mrs Anderson and Miss Bradley suggested and rap upon the door of Mr St John. I had no other recourse.

As I stanched my tears upon my well-worn handkerchief and trod the steps back from St James's to Park Street, I was overcome by a sense that my life, which for a short time I believed to be my own, was in fact not. Indeed, there seemed to be some sort of mechanism at work, something that pushed me this way and that, but towards what end I could not even guess. I found this vastly troubling, and the insights I was gaining too large for my heart and mind to fathom. I had no sense of what to expect from a meeting with my mother. Apart from Lady Stavourley's cold ministrations, I had thin experience of the affection that is meant to exist between a woman and a child in her care. I wondered what my mother would think of me. I wondered if she would have any love in her heart for an infant she had sent away so many years before. Indeed, had the situation been different, I would have been overjoyed at the prospect of locating my true mother, though, in truth, if the situation had been different, it is unlikely I would have sought her out in the first place! As you well know, until recent events, I had not been in the habit of associating with women of pleasure.

When I arrived at Park Street, I enquired as to the address of Mr John St John and was directed to the door of a very handsome house, not quite so large as my father's in Berkeley Square, but of a substantial width and made of Portland stone. I do confess that after my humiliating encounter with Allenham's butler, I was quite hesitant to try the knocker for fear of the reception I might meet. When the door was opened, I asked in a timid voice if Mr John St John was at home to callers. His butler examined my appearance and, seeing that I wore fur and carried myself in a manner befitting a gentlewoman, did not hesitate to show me into the drawing room.

It took all my courage to remain composed. As I sat in the shadowy room, I anticipated that the door could fly open at any moment and there would stand the mysterious figure of the woman who had ushered me into this world. But this was not what happened. Instead, after a short while, the tall, angular figure of a gentleman stepped over the threshold and stopped quite suddenly, almost too startled to greet me. His eyes fixed to me like tacks, his mouth parted.

'Miss . . . Miss Lightfoot,' he stammered, 'how . . . how may I be of assistance to you? Please, please, do sit down,' he added as he felt uneasily for the chair behind him.

'Sir,' I began anxiously, 'if you will forgive my uninvited visit, I have been informed by some friends that I should meet with Mrs Kennedy at this address.' I swallowed.

St John's eyes remained upon me.

'I regret to say that your friends have been misinformed,' he stated. 'Mrs Byram, as she was known, has not lived here for some time. She died nearly ten years ago of the consumption.'

Something within my stomach hardened as he spoke those words. My hope of meeting my mother had died stillborn, hardly hours after its inception. It took me a moment to digest this news, and the un-expected sadness that accompanied it. I sat in silence, St John opposite me, like two mourners at a funeral.

'Her loss is felt greatly,' he said after a time, his attention creeping towards a portrait which hung above the mantel.

Although half cast in shadow, I knew whose face must lie beneath it. She sat against a billowing backdrop of red drapery, with her hair piled upon her head in the fashion of twenty years earlier. I studied the image. It was one of those dramatic pictures painted with a flourish by Mr Reynolds, but I could see very little of the subject's expression or features.

'What . . . what has brought you to look for her?' asked St John, observing me take in the portrait. His question held an almost rhetorical tone, as if he had already formulated the answer and was merely testing it.

I hesitated, my gaze now transfixed by the picture of my mother. 'I have been led to believe that I am . . . her daughter.'

I regarded him, and he me.

'Of that, I am most certain,' he stated. 'I knew it from the moment I first set eyes upon you. You are a picture of her in miniature.' A smile flashed across his mouth, as quick as lightning. His brow trembled. 'But tell me, who is your father? Lord Robert Spencer? That devil Byram? Carlisle? Or Stavourley?' I watched his hands tighten around the gilt-edged arms of his seat. 'Or me?'

'I am the daughter of Lord Stavourley,' I replied, an imperious hint of Lady Catherine's voice within my own. 'I . . . I am the one Mrs Byram gave up when she married.'

'Ah yes!' St John exclaimed with apparent relief, his taut face now softening. 'You are the girl Stavourley took with him to raise in his nursery. Mrs Byram pined for you on occasion . . . but it was to be a clean break, you see. It had to be so. Mr Byram would not have you in his house after he married her, for you would have reminded him too much of his wife's disreputable past. He wished to make an honest woman of her,' St John snorted.

So the story my father had told me had been the entire truth of the matter. I looked again at the portrait.

'Robert Byram was the sort of man who wished to make his own fortune in life. When he married your mother, one might have thought he had reformed himself of his adventuring. He had played a few good hands at the table and made some prudent investments, and he wished to settle with a wife and a house in Marylebone. That lasted six years. He was in the Fleet prison by the end of it and Mrs Byram was left without any means.' He looked at me, disquiet in his eye. 'She was ill; dropsical at first and then the coughing fits began and she grew wasted and thin. She applied to me for assistance and I took her in. I would not leave her to rot with Byram in the liberty of the Fleet. I nursed her until she died, in my own house.'

True love, when it fills the features of one under its power, is most apparent to the naked eye. It warbles in the voice; it causes a tremor in the face and a glow in the eyes. It became obvious to me that St John was a man possessed by it still, by love, and regret, for I heard between the lines of his story that he wished it had been within his power to have married my mother and saved her from the miseries visited upon her by Byram.

'And pray tell me,' St John continued, his voice now lively and intrigued, 'however did you arrive here? Does Lord Stavourley know you have come?'

I shook my head. As I did, I felt another lie form within my mouth. I knew I must spit it out.

'Please, sir,' I began, 'I fear I am in a great deal of trouble. Lady Stavourley . . . she has turned me out.'

St John's eyes widened, though with amusement or scandal, I could not say. His expression begged me to continue.

It is a difficult thing, to hold the gaze of the recipient of a falsehood, and so mine wandered all about the room as I spoke.

'For many years she believed me to be the daughter of Lord Stavourley's brother, who died at sea. Until just these few days gone, she knew me as her niece . . . but . . .' I paused, not knowing where my tale was to lead me. 'But . . . there was some scandal below stairs . . . some story was put about of my true parentage . . .' Much to my surprise, the tears that had begun to form came entirely of their own accord and soon I was overcome with weeping.

'And what of Stavourley, what of your father in all this? Surely he would not turn his daughter out of his home?'

I recognized that I was a terrible liar. I was saved only by my tears and my inability to speak further on the matter.

'Oh sir . . . I flew . . .' were the only words I could manage. It was not entirely untrue, was it?

My patient host could see that my face was now awash with agony. I pressed my rag of a handkerchief to my eyes and attempted to catch my breath.

'I am afraid, sir, it was a most imprudent decision . . .' I hiccuped '. . . for I have no means and no friends. What little I possessed, a pearl necklace and eardrops, I was robbed of, right off the mail.'

'And you came here, to London, because you wished to find your true mamma.' He spoke in a sort of low purring.

'Nmmmm,' I moaned in agreement, 'and now you tell me she is no more . . . and I . . . I . . .' I fell into sorrows once more.

To this day, I am sceptical as to whether St John believed all of my tale. When I think back upon it, to one more experienced in life, my fibs would have seemed as flaw-ridden and transparent as a sheet of glass.

'There, there, dear poppet,' he said, obviously quite unaccustomed to comforting young ladies in distress, 'what sort of brute would I be were I to turn a helpless, motherless creature such as yourself loose on to the streets? You are my dear Kitty's own flesh and blood and she would roll over in her blessed grave were I to inflict such a cruelty upon you.'

I do believe St John was truly in shock, but I sensed that his disbelief was more on account of his sudden good fortune, rather than at my appearance alone, for how often do comely young girls at the bloom of womanhood arrive upon the step of a *roué* in his forty-fourth year?

'Why, never in my life did I think I would live to see this day!' he exclaimed, his gratitude thinly veiled. 'My dear, dear girl, you must make your home with me, for as long as you see fit . . . I positively insist on it . . .' he commanded. 'You are my Kitty's daughter, and that association demands that I protect you as I did her. I shall be devoted to serving you, Miss Lightfoot. Your every need and whim shall become my business. You may depend upon it.'

After such a gallant speech, I might well have believed him, had I not spied a certain glint in his eye which reminded me too much of that other gentleman into whose care I naively went: Mr Fortune. I do not doubt that St John meant what he promised, but I also understood that in this contract there would be clauses of which I was not yet aware. It is always the way with gentlemen such as these. I did not like this proposition one bit, and vowed to myself to quit this place as soon as I had received word of Allenham and his whereabouts. Until that hour arrived, I would accept what hospitality my host offered me, as cautiously as Persephone partook of Pluto's company.

I could not have imagined the speed with which St John was

prepared to take me into his household, but lust is a powerful engine. He sent immediate orders to his staff that 'Mrs Byram's apartments be prepared'.

'You will sleep in your mother's very bed, my child,' he beamed. 'You will have your hair arranged at her dressing table . . . Mrs Hooper,' he called out to his housekeeper, who stood at the door, 'do see if there are not some of Mrs Byram's effects which may be of use to her daughter.'

Of course, St John's behaviour was most generous, and to be sure I was grateful for the shelter he offered, but as he escorted me through the rooms of his masculine home, replete with walls of books, paintings of unclothed nymphs and the scent of uncorked port, I fear my mind was elsewhere. I could think of nothing beyond the moment when I might request writing paper and ink and send word to Arlington Street of my change of address. As I sat at my host's table, enjoying his dinner, he explained that he had cancelled all his day's engagements to wait upon me. He addressed me in a tender, instructive voice, the sort that a father might use with a child of five This, I am afraid to say, did not put me at ease. If anything, I began to I nurture a sinking dread of what might come once I was put to bed. Indeed, as the day became night, so his look of benevolence melted away to reveal the more predatory stare of a snake whose yellow eyes have fixed on its prey.

'We must attire you, Miss Lightfoot,' he simpered as he examined me from behind the hand of cards he insisted we play. 'Some of your mother's gowns may do nicely . . . the material, that is, for Mrs Byram was a good deal fatter than you.' He nodded with approval. 'They are fine fabrics, too expensive to waste but no longer *à la mode*. We shall have a mantua-maker refit them,' he said, walking his eyes across my décolleté. 'I should like to see you hold them against the cream of your complexion, my dear. Shall we retire to your dressing room, and you may amuse me with the sight of them?'

A sudden chill passed through me. St John had hardly permitted me to stray from his sight. He was so incredulous, so surprised by the gift Heaven had dropped into his drawing room, that he feared I would slip from his hands just as unexpectedly as I had been placed into them. An entire day had passed and my host had never offered me a moment of respite, never an instant where I might close a door behind me and collect my thoughts. Oh, my fingers positively itched to hold paper and pen so I could send word to Allenham! My hopes that he might come to me had not entirely faded. I held my thoughts close to me, as near to my chest as I pressed my hand of cards. Should my host suspect I had come to London on account of a gentleman whom I was now seeking, he would show me the door to be sure! There, with St John preparing to devour me, I felt very much like a mouse, backed to a wall by a cat, and I waited in terror for him to swing his claws at me.

'Sir, I beg you will forgive me,' said I, rising to my feet, 'but I am most tired from the day's events, and would wish to retire to my rooms.'

St John inhaled and settled back into his chair.

'Perhaps tomorrow then?' He raised his eyebrow, and then took my hand to his lips, much in the way of Mrs Anderson's lascivious guests.

I looked away demurely and left him.

Up two pairs of stairs lay my mother's rooms and entering them was, to me, like lifting the lid of a box of wonders. Although Mrs Byram had been dead since 1781, her devoted lover had maintained her apartments as if they were the temple of a goddess. I do not know the details of the story, but it seemed to me that hardly a vase or a jar, a mirror, warming pan, comb or pin had been removed. My mother had ceased to live, as did everything around her at the moment she expired.

The lights had been lit in this dressing room, and they glowed within the wall sconces. There upon her dressing table, a candelabrum cast its arm of illumination against the mirror, and upon the mantel, a row of small white vases were stuffed with the red berries and evergreen of winter. I walked about this place on light toes, almost fearful of waking the dead. I stroked her silver brushes and peered into the gold and porcelain patch boxes, still holding the moleskin circles and crescents that she had worn upon her chin and breast. A hardened circle of carmine lay in a silver dish, beside a thin, frayed brush. I did not wish to open the various jars of crusted creams and powders.

The housekeeper had done her master's bidding and laid over a chair what seemed to be three of my mamma's open-fronted gowns with their matching petticoats and stomachers. One was large indeed, but there were two, which I gathered she had worn in the final months of her illness, that were half their size. I touched them – the pink ruffle along the sleeve and neck; the satin, whose colour I could not identify under the dim light – and then retracted my hand quite suddenly. This felt like too much of an intrusion. Here lay what remained of my mother. Her blood coursed through my veins, yet she was no better than a stranger to me. Her effects held no warm remembrances, but felt instead like the cold shroud of a dead woman.

It was my good fortune that Mrs Byram's dressing room also contained an escritoire, still full of writing implements, sealing wax and paper. Although the ink had dried within its pot, it was easily revived by the application of some water. My heart beat steadily as I stirred it and then sat down to write another desperate plea to my love. Like my last attempt, it was a short note, informing him that I resided at the home of Mr St John, 'a friend of my late mother', on Park Street, Grosvenor Place. Once again, I begged for his forgiveness and for word of his whereabouts. After sealing it, I rang for a housemaid to prepare me for bed.

As she untied me I mentioned to her that there was a note I wished her to deliver. I drew it from my pocket along with my purse, which now held nothing but two pennies.

'Would you have me deliver it tonight?' she enquired.

I paused. It was now growing late, and to send someone from St John's house at such an hour might raise suspicion. My heart drooped.

'No,' said I, 'tomorrow morning, as early as you are able.' I placed one of the pennies into her palm. 'There will be another upon your return, when you tell me that it has been delivered and inform me of whom and what you saw when you delivered it.'

I was most grave in my manner in order to convey the seriousness of this errand, and impressed upon her that it must be done in secret.

I went to my mother's bed that night and, crawling beneath the coverlet, I imagined I lay in the very spot where she had died. The feather mattress had been plumped and firmed into a flat dome, which raised me as if my back rested upon a tablet. With the bed curtains pulled around me, I felt as if I lay in her tomb. However, this did not disquiet me half as much as the sudden realization that St John saw me as the resurrection of her. He believed his inamorata had returned to him, as if by some divine miracle. No sooner had this occurred to me, than I leaped from the bed.

The bedchamber had two doors. The first of these, which connected it to the dressing room, had a key within it. I hastily twisted it in the lock, but when I approached the second door, I noticed that the key had been removed. Placing my eye to the keyhole, I saw the outline of St John's as yet unoccupied bed and gasped. All at once his design became clear. Remembering too well what had nearly become of me at the Bull, I found myself for the third occasion in my young life dragging a chest of drawers across the floor to bar the route of St John's plotted incursion. It was a good stroke of luck that I thought to do it. No sooner had I been swept into the mists of sleep, than I was roused by the sound of my intruder. Silently and carefully, he had twisted the door handle, only to hear it collide noisily against the wooden back of a tallboy.

I cowered under the bedding, listening with fear to the smack of the knob against the chest, once, twice, thrice, before my embarrassed host realized he had been thwarted .

As the house filled with stillness once more, I lay, wound within my dead mother's sheets, my heart pounding in my ears. Staring at the hangings above me, I wondered how many more nights I was destined to pass behind a barricade, and whether or not my beloved would arrive in time to save me from its certain fall.

Chapter 22

I awoke to the same noise to which I had fallen asleep: the un-mistakable sound of a person trying the handle of a door.

'Madam, madam . . .' whispered the voice from my dressing room, 'there is a letter for you.'

My eyes had scarcely opened before the meaning of these words entered my mind.

'Letter,' I said aloud, scrambling to my feet. As the maid had not yet been inside to draw back the shutters, the room was still sealed in darkness. I turned the key and opened the door.

'I was to leave it by the side of your bed, but I found the door locked,' she apologized, while passing it into my hand. Indeed, it bore the name 'Miss Lightfoot', written in Allenham's script. I felt as if I might choke; my hands shook.

'Who . . . who gave this to you?' I demanded.

'I went to the house on Arlington Street, just after seven o'clock, as you directed,' said she, 'and gave the letter to a footman, who examined it and, if you do not mind me saying, was so bold as to open it and read its contents . . .'

I looked at her with astonishment, for such a presumptuous act was most irregular, unless, of course, he had received specific orders to do so.

'Once his curiosity had been satisfied, he bid me to wait and then went away and returned with this note, addressed to you.'

'And that was all?' I asked frantically. 'You met with no other person, you saw no one but that footman?'

'No one but a housemaid, who appeared, if I may say, quite idle, with no tasks to perform. It appeared to me that the family above stairs had gone away, for all was most quiet.'

'You have done well,' I commended her, placing my last remaining coin into her hand and fairly pushing her out of the door.

In a frenzy, I threw open the shutters and tore into the letter.

Gentle reader, had you been there to see me . . . My eyes wished to consume every word upon that sheet all at once! Oh, I remember it well. How could I ever, in all the days of my life, forget its contents?

'My dearest love,' it began, and at the sight of that salutation, I pressed my hand to my throbbing breast, as if to contain my heart.

I do not know where or indeed if this letter will find you, but I pray to God it makes its way safely into your hands.

As you may have surmised, circumstances beyond my control have called me away from you - and away from my home. I fear I am not at liberty to reveal the details of what has come to pass or of my whereabouts, but suffice to say, the situation was entirely unforeseen and unwished for by me. In short, I now find myself in a position from which I cannot be extricated. I cannot say for how long I shall be absent from you, nor am I able to present you with a reason for this cruel parting other than to say my life is no longer mine to do with it what I will.

Please believe me, my most Beloved Angel, the suddenness of what transpired caught me entirely unprepared or else I should have left you with some instruction. The circumstances of our separation are the cause of infinite pain to me, worsened still by the terrible confession I must put to you, that I have no means by which to support you in my absence. All I possess has been spoken for, and Herberton is to be let out with immediate effect. May God forgive me, dear sweet Henrietta! May you find it in your heart to forgive me for this most intolerable situation, for I can hardly forgive myself!

I fear I no longer bear the right to make any requests of you, but I beg of you to permit me at least one. Please, my dearest creature, do as I shall, and forever look forward to the moment of our happy reunion. You must live for this and do whatever you ought in order to ensure the safe arrival of that day. My brave, courageous love, remember always my words to you: that you have a strong mind. Let your reason be your guide, as well as the wisdom of your heart. Think of Monsieur Rousseau. Forgive yourself for any measure you may take that permits you to live and thrive. I shall never reproach you for any deed committed which has kept you safe and alive. In your dark moments, remember G & H upon the hearth. Remember your passionate Werther. Remember always the true pledges of love I spoke to you. Believe me, my dearest, most cherished Henrietta, you are the owner of my heart and, as such, it shall always be with you.

Until that blessed day when I take you in my arms, I am and will for ever be your adoring,

Allenham

My tears had begun to flow long before I had read the final sentence. Gracious heavens! I thought I might fall dead at that very instant, for my beloved's letter had delivered to me what I believed to be my mortal blow. Never could I have imagined that such injury might be inflicted by a mere sheet of folded writing paper. It entered my soul with the sharp force of a stiletto and I dropped upon the floor as if I had breathed my last.

No, I did not collapse into a faint like the heroine of some romantic tale. Those who have known true anguish understand that shock and pain course through the human body like currents of electricity. There is nothing genteel to behold about suffering. It is not done upon a couch. The victim does not lie angelically in a swoon. Instead, the limbs convulse and curl in pulses of agony. The body writhes and sobs uncontrollably. The nose streams, the eyes swell, air can hardly be drawn into the lungs. The moans and wails are incapable of being stifled.

Shall we leave this scene of distress? It does me no good to dwell here.

Over the years, I have put many remembrances out of my head. Beyond the sentiments relayed to me in his letter and its immediate and painful effect, I can recall very little. All is a blank. I kept to that bed-chamber for most of the day and dismissed the gentle knocking of the maids who enquired after me. I was ill and wished to be left alone.

I must own that, for a short time, I prayed for death, much as I had before when I first learned we were to be separated. I called up to Fate, and begged he would take me as swiftly as he had Lady Catherine.

One of us three must die! 'It should have been me!' I cried.

What poxy, foolish thoughts these were, but nevertheless, I savoured them a good while before they floated away.

It was the incessant discomfort of my churning stomach that eventually roused me from my black musings. It reminded me that I would not be ending one life, but two. I placed my hand over my belly and wept some more at the thought of what lay inside it.

Within me swam a most miraculous creation: Allenham and my form blended as one, swirling together, eternally joined as a single being. Oh, the sweet calm this knowledge bestowed upon me, though how sad indeed that he should not know of it! I would keep this child, this product of its parents' purest love, as close to me as I could. A rush of determination passed through me, that I should bring Allenham's child into the world and try with all my might to ensure that it grew and thrived. I stroked the spot where I believed the homunculus might lie. I was, dear readers, a good deal frightened; I was frightened and delighted all at once, and so dreadfully lonely.

Through my stinging eyes, I took in his missive several times more, and bawled like an infant at each reading. I wept because I knew not what to do. Allenham instructed me to live for the day of our reunion and to take whatever measures necessary to ensure it, *but I did not know how!*

I walked about the room, the letter enfolded in my damp palm, and gazed for a time through the window. My mother's comfortable and well-furnished bedchamber lay at the side of the house and, as such, provided a north view down the length of Park Street. I looked out at the row of attic windows where linen-capped maids moved about, and down upon the straw-strewn road where a beggar sat with a bowl in the melting snow, where two filthy children chased a dog, where a girl selling thread walked beside a man on a stick leg peddling needles. As I observed the trafficking to and fro, I saw how many possessed bandaged hands and torn skirts, ragged coats and thin capes. I thought of Miss

Bradley's words, her warnings to me. How indeed would I earn a crust? I had no means of making my way in the world. Privilege had rendered my hands too soft for work, my sensibilities too weak. With an infant in my belly and without friends to recommend me, I could never expect to serve as a governess or a companion. Should St John choose to throw me out, it would be I who trod the street in rags and torn stockings. It would be I who slept, like those despairing souls I had spied upon my entrance to this city, beneath the bulks of shop fronts, or curled like cats in doorways. It would be I who picked through the wilted radish greens beneath the market stalls, the rotten offal in the shambles gutter. Into what squalid corner would my child be born?

Oh you, you of birth and breeding, you happy bourgeoisie, you bankers and money-lenders, you ship-owners and sugar-traders, you who have never before opened the door to find the wolf's hot eyes upon you, you gentlefolk who have known no other life than one of ease, you may not comprehend the decision I made next, nor could you ever. Some of you, my fine readers, may think of hardship as too little coal for your fire, or being forced to remake your own gown for yet another season. You could never understand what I did at that perilous moment, when two lives dangled precariously between comfort and want, between life and a beckoning death. From the position in which I stood, the choice, dear friends, though repugnant to my tender heart, seemed most obvious. *Survive*, my beloved had written to me, *survive!*

Dinner had been called when I emerged from my rooms. I had rung for the maid to dress me. My linens had been laundered and both my gowns, the striped silk *robe anglaise* as well as my pewter-coloured riding habit, had been brushed down and pressed. I chose to wear the former, made from the blue, buff and grey striped silk my beloved had presented to me. I stood at my mother's dressing table and had the maid put fresh curls into my hair and smooth it with pomade. My neck and ears were bare without jewels. I feared I appeared plain; my face was so haggard and swollen from my distress that I resorted to applying paint, something I had never before ventured. I had not the first idea as to how to prepare it, but took some of the little hardened brick of carmine and rubbed it into my cheeks and on to my lips. I suspect it succeeded only

219

in making me appear more sallow – and ill. Thus prepared and smelling sweetly of orange flower water, I proceeded below.

I was directed into the drawing room where St John, looking most relieved at my appearance, rose to his feet immediately.

'Dear little girl!' he exclaimed. 'I cannot tell you what a fright you gave me! When I heard you had taken ill, I was simply beside myself. But you look most recovered now . . .'

'I am indeed recovered,' I responded quietly.

St John examined me, and then, like an uncertain suitor, suddenly pulled his eyes away.

'Miss Lightfoot,' he began, 'I should not like to think that you feel in any way . . . awkward here, that there is anything which might cause you unease . . .'

I recognized that St John, in his discomfited way, was attempting to learn if his failed attempt to enter my bedchamber last night had been the reason for my distress.

'Why no,' said I demurely. 'Mr St John, I apologize if I appear in any way ungrateful for your hospitality, for I can assure you . . . I . . . owe you . . . much . . .'

What magic my words performed. It was quite miraculous to behold, for all at once the lines of St John's face relaxed. Light filled his eyes and his mouth broadened into a gracious smile.

'Well, my dear . . . well, no, it is I who is most grateful, most grateful for your company, madam.' He then turned to a side table upon which sat a large, flat case. 'You had mentioned to me the loss of your jewels upon your arrival in London and I wished to make amends for this,' he said, humbly presenting me with the box.

I looked up at him, his towering height, his sharp, pointed features and slightly weathered countenance, with uncertainty.

'Go on then, you must open it.'

Inside lay a pair of pearls nearly as large as the tip of my thumb, set as eardrops on mounts of gold and diamonds. Surrounding them sat a fat double collar of the same.

'They belonged to your mamma,' said St John with pride. 'She wears them in her portrait.'

I peeled my eyes from the exquisite jewels and gazed at the woman whose face I had never before clearly seen. She sat almost in profile, an eardrop resting against the edge of her cheek. Her fair head was tilted and her pearl-embellished neck turned as she leaned dreamily towards her right shoulder. Her red, heart-shaped lips were softly parted, her dark grey eyes cast into the distance. In her I saw the shade of myself, many years older and wiser, a veteran of the dissipated world. Her features were as round as mine, her mouth as full, her nose as small and straight. To see the reflection of one's own face in an object other than a mirror is an odd thing indeed. I was dumbstruck by this image of my own visage on another.

St John approached me, delicately lifted the collar from the case and fastened it around my neck, his fingers pressing into my exposed skin. Carefully, he pushed the eardrops into place, running his hand across my cheek as he did so.

'How beautiful,' he breathed. 'You are as radiant as she ever was.'

I knew what was expected of me. I knew that if I were to remain here, in this haven of peace and warmth, where I should be fed and clothed and protected, that St John would demand something in return. Nothing goes for nothing in this world. Between my taste of life at the Bull and my introduction to the manners of London, I had learned this lesson quite quickly. I dread to think what might have become of me had I been dim-witted. No, I would give St John what he desired, but I too would exact a price, and it would be one that my self-satisfied host did not even know he paid.

And so I went to my bed that night prepared for St John to renew his attempt to visit me. I left both doors unlocked and unbarred, but before I did, I also took a precautionary measure.

As St John believed me to have my virgin's honour, it was beholden upon me to play my part, and to play it well. Should I shrink from this task, all would be overturned. I cast around my mother's dressing table for some inspiration. At first I alighted upon the scissors, and intended that I should make a small cut along my inner thigh, near enough to my privy parts that St John should think he drew the maiden's blood from me, but stopped when my eyes fell on the hardened brick of carmine.

Was this not a pigment like any I had mixed on my artist's palette? And had artists from time in memoriam not replicated the precise sanguinary colour upon their canvases? I paused in thought for a moment, and then rang for a servant to bring me a glass of port wine.

With some skill, I mixed a paste of reds, which I then took on my finger and pushed deep inside me. When St John fired his attack, I figured all would come loose, and my honour would be preserved.

I shall tell you, reader, this entire charade, this duplicitous and immoral act did not please me, not for one moment. What worsened it still was the thought that this deception was intended to secure yet another, larger falsehood. As I returned to my bed and extinguished the light, I lay perfectly still. I gently pressed my thighs together, fearing that my maidenhead might fall away before my seducer claimed it. My heart thumped very loudly indeed as I listened for his inevitable approach.

There were many things I had considered before I had gone down to dinner that night. I had resolved that if St John was to have me, he should also have my child. He should believe it was his own. He should never know of its true father, no matter how I pined for Allenham, no matter how determined I remained in my heart that we should be reunited. And oh, dear friends, I can assure you, this scheme disgusted me with the horror that you now suffer on my part! I recoiled at what I was forced to become – forced, yes, forced, I say, for you tell me, you disdainful censors, what other choice had I? Before you hurl this book across the room and condemn me with all the accusing disgust of Lord Dennington and his friends, I beg you to consider that I did it not to gratify some malicious urge within my breast but to secure the life of an innocent unborn. Were it in her power, no mother would willingly see her child brought into a life of poverty and illness. I would be a dullard indeed to let St John exact his pleasure from me without seizing the moment to place a cuckoo's egg in his richly adorned nest. Should my plan come to fruition, my child would enjoy all the gifts and protection of St John's wealth until the return of its true and adoring father. If not this, then what, dear reproachful reader, would you have done? Sent your infant on to the streets? To the foundling hospital? Or if they would not have it, would you hand it over to some slatternly nurse, who would allow it to starve? Have pity, my friends, have pity.

Just as I had predicted, my intruder tried the handle of my door shortly after my candle had been snuffed. I shut my eyes tightly at the sound of his feet, for it was all I could do to contain my horror at what I knew must come to pass.

'Henrietta, dear . . .' he whispered, 'I fear I heard you cry out. Are you well?'

'Quite well, thank you,' I murmured against my pillow. My face was turned from him, and a good thing it was, for his excuse to gain access to my bedchamber was so uninventive as to be laughable.

My answer did not satisfy him, and how could it have? He came for one purpose alone. He lingered and then placed himself upon the edge of my bed.

'Darling girl . . .' he ventured, beginning to stroke my hand, 'perhaps it was the torments of my own mind I heard. Oh dear, lovely creature,' he breathed, 'you have captivated me entirely. I am now without hope for happiness! Pray, my love, you would not see one who adores you so ardently in such anguish?' said he, moving his hand to my face.

I jumped involuntarily.

'Sir,' I commanded him, 'leave me be or you will indeed hear me cry out!' These words, my friends, are a true record of my sentiments, for nothing repulsed me more than his touch. Yet I knew St John would not desist. I recognized that my protests would only fire him further and that he expected me to enact the terror of a reluctant virgin on her wedding night. I would not disappoint him, though it sickened my heart to play this charade.

I sat up in my bed and drew the coverlet around me, but St John, as I had anticipated, saw this as a signal to begin his assault. Taking hold of my neck he pushed his lips against mine with great force. I struggled to repel him, turning my head and squirming.

'I beg of you, do not deny me, my love, my angel, for I should die if you do! I shall kill myself if I cannot claim your heart! What agony you cause me!'

'Sir!' I cried, as if reading from the very pages of Samuel Richardson's novels. 'I beseech you! Please! My honour! Oh God, preserve me!'

I shrieked as he lowered himself on to me and forced apart my legs.

What cruel devils are men. Had I been truly in a state of innocence, St John would have brutalized me. There was no tenderness in his actions, only the basest, most fiendish lust. He pushed one finger into my womanhood and I screamed, for not only did it cause me true pain and disgust, but I feared he would discover my carmine trick! Fortunately, the darkness kept my secret. In the morning he would find his nightgown, hands and member stained to his satisfaction.

How loathsome it was to have him inside of me. The act of love is repugnant when forced. I pity you brides who have no desire for your husbands, for it is this battery that you will forever know, with no understanding of what you might have enjoyed. There is no reason why any woman should be made to submit to a man for whom she does not feel affection. I confess, while he took his pleasure, I sobbed as if my heart would break, the name Allenham unpronounced upon my lips. With his kisses and hands, St John drew from me the sorrowful remembrances of true love. Under his touch, they rose like a ghost from a lifeless corpse. I can assure you, readers, the tears I shed were entirely real.

I wept for myself, for my tragedy, for this wicked deed, until my wailing was matched by his groan of exaltation. Then I fell silent. I could not help it. The bargain had been sealed.

Chapter 23

I must confess I had been so dreading my intimate encounter with St John that I could scarcely think of anything beyond it. Foolishly, I had not considered what he might demand of me afterwards, or that he would require me to roll upon my back whenever he desired it.

The first fortnight was tiresome in the extreme, for he would not let me be. His appetite, once whetted, did not diminish. Though, to my relief, there were some difficulties that slowed his progress.

A certain friend of St John's, to whom I shall soon introduce you, explained to me that long before my protector fell in love with my mother he had been a great enthusiast of women. As a result, he came to know the pox and the clap as well as every Polly and Betsy in Covent Garden. Too many doses of the mercury cure had – how shall I put it? – dampened his ardour. Raising it sometimes proved to be a problem, and, once up, it did not remain so for long. To be frank, I could not have been more pleased to discover this weakness, for it made my existence with him more bearable. Although my youth and beauty revived his powers, the effect was very much like a shovel of coal upon a fire: it flared to life, but soon burned out.

In that period, he passed every night in my bed, and did not neglect an opportunity to draw me upon his lap, or fondle my thigh, or reach his hand into my bodice. I learned to withstand these pawings and maulings with detached coldness. The act itself I found disgusting on most occasions, until I taught myself some resolve. By this, I mean that I learned to manage by lying perfectly still with my head turned away from him. I left him to grasp and fondle with his heavy hands and prob-ing mouth, while I floated my thoughts elsewhere, towards Allenham. St John seemed not in the least bit bothered that I flopped as if dead, for I suspect he had never known a bedfellow of his to do otherwise!

Now, I address my readers of the fair sex when I remark that there are few tasks more difficult for the female spirit to endure than intimacy with a man for whom one feels no passion. In my life, I have been asked by many a married lady, who whispers privately into my ear as we sit upon a couch, how I have learned to contend with the carnal demands of men. By this I have taken them to mean, how do I permit them to have their pleasure without expressing outwardly the revulsion and horror I feel within? I often respond to such delicate enquiries that it requires great fortitude. 'But how, *how*?' rejoined my desperate confidantes.

'It is not simple,' say I, 'but once the strangeness of the man has worn off, it is replaced by a certain familiarity, which in itself gives comfort. Whether he is grossly fat or noisy or covered with wiry hair, one comes to see his humanity. One knows him, and in the breast there grows, if not love, then sympathy, or sometimes a kind of gentle pity.'

'I suppose,' my questioner will often sigh, resigned to the difficulty of her position.

The one exception I make to this rule is that of strong smell. I cannot abide it, but I have found that most gentlemen will oblige a woman when she requires them to wash or apply some *eau de cologne*. In the case of St John, it was a small mercy that he believed in the use of per-fumes and pomades and always kept himself clean.

Necessity had driven me to depend upon St John, but I remained determined to reap what I had sown. I resolved to endure my situation only for the time it took to bring Allenham's child safely into the world. Until that day, my most heartfelt wish was to hide away from public scrutiny, to cower in my mother's set of apartments, but I knew that my keeper (as I now might call him) would have none of that. Reader, do remember I was not devoid of modesty or sensibility and, at the time, I did not believe this sort of life to suit me. I was still a young girl and had not yet shaken off the yoke of duty and goodness that had been set so firmly upon my shoulders. Notwithstanding Allenham's encouragement, I had no true independence of mind and no understanding of the world. I was greatly ashamed at what I had become and did not wish those who might recognize me to bear witness to it. More than anything, I feared that my father would see me or that Allenham would hear of my association with another gentleman.

On the day that followed the loss of my carmine maidenhead, St John declared that he would like to introduce me to his acquaintances and eventually to make a great show of me in his box at the theatre or to parade me through the Pantheon. We would dance and drink punch and be in company. The very suggestion of this brought an undisguised grimace to my face.

'No,' I protested, 'I would not like it. I should prefer to stay at home,' I added.

'Come now, my dear,' said he, approaching me and taking my hands in his. 'Do not act the fair, injured Clarissa. What came to pass last night happens to most women in their turn, one way or another. No young lady has ever died of it.'

My chin began to tremble ever so slightly. 'But I am ruined,' I muttered, which in part I knew to be true, but which I also understood St John expected me to say.

'Nonsense,' said he. 'I am here and I love you most ardently. I shall not desert you, little one.' He placed a kiss upon my cold lips.

'But what will they say of me?' I persisted, expressing a genuine concern.

'They will say you are a true beauty, one of the most alluring creatures in all of London. And they will say, "That St John, he is a fortunate gentleman to find an angel as lovely as Miss Lightfoot."'

I looked down at my feet.

'Tomorrow morning,' he announced, 'a mantua-maker will come to call. I have asked her to outfit you in entirely new apparel. You have seen your mamma's gowns; they now belong to you, and you shall have more beside. A silk draper will also pay a call so you may choose a few more fashionable fabrics to your taste. You shall have pretty little shoes and hats and bonnets and jewels, and all the fripperies that ladies delight in. Now then, does that cause you to smile? May I see your smile?'

He tipped my chin up and I squeezed a grin along my face.

I confess, dear reader, at the time, I was not prepared for how much I would enjoy these promised visits. My shame and awkwardness vanished almost as soon as I glimpsed the silk draper, who dazzled me with a rainbow of fabrics in every colour and pattern imaginable. So overwhelmed was I that I suggested he choose on my behalf, and so he selected a lavender lustring and tarnished brass tissue, which he assured me was *de goût* for this season. These materials were ordered to be sent to the mantua-maker, who arrived just as he was departing. Madame addressed me almost entirely in her native French tongue as she spent the better part of the morning pinning and tacking and measuring. Her two assistants helped her to straighten and pinch the florals, chintzes, silks, taffetas and Indiennes that had been my mother's wardrobe. She brought with her engravings of the latest styles and suggested that we attach collars here, and make a compress bodice there, that a belt be added to this and a fringe to that. St John lounged as a silent spectator in the corner of my dressing room, his face set in an expression of lustful approval, as skirts, petticoats, open gowns, stomachers and jackets were put on to and removed from my person.

Although I had witnessed Lady Stavourley and Lady Catherine beneath the hands of a mantua-maker, until then I had never before been the subject of such a fuss. I do admit, a visit from a fashionable manufacturer of ladies' attire never fails to tickle the vanity of most women, no matter how modest.

As I was later to learn, St John had it in him to be as much of a miser as a spendthrift, but his generosity on this occasion could not be faulted. However, his great show of extravagance was not entirely for my sole benefit. For those among you who are not familiar with the rules of the *demi-monde*, it is well known that a gentleman is judged not by how well he equips his wife, but by how handsomely he adorns his mistress. My keeper, unencumbered with a spouse and beginning to betray his age, wished to resurrect his standing by parading me about town. Of course, I was completely innocent of this at the time, and was willing to believe that St John's gifts were, as he claimed, 'a proof of his undying love'. What I had failed to recognize, in the grip of my naivety, was that St John was preparing me for my grand début. It was as if he had tripped upon an enormous unfinished diamond at his doorstep, and he wished to have it polished and set in gold, to wear for the edification of all who knew him.

The mantua-maker's visit was followed by a week of excursions to haberdashers, linen drapers, shoe-makers, milliners, glove-makers and perfumers, many of whom, I blush to say, recognized me from my previous life of virtue. They caught my eye, but looked away, not wishing to cause me embarrassment.

St John's carriage conveyed us through the streets of Mayfair and Piccadilly, from Bond Street to the rows of bow-windowed shops that lined the Oxford Road. He took a pinch of snuff upon his hand and commented to me with a sort of haughty indifference that it was his greatest delight to lavish fine gifts and apparel upon me. 'For,' he said, leaning against me and reaching beneath the hem of my skirts, 'I would not have you think me ungrateful for allowing me to take your virgin prize.'

I did so dislike it when he said such things. Worse still was his frequent need to finger that spot between my thighs which he believed his drooping manhood responsible for opening. I bit my lip and forced a demure smile, wondering how many more weeks might pass before my belly began to grow, and when it would be prudent to tell him of his approaching fatherhood.

It is true, my lot might have been far worse than this. When I chose my course of action I had reasoned that it was less abhorrent to tie myself to one man, and exist comfortably within his protection, than it would be to live as Miss Bradley and her sister, who were forced to entertain a range of gentlemen. And let us not forget that, when compared with the ranks of Cyprians who haunt the capital's streets and taverns, even my friends on Mount Street might be considered among the more fortunate of their profession. I can assure the most priggish among you that no woman enters into this life for the love of what she does, nor because she is lewd by nature. Circumstance alone is responsible.

As the evening of my 'presentation' approached, I grew increasingly apprehensive. St John, on the other hand, spoke of it incessantly. I soon learned that he had planned an entire occasion: there was to be a dinner and then a visit to his box at Drury Lane to see Mrs Jordan perform in *As You Like It*. This was to be followed by supper and music.

'You will be celebrated and admired by all, Hetty dear.'

'But I do not wish to be celebrated . . .' I protested.

'They will all adore you: Lord Barrymore, Sir John and Lady Lade . . .'

At the mention of these names, people of title and breeding, I bucked like a startled horse.

'Lady Lade? Lord Barrymore!' I cried in distress. 'But . . . but . . . I am not fit to make their acquaintance! Dear St John!' I pleaded. 'Lady Lade will not approve of me one bit! She will know I have been ruined! Oh, what shame this will cause me! What offence I shall give her . . . and any other ladies you invite.'

St John laughed heartily at my protestations. 'Little Hetty,' said he upon catching his breath, 'your innocence on this matter is precisely why her ladyship will love you.' He then put a gentle kiss upon my forehead, but my protector's assurances provided me with little comfort. I simply could not fathom what game St John played, for even I, as simple and innocent as I was, understood that no person of quality would tarnish their own reputation by publicly associating with a girl of my compromised position.

To be frank with you, my devoted readers, it would have been difficult to find a creature more confused than I. At this time, my mind was a turmoil of fears and longings. In the midst of it, St John persisted in carving from my girlish appearance his image of a perfect *haut ton demi-mondaine*. I was his Galatea and he was my Pygmalion.

Never in my life had I been the recipient of so many gifts, as daily arrived boxes and packages containing my new apparel. They were laid out in my dressing room like jewels before the Queen of Sheba. In spite of my depressed spirits, I was entirely dazzled by these glorious, shimmering gowns, trimmed with fringes and laces, reworked with modish furbelowed petticoats and shoes of matching silk and dyed leathers, bonnets and turbans, velvet ribbons, a large high-crowned hat, feathers, silk neckerchiefs and embroidered tuckers, sashes, satin girdles, brooches, shoe buckles, paper flowers and birds, a new pair of stays, silk stockings and linens, gloves in a variety of colours, in quantities to make the heart race! This, my friends, is what a young woman receives when she trades her virtue for experience. And you wonder why, every day, so many of our young girls in their simple dresses and thread stockings are tempted into vice?

When the fated day at last arrived, I was greeted shortly after twelve o'clock by an odd clownish sort of man and his rotund wife, whom St John introduced to me as my dressers for the evening. They, he explained, had dressed all the ladies of the *ton*, from the Duchess of Devonshire to Mrs Fitzherbert, and now were instructed to work upon me.

Within moments, the two were riffling through my gowns and accoutrements, chattering and arguing like a pair of squirrels. At last they chose for me a green and gold spotted open-front mantua with tassels and a matching forest-coloured sash. With it I was to sport a white satin petticoat trimmed with embroidered silk crape. My shoes, which were to peer out from beneath my finery, were of emerald satin.

After they had pushed and pulled me into my attire, I was seen to by a *friseur* who had come to perform some miracle of fashion upon my golden tresses, whereby he curled them loosely at the sides before bandaging my head in a mass of white silk, into which he inserted two vast green plumes.

Throughout this process of transformation, St John came frequently into my dressing room, examining and nodding, questioning the dresser or *friseur* in French, and, once convinced his money had been well spent, he would withdraw with a satisfied smirk.

As for me, coy, uncertain Henrietta, I lurked somewhere beneath the feathers and silk and the wash of rouge upon my face. I looked, as one might have said in my day, a picture of *le goût moderne*, but I did not feel at ease, for none of this frippery seemed to enhance my natural qualities. In truth, I could not take in what I beheld in the mirror, for although I recognized something of the young lady who stared back at me, I no longer knew her. I more resembled the portrait of my mother than myself. What would Allenham have thought of me, I wondered, or my poor dear father? While I was certain my beloved would have forgiven me, Lord Stavourley would have despaired at this sight; the shock of what I had become would have been too much for him to bear.

Since St John had taken me under his roof, thoughts of my father were never far from my mind. He joined Allenham as a constant presence in my heart. I could not be certain that Lord and Lady Stavourley were still at Melmouth, sunk deep in grief and hiding from scandal. What if they had returned to town? On occasions when my keeper's carriage passed the corner of Berkeley Square, I concealed my face. Whenever I stepped out into the street, I took care to see who passed. In those weeks, I came to fear the sight of my father almost as much as I dreaded dreaming of Lady Catherine.

After the *friseur* had departed, St John returned to my dressing room in order to prepare me for the arrival of his guests. It was then that the peculiarity of this entire situation struck me. This strange ritual was to be my début; a sort of backward coming out, a mockery of that which Lady Catherine had enjoyed.

My keeper, being a man quite fond of all things theatrical, wished me to make an entrance. I was to appear at half past three, once the sound of laughter could be heard within the drawing room. I nodded and swallowed. St. John could sense my anxiety.

'I . . . I am greatly uneasy, sir . . .' I began.

'Hetty, you have nothing to fear, my dear, dear girl.'

I twisted my fan in my hands.

'. . . I fear . . . I should be seen!' I whispered emphatically.

St John let out a cough of laughter.

'Who do you fear shall see you, my dear, whose attention you do not wish to court?'

'Everyone . . .' I stammered, before at last proclaiming my true fear: 'My father!'

My keeper's face was still for a moment. I suspect he had not considered this.

'I do not believe Lord Stavourley to be in town,' said he coolly. He then studied me from the corner of his eye. It was the first time St John had thrown me such a look, one of quiet suspicion. 'You have nothing to fear,' he repeated, and then, saying no more, took his leave of me and disappeared down the stairs.

Chapter 24

Oh, but I had all to fear! Reader, I did not know whom St John counted among his friends, or if they were likely to recognize me or deliver news of my life to Lord Allenham or to my father. How I fretted! My stomach had tightened into knots and I shook so violently that I had to lean upon the balustrade of the stair in order to steady myself.

The clock on the landing had struck half past the hour when I made my descent to the first floor. I could no longer bear to think what might await me on the opposite side of the door. It required a good deal of bravery to grasp the handle, and I did so with a cold, wet palm.

There, variously arranged upon the sofa and draped over the chairs, lounged two ladies, dressed as brilliantly as parrots, a gentleman in a suit of puce silk, another younger gentleman propped against the mantel swinging a horsewhip, and a third, older man with a wicked, drawn face. To be sure, they seemed the most reprobate crowd upon which I had ever laid eyes.

'And this, my good friends,' pronounced St John, whose lively conversation my arrival had interrupted, 'is the young lady about whom I have told you, my ward, Miss Lightfoot.'

I curtseyed gracefully to all the company, but soon realized that my formal gesture was lost upon a group already giddy from champagne and an afternoon of earlier amusements.

'Ward indeed,' hissed the aged snake upon the chair, taking me in with his bulbous, sagging eyes. He wore a rust-coloured coat, into which a nosegay of rosemary and white berries had been thoughtfully arranged. 'Such a manoeuvre, Jack!' he exclaimed. 'And all to exact your revenge on Stavourley after so many years.'

St John appeared quite taken aback at his guest's words.

'Ah, Selwyn, but how the years have dulled your sharp wit. It was not Stavourley with whom I had a bone, but that dog Byram.'

Mr Selwyn, George Selwyn, of late memory, recalled so fondly for his love of politics and public hangings, ignored his host's comment.

'Pray, Miss Lightfoot' – he turned to me – 'has Mr St John told you of the time your mamma vomited into his hat while we sat in his box at Drury Lane? She had taken a good deal of wine that evening.'

The entire room erupted into laughter.

'This is the stable from which you came, my little pony. The finest Irish hack in town, was your mother. Ridden by all in her day.'

'All but you, Selwyn,' declared the gentleman in puce, who I took to be Sir John Lade.

'Pshaw,' replied Selwyn, waving his hand. 'I would not have her.'

'You would have nothing, sir, above ten years old, which had not a snotty nose and lice,' St John volleyed.

'So fear not, Jack, I shall not be eloping with your Miss Lightfoot, for she appears older than that – though not by much.'

I must say, my ears had never been so affronted in all my life and I stood positively rigid with scandal as I listened to this exchange.

'Oh la, Miss Lightfoot!' exclaimed Lady Lade in the shrillest of London accents. 'What insult you have done her! Just look at her! How she blushes! You gentlemen should mind your damned tongues or you will frighten the poor creature to death.'

Gracious heaven, I knew not what to make of this scene. All at once I understood why St John had laughed at my misguided sense of shame, for, upon first acquaintance, there was not one among this licentious troop who had a scrap of politeness about them. How could it be that those with rank and title, gentlemen and ladies, conducted themselves with no manners at all?.

It continued much the same throughout the evening. Our dinner was served amid bawdy quips and banter, and I found myself assailed from every angle. To the left of me sat the old roué Selwyn, who sparred incessantly with his host. To my right, Lord Barrymore attempted to lift the hem of Mrs Mahon's skirts with his horsewhip. I watched her as she sat opposite me, wriggling and smiling with irritation. When he tired of this, he turned to me.

'Do you have a strong appetite, Miss Lightfoot?'

I had been taking dainty bites of a pigeon pastry at the time.

'Why, I do not believe my appetite stronger than that of most ladies,' came my innocent reply. The company began to titter.

'And do you find most ladies to have large appetites, madam?'

I thought seriously upon Lord Barrymore's question. The entire table seemed to hang upon my answer.

'No, my lord, I do not believe we do. As we are smaller creatures than gentlemen, we are more readily filled.'

At that, the company burst into hysterics, with Sir John Lade nearly falling upon the floor. I looked about me and smiled, though I did not comprehend what the others found so amusing.

'But, madam,' continued Barrymore, once he had contained himself, 'do you enjoy the sensation of being filled?' The laughter continued. 'Do you find St John . . . generous?' His lordship was attempting to maintain a sober face while all about him fairly wept at his jests.

I swallowed uneasily, now thinking something not quite right.

'Very much so. He is very good to me,' I said, glancing over at my contented keeper.

Defeated, Barrymore raised his glass to St John and proposed a toast. As he did, he gazed into my eyes and then down at my décolletage with a longing, wolf-like hunger.

'To John St John, who can fill a young lady . . . generously.'

It was several moments yet before Barrymore's double meaning dawned upon me. I was left speechless. Indeed, this entire circus had me lost for words. I stared and stared, until my eyes were as round as phaeton wheels.

Decanters of wine were emptied, beef, ragoûts, pies, puddings and sweetmeats were consumed in profusion, but in no way had this been an ordinary dinner. Never was there a suggestion that the ladies should retire – and why should they? There was no need to preserve the delicacy of the fair sex. Instead the merriment continued. St John called loudly for port, and then commanded that his 'cabinet of curiosities' be brought forth.

'Ah, generous St John . . .' purred Lord Barrymore. 'Now we shall see how you please Miss Lightfoot!'

I could not make much sense of this comment, or the humour it elicited from Mrs Mahon and Lady Lade, until St John's footmen appeared in the dining room carrying a box. Unlocking it, they laid its contents out upon a sideboard.

As we had only the candles upon the table and the wall sconces to light the room, I had some difficulty at first in detecting the nature of these objects, but Sir John Lade soon dispelled my confusion when, amid shrieks of laughter, he grabbed a long curved item and held it to the front of his breeches.

They were, as St John explained, treasures from ancient Rome, 'The venerable Priapus', he declared, protector of the home. St John possessed three of these within his collection, one of stone, and two of bronze, both of which were decorated with wings and bells. He jangled one above his glass of wine and proposed 'a toast to Dionysus and all his lively nymphs and maenads'.

At that moment, I believed I had seen enough. As St John's guests laughed and jeered, I began to wilt, turning my eyes to the hands I had folded neatly in my lap.

'They are his pets,' Selwyn, who sat beside me, said. 'Because his own fails to stand up, he collects those which will never disappoint him.'

A shameful smile twitched across my mouth.

He studied me closely. There lay a hint of sympathy in his gaze.

'You must learn his weaknesses, *petit chaton*, daughter of Kitty,' he advised me under his breath. 'Aside from your mother, there is one other thing which has been known to possess him and that is the gaming table. He is a slave to it.' Selwyn looked directly into my eyes; his teeth were as yellow as those of a rat. 'Should you ever wish to gain something from him that he will not concede, you must do so through the method of play.'

I sighed. 'I am afraid that I am not very adept at cards.'

'No, no, my simple child, not *cards*. You would not leave important matters to be decided by chance. No, I speak of *play*. The black art of the card table,' he said, pronouncing each word clearly.

I raised my brow in horror.

'Do not look so shocked, *chaton*. Your prudish innocence is growing tiresome. I shall demonstrate to you how it is done, and you will thank me for it. Mark my words.' He then examined my features and gave a satisfied nod. 'I doubt you are the ingénue you would have us believe.'

And so, following our dinner, when we repaired once more to the drawing room, the rather frail and stooped Selwyn called me to his side.

'Piquet, *chaton*. That is his game. Do not concern yourself with faro, for Jack is not so tempted by it, and it is too difficult to contrive a win if one is not the banker.' The old gentleman spoke to me from the side of his mouth, in the practised way of the conspirator.

'As there are but two players, it is quite simple to convey signals to your fellow sharper and thereby communicate what cards the opponent holds.'

Selwyn then spelled out for me a certain system of looks and expressions, each of which denoted a court card. 'Look directly ahead for a king, to your feet for a queen, to the right for a knave, to the left for an ace. And then to convey the suit, part your lips for hearts and purse them for diamonds. Place your lower lip over your top for spades, and your top over your lower for clubs. Now, madam, let us see how great a cheat you are. Jack!' he announced, above the intoxicated laughter. 'I should like a game of piquet.'

St John's ears pricked up like those of a hunting dog. He drew himself off the sofa with some difficulty. 'Piquet!' he echoed, directing a footman to bring the cards.

I was not certain if I could recall all the details of Mr Selwyn's method, or if I approved of it, especially as wagers were to be laid on the outcome.

'Stand behind Jack,' whispered Selwyn, as we approached the card table.

I took my place at the rear of my keeper's chair. In spite of being very much in drink, the prospect of the game positively animated St John. He rubbed and clapped his hands together in excited anticipation.

'Twenty guineas that Selwyn will have the game,' announced Barrymore, as he threw me a wanton look.

'And twenty again that it will go to St John,' responded Sir John Lade.

'That is an immoderate amount, gentlemen,' cautioned my keeper, turning to me and kissing my hand for good luck.

I wished he had not.

I did as Selwyn instructed me, and upon seeing that St John held a queen of spades and a king and knave of diamonds, I made the appropriate signals. The old man played his hand accordingly, and with each new card my protector drew, I informed my fellow cheat.

When at last the sixth hand in the *partie* was drawn, St John rubbed his brow.

'By God, Selwyn, fortune smiles upon you!' he exclaimed.

How wicked I was. I tried with all my might to mask the shameful smile inching over my mouth, and, in doing so, I made a fatal error. Not realizing what I did, I accidentally sent a signal to my conspirator, which caused him to lose the final round. Ultimately, this was a good thing, Selwyn informed me afterwards. 'One must always conceal the mechanism of cheating by losing a game every now and again.'

To tell the truth, I was not proud of what I had done. I could not imagine what my father would make of me, or my beloved Allenham.

'Do not wear such a grave face, *chaton*,' Selwyn scolded me, as I resumed my seat in the drawing room. 'It is doubtful that any of those present will pay their gaming debts, and your artfulness has not caused anyone's ruin.'

'But it is dishonest.'

'Bah!' spat Selwyn. 'Enough of your schoolroom morality. If you are to make anything of yourself, you must know how to survive among these rogues and whores.' He then leaned in very close to my face. His cheeks puffed and sagged like a pair of bellows as he spoke. 'You do not think Lady Lade arrived at her position through shows of piety and innocence? She was far worse off than you when Sir John found her. He plucked her from a brothel. *Think*, girl,' said he in a low, raspy voice.

'You have so much the look of an angel, you are the perfect golden-haired child. No one will ever suspect you of anything, *ma petite*. That is your greatest gift. Be clever with it.' He tapped his finger to his forehead.

I considered his words as we rode to the theatre in St John's coach, which stank of wine and sweat. Barrymore, whose eyes had been fastened to me since our exchange over dinner, had pushed his way into my keeper's carriage, while the others rode with Sir John Lade. It was not yet seven o'clock and the feather atop my head had begun to droop, along with my tolerance for the company. Lord Barrymore was slumped upon the seat opposite us, his face flushed red. With every bump of the road, his head joggled this way and that. He watched me keenly, like a cat before a bird's cage.

'St John, you are a fortunate devil,' he sighed. 'How a fresh little piece like Miss Lightfoot should find her way into your bed is a miracle indeed!'

My keeper proudly took my hand and offered Barrymore a haughty smile. 'You forget, my lord, how much experience separates a man of forty-three from a boy not yet twenty-one.'

The young Earl, too drunk to offer a witty response, shifted in his seat and growled with jealousy. St John, clearly enjoying his guest's envious looks, sought to taunt him further. Placing his hand beneath my chin, he roughly pulled me to him and smothered me under a heavy kiss.

My stars! Between Barrymore's offensive manners and St John's arrogance, I knew not who was the more unbearable of the two. To say I had never before been subjected to anything like this, that I was scandalized to my very core, would be the mildest of understatements. Selwyn was correct. Were I to have any control over my life, I would have to take some matters into my own hands.

We arrived quite late to the theatre, as was the custom for fashionable society. The large crowds who regularly gathered to see the great Mrs Jordan perform had long since jostled their way into the pit, leaving the theatre entrance clear for the arrival of the *haut ton*.

As we stepped from St John's coach, he carefully guided me away from Barrymore and beckoned Mrs Mahon to my side. Here, dear reader, I would be most negligent if I did not pause to describe the tiny, doll-like woman who took hold of my opposite arm.

Mrs Gertrude Mahon was, to be sure, an extraordinary creature. I do not doubt there will be some among you who remember her fondly. While I stood at scarcely five feet high, Mrs Mahon was smaller still, by at least an inch or two. Although no longer in the bloom of her youth, she moved with the sprightliness of a girl. From a distance, one would think her half her age, a young miss of seventeen, but under the light of the chandeliers the creases beside her eyes came plainly into view. Long before my birth, she had reigned as the Bird of Paradise, a giddy thing, fond of outrageous fashions and carriage-racing. Now, she seemed more a seasoned, worldly dame than a showy, excitable flibbertigibbet.

'I shall preserve you from Lord Barrymore's attentions,' she reassured me under her breath, 'but only if you do not wish to invite them.'

I offered her a puzzled look. She merely smiled and placed her gloved hand over mine.

'Why, child, you are a knot of nerves,' she exclaimed. 'What frightens you so?'

I shook my head. 'Oh Mrs Mahon, I am terribly shy of public places,' I stammered.

She rolled her eyes at me. 'Dear girl, you have nothing to fear. The theatre is a dark place and few among the audience will recognize you from the boxes. Your face is not yet known among the *demi-monde*.'

These were false assurances indeed. What I did not know was that my keeper had artfully arranged my entrance to attract as much notice as possible from his friends and rivals. Gentle reader, I do not doubt you have observed what takes place in a theatre. By this I do not mean the performance upon the stage, but what occurs among the audience. There is a silent language of the boxes. Who sits beside whom speaks of reputations: sullied or rising, virtuous or questionable. Even I, a relative stranger to the fashionable world, understood the rules of this, which is why my pace began to slow as soon as we passed through the foyer. My fears of being recognized grew with every step we made towards St John's box. I knew not whom I would encounter when I came through the door and into the full view of the audience. 'Dear Lord, protect me from scrutiny and recognition,' I prayed silently.

Mrs Mahon sensed my hesitation, for I felt her pulling me along as we proceeded through the corridor to the box.

'St John is a great lover of the theatre,' she chatted away merrily. 'He has recently turned himself into a playwright. Has he not told you?'

I could say nothing, but walked with my eyes straight before me.

'Why, his play *The Iron Mask* has just been performed and last year his opera, *The Island of Sainte-Marguerite*, was staged here at Drury Lane.'

The door to the box was opened for us.

'Lord Barrymore has built his own theatre at Wargrave. No doubt we shall soon pay a visit there.'

Barrymore, Sir John and Lady Lade and Mr Selwyn moved through and took their seats.

'They say it is the finest theatre ever built by a gentleman . . .' she continued, taking me directly to the front of the box. 'There now, Miss Lightfoot, do have the best seat. Yes, there beside St John. I shall sit here, to your left, so no harm comes to you from the charming rascal.' She nodded at my keeper, who now held his head like a king.

If St John had placed an advertisement in the *Morning Chronicle*, there could not have been a greater declaration of my new life than my appearance there, between the infamous Bird of Paradise and the renowned rake John St John. How I wished I might disappear into thin air! I immediately drew up my fan to hide myself as my eyes adjusted to the dimness of the playhouse. It was then, gnawed by terrible anxiety, that I began to search the audience for the faces I most dreaded to see.

Immediately I spied two of Lady Stavourley's associates, but saw no hint of the Countess herself beside them. My heart thudded violently as I continued to squint at the faint outlines of the figures before me. There were Lord and Lady Bessborough in one box with Mr Fox, Lady Dundas and Lady Melbourne on either side, Lord Jersey with two well-dressed officers and ladies I did not know. I looked as hard as I might against the cast of the chandeliers, and after some time determined that my father was not present. I exhaled with relief, but continued to pass my eyes over the crowd, searching for the face of my beloved among the assembled throng. It was folly, and I knew it, for I understood I would not find him. He was no longer here, but until I learned where he was, my heart would never sit still. It was only when Mrs Jordan made her entrance, raising a storm of huzzahs and applause, that I gave up my quest and turned my attention to the stage.

How they cried for her, the adored Jordan. Seeing her step out on to the boards as Rosalind, in her flowing pink gown, lifted my spirits mightily. I could not help but recall the other occasions when I had seen her, dressed as a boy, or marching about the stage as a wilful girl, drawing roars of approval from the audience. Polite young ladies were not encouraged to admire actresses, but I had always thrilled to her performances. I could not think how it would feel to be so esteemed, so universally loved.

I had watched the first three acts of *As You Like It*, completely immersed in a reverie, before something caught my eye. Not two boxes to the right of where I sat, I spied a familiar silhouette. In fact, it was one I had sketched and cut myself not two years earlier as we had sat in the drawing room at Berkeley Square. Unable to contain my horror, I let out a loud gasp, which drew the looks of everyone around me.

'Miss Lightfoot!' cried a startled St John. 'Whatever is the matter!'

I immediately rose to my feet as Mrs Mahon grabbed for my arm. By then the tears had begun to gather.

'My father . . .' I murmured with my hand pressed to my mouth. 'You said he was not in town!' I exclaimed. At that point, I imagine all within sight of our box were following our drama. I pushed my way between Sir John and Lady Lade in an attempt to escape. St John came stumbling after me, amid bemused looks and questions from his friends. He pursued me out of the box door and into the corridor where we stood against the shallow illumination of the sconces. I had only glimpsed my father fleetingly, but that small dose of him had been enough to fell me entirely.

'I must quit this place at once!' I cried, now in a true panic.

'Why? Whatever for? Henrietta, whatever has come over you?' He grabbed hold of my arm as if to shake me.

'Lord Stavourley!' I wailed in a fit of hysterics. 'He is here!'

St John's face dropped. 'Are you certain of it?'

'Indeed, sir,' I wept. 'Oh, I am ruined to be sure! Oh, the shame of it!' I then lifted my skirts and began to flee down the corridor.

'Miss Lightfoot!' called St John, running like a footman behind me, until, nearly winded, he caught me and held me still. 'Madam! Compose yourself . . .'

But I could not. Something had occurred within me that I could not explain. For all that had befallen me, I had maintained myself well, but the sight of my father had unravelled me entirely, as if a thread had been pulled that unwound all my fortitude.

St John passed me his handkerchief as I sobbed loudly. He stared at me for a good while.

'While I am greatly moved by your distress, my dear, I cannot imagine how the briefest sight of Lord Stavourley could have sent you into such a fit. Why, you do not even know if he saw you.'

'No, I do not,' I confessed, blotting my eyes. My paint and powder were now flowing down my face in great rivers.

'Why, you are so transformed, it is unlikely Lord Stavourley should have recognized you in your finery!' scoffed St John, in a manner I found rather callous, for that was precisely the cause of my shame.

It was only with hindsight that I appreciated the truth of his comment. Had I been able to gain control of my senses, I might have understood this, but I was too far gone to think rationally. In truth, there was another matter devouring my mind. Thoughts of the child growing in my belly plagued me. Every day and night I feared discovery. The attempts to hide my morning sickness, the counting of the weeks and the complete absence of female counsel: these things played upon me constantly.

Nothing that St John said to me could possibly have stanched my tears. I no longer had command over myself.

'Oh dear, Jack . . .' I began, wringing my hands.

St John studied me.

'Oh . . . dear . . . oh . . .'

'What, madam? What?'

'Oh for dear life, sir, I am with child!' I cried.

My keeper's face went entirely still. Hardly a twitch passed over it. Then his eyes widened, by degrees.

'Can you be certain?' he whispered.

'I am certain.'

He turned his back on me and took several steps towards a servant.

'Find my man! Have my coach brought round at once!' he ordered. 'Miss Lightfoot is ill and must return to the house immediately! Now! Go!'

It all happened so rapidly. St John seemed to disappear in a flurry. I was bundled into his coach and sent charging off to Park Street, my tears never drying for an instant.

Once in my rooms, I was undressed and put to bed, thinking all the while that this was to be my final night in my mother's home. In my heart I was certain he knew the truth, that the child inside me could not have been his. I could sense it in his look, the manner in which he glared at me. This was the end! He would turn me out for sure! The fate of those weary creatures I had observed from my window would soon be mine too. I was destined to tread the streets, to sleep in corners, to freeze and starve. How I suddenly came to appreciate the coal in the fire, the warming pan on the mattress, the soft night clothes upon my back!

I knew I would have no sleep that night. Instead, I lay awake, awaiting the sounds of St John's return, the creak of floorboards, the closing of doors, knowing that his homecoming would seal my fate. But this never came. Only the clock upon the landing filled the silence, striking out the hours: twelve, one, two, three, four . . .

Chapter 25

'Never have I known a woman to commit a more thoughtless deed than yours, madam,' scolded Mrs Mahon from the side of my bed. I had hardly awakened that morning before she appeared at St John's door begging to call upon me. She was shown into my bed-chamber as I sipped my dish of chocolate, my eyes swollen from grief and lack of rest.

'No sooner have you been taken under the wing of a devoted keeper and plied with gowns and gifts than you seek to overturn it all!' she exclaimed.

Her reproaches filled me with self-pity. I could not meet her gaze.

'I did not know what else to do,' I said in little more than a whisper. 'I know not what will become of me now . . .'

'I should think not!' huffed Mrs Mahon. 'Dear child, you have not the slightest understanding of how to manage things.'

I regarded her and she me. It was then that I recognized I had not the faintest notion of what she spoke.

'Manage . . . what things?' I asked coyly.

She sighed. 'Only the most fool-headed girl would announce to her keeper that she is with child without first learning his thoughts upon the matter. You have not been under his roof a full month and you are out with it, quick as that.' She snapped her fingers. 'I do not suppose you ever enquired if he would welcome a child? Goodness, girl, how can you even be certain you *have* a child in your womb? Have you felt the quickening? Have you felt it move?'

I stared at her blankly, as stupidly as I had at Miss Bradley and her sister.

'No.'

'Then what makes you so certain?'

'I have not bled and I have been ill these several days.'

The Bird of Paradise sighed again and folded her arms. 'I suppose it is possible.'

'He has lain with me almost every day and night since I arrived,' I added, in an effort to shore up my tale. I observed her expression closely, recognizing that Mrs Mahon was likely to know a good deal more about matters of conception than I.

'I do hope, for your sake, Miss Lightfoot, that you are correct in this instance.'

'Why?'

'Because St John has passed the entire night toasting the health of his unborn child. He has told half of London that he is to be a father,' she exclaimed. 'But if you prove to be wrong, or if you miscarry, he will be made a laughing stock. Then you will find yourself on the street – unless Barrymore will have you.'

None of this made any sense to me. There seemed no reason in it.

'But you made it sound as if he would be displeased to find me breeding.'

'A good many gentlemen would be. For most men, a mistress with a baby is as desirable as a dose of the clap. Few, like St John, who have no offspring, welcome such news. You are fortunate, my dear. I have known too many ladies of our sort made destitute for allowing their bellies to swell.'

To be frank, I was quite appalled by this. I thought of Allenham, who I was certain would be overjoyed at the news of his impending father-hood. He had promised me that he would love any child of our union. He had promised.

'St John will not abandon me,' I breathed with relief.

'I dare say he will not.' She smiled. 'But you have a good deal to learn, madam. You must think before you speak, always. The slightest slip may endanger your comfort.' Then she paused thoughtfully. 'If I may say so, dear Miss Lightfoot, you are far too honest. You wear your thoughts upon your very face; you make no effort to disguise them. You are artless to a fault.'

'But an honest character is a good one . . .'

'As is a modest and virtuous character, but that is not the world we inhabit, my dear. You will be eaten alive. Your bones will be picked over by the carrion birds of the *haut ton*. We must rescue you.' She studied me with a sympathetic smile and then pulled the bell rope. 'Come now, you must dress. There is someone I should like you to meet.'

No sooner had I been attired than I found myself sitting in Mrs Mahon's coach en route to Grosvenor Square, where we were to call upon Miss Mary Anne Greenhill, 'the Greenfinch', as she was called by the fast set.

'They think themselves very witty for inventing such names for us. I am "the Bird of Paradise" and Sarah Adcock is "the Goldfinch". Mrs Irvince is "the White Swan" and Mrs Corbyne "the White Crow". It is all quite silly,' Mrs Mahon explained. 'The Greenfinch is very much in favour at the moment, as you will see by the manner in which she lives. She has the run of her own house.'

'Do you mean she is the housekeeper?'

My tutoress laughed heartily. 'No, I mean that Lord Sefton, who keeps her, has provided her with these lodgings. She has no boarders and comes and goes as she pleases. His credit pays for all that you will see.'

We were greeted at the door by a footman in livery, who showed us through a glittering entry hall and up a set of gold-painted stairs to the drawing room. There we found Miss Greenhill, in an elegant gown of striped yellow satin, stroking a nervous white lap dog.

'Mrs Mahon,' she exclaimed, rising to her feet and holding out her cheek for a kiss. Her brown hair had been arranged in modish, free-flowing curls, encircled by a thick blue bandeau of silk, which sat across her forehead. Although she appeared extremely youthful, her air was greatly affected.

'Miss Greenhill, may I present to you Miss Lightfoot, who is in keeping with the Honourable John St John.'

As we made our courtesies, I could feel my hostess's hot eyes upon me. I watched her pupils shamelessly wander over my floral patterned gown and study the material of my gloves. Indeed, there was not one inch of me that escaped inspection. The paste buckle of my belt, my pink slippers, every detail and bow upon my hat was examined before she addressed me with a fixed smile.

'Please, Miss Lightfoot, Mrs Mahon, do sit.'

A Wedgwood tea service and a collection of highly polished silver was brought and laid before us. Two servants fussed with an enormous kettle of hot water, while Spark, Miss Greenhill's dog, hopped between their legs.

'Dear Miss Lightfoot,' she began with breathy excitement, 'do tell me all about Mr St John. Does he keep you well?'

I did not quite know how to respond to such an indiscreet question.

'Why, I suppose so,' I commented, taking a sip of my tea.

'Is he generous? Has he showered you with gifts?' She giggled.

I turned to Mrs Mahon, hoping she might offer an appropriate response, but she merely returned my look.

'Oh, he has been most generous . . .'

'Has he bought you fine silks and laces?'

My hostess's questions were now causing me some uneasiness.

'Have you had many gowns made up? Is that lovely gown a gift from him?'

'Yes . . .'

'And has he bought you many jewels?' She tittered excitedly, her bright green eyes sparkling like emeralds.

'Not so many, yet . . . but he has been generous. When he learned that I had been robbed of what few jewels I had, he immediately gave to me some pearls that had belonged to my mother.'

Mary Anne Greenhill stared at me, her tight smile unmoving. I could not begin to fathom what thoughts were circulating inside that head of curls.

'The Earl of Sefton has been most generous too. I declare, he must be the most munificent lover in all of London, and handsome as well.'

'Not so handsome . . .' Mrs Mahon corrected her, thinking no doubt of the unfortunate Earl's hunchback.

'Perhaps not,' Miss Greenhill smirked, turning her eye to me, 'but he is young . . . and terribly wealthy.'

It was then that my wise tutoress interjected, 'You see, my dear, Miss Greenhill has been exceptionally clever in catching Lord Sefton and she is no older than you—'

'Seventeen,' boasted my hostess, 'and nearly two years in keeping with his lordship.'

'Two years?' I echoed in disbelief.

'He has been very content with me.'

'Miss Greenhill is the daughter of a tailor in Holborn. One of six girls.'

'My eldest sister is also in keeping, but only in Bloomsbury. Her lover is a wine merchant. She has not done so well as me.' The pretty braggart blew on her tea and then took a delicate sip. 'His lordship is so pleased with me that he pays all my debts without a single question asked. He has permitted me to decorate the entire house to my taste.'

Her drawing room was indeed quite ornate, as well furnished with expensive carpets and cabinets as my father's. The sofa and chairs were upholstered in cerise silk, dotted with a white fleur-de-lis pattern, while the walls and ceiling were a riot of fashionable plasterwork in curls and swags.

'Oh!' she exclaimed, as if suddenly recalling a matter that had slipped her mind. 'You must see what little treasure he presented to me not three days ago!' She went to pull the bell rope, and then, catching my eye, stopped. 'No, I shall not ring for it. I shall take you to my dressing room directly.' And with that, we rose abruptly from the tea table and followed Miss Greenhill as she and Spark bustled down the corridor.

Only a pasha's tent could have rivalled the splendour of the Greenfinch's dressing room, with its flounces of aquamarine silk and chartreuse damask. Everywhere gold leaf and mirrors poured light into the room, while in the far corner sat a vast birdcage in the shape of a Chinese pagoda. Its occupant twitched and fluttered at our approach.

'Is it not the most fetching piece?' she declared, holding out a small circle of diamonds. 'It is a buckle for me to wear upon the band of my new hat.' She beamed, gesturing to her maid to bring the piece of millinery.

A green, high-crowned creation was offered to me for inspection. Once the Greenfinch was satisfied that she had raised my jealousy, she turned to Mrs Mahon with a lowered voice. 'But you should see what arrived from Captain Hervey-Aston yesterday.' She nodded to her maid, who unlocked a drawer and brought out a pair of ruby earrings.

My tutoress and Miss Greenhill gasped and squealed. I must confess, I was somewhat confused by this. The Bird of Paradise looked over her shoulder and noted my puzzled expression.

'I do believe Miss Lightfoot is scandalized!' She laughed, placing a gentle hand upon my arm. 'Dear girl, it is no crime to accept gifts from other admirers. Why, a lover is not a husband, and any lady in our position would be a fool to discourage the advances of other beaux.'

'But would Lord Sefton not be angry if he learned of it?'

'Of course he would,' answered the Greenfinch haughtily, 'but he will not learn of it, will he?'

'And who is to say Lord Sefton might not lose his fortune tomorrow, or die from an accident, or tire of Miss Greenhill? Why, such a thing has occurred to me on several occasions. Nearly every day a mistress is jilted for some reason or other. If she had not other admirers, whom might she call upon in her distress?' my kind adviser explained.

'But . . . certainly . . . Lord Sefton loves you . . .'

'Love?' they both echoed.

'Well, in a fashion, I suppose he does,' mused the younger of the two.

'You believe a man's love will outlast his purse?' Mrs Mahon sniffed. 'I shall tell you this, Miss Lightfoot, when a man finds he cannot pay his debts or your mantua-maker, he will throw you over, quick as lightning. That is the truth of it. Do not think St John any different.'

I was terribly chastened by her words, but not entirely inclined to hear them. After all, my keeper believed I carried his child. Why should he want to be rid of me?

Mrs Mahon tilted her head sympathetically and then reached for my hand. 'Henrietta, if you permit me . . . I do not mean to frighten you, only to offer you guidance. You are so very inexperienced. I should hate some harm to come to you on account of your simple, countrified notions.'

'We only mean to instruct you, Miss Lightfoot,' added Miss Greenhill with a condescending smile.

'Your naivety is charming, but dangerous, dear. One must always keep an eye to one's future. Guard one's interests in the face of adversity.'

'And you could have any gentleman you desired, Miss Lightfoot,' exclaimed my hostess, her features hardening with jealousy. 'You are a true beauty.'

'She is correct. You might have any man you choose,' encouraged my tutoress.

I shrugged and looked away. 'But I do not choose it.'

Oh reader, what was I to say? In truth, I had no wish to live my life in this manner. My desire was not to collect suitors and jewels, forever moving from one man's bed to the next, pretending to love. My only wish was for the safe delivery of Allenham's child, my only aim to secure my current place of refuge until my beloved and I could be reunited. I wanted no other lover but him: my true husband, the keeper of my heart. But I could not confess this to them! No, my friends, I could not betray a single word of my hopes; not the slightest longing or moan of pain for my absent love could escape my lips. I would have to remain entirely silent, for my survival and that of my child depended upon it.

On the night of St John's gathering, Mr Selwyn had recognized something within me, to which even the Bird of Paradise was blind. He knew I carried secrets. He had seen that I was not the ingénue I pretended to be. Selwyn did not teach me to deceive, for I had taught myself that art already.

Mrs Mahon sighed. 'Then you are foolish, and I am certain you will come to change your mind.'

I regarded her, my eyes now full of shame. 'Perhaps,' I muttered, 'though I should not like myself very much if I did.'

Chapter 26

Never was there a man more thrilled by the prospect of fatherhood than St John. Such a change came over him in the following months that his friends found him near unrecognizable. Gone were his cold reserve and his tendency to meanness. Lightness and benevolence glowed in their place.

'There is a rumour put about that you now feed your servants upon beefsteaks, Jack,' quipped Mr Selwyn one evening as he sat at St John's dinner table, consuming potato pudding and tripe.

My keeper smiled in a soft, saintly manner, but did not reply.

'I shall have you know I disabused that person of their absurd notions. I said that anyone who knows Jack's reputation for economy would understand that to be a gross falsehood.'

Selwyn waited for a witty retort from my keeper, but St John was in too serene a state of mind to spar with his friend. 'Perhaps the gossip-mongers of Mayfair are correct, sir. What then?'

'Then heaven preserve us! For when this child is born, it will be the complete ruin of your miserly character!'

Indeed St John seemed a man transformed, and I could not help feeling a certain ache of guilt when I looked at him, particularly upon those occasions when he wore such a contented expression.

As for me, the promise of motherhood held all manner of confusions, fears and joys. I found the changes that came over me mysterious and unsettling. No sooner was I free of morning sickness than great red patches began to appear upon me. I was subject to all variety of swellings, itches and soreness. At first I believed this to be an infestation of bedbugs or fleas, until Mrs Mahon instructed me that such discomforts were usual in my condition. She had my maid make up a comfrey unction and sent me some nettle tonic, which relieved me greatly.

Within a month or so of my outburst at the theatre, my belly began to spring forth. How curious it was to observe my expanding middle. Each morning, I stood before my mother's looking glass, gazing at my silhouette. The bulge seemed to grow quite rapidly. At first it was a hard, small dome, the shape of a wide pudding. Then it began to inflate like a balloon. At about this time, I felt the quickening, the gentle flutters of the creature swimming within me. 'That is when one knows for certain that the infant lives,' Lady Lade assured me, though how precisely she, a woman with an empty nursery, understood this, I had yet to learn.

Soon, my figure was so enlarged that I could scarcely bear to have my stays laced. My bubbies, which had always been well made and ample, suddenly appeared to double, and then to triple in size. Far from repelling St John's desire, as I had hoped, my strangely bulbous figure seemed to inflame my keeper further. His hands could not be kept from my tender bosom, though the child inside me was spared a regular battering owing to the inconstancy of his manhood, and for this I was grateful.

It was only in my private moments, as I reclined awkwardly in a chair, or rested in bed, that I allowed myself to think of Allenham. I laid my hands across my belly and imagined the infant, built of both our pieces, floating within my womb. My beloved lived within me. I spoke to him there, stroking my mound and bidding him to return to me, willing him to my side. But he did not hear me, and the months continued to pass.

By the arrival of spring, all the attire that had been made up for me required alteration. 'Alas, this is always the case,' the mantua-maker confessed to me. 'A young bride outgrows her wardrobe within a year.' She gave me a wink, knowing all too well that I had never been a bride. She also advised me to give up my stays for a pair of jumps. What a shame it is that you ladies no longer wear these old-fashioned half-corsets, for they leave the waist entirely free. Such relief they provided me, I cannot begin to express!

In truth, had it not been for the wisdom of my mantua-maker, and the knowledge of Mrs Mahon and Lady Lade, I would have been lost indeed. A young lady is never more in need of female counsel than when she finds herself breeding, and, to be sure, it is remarkable how many perfect strangers are willing to dispense advice. Why, in my state, I seemed to attract the notice of every *demi-mondaine* in London. While some were quick with smiles and gentle words, others threw me jealous looks. And this, dear reader, was precisely what St John wished them to do.

Now, friends, you know me to be of a modest nature. You know that I would never willingly seek such attention, but St John was of a different character altogether. He was both proud and vain, and desired all of London to know that I was with child, and that he was the cause of it. He would push me before every rival and friend alike, so that they could examine the evidence for themselves. It might have served him better to have simply pitched a marquee in Green Park, stood me upon a dais and invited all and sundry to have a peep. Instead I was subjected to a tour of every public place in London. We attended every rout, every play, opera, exhibition or musical party. As both my belly and the season came into full bloom, he took me through Hyde Park in his calash, directing his driver to stop whenever he spotted some distant acquaintance or other. In May and June, I moved like a slow, heavy galleon through the crowds at Vauxhall, Ranelagh and Sadler's Wells, while a visit to Epsom, further afield, very nearly brought about the death of me. Having survived the pitted roads, I found myself wilting beneath the heat of the crowded assembly rooms.

'Dear Jack,' I often pleaded, as I stood fanning myself, 'may we sit? I fear my back shall give way.'

'But there is the Earl of Egremont' or 'But I spy Lord Pitt Rivers' – or some other rakish friend – 'who I am certain would desire an introduction,' he would say, and so I remained upon my weary feet.

I was displayed like a pregnant mare at a horse market; led from this paddock to the next, my keeper patting my vast bulge every so often. I could do little else but tighten my lips and hold my tongue at this mortifying treatment. Is it any wonder that this absurd spectacle soon found its way into the intelligencer columns of the newspapers? All of London laughed at St John, who was described in the *Morning Post* as 'the virile Jupiter', who 'in striking Miss L---t with his bolt of lightning, has turned her from vestal virgin to high priestess'. Oh, the shame of it! I do not doubt that this was how my father came to hear of my disgrace. Indeed, it was not until much later that I learned he had not seen me at the theatre that evening, as I had feared. No, he learned of my circumstances in the months that followed, and I dare not think what injury this discovery did to him.

It is a testimony to St John's extraordinary vanity that he remained deaf to all forms of mockery. Men believe what they wish to. He even failed to hear the loudly whispered suggestion that he might not have been 'the author of Miss Lightfoot's round belly'. Instead he chose to triumph in his title of 'the virile Jupiter'.

Contrary to what you may have heard from my enemies, the notorious Roman feast hosted by Mrs Catherine Windsor of King's Place was not of my design. The scheme was entirely St John's. The notion of celebrating the ancient festival of the fig, Nonae Caprotinae, seemed to him a fitting tribute to my maternal condition. I was told little of this plan, only that I was to figure as the honoured guest.

'You will be venerated as the fertile Juno, my dear,' he announced. 'It will be a masquerade and supper in Roman dress, attended by all who know and cherish you.'

I regarded St John with uneasiness as I stroked my moon-shaped belly. As you might imagine, by July, the awkwardness of my situation was beginning to prey upon my mind regularly. By my reckoning I was near eight months gone, though my duped keeper thought me no more than six. My time of confinement was fast approaching, and I wished for nothing more than to pass the ensuing weeks in the privacy of my rooms thinking on what I should say when St John's child arrived two months earlier than expected!

'Oh Jack,' said I, 'I am much indebted to your kindness, but I find myself so inconvenienced by my size that I doubt if—'

'I shall not hear it, madam.' He silenced me with a wave of his hand. 'You will have a couch upon which to lie and slaves to do your bidding.' Then he smirked. 'Dearest girl, your comfort is always my greatest concern.'

As the feast of the fig approached, my keeper's anticipation grew. This was to be an entertainment to rival the finest theatrical performances, he promised. 'Not since the days of Mrs Cornelys' masquerades will London have seen anything quite so elegant.'

Such an event required a suitable costume, and my keeper went to great lengths to secure one for me. I, like everyone else, was to sport the robes of antiquity, but mine were made of a fine drape of orange silk and held in place with brooches in the shape of palmyras. I wore gold-laced sandals upon my feet, while my hair had been set in a flow of curls, on to which a laurel wreath was placed. In one hand I held my gold mask upon a stick, while in the other I carried an enormous cluster of Juno's peacock feathers, which St John had ordered a fan-maker to create especially for the occasion.

As we rode to Mrs Windsor's house on King's Place, it occurred to me that until I had met St John, I had never heard this street mentioned, yet among his set, it seemed to be the most fashionable address in town. They were always speaking of it with a smile or jest, or commenting upon some tempting beauty who lived there. As you might imagine, this made me vastly curious. I believed I was to attend a ball at the home of a fashionable, though dissolute grand dame. By then, I was no longer so innocent of the manners of the world. I had come to accept that I would never again cross the threshold of a respectable home, but neither had I imagined that St John would bring me to a brothel for a night of entertainment!

To be sure, King's Place and its row of smart townhouses appeared like any other in St James's. But for the crush of sedan chairs and carriages, there was nothing extraordinary about it. Mrs Windsor's home, too, was laid out in a plan identical to most. We entered through the door into a broad, lavishly decorated hall. It was here that we were greeted by the hostess herself, her weathered cheeks bright with rouge and her generous figure swathed in red robes.

'Ah, the blooming Miss Lightfoot,' she exclaimed, greeting me with a kiss. The intimacy of that gesture startled me. 'Mr St John has done well to have found you – such beauty and freshness in one form is rare indeed.'

The virile Jupiter offered her a gracious bow.

Had I been more familiar with women of Mrs Windsor's sort, I might have known who, or rather what, she was from the moment of our introduction. Why, she examined me as a butcher might a leg of lamb, her eyes weighing my flesh and imagining the price she could exact from the sale of it. No doubt, under normal circumstances my sense of alarm would have been raised, but I fear my powers of judgement were far too distracted by the dazzling surroundings to have been of much use to me.

The old bawd had gone to quite an expense to adorn her palace. The hall in which we stood had been decorated with garlands and billowing drapery. Everywhere were to be found hanging oil lamps, cushions and low sofas, so that the entire interior appeared like that of an emperor's tent. Across the mirrors were draped swags of greenery, while vast urns of orange blossoms and horns of hot-house grapes and figs were laid upon the pier tables. The thick summer air was enriched by the deep scents of wine and frankincense, wafting in clouds from the perfume-burners.

No sooner had I taken in these delights than into the hall ran two laughing nymphs, clad in nothing more than gold sandals and laurel wreaths! Imagine my surprise again when they were followed by a pair of masked gentlemen in senatorial robes, who threw them upon the sofas and began to ravish them like satyrs!

I declare, I believe my mouth fell wide open. I averted my gaze and began to colour, brightly. With a wry glance, Mrs Windsor took my hand and began to lead me and my keeper to the staircase.

'There will be much more of that to come, what hey, Mr St John?' teased our hostess.

I shot him a horrified look. It was then that my whereabouts became plain to me. I wondered what he meant by such an offence, by organizing this occasion in a brothel. St John read my thoughts immediately.

'My dear little Juno.' He wagged his head. 'Your sensibilities are so delicate as to cause you to feel dishonoured . . .'

I began to speak, but he halted me.

'You must know that this is no ordinary establishment. Mrs Windsor's home is open only to men of title and wealth. Why, you might have seen your own father here before your birth.' He sniggered.

I bristled at this.

'Miss Lightfoot, I would have you know my house is considered the finest of its sort in London. Indeed, the royal princes are regular patrons,' Mrs Windsor added in a whisper.

We continued up the stair, which was dressed in tendrils of ivy and papier mâché grapes, and passed into a large double drawing room. The dancing had already begun, but at the grand dame's arrival, the musicians were ordered to change the tune and beat out a march. With my hand in hers, she brought me to a low couch, which lay beneath a canopy of yellow-fringed gauze.

'Juno assumes her throne!' she proclaimed. 'All hail, mother Juno!'

The assembled guests let forth a great huzzah.

Reader, let it be said that I knew from the moment I took to my couch that I was not the honoured guest at this event. He took his place beside me, upon a couch of his own. Reaching for a glass of wine, St John raised a toast to 'Fertility, virility and pleasure'. I would that he had toasted my safe delivery and the birth of a healthy child, but such trifling matters were, at that proud moment, of no real concern to him.

I must admit, it took some time for me to grow accustomed to the strangeness of my surroundings. That I should find myself in a brothel, no matter how grand, shocked me to my very core. Never did I think in all my life that I should have cause to enter such a place, and at first I sat uneasily upon my couch, attempting not to gawp as revellers breezed in and out of the ballroom in various states of undress. However, after a spell, my sense of scandal began to abate, as it had with virtually every other lewd and licentious situation into which St John had thrown me. It may even surprise you to read that I eventually came to enjoy my reign upon the throne that evening. As my fellow guests lifted their masks to address me, I was pleased to see many familiar faces among the sea of strangers. Shortly after our arrival, the Bird of Paradise arrived upon the arm of the old Duke of Queensberry and Sir John and Lady

Lade appeared not long after. My condition prevented me entering into the dancing, so I lounged for most of the evening upon my couch, fluttering my enormous fan of peacock feathers and receiving flirtatious looks from a good number of admirers. Only a brave few dared approach me, for the virile Jupiter guarded my throne with the ferocity of Cerberus. As you might imagine, dear reader, jealousy had lately taken root in St John.

Suspicion is the price for excessive pride. A man who boastfully displays his riches to all the world is soon convinced that he will be robbed of them. And not without reason, I hear you say. Those of you acquainted with the habits of the *demi-monde* know this to be too true.

Although I had dismissed Mrs Mahon's earlier attempt to instruct me in the ways of the mistress, she would not be put off so easily.

'I impart these lessons to you for your own benefit, my dear,' she had lectured me one evening as we took a turn, arm in arm, through the Pantheon.

'But why would I need the protection of another gentleman when St John has displayed such devotion to my happiness and to that of my child?' I sighed, now growing weary of her pestering.

My tutoress rolled her eyes heavenward. 'And what if he tires of you?'

'But I am to give him a child. Certainly, he would not tire of the mother of his child.'

At that, Mrs Mahon let out a yelp of astonishment. 'My dear,' said she, 'I have given three men four children, and for what? One has paid me an annuity of a hundred pounds per annum. Men are more fickle than women in their desires. They are like bees, forever moving from one flower to the next.'

I feared the truth of her words, though I simply could not see St John tiring of me, the daughter of his Kitty, his *petit chaton*, the very incarnation of the woman he had lost. And certainly, *certainly*, I assured myself, Allenham would have returned to me by then, for every day I lived in expectation of a letter from him.

The Bird of Paradise gave me a look of exasperation. 'Hetty, are you so ignorant of your charms that you cannot see them in the looking glass? Heavens, my girl, you are the Goddess of Beauty herself! Can you not see why St John wishes to display you?' She wore a look of wonderment as she addressed me, as if I were some feather-brained ninny. 'The gentlemen of this town talk of little else beyond your golden hair and round blue eyes. Why, you might play the bee, not the flower. I declare it, St John has all to fear once you are delivered and freed of your condition,' said she, casting a glance at my belly. 'Barrymore. Permit his advances. I shall arrange for an assignation at my lodgings.'

Zounds! If St John only knew what treachery his trusted friend proposed! After all, it had been he who had suggested that Gertrude Mahon act as my tutoress, my chaperone through this garden of dangers. He believed he had employed an angel, when in truth he had engaged a serpent.

'No.' I spoke firmly. 'I do not wish it.'

My friend tossed her head. 'Then it is no affair of mine.'

But this was not the end of it. That evening at Mrs Windsor's, as I presided over the company, she sat beside me on my couch, again whispering into my ear.

'Just look about you now, Hetty, at the wolves circling this room, smacking their lips while St John sits not two feet from us. Why, in the time we have sat in conversation, I have seen Lord Grosvenor gaze upon you in the hopes of catching your attention, and Colonel Wheeler there who is dressed as a centurion . . . see, he looks again . . .'

Only the approach of Lord Barrymore brought a halt to her scheming. She rose from her seat and made a coy curtsey before drawing him down so she might whisper some mischief into his ear. She glanced back at me as she departed, and flashed me an impish smile.

His lordship remained teetering before me, as drunk as he had been upon the day we first met. He paid his respects to St John and then waited until my keeper was engaged in conversation, before slithering into the seat beside me. He began to stare at me, though I turned my head from him and waved my frothy fan between us. He moved closer still, keeping one eye fixed always upon St John.

'Angel,' he breathed, in great sour clouds of wine, 'have you no knowledge of your pregnant charms?'

I ignored his taunts.

'A woman round as the Madonna is a great temptation indeed.' He began to laugh wickedly. 'You see, dear Miss Lightfoot, a womb filled with another man's infant betrays no secrets. One can spill as much seed as one likes upon the ground and yet it will never take root.'

My face was growing hot with indignation.

'Do not fret,' said he, sliding nearer to me still, 'there is no risk to be had. No one will know I have been inside you, and your large belly will not hinder us. I shall take you from behind, like a true Roman.'

At that I moved quite violently away from him and attempted to catch my protector's eye, but St John was too engaged to notice.

'*Tempus fugit*, my dear,' Barrymore murmured, shutting his eyes in imagined bliss. 'You will not remain in such a convenient state for long. Make haste.'

At that very instant I was preserved from Barrymore's advance by the approach of one of his friends.

'My lord,' called the gentleman attired in a vast gold breastplate and helmet. He was short and as broadly built as Mars himself.

'Ah, Quindell!' exclaimed Barrymore. 'May I introduce to you Miss Lightfoot?'

'The ox-eyed Juno,' he gushed, quoting from Homer and making a deep, theatrical bow. 'Madam, you grace the mortal world with your beauty. '

'Miss Lightfoot will not permit anyone to make love to her, Philly. I have tried and failed.'

But this did not deter Mr Quindell, who at that moment removed his mask to better feast his wide-set eyes upon me. He wore the dumb expression of a man enchanted.

'You cannot put me off so easily, my lord,' said he, going down upon his knee and taking my hand in his.

'She has eyes for no one but St John, her keeper.'

Just then, Quindell's face changed. He looked over at the virile Jupiter, who was rapt in conversation with a gentleman in an orange mask.

'St John?' He snorted, and then began to chuckle. 'Why, John St John?' he said again, in a louder, more assertive voice.

I knew then that my keeper had heard him, but rather than turning to Quindell, he leaned nearer to the masked gentleman, as if to hear him over the din.

'St John owes Quindell a great deal of money,' explained Barrymore with a hiccup. 'Why, most of London owes Quindell a great deal of money.'

I looked at Barrymore with a startled expression.

'I know nothing of this,' I muttered in disbelief. 'Why? However did this come about?'

'Oh madam, this is no new state of affairs for Mr St John,' stated Quindell, raising his voice further. The debtor continued to play deaf. 'His losses at the gaming table are quite considerable. He has assured me on many an occasion that he will shortly be in receipt of his income from his nephew, Lord Bolingbroke, but that was near eight months ago. If you would be so kind, Miss Lightfoot, might you have a word with Mr St John on my behalf? Remind him, in that way that only an alluring creature can, what he stands to lose.'

I nodded warily, not knowing what to make of this distressing revelation, and thinking all the while of Mrs Mahon's cautionary tales.

Gracious heaven! If you had seen St John's expression upon our return home . . . The inside of his coach positively rattled with the sounds of his fury. His eyes shot forth with thunderbolts; his face was as red as a screaming infant's.

'By God, that man wished to make a fool of me,' he spat. 'Never have I been subjected to such an insult! To have one's debts cried publicly before one's friends – and upon this night of all nights! What am I to make of this? Dear Lord, I should have called him out! Yes, I shall. I shall do it. There is no other remedy for it . . .'

I attempted to calm him, to convince him that a duel would not resolve the issue, but he would not have it. He would not hear a single word I said.

'And to think, this . . . this . . . sugar merchant's son holds some of the greatest families in the land in his debt! Why, who is he? Some . . . some ingrate Barbadian planter? That this Colonial should speak to me with such disregard – it is an abomination, an affront to all that is right and just, I say!'

Oh, and would that it had ended there.

St John's pride was vast, but it was not robust. He did not forget an insult easily. He brooded upon the matter all the next day and the one after that. Indeed, nothing seemed to lift his mood from the dark space where it lay. I crept around on quiet toes as he stewed in his study, emptying the contents of his cellar into his wine glass. On several occasions I rapped upon his door, but he only groaned.

'It is I, your *petit chaton*.'

'Leave me,' he growled. And so I did.

I confess, my keeper's melancholic behaviour troubled me greatly. I had never seen a man so glum, nor did I know when this storm was likely to blow itself out. Happily, his proposed challenge to Quindell came to nothing: he had not the resolve to fight a duel. In fact, little could stir him from where he sat, wallowing in his sorrows. Little, I say, but his unquenchable thirst for that proverbial medicine which dulls all men's pains.

I suppose this was what drew him down the back stairs to the kitchen. There is no other explanation for why he would have been making use of the servants' passage. He must have been very drunk indeed to decide to fetch a bottle from the cellar rather than to ring for it. In any case, it was here, quite late at night, that he came upon Mary, the girl who tended me. He found her with a candle in one hand and a letter and packet in the other.

'Who sends a message at this hour?' grumbled St John, ripping the parcel from her. Mary was powerless to resist, she later claimed to me. Her ill-tempered master had it from her so quickly that she had no time to protest.

Perhaps you have already guessed from whom this secret dispatch came. Barrymore, of course. He had paid Mary a guinea to bring the gift to me without St John's notice.

The first and, dare I say, the last I knew of this was when St John threw open my dressing-room door.

'And now, madam,' he shouted, 'the truth of the matter is known!'

Goodness! I very nearly jumped from my skin.

'Dearest Jack,' I pleaded, greatly confused, 'whatever do you mean by this?'

Truly, I have never seen an expression so twisted with fury as his. He reached into his pocket and drew forth a rumpled letter.

'"Fly away with me,"' he read in a cold voice. Then he turned his sharp eyes upon me. 'It is from Barrymore, but I expect you knew that.'

'Dear Lord, sir!' I exclaimed, rising to my feet at his accusation. 'You cannot think I would have courted his notice! Why, I have rebuffed his attentions upon every occasion since our first acquaintance! You yourself have witnessed this . . .'

St John would not be moved by my words. Instead, he felt inside his waistcoat pocket and pulled from it a little object tied up in a piece of white silk. Angrily, he unpicked the knot and then slowly removed the item. There before me was a small gold watch, its pretty face painted with roses and the phrase '*Tempus Fugit*'. He dangled it from his fingers like a mouse held by its tail, as a sneer of disgust settled on to his lips.

' "*Tempus Fugit*", indeed,' he snarled before dropping the object upon the floor. With a heavy foot, he then pounded his heel upon it and crushed it mercilessly into pieces.

Chapter 27

And that, dear friends, brought about an end to my period of peace beneath St John's roof.

It must be said that my keeper was no Othello. I have known some ladies to suffer greatly by the back hand of their lovers and husbands. The slightest hint of suspicion or a flirtatious look results in a bruise or a fall down the stairs. But fortunately, this was not the way with St John. No, he contained his passions behind his pride, while fury and suspicion ate through his insides like a tapeworm. His expression may have appeared calm and sanguine, but beneath it, his vengeful heart raged.

After his eruption, there was no further mention of 'the affair of the watch'. St John broke with Lord Barrymore, whom he decried as a 'scheming rascal', a man 'incapable of loyalty' and 'bent upon ruining the happiness of his friends'. He was banned absolutely from paying me any address whatsoever. And that was that, or so I believed.

'The world is composed of schemers,' he muttered one evening as we sat alone at dinner. St John would have no one round our table until he had licked his wounds completely clean. 'Plotters and dissemblers and frauds,' said he, examining me over the edge of his crystal wine glass. 'Hmm, madam? What say you to that assertion?'

I swallowed with some difficulty and studied my plate.

'I believe you see enemies in every shadow, sir.'

St John puffed out a laugh.

'I have good cause for it, have I not? Are you not a schemer and a conspirator?'

I was indeed, and a far worse one than he could have imagined. Unthinkingly, I folded my hands across my broad belly.

'I have no love for Lord Barrymore, sir, and you know this.'

St John smashed his hand down upon the table, sending both me and the tableware into a jump.

'Damn that devil! I do not mean him. I mean the others . . .'

'There are none, sir. I have pleaded this to you before.'

'When you learned of my debts you began to scheme your escape. Do not deny it, *chaton.*'

'No, you know that not to be true!' I protested, lifting myself from the chair. I own, I could not bear this inquisition, for I was certain that with enough cunning he would winkle out of me the dreadful truth of the matter.

'I shall watch you like a hawk, madam!' he cried as I fled from the table. 'You will feel my eyes upon you for ever more!'

While I had escaped St John's scrutiny on that evening, I could not avoid it altogether. The grumbling and the questioning now came at regular intervals, so that I attempted whenever possible to avoid spending time in his company. Worse still, I found that something in his demeanour had altered quite significantly. He had taken on a sourness.

'Jack has often been prone to depressed sprits,' Mr Selwyn explained to me, 'but I have not known him to be so distant and bitter since your mother's death.'

St John had retreated into himself. He seldom engaged me in chat and often sat sullenly beside me at the opera or while sipping tea. To be sure, he was not indifferent to me – quite the contrary! Just as he had promised, there was rarely a time when I felt free of his gaze. Even as he sat at a card table, when it seemed as if his attention was consumed in a game, I felt the presence of his scorching black pupils upon me. He followed me wherever I chose to recline or stand, and studied the recipients of my conversation. Heaven forbid that any among them should be male. Why, he would be upon his feet before they could so much as make a bow to me. Suddenly he would appear, having slipped sylph-like to my side, to place a firm hand upon my elbow and turn me from their attention.

He studied me too closely. When I spoke, I felt him observing the very movements of my mouth and brow, as if he hoped to find some poorly disguised falsehood upon them. He was forever paying me that look of incredulity; that suspicious sidelong glance, inspecting me like a beady-eyed bird.

'You are scheming something,' he would say to me as I read or embroidered or dined, occasions when he had not the least cause to suspect any treachery whatsoever. 'You have the look of a schemer, just like your mother.' Such spiteful accusations would often reduce me to tears, tears of shame and fear.

'Oh Jack,' I would weep. 'How could you be so cruel, when you know I carry your child?'

Reader, how I detested this deception. I was certain he would find me out. I knew that the day and hour of the discovery of my hideous fraud would soon be upon me, and I quaked with dread at the thought of what would ensue. Heaven preserve me, I exclaimed to myself, when had I become so base and artful in my ways? Invariably, I would soon be reminded of the reason when the child inside me fluttered its feet.

During the month that followed the Roman feast, St John forbade me to associate with anyone who was not of the fair sex. Perhaps the greatest absurdity in all of this was that he had chosen Gertrude Mahon for my chaperone. Had he known what strategies were being hatched by the dear Bird of Paradise, he would have fairly extinguished himself in a fit of rage.

Wherever we went in company, she attended me, sporting one of her vast, colourful hats, so that 'we might draw the male eye', she whispered with a knowing look.

'Oh no, St John will murder me!' I breathed with genuine fear, but she only laughed.

In those last weeks before I was brought to bed, Mrs Mahon became my constant companion. When I was not receiving her visits and those of my other associates, Lady Lade, Miss Greenhill, Mrs Cuyler and Miss Ponsonby, she was escorting me out in her coach to call upon the *demi-monde* in their drawing rooms and to make excursions to all manner of places.

You are surprised by this, by what polite and regular lives we led? Why, what else do you think we might have done? You cannot believe that because a lady loses her reputation, she goes without society? Dear me, no. This is not the case at all. We amused ourselves no differently from any set of married ladies: eating ices and sweetmeats at the Pot and Pineapple, visiting Mrs Salmon's waxworks, Kensington Gardens, and all the shops between Mayfair and the Strand. To be sure, I had more friends once fallen than I might ever have hoped to make while virtuous.

On one occasion the Bird of Paradise suggested that we, and the gentle but flighty Caroline Ponsonby, pay a visit to Rackstrow's Museum on Fleet Street. There, an officious woman showed us through the jumble of rooms, in which were displayed an assortment of marvels, including a full skeleton of a whale, Egyptian mummies and a collection of anatomical waxworks made so lifelike that the vessels ran with blood. We gasped and exclaimed over these wonders, though the dim-witted Miss Ponsonby could not make sense of half of them.

'And this model should be of great interest to you, madam,' said our guide, addressing me. She then pushed us towards a waxwork specimen unlike any I had ever seen. There, before us, was a cross-sectioned woman, heavy with child. Every vein and sac, every organ imaginable, including those of the infant within her, was open to view. Our guide then pressed some hidden lever and, as if by a miracle, the object began to breathe. Air poured through her lungs and sent all the fluids coursing through both bodies, from mother to child and back again. To see the creature within me illustrated so plainly filled me equally with wonder and horror. Though, to be sure, what alarmed me most was not the spectacle of the inner workings, but the size of the infant. It appeared so large and its passage to the world so small that I was immediately overcome with a sense of terror. Mrs Mahon and Miss Ponsonby, noticing my distress, instantly removed me to a quiet chair.

Later, in Gertrude Mahon's coach, my friend comforted me.

'Dear Hetty,' she began, 'you need not fret, for every day women are brought to bed safely. Nature has formed us for birth. You must trust in her.'

I nodded, though her words did not entirely calm my anxieties.

'You are young and strong and will fare well.' She took my hand and gave it a squeeze of reassurance. 'Come now. Think no more of it. Let us go to Parson and Son and purchase something for your childbed linen.' She smiled. 'A bed gown or lace cap or some such item.'

Her tenderness was not lost on me, a girl who had never known a mother's affection. It must be said that, while I had been somewhat suspicious of Mrs Mahon at first, my heart began gradually to soften towards her. I saw that she was no mere schemer who simply wished to amuse herself by meddling in my life, but rather that her intentions were for my happiness.

'I have seen no small share of myself in you,' she confessed to me. 'When I eloped with that blackguard, Gilly Mahon, I knew nothing of the world. I was not much older than you when he abandoned me to my fate – and would that I could preserve you, or any young miss, from my youthful errors.' She sighed and shook her head. 'Take care to listen, not just to my words, but to all you hear. Intelligence, my dear,' she warned. 'Do not dismiss gossip, for you can learn all you need know about yourself from it.' And this, faithful reader, was why my wise friend was intent on introducing me to every one of her associates.

One morning, I was fortunate enough to be granted an introduction to an old, cherished companion of hers, Mrs Armistead, who was then the mistress of Mr Fox, the politician. 'She is not often in town, as she and Mr Fox live quite privately in the country.' She smirked. 'In truth, they are as good as married.'

Indeed, it was not until I had entered into this way of life that I had even known that my father's close political associate kept a mistress. The unkempt, loud Mr Fox had been grudgingly received by Lady Stavourley at Melmouth and at Berkeley Square. She did not find him charming, though I suspect her dislike of him stemmed more from his association with the notorious Elizabeth Armistead than it did from his unwashed linen. As you might imagine, I was a good deal curious to meet this lady, though prayed I should not encounter her keeper, who I feared might remember the tow-haired little Henrietta who ran about the rooms of Melmouth.

When we arrived, her dressing room was already filled with boisterous acquaintances. The Greenfinch sat in the corner with Spark upon her lap, her white muslin gown spread proudly around her. Mrs Armistead sat before her dressing table, looking as plump as a plum in a lavender summer gown. As her maid arranged her hair, she held forth, chatting and blowing gossip about the room with the ferocity of the four winds. My friend made an introduction and I curtseyed to my hostess as best as my bulge allowed.

'Ah,' said she, her face flushed with heat, 'you are Mr St John's catch. I have heard much about you.' She examined my belly and smiled. 'So, it is proved then, he has made good on his manhood at last.' The company tittered at this. 'But tell me, is it true what they say, that he is ruined?'

I looked at her and then at Gertrude Mahon. 'Why, why . . . I have not heard anything as to this.'

'They say he owes money to every man in town, that he has run through his income and Lord Bolingbroke will make him no more advances upon it.'

'I . . . have not . . . heard anything of this matter,' I responded uneasily.

Just then, Mrs Mahon laid a hand upon my arm. 'I have warned Miss Lightfoot that she must be prudent and cast her sights abroad for another keeper, but she pays no heed to me.'

'If St John cannot discharge his gaming debts, then what hope is there that he can keep you in French silk for much longer?' added Miss Greenhill from across the room.

'My dear,' said Mrs Armistead, straightening herself in her chair, 'one is never entirely safe. Why, although Mr Fox loves me to distraction, and I him, I have in my mind the names of two men who would come to my rescue should some calamity befall me. Of course, I should never be so foolish as to let him know that.' She smiled, flashing her sparkling violet eyes at me. 'You must consider your future.'

'Poor Lord Barrymore is broken-hearted on account of you,' scolded Mrs Mahon.

'But I am not to blame for that! St John found him out . . .'

'Mr St John believes you will abandon him as did your mother,' the Bird of Paradise replied. 'He keeps you locked away in a manner that is detrimental to your prospects, my dear.'

'Have you not heard? The *Morning Post* has called you the Fair Princess in the Tower!' sang out Miss Greenhill with a satisfied smirk.

'Why not fix your sights on one of Lord Barrymore's brothers?' offered Mrs Armistead. 'I hear that Mr Henry Barry is turning out as much of a rakehell as his lordship.'

'The crippled one? With the limp?' said Miss Greenhill, crunching her nose in disdain.

'A fine thing for you to say when Lord Sefton is a hunchback!' shot back Mrs Armistead.

'There are many others,' Gertrude Mahon interjected. 'We are to visit Ranelagh Gardens in a few days' time and I shall arrange to have St John distracted, so that we might take a turn around the grounds. One never knows who is to be met in such a place. It may be the making of you, my dear.'

So, gentle reader, you see quite clearly, it was not I who laid these stratagems, but those who could not possibly have known my inner thoughts. I must confess, there were times when I felt myself a leaf upon a fast-moving stream. I was forever pulled this way and that, dragged into eddies and floated into dark pools, where I never wished to go. To think I had once believed myself to be the mistress of my fate seemed to me at that moment preposterous. On my inside, an unborn child determined my life, and on my outside, it was St John. All around me were other forces, equally wilful. The words I had once read, Werther's liberty to roam, to love freely, Monsieur Rousseau's call to live from the heart: all seemed to me nonsense, absurdity. We were, none of us, unshackled. Even my dear, lost Allenham complained that his fate was no longer his own. Oh, thought I, sinking under the weight of these reflections, had I made any error in my life, it was to believe in the philosophy of men.

So, perhaps it was with some resignation to finding another protector that I permitted the Bird of Paradise to launch her scheme on the night of 12th August 1790; a date I recall very clearly indeed.

Over the months, I had carried both my secret and my child

remarkably well. Such was the case that by late July, when I might have rightfully entered my period of confinement leading to the birth, I did not appear so vast as to rouse suspicion. I had not worn my bulge as do many women, as if they carry Mr Lunardi's balloon beneath their skirts. Instead I bore a closer resemblance to those portraits of the Madonna, with a ripe but modest pear shape. I am ashamed to admit that it was this small mercy that enabled my deception to be such a successful one.

Although I had no true understanding of what the birth might hold, I knew it to be a hard and terrible course. I lay many nights unable to sleep for the heat and the discomfort, but also on account of my anxieties. I knew that the great falsehood was soon to come out of me, in one way or another. There were indeed so many things that plagued my mind: the pain, the chance that my life might end where my child's began. I feared, too, that my labour might set in when I least expected it. To be sure, I had my linens in place, and all the equipage for the arrival of the little stranger, but I had made no arrangements for a nurse. How was I to explain my need for one so early, when St John believed me but seven months gone? With his hot eyes upon me at every turn, I was too fearful to make more than a peep in his presence. All might be undone by a simple indiscreet word – and then where would I be? Condemned to give birth in the squalor of a lying-in hospital, or alone in a draughty garret? Left to bear down atop a hessian sack, with rats in place of a midwife and servants? Oh, the cursed thought of it! No, no, this would not be my fate. I had not come so far and endured so much to be thrown out at the critical time. And so I continued to hold my tongue and swallow my fears, fretting all the while that the child should come at a moment when I was furthest from my bed.

The pains began on the afternoon of the twelfth – the very same day that we were due to visit Ranelagh Gardens, and upon which Gertrude Mahon had proposed executing her plot. In those nine months, I had experienced so many strange sensations that at first I did not make much of the cramping along my back and middle. Had the feelings been accompanied by my usual sense of exhaustion, I might have begged to remain at home that night. Instead, I felt strangely bright and lively. My inexperience prevented me recognizing these to be the first twists and pangs of labour.

It was Mary, the housemaid, who first noticed that my face was drawn with discomfort as she assisted me into my lawn gown.

' Do I pull you too tightly, miss?' she enquired.

'No, the baby kicks,' I explained, rubbing my protrusion. But Mary, who was one of seven children, knew more of birth than I. She examined me sceptically as I moved slowly through the door of my dressing room and down the stairs to greet St John.

It was not until the coach was halfway through Hyde Park that I began to contemplate the possibility that my pains might be of a more serious nature. Although the evening was a clear and mild one, I suddenly found myself growing unusually warm, and asked St John to take down the window. This he did, and then began to eye me like a toad examining a gnat.

'Your face has gone quite red.'

'It is the heat,' I remarked, waving my fan before me.

'Why did you not request the window to be taken down earlier?'

'I did not suffer from the heat earlier,' I answered plainly. I could not comprehend the point of his enquiry and continued to gaze out at the dusk-lit landscape. 'Madam!' he snapped just then. 'Look at me when I address you.'

I turned my surprised gaze to him.

'To whom have you just sent a signal?'

'What?' I responded, with true confusion.

'Whom do you expect to see along this road? Some paramour of yours, I expect. You wish to signal to him that you are in my coach? Are you warning him to beware of me?'

'Why, that is quite absurd, sir,' I responded. 'A more ridiculous thing could not have been invented.'

I shut my eyes and steadied my resolve, for I knew I was about to be subjected to another of St John's interrogations.

'Do not mock me, you little minx. You are plotting something. Have I interrupted some scheme of yours?'

'Sir,' I breathed, with more than a hint of exasperation, 'I have been faithful to your affections and always showed you the utmost adoration and gratitude, and yet I am constantly subject to your suspicions. What more need I do to convince you that I am true, dear Jack?'

For once, my words seemed to silence him. He moved back against the seat, slightly shamefaced, and said nothing more until our arrival at Ranelagh.

With some awkwardness, I was handed out of the coach and into a scene of lantern-lit trees and distant music. Jig dancers and fiddlers gathered not far from a line of coaches, while a group of roistering sedan chairmen drank and sang along to the tunes. It was only then, when my feet touched the ground, that I felt the full force of the pain upon me. My face twisted in distress and I drew a large breath of air. The pangs were now much sharper than they had been earlier in the day. It was at that instant that I knew for certain my labour had begun. All the colour ran from my face as I prayed the infant would do me the courtesy of waiting until I arrived home. Perhaps, perhaps, I began to reason with myself, perhaps I might will it away. Bravely, I continued beside St John, slowly padding along, halting every so often to catch my breath. Truly, men can be such imbeciles. He had not even the sensibility to see how I suffered.

It was a great relief to me to come upon Mrs Mahon and Lord Beauchamp, who was one of several gentlemen who financed her whims. She had also the infamous Lady Grosvenor in her company, along with Colonel Porter, the Countess's *grand amour*. I do not know what she and the Bird of Paradise had devised between them, but upon greeting me, she gave me a strange, calculating smile.

Much to my annoyance, St John insisted that we stroll along the hedge-framed avenues before taking some refreshment. Knowing that this would cause me no end of discomfort, I regarded him with a pleading, flushed face.

'Dear madam,' said he, shaking his head ever so slightly, 'what objection have you to taking the air on such a fine evening as this? Certainly your condition might benefit from it.'

'Sir,' I began, 'I fear I am so heavy upon my feet this evening—' I broke off with a wince.

It was then Mrs Mahon bustled to my side and gently took my arm. I wore a pained expression, which I believe she mistook as a show of my disapproval for her plan.

'Dear little *chaton*, why are you forever crossing me? I ask for white and you insist on black. I wish to go right and you beg that we move left.' His sentiments were threaded with anger. St John tightened his lips, deliberating over his next words. A vague, cruel smile then moved across his mouth. 'A thought has plagued me greatly,' he began. 'It has played heavily upon my mind since the day you first appeared in my parlour. At the time, I was so overcome by your resemblance to my Kitty that I did not permit myself to pursue the question, but now, after I have seen the deceitfulness of my friends, I am filled with doubt once more.' St John inhaled deeply. 'Why did you introduce yourself to me as Miss Lightfoot and not Miss Ingerton, which surely was your given name?'

I confess, his enquiry knocked me utterly speechless. I had not expected such a vicious attack to be launched upon me – and here, in such a public space as this! To make matters worse, I was so in-experienced in the art of lying that I had never once considered this hole in my story. I had no explanation prepared. I could think of nothing to say. The man had caught me out entirely. Let this be a lesson to any who set out to deceive: think through your narrative, tie it as tightly as a sail, or it will eventually take you off course.

I felt Gertrude Mahon's fingers tighten upon my arm, as if she too had been startled by this question. I stared at St John in horror, my mouth agape.

'As our friend Mrs Mahon will affirm, whores change their names as frequently as they change their chemises. They often wear the surname of their current keeper – why, you could be known as Miss St John, should you ever choose to return to the streets . . .' said he, raising his eyebrow provocatively. 'But you were not a whore when you came to me, Hetty, were you? You were a virgin, and you stained my sheets – or so it appeared. So why, dear creature, why would you choose the name Lightfoot over the distinguished title of Ingerton?'

Now the Bird of Paradise was also staring at me, wishing to know the answer and wondering what I might say. I felt the dread, the panic growing in my breast, my hands beginning to tremble, when all at once I was felled by a great swell of pain.

'Oh!' I cried out, wrapping my hands around my belly. Indeed, the cramp along my back was so violent that it brought tears to my eyes. 'Oh!' I moaned again. 'Sir!'

'Dear God, man!' Mrs Mahon shot at him. 'See how your jealousy has disquieted her! Will she have no peace till you have caused her to miscarry? And this the child you have crowed about to all of London? For shame!' My friend placed her arm about me and kissed my cheek. 'With your leave, sir, I shall take this injured creature to where she may recover, unharmed.'

St John had not been expecting such a chastisement, and as we pulled away from him, Lady Grosvenor quickly took up his arm, which I believe had been their plan all along.

By the time Mrs Mahon directed me down a narrow avenue of cherry trees, I was fairly panting.

'How clever you are, Henrietta!' she squealed, taking both my hands in hers. My face was flushed red. 'I could not have contrived it better myself.'

I nodded, forcing a smile upon my face.

'But tell me, dear, *who* is the father of your child, for it cannot be St John, can it?' she asked, her eyes wide with the thrill of intrigue.

I could not respond. Indeed I would not respond, no matter how great the pain I was forced to suffer. Such a revelation would be the end of me. I drew in a long breath.

'There has been no one but St John.' I attempted to hold her gaze, but failed as another ache rippled through me.

'Henrietta? Are you quite all right?'

'No.' I moved my head. 'I fear I am not.'

'But surely, the child cannot be coming now . . .' She drew back to study me, her expression growing ever more suspicious. 'Are you quite certain?'

'I believe so, the pains have been quite severe for these past hours.'

'Little Miss Lightfoot,' said she with a wry smile. There was more than an ounce of admiration in her tone. 'Do not fret, my dear, I shall not reveal the truth.' Her arm was now about my back, her other hand clasping mine as she whispered into my ear. 'Now tell me, who is the father? Certainly not Barrymore . . . ?'

Just then I was subject to one of nature's great humiliations. When a woman begins her labour she relinquishes all control of her faculties. It is the child, the homunculus inside of her, who determines the workings of her body; from that moment she is merely the carriage, and the infant the driver. I was to learn this quite suddenly when, without warning, a sudden gush of water flowed from between my legs. It came with such force that it drenched my blue embroidered slippers, and even, I blush to say, splashed the hem of Mrs Mahon's skirts!

We both looked down at the damp ground beneath our feet. I was more mortified than words could express, but my companion rang out with laughter.

'Madam,' she exclaimed, 'I do believe you are in need of a midwife!'

Chapter 28

With the assistance of Mrs Mahon, I was taken from Ranelagh to a clapboard house just beyond its gates. It was a rambling old place, which looked to me quite disreputable, part inn and part lodging house, set far back from the road. It was the sort of establishment of which, until recently, I had no knowledge. The Venetians have a particular name for such places: *casini*, rooms to which couples might retreat for assignations; and in my day, houses such as this were to be found at the outskirts of most parks and pleasure gardens.

The proprietress, a Mrs Perrot, was an acquaintance of Mrs Mahon's, and upon seeing my condition, she calmly wiped her hands upon her apron and called for one of her maids to fetch the midwife. The other servants were then sent into a flurry, directed to bring the bedding, fresh water and rags. With the aid of both women, I was taken up the stair to a whitewashed room, where sat a large wooden-framed bed, a small table and two spindly chairs. Two candles and a lamp had been lit, which cast no more than a thin light around the space. I confess, upon seeing that place, I was filled with an indescribable terror, as if some voice had whispered inside my head that this cell was to be my death chamber.

Gertrude Mahon held my hand as we watched the servants lay Mrs Perrot's stained linens and wadding upon the mattress.

'You are not the first to be brought to bed in my house,' stated the proprietress as she examined the bed. 'But I shall charge you a shilling for the rooms on this floor which cannot be filled on account of your screaming,' she added coldly.

Once the bed was made up, I was stripped down to my chemise, which was already soiled with sweat and all manner of unpleasant fluids. Had the pains not been coming with such intensity, I might have felt a good deal bashful about this, but at that moment I was so stricken with discomfort and dread that I was well beyond regard for polite manners.

I do not mean to frighten those among my readers who have no knowledge of the childbed, the spinsters and young brides, nor do I wish to be indelicate, but birth is a most horrifying experience at the best of times. I was by no means prepared for it. The filth of child-bearing is beyond all reckoning: the vomiting, the purging of my waters and my bowels, oh and, dear God, at the end, the blood, how it poured forth from me, sinking deeply into the lumps of wadding upon the bed. The acrid stench of the lying-in chamber is disgusting, to be sure.

I lay upon my back, shuddering with agony for what felt like an eternity. The pains came, one wave breaking upon the other, each seemingly greater than the last.

'Where is my midwife?' I begged Gertrude Mahon, who had hold of my hand.

She stroked the hair from my brow and then began to blot it. 'She is not far, I should think. Not long now.'

I moaned and then began to quake.

'I fear it will come without her . . .' My voice was strained and harsh. 'Oh Lord, save me!' I cried out.

'Hetty, hush, child, hush.' She spoke in soft, calming tones. 'Nature will take her course.'

Heavens, I was grateful for her devotion to me that night. The feel of her gentle touch turned my frightened tears into ones of sadness. I wished at that moment that I might tell her of Allenham. My heart ached to confess what lay within it. Instead I shut my eyes and sobbed, allowing myself to remember his bright face, the squared features, the strong chin and clear eyes of shining blue. Did he know where I was? That I lay here, perhaps breathing my last so I might bear his child? 'Where are you?' I asked, again and again, which only caused my tears to flow more copiously. At last, fearing that I should utter his name, I bit down heavily upon my lip.

The night was passing and neither the midwife nor the child had yet appeared. Still, my birth pangs continued, brutally, racking my back as if they might break it. I had been bearing down for hours, just as Mrs Mahon had instructed, attempting with great fury to push the infant from me, but to no avail. It remained stuck fast. I was growing weary, shivering with distress while sweating from the heat.

'I shall die . . .' I groaned to Mrs Mahon. 'I shall die here . . .'

Just then there was a great commotion in the corridor and the midwife came through the door. She, a tall, manly woman, entered with a young girl apprentice, who looked on the scene with mild horror. The room was so gloomily lit that, although they brought with them a lantern, my tired eyes could scarcely make them out.

'You will forgive me, miss,' the woman addressed me, 'for Mrs Reid was brought to bed of a girl this evening and it is a fair walk hence from World's End.'

She swung her light over me and it was then I noticed her fingernails, still blackened with Mrs Reid's birthing blood. I gazed over at my friend, my expression imploring her to observe the woman's unclean hands, but Gertrude Mahon just smiled and stroked my head.

'All will be well, dear, if you do as she bids you.'

The midwife went between my knees and pushed her hand into my cavity. By God, how I howled! The agony of it! The sense that I was soon to die gripped me so fiercely that I could think of nothing else. I was tortured and torn, and was to be slowly disembowelled by the writhing knot inside of me. I believed then that this woman intended to wrench apart my womb. I imagined my innards slithering out, like those of a steaming pig hanging in a butcher's yard.

'The infant is turned,' she announced, her hand still within me. I felt the chill wetness of my blood all about.

As my eyes fluttered open and shut, my body was taken with spasms. 'So here it will end,' I heard my voice from within my head. 'Allenham, my dear, dear George,' I called to him, willing him one final time to my side. I cleared a path for him through the heavens, it lay open and waiting, but he did not come. My vitality was burning away. I was bereft of strength, and after treading such a long and harrowing course, had begun to consider that death might be a comfortable bed in which to lie.

A just punishment. A divine retribution for your sins, I heard. I knew not where these words came from, though in my confusion I guessed them to be my own.

A cloud settled upon my senses so that all noises became no more than a humming din and all sights no more than mere outlines. The lantern hung over me, like a pole star. Against its light, I strained to focus my vision upon the circle of women gathered around me. Beside the midwife in her frilled cap stood her youthful apprentice. To my right appeared Mrs Mahon, her face now cast in an anxious expression. Soon there was another figure, whose form appeared quite hazy. She moved along either side of me, shifting her position to gain a better view perhaps. I took her to be some servant of the house, though I knew not what her purpose there might be. It was only when she stood beside the lantern that I saw her face.

'You will never keep him!' Her mouth framed the words, though no discernible sounds came from it.

Her unexpected appearance put a burst of breath back into my lungs 'Cathy!' I wailed in horror.

'It is nearly at its end, madam,' said the midwife, 'the head is almost through.'

I grunted and thrashed in a final thrust of pain as I felt my child being tugged loose of me.

And then, all at once, he came free.

I saw before me the bloodied, slime-covered form of my son, dangled by the ankles as if he were a plucked goose. The midwife tapped upon his back several times before his tiny mouth parted and issued forth a long, shrill wail.

'A boy!' she cried.

'A boy!' echoed Gertrude Mahon.

But at that moment, I hardly heard their news. I was too stunned, too frightened to speak, until I knew for certain that she and her shadows had gone.

Chapter 29

George Allen St John. The names were my choice. I had bestowed them upon him as soon as he was laid into my arms. The infant's 'father' was at that time yet to be located. When I was taken into her house, Mrs Perrot had sent two of her servants to trawl the avenues of Ranelagh. Eventually, St John was found at his home, popping with rage in the belief that I had run off with the help of Gertrude Mahon. When it was explained to him that, in fact, I had been brought to bed of a son, *his son*, at a house near Ranelagh, he was utterly dumbfounded. At four o'clock in the morning, he raced to my bedside and, upon seeing me with the infant, fell to his knees in a fit of tears. At that moment I understood that it would not have mattered what I called the boy. Why, I might have named him George FitzAllenham, and St John would have neither raised an objection nor questioned my decision. He was in raptures. Indeed, I have never seen a man so entirely subdued by a child. When Mrs Mahon explained to him that an attempted robbery in the gardens had startled me into an early labour, St John seemed entirely uninterested. He cared only that his son was well and healthy.

As you might have gathered from my story, the birth had brought me very close to death, so that it was nearly three days before I was fit enough to return to Park Street. In that time, a proper nurse had been located for Georgie, who squawked and cooed and drank a good deal of milk. It seemed an odd thing to me to hand over my child to another woman's bosom, when my urge was to clutch him to mine, but Mrs Mahon assured me that it was for the best, as I would be likely to drive St John away if I always had an infant hanging from my breast.

'Sentimentality will do you no favours, my dear,' she counselled me as I sat abed adorned in my new linens and lace cap. Sweet, warm Georgie gurgled against me. Her words caused me to frown.

Noting my expression, she began to shake her head and then rose from her seat in order to shut my bedchamber door. 'Now hear me, Henrietta,' she began, her voice a low whisper, 'if you wish any command of your life, you must not permit your heart to rule your head. You have been exceptionally foolish in your devotion to St John and never once heeded my advice. Now you have only him on whom to rely, so take care not to drive him away.'

For the first time ever, I glared at Mrs Mahon and then dismissed her with a laugh. It was ungrateful and impertinent behaviour, but I was growing weary of her designs for me. At eighteen, I believed I knew best. I was now a mother and no one should tell me how to mind my life and that of my child.

'St John adores Georgie and would want only what is best for him.'

'And what is best for your son, madam, is that St John remains fore-most in your affections – so it is true for all men! The moment you refuse St John's advances in order to coddle your child, to suckle him, to stanch his tears, is the very instant you have lost your keeper, and all your peace and comfort. He will find another to take your place. Remember this, Hetty: you are not a wife. He has no duty to you. You are indeed blessed that St John adores little George, but to play wet nurse to your own infant is an indulgence that a woman of your position cannot well afford.'

Gertrude Mahon's advice was correct, of course. Many years later, I found myself repeating her words to other young ladies who trod a path similar to mine. You see, she was that rare thing among the *demi-monde*, which is to say a true friend. She wished the best for me, as might a mother or an elder sister, but I was still too inexperienced to appreciate her wisdom. Safe in the knowledge that St John loved Georgie, I saw only the advantages to be gained in the immediate present.

Long before Georgie's appearance, St John had ordered the conversion of several rooms in the attic for the purpose of creating a nursery. He took great pleasure in this and in commissioning the furniture: acquiring the cot and tallboys and a nursing chair. During my period of lying-in, the house on Park Street was a scene of familial bliss. My keeper hovered frequently beside the infant's cot, begging like a young girl for permission to lift the boy. His face beamed with wonder as he admired the child's wide blue eyes and dark patch of hair. At first, I must confess that Georgie's appearance caused me some concern, for there was a good deal of Allenham imprinted upon him, but doting adults see only what they wish to in a child's features; and where I recognized my beloved, St John recognized only himself.

During that month, visitors bearing well wishes came and went regularly. To be sure, I drank so much caudle that by mid-September I could scarcely tolerate the sickly, spiced taste of it. It was offered along with seed cake to all of my lady callers, each of whom wished to admire and coo over the head of my angelic Georgie.

At first I found it curious that Lady Lade, who had the least feminine charms of any woman of my acquaintance, seemed most possessed by the little infant. She, more than any of my companions, fussed and bustled about him, rocking him in her arms while mimicking his yawns and burbles. This attention from the swaggering woman, who seemed more devoted to horses and swearing, surprised me immensely.

'Ho,' she exclaimed as she attempted to silence his wails with some gentle bouncing, 'he has a pair of lusty lungs, just like my Jemima.'

I turned to her with a puzzled expression.

'Why, in all these months I have never once heard your ladyship mention a daughter.'

'I had two. And a son. He is in the army, I know not where.'

The room, in which sat Mrs Mahon, Miss Greenhill and Miss Caroline Ponsonby, fell suddenly quiet.

'And they are Sir John's children?' I enquired with some hesitation. The others watched me closely, knowing that I had ventured on to precarious ground.

'Of course not,' she snapped, and then laughed. 'Too much damned pox in my veins to bear him a child. I bore the others when I was young. The boy, Billy, was named after his father. Raised by his relations in

Ireland. The girls, twins, were by that devil John Rann, who had my maidenhead when I was fourteen. One is married to a goldsmith, and Jemima is in St Marylebone's churchyard.'

'Oh,' said I, meekly, ashamed to have raised the matter, 'how unfortunate.'

'No,' came her quick reply. 'Children come and go, that is the way of things. You think I desired those three? Why, I could not get them out of me! I took rue and ergot and pennyroyal. I had my cold baths. Still they stayed fixed. The others were got rid of with more ease.'

I attempted to disguise my shock at her revelation, though I am not certain I was so successful.

'Hooper's Female Pills. They are the best for clearing the womb, if you swallow the entire box at once,' announced Miss Ponsonby with an air of authority.

'Oh no, dear,' began Gertrude Mahon, 'if you take too many of those your teeth will turn black and fall out. Blatchford's elixir is unrivalled in its effectiveness.'

'I have used it and it did not work,' pouted Miss Greenhill.

'But you miscarried,' added Mrs Mahon.

'Yes . . . but I believe that was on account of a poisoned oyster, not Dr Blatchford's mixture.'

'Pah! Oysters!' cried Lady Lade, rumpling her nose in disgust. 'The best use for one of them is to push it up your cunny!' Her quip caused the company to fall about laughing.

'I once moulded some wax into a flat plug and put it in me,' added Miss Ponsonby in her high, nasal voice.

'Did it work?' asked the Greenfinch.

'For one or two attempts, I believe it did, but the sponge and vinegar is best, for the wax came loose and does not take up the seed as does a sponge.'

'I have become very clever at preventing Lord Sefton spending his seed in me, for I pull him out just at his moment of bliss.'

'And he tolerates it?' asked Mrs Mahon.

'Not always, but I use a douche of lime water if he does, to great effect,' she simpered.

'Well,' said Miss Ponsonby, 'he should be grateful you manage your-self so prudently, for it is far more difficult to be rid of the ones that are born . . .'

Just then, Georgie began to scream loudly. I rose and went to him directly, taking him from Lady Lade's hands.

'I do believe he heard you . . .' said I with an uneasy laugh.

It was not as if I had never been privy to such conversation before, for female matters are forever a topic of discussion among the fallen sisterhood, but the coldness of the exchange struck me especially hard. Prior to my life in London, I would never have imagined that the birth of a child would not be a welcomed event, and had foolishly taken for granted that St John would treat Georgie with such benevolence. Why, Mrs Mahon and Lady Lade had entertained me throughout my pregnancy with terrifying tales of infants who, on the orders of their fathers, disappeared into laundry baskets and rivers, never to be seen again.

But I had nothing to fear. St John was the most doting of fathers. He never tired of fondling his son – scarcely a day went by when he did not bring the boy out to be dandled over his card table and toasted by his raucous companions. Indeed, I believed that my keeper desired nothing more than to pass his entire life, like me, staring down at Georgie as he slumbered and flexed his wee fingers. What happy days were these, thought I, in a type of blind delirium. There seemed no more perfect paradise than the tranquil nursery where I cradled my boy and admired the yellowing leaves from the high attic windows. To be sure, I had not felt such contentment since Allenham closed the door of Orchard Cottage behind him. But dear Gertrude Mahon was correct in her assessment of me: I was desperately foolish. I was a ninny, a giddy-brained little girl. I thought I had seen enough of the world to know my own mind, when I had hardly done more than glimpse it.

Had I listened to her, had I been reasonable, I might have spared myself a great deal of disappointment and pain when St John announced his intentions to me. As it was, it came quite unexpectedly one morning as we enjoyed breakfast.

'It is time Georgie should be sent out to nurse,' he stated, as he sucked at his cup of tea.

'Sent out?' I echoed.

'Yes, it is time. For the child's own good. A house such as mine, full of dissolutes and whores, is no place for him. And the air is better elsewhere.'

'But, surely the nurse we have . . .'

'No, Hetty, you shall not contradict me. Gertrude Mahon said you would object and I must not permit you to sway me on this. You do not know as well as she about these matters.'

'Gertrude Mahon!' I blurted, feeling utterly betrayed that my friend should have advised on such a cruel course of action.

'Do not be so quick to accuse, *chaton*. She merely convinced me of my own sentiments,' said he, straightening himself in his chair. 'I am far too sensitive a father and I shall weaken my child through my own sentimentality. Georgie is to go to a nurse in Primrose Hill tomorrow. Mrs Mahon has been good enough to fix it for you. She knows what is best, Hetty, where you do not.' Then he sent me a disapproving look. 'And she warned me to prepare for your protests.'

At that pronouncement, I exploded into a shower of tears and ran from the table. How my friend had betrayed me! She understood that Georgie's removal would break my heart, and yet she conspired to have it done. Never could there have been a more unforgivable deed than this!

'Henrietta . . . Henrietta!' I heard St John calling, but it was no use. He would never have convinced me of the correctness of this plan, nor of the good intentions of the friend who had pushed a dagger into my maternal breast. Naturally, it was only after the deed had been done that I came to see the merit in it, and to comprehend the wisdom of her experience.

I wept the entire distance from Mayfair to Primrose Hill, which lay across tawny autumnal pastureland a few miles to the north of London. I clutched Georgie to me, my sobbing causing him to accompany me in my sorrowful song of parting and sadness. By the time we arrived, I had soaked his blankets and linen with my tears.

It was not such a terrible place, the clean, whitewashed cottage to which he was sent. Mrs Brown was a full-bodied woman of no more than twenty-six, with two children and an infant of her own. Her face was ruddy with health, as were the cheeks of her girl and boy. 'The older ones have taken the inoculation,' she assured me, rubbing their tow heads, 'so there will be no smallpox here. No, we are a healthful house-hold,' she boasted, before adding that no one ever went hungry, for in addition to her own two breasts, they owned 'two fine cows as well'.

I suppose this went some way towards easing my distress, but it failed to cure it altogether.

'Mrs Brown has nursed two sons of the Duke of Portland,' St John said upon our return, attempting to comfort me, but I said nothing. Tears were all I could produce.

I wished myself dead in the days following our visit to Mrs Brown. I lay in bed, entertaining all manner of thoughts. I imagined that my boy should be overlaid, that one of the nurse's stupid children would drop Georgie or one of the cows might kick him just when he was learning to toddle about on two feet. Oh, I could not count how many possible fates awaited him! And when I had finished enumerating those, I wept over Allenham, that the only remembrance I had of my true love had now been stripped from me. When I had embraced Georgie in my arms it was as if I had held his father as well. 'Dear God, where is he?' I sobbed. 'When in heaven will he return to me? Surely, he must know,' I told myself. 'He must know I have had his son.'

To be sure, I truly indulged in my melancholia upon this occasion. I wallowed in my depressed spirits, behaving much as I had observed Lady Stavourley in her times of unhappiness. I refused to dress and believed myself ill. Foolishly, I even dared to turn St John from my bed, prompting him to think me hysterical.

'Hysterical women require a visit from the surgeon to cure them of their distemper,' he threatened me with a wagging finger. So, the following day, the surgeon arrived to cup me. As this had no effect, in a rash final attempt to revive me, he sent word to the Bird of Paradise.

As I had lain in bed, Mary entered and announced that Mrs Mahon was below, wishing to call upon me. The mention of her name drew such hot indignation from my heart that I sat up straight.

'I shall not see her!' I declared. 'Tell her that I am not at home to a Judas, nor shall I ever be again!' With that, I fell back upon my pillow in a torrent of tears.

And this, dear reader, was how I repaid that woman's kindness to me.

After that disheartening episode, I can only say that I am grateful to Fortune for interceding on my behalf. With hindsight, I came to appreciate how the loss of Georgie spared me from complacency. It was not my destiny to remain at Park Street; indeed I had almost forgotten what were my intentions when I had arrived at this place. I was only reminded of them again when Lucy Johnson appeared in my dressing room.

I have heard it said that when a great thing departs one's life, the space is soon occupied by the arrival of something of equal importance. While I cannot say that Lucy Johnson filled the emptiness left by my son, her presence did significantly alter the course of events. And to think I very nearly sent her away.

Nearly a fortnight had passed since I had parted with my Georgie and St John wished that I should leave it a few days more before I paid him the first of what would become my thrice-weekly visits. Need I say that this news did not have an uplifting effect upon my spirits? Although I now no longer lolled about in my bed, I did little more than stare at the rain-splashed windows and imagine my son's hungry cries. My misery had begun to offer me the sort of comfort that a drunkard finds in his bottle of brandy; I wished to be alone with it, to savour its stupefying effects, so when Mary rapped upon the door with a message I had no wish to hear it.

'Madam,' she whispered, poking her head round the door, 'there is a girl come to speak with you.'

'I know no girls who would wish to speak with me.'

'She insists you will know her.'

'What is her name?' I asked, attempting to muster the thinnest of interest.

'Lucy Johnson, madam.'

'I know no one by that name.'

'She says she is of number five Arlington Street.'

At first I did not think I heard Mary correctly, or perhaps that I had imagined she spoke the address.

'Arlington Street? Number five?'

'Yes, madam.'

Suddenly, I found my heart in my throat.

'Well, well, do show her in, Mary,' said I in a trembling voice, arranging myself upon the sofa and nervously smoothing my skirts.

After a minute or so, Mary reappeared alongside a young woman in a brown woollen cape, a starched white apron peeking from beneath it. She hardly dared look at me as she folded herself into a polite curtsey.

I instantly recognized her as the maid I had spied listening to me plead with Allenham's butler. Her auburn hair and freckled features made her unmistakable. I dismissed Mary and waited until the door shut fast behind her.

'Lucy Johnson, of number five Arlington Street?'

She curtseyed again. 'Yes, madam.'

I swallowed anxiously. 'Do you come with a message?'

Lucy Johnson corrected her posture. 'No, madam, I come begging a place in your household.'

I sighed inwardly at this announcement, but remained intrigued by her presence.

'But you have a place in Lord Allenham's household.'

'Not beyond this week, madam. The house is to be closed up. His lordship's cousins, Sir Folbert and Lady Jervas, who had rented it earlier in the year, have now gone abroad. I have been told I must find another place, but I have only a reference from the butler, not his lordship or his cousins, and that does not go far for securing another place, not as far as a letter from a person of breeding, madam.'

'The house is to be closed up?' That was the only information I had correctly taken in. 'By whose orders? Where is his lordship? Have you received word that he will not return?' I heard the pitch of my voice begin to rise, and immediately and rather ashamedly attempted to compose myself.

Of course, Lucy knew too well that this information should pique me.

'I was told his lordship is to be gone for some time.'

My face fell, like a banner stripped of the breeze. I looked down at my lap, unable to think what to ask next. This news had pricked the small bubble of hope that I had managed to carry within me over the past months. Lucy stood patiently, observing my distress.

'I . . . I saw you, madam, come to the house, begging to see his lordship,' she began, her tone now more tentative and confessional. 'I said to myself, this lady has some business with Lord Allenham. I read the message you sent round by one of your servants. I know I ought not to have . . . but I remembered your address . . . I remembered it, thinking there might be a time when I am in need and she is in need and I can give her something she would want . . .'

At that I looked up and locked my eyes upon her.

'Do you wish to find his lordship, madam?'

I continued to stare at her, my mouth parted in disbelief.

'I can tell you where you might find him, but first, madam, I ask for a place in your household.' She dropped another deep, obeisant curtsey, knowing all too well the boldness of her proposition.

I rose unsteadily to my feet, my face and neck flushed with heat.

'Yes,' I whispered. 'Yes, yes, please. You shall have a place,' said I, between frantic breaths. 'Please . . . please sit, Miss Johnson,' I stammered, my eyes roving the room while I decided upon my course of action. By God, I would not permit this girl to leave St John's house without disgorging her information. 'I must first make an enquiry,' said I, reaching for the door. I had to find St John immediately.

I rushed down the stairs in search of my keeper, and found him in his study, hard at work on a play he was devising, *Icarus Aflame*.

'Sir,' I said, startling him from his pen. He took in my flustered expression with a puzzled look.

'I have in my dressing room a girl who comes to me for a position . . . as a lady's maid. You know I am in need of one, sir, for while Mary is diligent, she knows nothing of dressing me properly and I am always scolding her. I should like very much to hire her. Oh Jack, it would make me so happy to have the company . . . with Georgie now gone . . .'

'Say no more, *chaton*.' He dismissed me, waving his hand. 'Do as you will.'

'Bless you, dear Jack. Bless you,' I thanked him with a smile more of relief than gratitude. I turned on my heel – no, rather I spun on my heel to leave, when his voice halted me.

'Who sends her?'

I looked back at him.

'Which house does she come from? I should not like a thief under my roof.'

'Lord Kerry,' I lied, hardly drawing a breath to do so. 'Who you know to be a relation of Mrs Mahon's. The girl was employed by a cousin of his . . . who has lately gone abroad.'

There was a pause.

'Very well.'

I flew up the stairs to my dressing room, fearing for a moment she might have abandoned me, fretting that she would disappear along with her most precious secret, but she remained where I had left her, with no evidence that she had slipped one of my patch boxes or silver-topped bottles into her pocket either. She gazed at me with a hopeful smile.

'I should like to take you into my service as my maid – from today.'

'Oh thank you, madam.' Lucy beamed as she bobbed. 'I am ever so grateful. I shall serve you well.'

Then, sobering herself, she raised her head and with a proud look stated plainly, 'Lord Allenham is in Paris.'

Chapter 30

You might be asking how it was that I could remain in St John's house for a moment more, now that I knew where my Heart of Hearts resided. Why did I not upon that very day retrieve my son from the teats of Mrs Brown and make post-haste for Dover? Well, think on the matter, dear reader. Such things are never as simple as that. Journeys require a good deal of preparation, and a vast sum of money. I had neither anticipated the receipt of this information nor hidden away the cost for such a voyage. I could no more spring myself free than could a prisoner unlock his own shackles. But this is not say that I did not react swiftly to this news. Ah no, the revelation of my beloved's whereabouts altered everything.

By this point in my life, I knew very well the danger of betraying the inner workings of my mind to St John, and so it was necessary for me to remain as calm and easy as I had been before this turn of events. While I worked hard at maintaining a composed outward demeanour, the inside of my head sparked and raged with the fury of a foundry. My heart raced as I lay beside St John that night. Sleep would not come to me and, in a torment, I rolled from my bed to collect my thoughts elsewhere. For a spell, I paced the boards of my dressing room, but, fearing that the creaking of my steps would rouse my keeper, I soon fled downstairs to continue my exercise in the parlour.

I sat myself upon the sofa, the very seat where my first interview with St John had taken place, and there I found my answer. It was as if she had been waiting for me: my mamma, gazing down from her portrait.

The room had been entirely dark, but for the sparse illumination provided by the night sky. Through this cast of starlight, the white paint Mr Reynolds had used in rendering my mother's pearls glowed against the blackness. 'Here are the means for your flight,' she said to me, through her silent, dreamy smile. 'These are my legacy to you.'

I could not begin to calculate their worth, nor had it ever occurred to me to do so. I had not a mind as mercenary as some of my acquaintance, who knew the value of their jewels down to the ha'penny, but I guessed that these items, along with several other brooches, necklaces and eardrops that St John had given to me would amply purchase my passage to Paris. My pulse quickened at the thought of how I might do it. I would flee to Dover by post chaise before boarding a packet ship to Calais. From there, I had heard there was the diligence which travelled the route from the port to the French capital. I would retrieve my son, and with him in my arms, I would slip away under cover of darkness. Of course, I knew not what to expect from a voyage to the continent, but having undertaken two journeys on my own initiative already, I believed myself capable of adding a third to that list. By Jove, so long as I knew that Allenham could be found at the end of my travels, I should crawl the distance to find him upon my very knees!

I believe Lucy had some inkling of my thoughts before I had so much as mentioned my plan to her. I wished not to be hasty in my judgements, not to make the impetuous mistake of thinking her trustworthy when she had yet to prove herself to me. Mrs Mahon had scolded me for my rash, thoughtless behaviour and I wished to demonstrate, if only to myself, that she had been wrong in her estimation of me. Oh, but I positively burst to execute my scheme – and I required Lucy's collusion so that it might work. Alas, my eagerness consumed me and, in the end, I allowed no more than four days to pass before I revealed my hand to her.

When I rang for her on that day, I made certain to shut and lock all the doors to my apartments behind her. Then I put myself upon the sofa and beckoned her to come and sit close beside me, which she did with hesitance and an uneasy expression.

'I shall be requiring you for a very important task.' I spoke in hardly more than a whisper. 'I am in need of money and shall be dispatching you to the pawnbroker to sell some of my possessions.'

Lucy nodded.

'Mr St John is to know nothing of this. Do you understand?'

'Yes, madam.'

'Let no one among the staff guess at your actions either, for if you are found out we shall both be undone.'

She regarded me with watery, dog-like eyes.

I then went to my rosewood box of jewels, the casket that had once belonged to my mother, and unlocked it. From it, I removed the flat case that contained the collar of pearls and the two large earrings, and committed it into Lucy's hands.

'Bring this to Dubois, the pawnbroker on Piccadilly, near the church of St James. Mr St John is to dine with Lord Charles Spencer and his wife this evening, an occasion to which I have not been invited. Wait until he departs before you set out. Tell Mr Dubois that your lady is in need of funds and hopes to fetch a good price for the jewels, but do not sell it to him until you have told me what sum he has offered. That is all for the moment,' said I, dismissing her.

She curtseyed.

'And Lucy,' I whispered to her before she quit the room, 'make certain to hide it well beneath your cloak.'

I then sent away my accomplice with her pocketful of treasure – and waited.

It must be said in her defence that I, too, believed St John had departed. Like Lucy, I, too, had seen the coach before the steps of the house and then heard it pull away. What neither of us knew was that it had left without its passenger. The coachman noticed that a horse had thrown a shoe and so the entire apparatus was made to return to the mews. St John had been standing in the window, idling away the time, awaiting his driver's return, when he observed Lucy steal away, concealing what appeared to be an object beneath her cloak. He sprang as quickly as a hawk upon a vole and, within an instant, had sent his valet barrelling down the road after her. A terrible scene then followed in the hall, and it was the racket produced by this that alerted me to the failure of my plan.

I flew down the stairs and there found the housekeeper, St John's valet and my protector encircling my poor, dear Lucy like a gang of villains. St John had retrieved the box, which he now held in his hand.

'Oh dearest Jack,' I cried. 'She is not to blame! She speaks the truth!'

They turned their heads, surprised to hear me plead my maid's case.

'I have found her attempting to steal your jewels, madam,' St John shot.

'No, dearest angel,' I panted, 'I gave them to her . . .'

'Your mother's jewels, Henrietta!' stormed my keeper, redirecting his ire towards me. 'What? What sort of deception is this? Are you in want of money? How can that be, madam, when you hardly approach the gaming tables? What are you in need of that I have failed to provide?'

Oh, my mind raced like a Derby champion.

'I wished to buy some trinkets for my boy, perhaps a silver rattle . . . or . . . or a teething coral.'

St John eyed me in that sidelong manner I feared. He breathed slowly, his nostrils flaring as he considered my tale.

'You wished merely to buy the boy a trinket, you say?'

'Yes, sir.'

'But which boy?'

I squinted at him, not quite comprehending his meaning.

'Which *boy*, madam?'

'Why . . . your . . . your boy, Jack,' said I, meekly.

He shook his head. 'No, that is a falsehood. My son has no need for silver and coral gewgaws. He has enough at his disposal. I see to it that he wants for nothing.' He returned his searing eye to me. 'What were you after, madam?'

'I have told you, Jack.'

Each of the party stood in silence, their gazes nailed to me.

'You wish to buy the boy a trinket!' He sniffed out a laugh. 'I would wager the boy you wish to ply with a gift would far prefer a pair of gloves . . . perhaps a horsewhip? Or perhaps, even, a watch?'

'No, sir,' said I sternly. 'You are quite mistaken on that account.'

'You, madam, are the most artful, deceitful liar that ever wore shoes, and this time, I shall prove it!' And with that St John dashed up the stairs to my dressing room.

Dear Lord, I had no notion of what his intentions were when he arrived at my dressing-room door. His face was a hideous mask of fury; his fists were clenched with rage.

I ran behind him, with Lucy at my train.

'Jack!' I cried. 'Jack, why do you persecute me so? I have done nothing to merit this!'

He pushed open my door and stood at the centre of the room, his eyes scanning it for some unknown object.

'Madam, I would have the key to your jewel box. And yours as well, hussy,' he said to Lucy, holding out his hand. After we had relinquished them, he went straight to the rosewood box.

'If I find any item in here which is not of my giving, if I find any gift from a gentleman not me, I shall send you from my house directly!'

He was so brutish, his temper so foul, that I began to grow quite terrified, though I had no cause. Of this invented crime, I was entirely innocent. Still, his shaking hands unlocked the casket and tore through the contents. He pulled from it all of his earrings, all of his hair slides, the two modish filigree necklaces that had been given to me, the emerald brooch, the brooch made of brilliants and every other present besides, and yet he failed to uncover any proof of my infidelity. But it did not end there. Unsatisfied with his findings, he then went to my dressing table and lifted every lid. He emptied a glass jar of marchale powder, and another of pomade. He forced Lucy, who now was sobbing audibly, to unlock every door of my clothes press, every cabinet and every drawer of the tallboy. He opened my escritoire and ran his hand through it.

When he had completed his examination, he drew a long, angry breath and glared at me.

'Do not think you can hide so much as a pin from me, madam. I will discover all your secrets. You are a whore, and I have learned that whores are not to be trusted, no matter how sweet their dispositions.' He then slipped the two keys belonging to my jewel box into his waistcoat pocket. 'From henceforth, I shall be the master of these,' he announced and, with a nod, departed.

It was that incident, dear reader, which caused me to consider quite carefully my future. St John had confiscated my jewels, thereby robbing me of the means of funding my escape. This in itself was a terrible hindrance, but worse still, the discovery of my plot to sell my mother's pearls had served to reawaken his tyrannical jealousy, which Georgie's birth had temporarily conquered. I should never again be free of his gaze, and if he never permitted me a moment's peace, I should never be at liberty to plan my flight. I had no more than a handful of pennies at my disposal, and while he observed me, I was not even free to sell my clothing or trinkets. Should an item be missed, he was certain to question me as to its whereabouts. I knew then that to flee this prison would be impossible.

Friends, had this been nine months earlier, I might have collapsed upon my floor into a sobbing heap of silks and chiffons, but in the passing of that time, my character had been altered. I had seen much and gained no small share of wisdom. Among the many lessons I learned was that it was far better to meditate upon a problem than to fall into hysterics on account of it. Allenham had once remarked upon the strength of my mind. Was it not better to make use of that sharp tool, rather than to dull it with despair and weeping? This is not to say I did not shed a tear or two, but I soon blotted them away and applied myself with great determination to resolving my dilemma.

You may think me a radical, but I have always been of the mind that womankind is rendered helpless by her dependency upon men. We require husbands, fathers, sons and brothers to sign our documents and to speak for us. Why, I had no bank account, no assets, no protection from the law. Even today, in this modern era of steam power and gas lighting, I still require a man to defend my interests. Imagine me then, in my youth, without a father or brother to protect me, and my son too young by far to speak for his mother's cares. At St John's mercy, I was no better than a rabbit in a trap, and the more I contemplated my predicament, the louder I began to hear Gertrude Mahon's warnings in my head. I soon came to understand too well her insistence that I have in mind a number of possible admirers into whose guardianship I might throw myself, should circumstances dictate. What a fool I felt.

'I know not what to do,' I confided to Lucy the following day. 'I must take my leave of this place,' I said to her in an agitated whisper.

I believe Lucy understood my meaning directly. She would not confess to it at first, for fear of seeming impertinent. She knew her role, and my association with Lord Allenham was no business of hers. But, to be sure, my maid was no dullard. Her impish smile and darting hazel eyes betrayed the quick wit of an urchin. I suspect she had knitted together the strands of my story well before I drew her into my confidence.

At first she was shy of offering me advice, but then, when she saw my eyes imploring her, she laid down her darning.

'Might you flee to someone, madam?' she asked timidly.

'No,' I remarked with sadness, 'I am quite alone in the world, Lucy.'

'Have you no friends who might take you in?'

'No one.' I thought at once of Mrs Mahon and closed my eyes in shame. 'No one who would not betray me to Mr St John. And how might you pack my belongings? How might I prepare to flee without his notice? I could not very well abandon this place with only the clothes upon my back. What should I live upon? Even the kindest of hostesses would not pay for my maintenance.' I had begun to wring my hands in distress.

'Then, madam, if I may be so bold . . . you must find yourself another gentleman.' Lucy did not wish to meet my gaze as she offered her suggestion.

'But I do not wish to find another gentleman!' I inhaled sharply. 'I wish only to fly to Paris – at once.' And there, if she had not guessed it already, I confessed to her the truth of my situation.

Lucy did not respond for some time to my revelation. Instead she turned over the stocking she mended.

'Madam, if you are clever . . . and willing . . . there are ways in which . . .' She stopped and shook her head.

'Continue,' I urged her.

'Begging your pardon, madam, it is to your credit, but I do not think you have enough of the vixen in you to attempt such a thing as I was to propose.'

'Tell me, girl,' I pressed.

'I had once a mistress, a noblewoman who had ruined her reputation with a captain, and when she found him unfaithful to her, she wished to part with him. He would not have it, and so she permitted another spark to make love to her, and when the captain found them together, he called the other gentleman out to the Powder Mills on Hounslow Heath to fight for her. Her gentleman wounded the captain, though not fatally, but as he had lost the challenge, the captain was made to give her up. I boxed up all her apparel and trinkets, which were then sent to her new abode.' All at once Lucy began to giggle and hid her face behind her hand.

'What?' I demanded. 'What then?'

'Oh madam,' she gasped, composing herself, 'begging your pardon ... My mistress, she was a sly one, for no sooner had she quit the captain's house for her new gentleman's lodgings than she eloped with a musician! She sold all the clothes and jewels she acquired from the captain so she might make a life with her musical lover. The poor blunderhead who freed her from the captain was left no more than her garter ribbons to show for his efforts!' she exclaimed.

Had I been another Henrietta, that child who had thrown herself upon the world a year earlier, I would have bristled at this fable. In truth, I doubt I would have grasped the meaning of it, and certainly the ingenuity of its heroine would have been lost on me entirely. Although it must be said that the lady in question's conduct was less than exemplary, I was desperate for a plan, and her cunning strategy brought a thoughtful smile to my lips.

Chapter 31

Quite as I had anticipated, my situation with St John grew ever worse following that fateful encounter. He was now more convinced than ever that I should be kept under the strictest of guard. Indeed, his suspicion had been fanned to such a heat that he positively forbade me to leave the house. He would have permitted me to go abroad in the company of Mrs Mahon, he informed me, 'But as you have unwisely broken off that friendship and as I trust no others among your coven of associates, you shall remain at home, unless escorted by me.'

The one exception to this sentence of imprisonment was the thrice-weekly visits he allowed to Georgie. These I might make without him, so long as Lucy accompanied me. At first I thought it peculiar that he should permit me this liberty, but I might have guessed at his motives. My faithful Lucy, who was proving her devotion to me by the day, revealed the truth of the matter.

'Two shillings,' said she, 'he promised me for reporting all your movements to him. He wished me to keep watch over you, to tell him if you paid visits to any other person besides Mrs Brown.'

I was indignant upon learning this. That he should treat me as a villain was more than I could bear. I expressed my deepest gratitude to Lucy for her loyalty, and promised her that I should forever be a kind and generous mistress.

'Madam . . .' She hesitated. 'Should you go to Paris . . . might you be inclined to keep me for your maid?'

To be sure, this girl was bold. She knew the value of things and had learned how to acquire what she desired. Some might call this designing. Certainly, it was impertinent, but I had arrived at a time in my life when I was coming to admire traits that I might once have thought despicable. Now I saw their necessity. Lucy would prove an asset to me.

'Yes, Lucy. I should want a maid as constant as you at my side, always.'

She made a triumphant smile at me, and I at her. And so, from that day, our pact was sealed.

I must confess, Fortune truly walked beside me in those months of winter. I cannot ascribe any reason to this. I suppose the winged goddess had abandoned me for so long that she now wished to make her peace. This she did in spades, for no sooner had she sent me Lucy, then she blessed me once more by delivering Philip Quindell.

Shortly after Georgie's birth, it emerged that St John's eyes had not been the only pair keeping watch upon me. Over the course of several months, a young man had been standing on Park Street, sheltering in some inconspicuous corner or shadow. He had been paid to do so; to wait, to observe and to report my movements. His master wished to know how frequently I emerged from the house and if I went abroad unaccompanied by St John. Eventually, when the trap had been set and the time deemed appropriate, he was instructed to pounce. This event came to pass on a sleet-washed afternoon in early 1791.

Lucy and I were setting off to pay a visit to Georgie. No sooner had we stepped into St John's coach than we found ourselves being pursued down the road.

'Miss Lightfoot!' the runner called out after us. 'Miss Lightfoot!' he cried again, this time waving a sealed letter.

I ordered the coachman to stop and took down the window.

The poor lad could hardly speak.

'Madam, my master Mr Quindell bids you read this,' he panted, pressing the note into my hand. He then tipped his hat and backed away into the eddying traffic of the street.

Bemused, I examined the letter. Quindell, thought I, recalling the short, dark-haired gentleman who had knelt at my feet during Mrs Windsor's Roman feast. This came from St John's creditor, the man who had mortified him before his friends. Certainly, it could not be good news. Anxiously, I broke the seal, but was greatly surprised by what I found inside.

> Madam,
>
> I was rendered insensible with love from the moment I beheld your beauty. Delightful Juno, I am your priest entirely. Honour me with your attention. Lower yourself to accept my mortal professions of devotion. Since the day I heard you had been safely brought to bed, I sent a boy to watch at your window and to deliver to me any news of you. If you wish me to appear in his stead, close two of your dressing-room shutters on the morning you intend to set out in your coach. Until that moment and for ever after, I shall remain your devoted slave,
>
> P. Quindell

'Gracious heaven,' I exclaimed with astonishment. I had not anticipated this. I pressed the letter to my bosom and paused for thought. I attempted to recall all that I had heard about Philip Quindell, the absurdly wealthy heir of a sugar fortune, the young gentleman who scattered his credit and coin about London as if it were seed corn, lending it to any who asked, throwing it about on waistcoats and coaches, cards, horses and the nymphs of King's Place. It was then that something like a whip snapped in my mind and all at once a mechanism began to turn. The hammers were lifted and came pounding down upon thoughts, thoughts that eventually were fashioned into a plan, a plan that took its inspiration from the one Lucy had recounted to me. By the time I had returned from my visit to Georgie, my second strategy for an escape had begun to take form.

Three days after I received Quindell's letter, I rose from my bed and closed two of my dressing-room shutters.

'I shall go to Mrs Brown's this afternoon, Lucy,' I instructed her. 'Mr St John will be out.' My maid's mouth carried a vaguely discernible smile. She already knew whom we were to find en route there.

At precisely one o'clock, the coach was brought round. Upon being assisted inside, I looked over my shoulder to see the figure of a gentleman, sporting a fashionable black hat and a tailored blue great-coat, idling down the road. I instructed St John's coachman to take me as far as the corner and to stop. There, Lucy stepped out and waited. The well-dressed figure made his approach slowly, carefully surveying the road and those who traversed it, before stepping around to the far door and silently entering my compartment. Then I tapped upon the roof for the coachman to make haste to Primrose Hill.

But for my brief introduction at Mrs Windsor's, I knew very little about Quindell. I knew nothing of his character, only that he was a young, excitable wastrel. 'The Prince of Wales calls him the Boy Barbadian. His adventures regularly feature in the Intelligencer of the *Morning Herald*,' the Greenfinch had informed me. 'He is forever the subject of gossip . . . much like me and Lord Sefton.' She sighed contentedly.

Beyond this, I had no clear notion of what was to be expected from Mr Quindell, but, upon the moment I permitted him into my coach, I soon learned. He dispensed with all pleasantries and immediately attempted to steal a kiss. Offended by his forwardness, I batted him away.

'What do you mean by this?' I scolded.

'Oooh,' he moaned, as if in agony, and slid down upon the floor of the carriage. 'Your forgiveness, goddess, for my brutish, mortal ways.' He then took my foot into his hands and kissed the tip of my shoe. 'I shall rise upon your command.'

I knew not what to do with this ridiculous wretch. I merely stared at him with a look of disdain. Eventually, he gave up his game, rose from his knees and assumed a position on the seat opposite.

'What is it you wish from me, Mr Quindell?' I enquired, stony-faced.

'I wish to be your priest, my lady. I wish to worship you, to be your slave, your acolyte. I wish for nothing more than this, to dedicate my life to your happiness, which I believe is the only channel through which I may find peace. I am in love with you, Miss Lightfoot. From the moment I gazed upon you, the most perfect vision of womanhood I have ever beheld, I was enchanted.'

'But I belong to Mr St John, sir,' I responded coolly to his plea, 'and he has been a most generous and kind protector.'

'Generous?' He snorted with indignation. 'That rogue has not a generous bone in his body.' Quindell was now quite fired. 'Tell me, Miss Lightfoot, what means does that dog have of providing you with happiness? He has no estate of his own and has lost his seat in Parliament. He has a mere five hundred pounds per annum to live upon, which is just as well for a country squire, but is not a respectable amount for a man of fashion who lives in town. By Jove, he has not even the means of paying his debts to me. He has failed to take a wife, as no lady of quality will have him for so reduced a sum. So why then, my beautiful creature, might he be entitled to own you?' Quindell then grabbed my hands in a manner so brusque that it startled me. 'Dear Miss Lightfoot,' he begged, 'dear, dear, goddess, what must I do to win you? I shall die if I do not taste the sweetness of your lips, those lips which St John may make a meal of whenever he chooses. May Venus have mercy upon me!'

Quindell was such a child. His unskilled and impulsive manner of making love did not endear him to me. His pleadings were met with silence, but not because I wished to rebuff him, rather because I wished to consider them with care and thought.

It was at that moment that I came to recognize an important truth. Mr Selwyn had attempted to impart it to me many months ago, and dear Mrs Mahon, whose advice and urgings I had so often dismissed, had wished me to learn it too. Why, even Lucy Johnson had recently illustrated this principle to me. Quite plainly, life was but a game of bartering, of requesting one thing for another. The more I contemplated this, the clearer it seemed to me that the entire world turned upon this principle. Lucy desired a position from me, and this I gave to her in an exchange for something I desired: information. I required a place in which to bear my child safely, and St John wished to have a replica of his old mistress. Now Quindell desired my love and I was in a position to request something in return. I desired my freedom and, if I moved wisely, I might very well be able to secure it.

'You would like to know what you might do to win me, Mr Quindell?' I began, preparing to make my offer. 'Then I shall tell you.'

He moved nearer to me, a smile of intrigue creeping across his face.

'You say that St John is a good deal in debt to you?'

'Yes.'

'And you would wish to have those debts honoured, would you not?'

'Very much.'

'Well, sir, I believe there is a way in which all of your aims may be met.'

'How so?'

'Challenge Mr St John to a game of piquet.'

'Piquet?' puzzled Quindell, 'But certainly, faro . . .'

'He does not care for faro, but is positively enslaved to piquet. I can assure you, sir, he will be unable to resist such an invitation. Once he commences a game he is loath to quit it until he has won, so you must play for high stakes.'

'I do not see how . . .'

'Please, Mr Quindell, I shall explain myself. You will set the wager before the game commences. If he wins, you will agree to discharge all of his debts. I tell you, sir, he will not be able to resist that opportunity.'

'And if I win . . . ?'

I did not mean to appear coy. In truth, what I was about to propose so disgusted me that I could not meet his gaze. By uttering it, I would bind myself to him, he whom I neither trusted nor knew. I drew a long breath.

'If you win, sir, I shall be your prize.'

Quindell could not believe his ears. He stared at me for a moment.

'Do you suggest that I . . .'

I forced a smile. '. . . Play for me.'

The Boy Barbadian's face lit up like the morning sky, and I watched the sun move across his countenance as he contemplated the idea.

'But I mean to win you, Miss Lightfoot. I shall not accept less. So how do you propose I engineer chance?' said Quindell, thinking he had found a hole in my plot.

'You do not expect that matters of importance should be left to chance?' I replied, quoting my friend Selwyn.

Quindell paused, uncertain of my meaning. He knitted his dark

306

brows together and rolled his grey eyes. He was not especially quick-witted.

'You do not mean to . . .'

I gave a very subtle nod.

Then, all at once, a delighted look of shock passed over him, and he roared with laughter.

'Great Jupiter, madam!' he cried. 'You are a genius!'

Chapter 32

M y actions did not give me ease. No, dear friends, that evening, I returned to Park Street in a tremble. I felt ill, sickened by my devious proposals. I sat before my fire, wishing to warm myself through, but the coldness of my scheme had settled so deep within me that I could not cease my shaking.

To cheat a person at cards was no harmless lark. This ploy I had suggested would not be a mere trick to entertain an old friend. No, what I proposed was the lowest of deeds, a punishable offence. Should I fail, should St John uncover this deception, my comfort and happiness would be at an end for certain. I might even find myself a prisoner, languishing in Newgate. Allenham had urged me to survive, to do what I must to preserve myself, so long as I remained *safe and alive,* he had written. This risk I took for him, so I might free myself to be at his side.

'To what depths have I descended?' I moaned as I sat at my mother's dressing table. Lucy stood above me, removing the combs from my hair. I had confessed my entire strategy to her, though it caused me a good deal of shame to do so. I proposed to make my escape from St John, much in the manner of her former mistress, but as I could not tolerate the thought of a duel, I would contrive to bring them together over a carefully manipulated game of cards.

'My stars, madam!' my maid positively whooped. 'You are sharp-witted, to be sure.'

I checked her with a solemn look and she soon contained herself.

'I do not relish committing a crime, nor using two gentlemen ill, Lucy. It is a devilish plot.' I sighed

Lucy continued to unpick my hair with a quiet, thoughtful expression.

'We do what we must, madam,' she muttered.

I turned to her with sad and questioning eyes.

'My ma, those were her words. We do what we must, not always what we ought.'

'Certainly,' said I, 'we should do what we ought.'

'If I may say, madam, it is for men to do what they ought and women to do what they must. We have not the choices they have. If we desire something, we do what we must to have it, or else . . .'

'Or else?'

'We have nothing, madam. Nothing that is ours, at least. Nothing we desire in life. We are drudges, no better than a horse or an ox.' She reached for my nightcap and began to fit it atop my head. 'No,' she sighed, 'we do what we must.'

I watched her in the looking glass. There was truth in her simple philosophy, though it was one which seemed to rub against all that I had ever learned. It was love that first compelled me to do what I must, rather than what I ought, and, having begun upon that course, it seemed I was fated to continue along it. Certainly, I reasoned, Allenham would not oppose this system of beliefs, when his prophet Monsieur Rousseau seemed to live by this code. *Think of Monsieur Rousseau*, he had urged me in his last letter. I recalled those evenings at Orchard Cottage when we had read his *Confessions*. How shocked I was to learn of the philosopher's misdeeds, his base, human desires, his petty acts of thievery, his deceptions, his abuses; and yet how all the more surprised I was to see that my beloved overlooked these ills, and venerated the author for being true to himself. Might Allenham forgive me as easily? I feared he would not.

Never had I imagined myself capable of being a shrewd, conniving creature, but upon that day, that was what I had come to be. There she sat, gazing back at me from the candle-lit looking glass. I was saddened to think how I had grown into the very scheming harlot St John had accused me of being, but what other choice had I? Indeed, I quite shocked myself at how artfully I had manipulated Quindell. Admittedly, my schooling in this subject had been extensive, as my friends spoke of little else but how to get a keeper to do one's bidding. It was their words that guided my actions, and I believe I acquitted myself well, whether I wished to or not.

Before Quindell had quit my carriage I had known that I must make very clear the specifics of my demands. I was not accustomed to such bartering, and could not imagine how he might respond.

'Mr Quindell,' said I, gathering my courage, 'in exchange for . . . my love . . . I wish to have my own lodgings. I . . . wish to be kept in a fashionable manner, and no longer to live *en famille* . . . as if I were . . . a wife.'

He turned to me with an incredulous look and then burst into a laugh.

'Why, of course,' he exclaimed. 'Any other arrangement would be preposterous.' He then stepped out of my coach, a picture of swagger and confidence, before leaning in to address me through the window. 'All the *ton* thinks St John ridiculous. He keeps you as a miserly shopkeeper might keep his spouse.'

I smirked at this admission, for I was amused to learn what society made of my gaoler, but also because I could scarcely believe what had occurred. The simplicity of the transaction, the ease with which I had arranged an escape to my freedom, seemed remarkable.

Before you judge me too harshly, reader, I ought to explain. There are many among my sex who wish a gentleman to run through every penny at his disposal in purchasing trifles and gifts for them. But this was not my intention in allying myself to Philip Quindell. What I desired from him was not his limitless credit, ten hundred new gowns or a neck hung with jewels, but rather that he should simply unlock my cage.

In truth, by the time I had made my proposition, I had contemplated the matter quite closely. If I were to execute a plan similar to that of Lucy's former mistress, I recognized that I required a private abode of my own. It was necessary that I had a place, unobserved by my new keeper, where I might prepare for my journey to Paris. It would be to this address that St John might send my clothing and effects, and from which I might pawn every expensive bottle and petticoat, each unnecessary hat and brooch, till I had accumulated the price of my passage to France. In fact, I figured, the matter might be concluded so quickly that I would hardly be resident at my new lodgings for more than a handful of days before I made my escape.

Apart from the dangers of complete ruin, which were considerable, that which also gave me disquiet was the character of Philip Quindell. Indeed, the man was no better than a capricious puppy and had little by way of intelligence. I recognized immediately that he would require guidance in this scheme. This, I dreaded, for to suggest a plan is one thing, but to see to its successful execution demands courage and skill, and I believed myself sorely lacking in both of these qualities. Nevertheless, I prepared myself.

On the morning following our meeting, I set about composing a series of signs and signals to be used at the card table. I scribbled each down, attempting to make them as simple as possible, for my liberty was to be won or lost upon the ease with which Quindell could commit them to his memory. Each suit was given a gesture: hearts – I placed my hand to my neck or bosom; spades – to either ear; clubs –to my chin; and diamonds – to my lips. The royal cards were each to be signalled with a look: king – up; queen – down; knave – to either side; while the numbers were to be displayed upon my fan. Quindell was to count the spokes I revealed; one was an ace and so on.

Devising this act of brazen dishonesty distressed me so much that by the time I had committed the strategy to paper and then copied it out for my conspirator, I felt so faint and unwell I was forced to lie upon my sofa in order to recover. Once I had regained my nerve, I wrote under a separate cover that I wished him to commit the contents to heart and to destroy the incriminating note once he had done so. I then sent Lucy off with the two sealed packets. 'Blessed Fortuna,' I prayed as I watched her steal down the road, 'do not abandon me just yet.'

Faithful reader, I had no knowledge of when my day of judgement was to arrive. When I dispatched my message to Quindell, this had been left entirely to the Fates. I thought it likely that St John and I should, within a few weeks, or even a month, happen upon Quindell at an intimate gathering, when a game of cards would then be amicably proposed. In my heart, I knew that chance would fix the date of our meeting. Indeed, this is precisely what came to pass, though not at all in the fashion I might have wished.

In the very week that I set the wheels of my devious design into motion, St John and I were to attend a ball and supper at Carlton House, which was then the home of our late King George IV, when he was still Prince of Wales. My friends, do remember that this was an age quite different from the present one. Women of my sort were very much in favour with the Prince and his circle; indeed, never will you have seen a greater gathering of libertines and reprobates than was to be found in his gilded rooms. Lord Barrymore and his brothers, Mrs Mahon's lascivious Duke of Queensberry, and the stinking Duke of Norfolk, who would sooner bathe in rum punch than water, were all numbered among his closest associates. To be sure, no person who wished to preserve their reputation in respectable circles was to be seen at occasions such as this one. Should you wonder at the tone of the evening, I need only explain that the guest of honour was not to be a foreign head of state or one of the Prince's royal sisters. No, it was to be the Prince's jockey, Samuel Chifney, who attended the ball upon Escape, one of His Majesty's champions. The horse bucked and bridled, soiled a carpet, kicked over a chair and nearly tore Mrs Farren's train before being led back to the stables. But here I get ahead of myself.

Suffice to say, although I had been introduced to the Prince before, it had only been in passing, at the opera. Never had I imagined that I should be honoured with an invitation to Carlton House, and from the day of its arrival, lived in great anticipation of the event. I passed a good deal of time deciding on the gown I should wear and how my hair ought to be arranged; whether it should be set into flowing curls or wrapped into a turban, whether I should sport two feathers or simply a large one at the back of my head. Not once did I bother myself by thinking on other matters; such as who else might be present that evening. Why, had I not received a message from Philip Quindell on the day before, I dread to think what might have been the outcome.

'My dear Goddess,' he wrote:

> I have reason to believe I shall have the honour of claiming you
> for my own tomorrow night. Sweet Juno, I count the hours, the
> very minutes until you are in my arms and freed from that
> tyrant, who has no right to your charms. Make haste to the card
> tables! Do not delay! I cover you with a thousand kisses,
>
> Q

Gracious heaven! His words struck me with the force of lightning. It
would be tomorrow; the event I both prayed for and dreaded. My head
began to spin and I swayed upon my feet. Could it be? thought I, allowing my heart to swell with hope. Was it possible that I should be with
my beloved in Paris in a week's time? But I calmed myself; I steadied my
nerve. There was much still that lay between St John's house on Park
Street and Allenham's arms in France.

I went to a small porcelain box of toothpowder that I kept upon my
dresser, and carefully removed the hidden note containing the code.
After I had taken a moment to rehearse the signals in my mind, I threw
it upon the fire. I then went in search of an appropriate fan.

The selection of this object required a good deal of careful consideration, for she would be the tablet upon which my bid for liberty would
be written. I riffled through my modest collection. It was essential that
she not be too showy. Her design must not be too complex or appeal-
ing or I would be likely to draw too much attention. Her spokes must
be clearly visible, not painted to fade into the pattern of the silk, or
made of perforated ivory, which would be too difficult to make out. I
chose from among my menagerie a simple, elegant piece; her handle
was of dark japanned wood, set with a few paste jewels. I held her to the
light. The outline of her black spokes showed through her pale pink silk,
like a lady's figure through a chemise. I chose her for my accomplice.

And so, dear friends, my treachery was prepared. I went to my bed
that night, but had scarcely any rest. St John lay beside me in a deep
swoon, entirely innocent of my designs. Oh, how my head flitted this
way and that. I rolled in my bed covers. I recited the code to myself
again and again, but still my pulse raced. What if Quindell failed me?

Where should I be then? I turned and studied St John, breathing like a child on his pillow. His long, sharp features did not appear so menacing when held in sleep. Would you cast me out? thought I. Would you have me sent to prison with Quindell for defrauding you at cards? He had it in his heart to be foul, cruel and spiteful. 'Oh, would that I should never again have to share your bed,' I sighed at him and then gently shut my eyes. I willed Fortuna to my side. I willed Allenham to me, just as he claimed I had done when I first flew to him at Herberton.

I willed him near to me. I willed myself down a road that ran through many miles of grass. I drew him nearer. I saw him come to me from the distant horizon, a tall figure approaching, hidden beneath a hat. And as the distance between us grew shorter, so did the person before me. With each step, I spied more. I noted that the hat was in fact a cape, and the man was in fact a woman, and before I could pronounce her name she was standing before me, her mouth drawn back in a dog's snarl.

'I shall sour every joy! I shall blacken every triumph!' she barked. 'You will never escape your prison – I shall see to that!'

My eyes sprang wide. Gasping for my breath, I drew myself upright. 'Cathy.' I covered my face and moved my head, wishing to free it from her image, hoping to empty my ears of her dreadful curses. 'Prison . . . prison . . .' I whispered in horror. Was this some prophecy? Now I did truly begin to shiver, for there, wrapped in the gloom of the bed hangings, I ventured to consider this possibility. Carefully, I picked over her words, recalling those hateful sentiments that she shot at me through my nightmares. 'You will never keep him,' she had mouthed to me as I lay upon my childbed, Georgie not quite born. I had dismissed that vision as nonsense. At the time, I believed she spoke of Allenham, but now, with hindsight, I saw to whom she referred: my son, who would be taken from my arms.

At that distressing thought I began to weep and, not wishing to wake St John, I removed myself from the bed. My heart went into a frenzy. My mind bolted from all restraints. I was a child of reason, but to my troubled soul, this presentiment seemed to contain some irrefutable truth.

'Prison.' My hands and feet grew suddenly numb. I could not bear to contemplate it further. I wished to move, to run from these thoughts. I threw open the doors to my dressing room and then to the corridor beyond it.

I cannot say why I longed to look upon my mother's face, or why it should then offer me some comfort, when in times before it never had. She had been no better than a stranger to me, a sumptuously painted portrait of a favourite mistress, a heavy collar of pearls, a set of sheets upon a bed, a dried block of carmine. And yet I longed for her. I wished that she might calm me.

So I crept into the night-filled parlour, just as I had done weeks before. There, I settled myself upon the sofa, directly beneath her gaze, and allowed the light touch of her smile to fall upon me.

Chapter 33

Had I not dreamed of Lady Catherine, had I not entertained her words as a prophecy of my ruin, the night ahead of me would have filled me with sufficient dread, but now I was nearly beside myself with anxiety.

I was not at home to any callers that morning, and locked myself away, having first sent Lucy out for some syrup of motherwort, which I then sipped throughout the day. I ingested a good deal of this cordial, perhaps more than I ought, but the result was a good one for, by the time I was dressed that afternoon, I found myself in possession of a clear head. I would require it, and a vast amount of fortitude, for the evening was to prove a lengthy one.

Would that we could have repaired directly to Carlton House, but that was not to be the order of events. The ball would not begin until after the theatres closed, and we, like the Prince and his beloved Mrs Fitzherbert, were to attend a performance of *The Haunted Tower* that night. I feared that my nerve would not withstand the hours of antici-pation, and that I would betray myself to St John. Indeed, I scarcely spoke to or looked upon him that entire afternoon, but he had grown so accustomed to my reproachful silences that he thought nothing of this.

As I had feared, once we arrived at the theatre the effects of my medicine had begun to wear thin. Slowly, my sense of agitation returned. I shifted in my seat, adjusted the ribbons on my sleeve, and fingered the jewels at my throat, until St John paid me an exasperated look. At that, I corrected my conduct and surveyed the faces among the audience. It was then that I noticed the outline of Philip Quindell in a box opposite, peering at me through the darkness. His eyes glowed like those of a wolf in the woods. I squeezed my fan in the palm of my hands. My mouth ran dry.

Barely a bite of dinner had passed my lips that afternoon. My stomach was too full of worry to desire food. The light-headedness I experienced while St John's coach conveyed us along Pall Mall to the illuminated windows of Carlton House had as much to do with my lack of nourishment as my nerves. Everyone in my company, including St John and Sir John Lade, was so soused in drink that they failed to spot my unease. Only Lady Lade poked me with her fan.

'What ails you, chicken?' said she, leaning into my ear. I shook my head and then cast my eyes at St John who was laughing riotously at Sir John's impersonation of Lord Derby.

'Him.' She sniffed and nodded, before laying a sympathetic hand upon my shoulder.

The windows of Carlton House blazed like stars through the profiles of the stark winter trees. Indeed, there were few houses in London grand enough to burn so many lights at once. To be sure, it was a remarkable place, and more like an opulent fairy palace than a habitable abode. Its interior was lined with marble, every column touched with gilding, every curl and swirl of plasterwork washed with colour. The elaborate gold stair seemed to twist upward into the heavens. Everywhere, lanterns, candelabra, torchères and chandeliers flamed and danced like sprites, while clocks ticked and looking glasses glittered from each corner. I had been quaking like a jelly until distracted by these splendours. For a brief few moments, I found myself at ease, marvelling at the walls of paintings by Rubens and Van Dyck, and the bronzes, marble busts and precious Chinese jars that towered above my head.

I might have lost myself among these treasures had St John not roughly taken my arm.

'Sir, your grip is too tight,' I complained.

'You would rather I set you free, to run amid these dogs?' He muttered beneath his breath. In every corner the man spied a rival, a betrayer, a schemer ready to divest him of me – and his judgement was not incorrect upon this occasion. It was not merely the presence of Barrymore and his brothers which had raised the alarm: that matter was seen to by Lady Lade, who had been charged with keeping his lordship at least one room from us at all times. No, the threat was far worse than this alone. The palace swarmed with pleasuremongers, rakes and nymphs of every rank and description; ancient bawds who still painted their faces with white lead, pox-ridden debauchers, perilously young whores, and the black-leg racing set, who never saw fit to remove their tall boots. In St John's eyes, the rooms writhed with predators and he was loath to leave me unattended for more than a heartbeat.

Nearly an hour had passed before we came upon Quindell. On seeing him hovering about the card tables, my stomach fell to my knees. Indeed, I felt as if I might be sick. Within an instant, my conspirator caught my eye and charged upon us. He bowed to me, quickly, aggressively, and then turned his fire on St John.

'Ah, Mr St John, sir, I have often wondered where you hide yourself,' he exclaimed with good humour, 'so few have been the occasions on which our paths meet.'

St John hesitated, realizing too late that he had been sprung upon by a creditor.

'You have been at work, I hear, composing a play. Another play, Mr St John? Why, what a marvel you are. I suppose when one is occupied with the art of play-writing one has time to think of little else.' Quindell raised an eyebrow. My keeper knew precisely to what he referred.

St John opened and closed his mouth several times and cleared his throat uneasily.

'Mr Quindell,' he began, lowering his voice, 'with all due respect, I do not believe this to be the time or place to raise such an issue. If you will see fit to call upon me tomorrow . . .'

'And find you not at home, sir? You think me both rich *and* stupid? No, I am afraid this will not do, Mr St John. I have permitted you a certain clemency for long enough and I should like this matter settled at once. This evening, in fact.'

318

I looked at my protector, his face now flushed scarlet.

'Sir . . .' he lowered his voice yet further, almost below a whisper, 'I am afraid . . . you put me in some difficulty by this. I have not the funds immediately at my disposal . . .'

'Come now, Jack,' said Quindell, placing a firm hand upon St John's sleeve, 'that is not how I intended it. No, no, that is not in the spirit of a sporting gentleman. No, we shall play for it, sir. At the tables. Piquet, that is your game, is it not?'

Though obviously bewildered, St John gave him a nod.

'I shall make you a wager; if you win the game I shall absolve you of all your debts to me. In fact, I shall offer you that satisfaction, regardless of the outcome.'

St John furrowed his brow, perplexed by this offer.

'I do not follow . . .'

'You, sir, will be free to walk from the table and owe me not a penny. But if I win, then I shall name my prize, on the condition that you must give it over to me directly.'

'Pah!' blew St John, now believing he had the measure of his young challenger. 'You ask me to enter into a wager where I know not what you propose to take from me! Why, that is madness.' St John's eyes glowed with contempt. 'You may have my property off me, you may demand I pay you an annuity for the rest of my days, or any such outrage.' My keeper folded his arms and scowled at this mean little mushroom of a man. He was not so foolish as that.

Quindell paid him a generous bow.

'Consider then, sir, that I shall call upon you tomorrow with the bailiff. Two thousand three hundred pounds is not a trifling sum. I shall have your fine coach from you, those horses you keep and any possessions I see fit to claim.'

St John's eyes broadened, and he flared his nostrils in a show of fury. By God, he wore such hatred on his face!

'Damn you,' he muttered through his clenched teeth. 'If that's your price, then I shall play – and I shall permit you to choose your prize from among my possessions, *without* the presence of a bailiff.'

Poor, dear St John. He moved as if in chains to the green baize-lined card table. Once in his seat, he raised his head imperiously. Beside his tall, thin figure, the square-built Quindell seemed like the court dwarf. Dutifully, I took my place behind my keeper's chair, my breast heaving with fear. In my hands I clasped my fan so tightly that I fretted it might break.

There had been no opportunity for Quindell and me to rehearse our strategy, and this disquieted me. My head began to spin with images of unspeakable horrors: destitution, disgrace, prison. *Prison.* I quivered. No, I would not permit my mind to launch upon that. I dared not give credence to her curses now. Now I required all my wits about me and I banished her absolutely from my thoughts.

As the first hand was dealt, word had begun to spread through the rooms that this was to be no ordinary game. A matter of honour was at stake, it was whispered, though no one knew precisely what that was. The mystery drew spectator upon spectator to the table, whereupon further wagers were laid in favour of the elder or the younger of the two players. I noted Queensberry among the faces, and then Sir John and Lady Lade, and eventually Barrymore and his limp-footed brother as the crowd expanded. They muttered and jostled. I was nearly pushed from my spot by the rude elbows of two giggling whores.

Quindell raised his wide-set eyes to me as I hovered above St John. That was his cue and he wished me to give him a signal. This was it; my bid for freedom had arrived. My thudding heart inched upward into my throat. Anxiously, I glanced down at my keeper's hand. He shed his lowest cards, which left him with two useful ones: the queen of spades and ace of diamonds. I unfurled one spoke of my fan and, upon my sign, Quindell shuffled his hand. I attempted to form my face into an expression of indifference while he played his cards.

'Good?' he enquired of St John, as one does in piquet.

St John grimaced. 'Not good.' And with that, Quindell had taken the first *partie.* Thirty points had gone to him and there were seventy left for which to play.

The spectators crushed closer to the table.

'A hundred says Quindell takes the game,' announced Major George Hanger, one of the Boy Barbadian's raucous associates.

'I shall see you on that!' exclaimed a voice from behind him.

I held my breath while Quindell drew a new hand, and St John received his cards. Tightly, I pressed my eyes together and then opened them upon my keeper's cards. A knave of clubs, a king of diamonds and a queen of spades made part of what appeared to be a strong hand. I fretted that Quindell could sense my concern. I signed to him; perhaps my motions looked more like agitation than code. He put down three of his cards and St John one.

'Good?' posed the younger man, his face an anxious mix of concern and resolve.

'Very good,' parlayed my protector. He showed his hand and stole a total of forty-five points.

A huzzah went up from the mass of faces. Quindell avoided my gaze.

I felt myself begin to quake quite noticeably. What had gone so wrong, thought I? Perhaps he had won the first hand through good fortune alone. Perhaps he had not committed to memory any of my signals, or was too much in drink to recall them. By the next hand, I would know the truth of the matter.

The cards were dealt, and St John found himself with a hand of middling worth: queen of clubs, a nine and an eleven. I carefully picked out the spokes of my fan. I fluttered it with eleven spokes clearly visible, before retracting it by two. Certainly, if Quindell did not play this *partie* accordingly, he was a blockhead, a simpleton, an idiot. I gritted my teeth.

'Good?' questioned the chestnut-headed young man.

'Damnable!' responded St John, throwing down his hand, his fist shaking, his face now so red that I feared he might split his skin. Quindell nearly jumped from his seat in a cheer. He had secured a further forty-five points and stolen the *partie*. If he was to win the next hand . . . well, dear readers, I would have gained my freedom. I looked away, attempting to mask the faint hint of a smile that crept over my face. My nightmare had been but a meaningless dream, conjured by my frightened mind, I reassured myself.

It was at that moment that the crowd, which now stood five or six deep around the table, began to part.

'What the devil is this?' came a jovial voice. 'Philly Quindell and Jack St John at a hand of piquet! By God, gentlemen, there must be a great prize at stake here!' The Prince stepped rather unsteadily towards his card table, with the round-figured Mrs Fitzherbert upon his arm like a counterweight. The entire gathering and the two players rose and bowed.

'We play to settle a debt, Your Royal Highness,' said St John.

The Prince sent out a sputtering laugh.

'Dear Jack, I cannot imagine it is Philly who is indebted to *you*.'

The entire room roared with amusement, and St John, not one who was bred to entertain a gallery, forced a smile.

'Fear not, Jack, Philly owns more of me than he does of you!' said His Royal Highness, before waving his hand in a dismissive manner, 'Play on, gentlemen, I should not wish to distract you from your wager.'

It was then, in the midst of this commotion, that a calamity befell me. In positioning themselves at the side of the card table between both players, the broad-waisted Prince and his double-chinned wife displaced all the spectators who surrounded them. It was as if two fat stones had been dropped into a pool, sending out ripples of movement among the observers. I was momentarily carried upon a wave that took me from the back of St John's chair into the crowd. I gasped, and in swimming through the current back to my position, I let slip my fan from my shaking palm.

The final hand was being dealt as I dived beneath the card table, feeling for it in the gloom. Its dark handle rendered it virtually impossible to find. *Oh dear, dear Fortuna*, I nearly began to weep, *do not abandon me now. Not now, I beg you!*

St John was shuffling his hand. The seconds passed, moving further and further onward, leaving me behind. I struggled, patting my hands all about me, knowing that soon the cards should be called and the *partie* decided. Oh dear God, I beseech you . . . Cathy, let me be! My fingers felt along the Turkish carpet, until, stretching them outward, I sensed the smooth handle within my reach.

I came above the table, ruffled and frightened. Quindell's eyes were frozen with terror.

'Why, Miss Lightfoot, do you make a habit of polishing Mr St John's shoes while he sits at the card table?'

The company laughed, but I looked at him quite startled. Foolhardily he had drawn all the eyes of the room upon me, upon us, and what I was to do next.

I glanced down at St John's hand and, comprehending that I now stood upon centre stage, caught my breath and opened my fan. I showed ten spokes and pressed them to my lips.

'Sir, I do beg your pardon . . .' I answered demurely, making no pretence at wit. 'I had . . . dropped my fan.' I closed my pretty little accomplice one spoke further, then looked coyly to the side to denote the knave I had seen in St John's hand.

Quindell's face hardened and he licked his lips.

'Good?' enquired St John, his voice cracking with nerves.

The Boy Barbadian sucked in his breath. He raised his eyes to me with such desire that I thought he might leap across the table at me.

'Very Good Indeed!' he declared, slamming his hand upon the table.

The crowd hollered and huzzahed. 'Quindell! Quindell!' a collection of blacklegs cried, championing his name.

Oh reader, I did everything in my power to contain my desire to do the same. When I saw the cards he flung upon the table, the winning hand that secured my release, I wished to squeal with joy, I wished to jig a merry dance. I wished to fly from that room as fast as I might. Had it been possible, I would have boarded a stage to Dover at that very moment! Inside my head I both triumphed and sighed with relief. Prison, indeed! I laughed at my own foolishness, while gleefully dismissing the spectre of my sister for what it was: a mere irrational imagining prompted by my own fears. Here the truth lay before me, upon a card table.

My head spun like a Catherine wheel but I forced my expression into blankness, and emitted no more than a politely surprised gasp. The deal was yet to be completed, and my heart thudded in anticipation.

All about me the cheering and high spirits continued. The Prince lingered at the edge of the table, inspecting the final play, greatly amused by the tournament that had transpired in his card room.

'Now, Philly, has the matter been settled?' he enquired.

'Not just yet, Your Royal Highness,' responded Quindell with a half-smile, gathering the cards spread upon the table.

St John had yet to move or make a sound. He had been sitting, silent and stoic, a vanquished man, preparing to submit to his punishment.

'You may call upon me tomorrow, Mr Quindell,' said my keeper, preparing to push himself up from his seat.

'That shall not be necessary, Jack,' he responded, raising his eyes to mine, 'for I shall claim my prize now.'

'Your prize, sir?'

'Miss Lightfoot . . . if she will agree to become mine.'

St John's face fell as hard as the walls of Jericho, his entire arrangement of features seemed to bow and collapse under the shock.

'You cannot mean . . . How dare you?' he growled.

'You agreed to my terms, sir. Certainly you are prepared to honour your word?'

My keeper then turned his thunderous face to me.

'You . . . This was your doing! I might have guessed . . .'

'Ah! But does she accept you, Philly?' interrupted the Prince, rapt by the unfolding of this comedy of errors.

My mouth trembled. I looked away nervously, not daring to meet St John's fiery, accusing eyes.

'Yes,' I pronounced softly.

The Prince crowed with delight. 'All for the love of Miss Lightfoot!' he cried, reaching for my hand.

It was a merciful thing that Mrs Fitzherbert had long since abandoned the table for more intriguing spectacles, for His Royal Highness pulled me from behind St John's chair and drew me to his side. For a brief instant, I flashed my gaze at the Prince, and beheld such a vibrant pair of marble blue eyes that it brought a blush to my cheek.

'A kiss? Will you favour me with just one kiss, before Philly makes you his own?'

I did not dare note the expressions of either of my keepers, old or new, for I understood it not to be in their command to refuse such a request. Now I coloured even further, for it is one thing to be a guest at the Prince of Wales's gathering and another thing entirely to be admired by him. I had hardly more than nodded a coy approval, before he had his hand upon my cheek and his lips pressed to mine. Once more, the sound of cheering went up around me.

It was over that quickly. Indeed it was no more than a fleeting gesture of approval but I was most overcome to have been the recipient of it. In fact, I believe you would think me dishonest if I did not here admit that, among the many kisses I have received in the course of my days, this one I recall with great fondness. I was so very young and beautiful then, in a palace that danced with splendours. On that night, the eve of my promised release, all possibilities spread before me.

The Prince and the revellers who encircled him drew us into their orbit as they laughed and jested. There was a good deal of drink; champagne and brandy were poured into our glasses. I could hardly see over the heads of the gentlemen and bejewelled ladies who surrounded us. When at last a clearing did appear between the embroidered coats and trains of silk, I glanced back at the table. Not surprisingly, St John had disappeared.

The festivities carried on into the morning hours, as most celebrations at Carlton House were prone to do, while the company sank further and further into drink and debt. During the course of the evening, I found myself separated from Quindell and wandering from room to room among the boisterous guests. While passing through the echoing octagonal entry hall, I felt an unexpected hand upon my sleeve.

'Do not think I did not foresee the arrival of this day, *chaton*.'

I looked up to see St John, his posture stooped from drink, his eyes red with exhaustion.

'You are no different from your mother,' he sniffed. 'Take your pleasure with the idiot Barbadian. Amuse yourself, but you will return. This I know.'

I turned from him, not wishing to demonstrate my ingratitude, or to disappoint his hopes.

'You have given me a son, dear little *chaton*, and for this, I shall always be indebted to you. But do not forget, madam, he is *mine*. He belongs to my house, as you no longer do,' he warned, before turning upon his heel.

I remained there, fixed in place, watching him withdraw down the stairs. As he reached the door, he stopped and glanced back at me, his features set in an unmoving, icy expression.

Chapter 34

There was, of course, one point of business left to be transacted before Quindell would grant me the keys to my liberty. This, as you might imagine, I dreaded. Let none of my fellow lady-memoirists convince you to the contrary: it is no joy to lie with a disagreeable man, a man for whom one feels not even an amicable warmth, not the merest modicum of admiration or affection. But this one task I would bear with good cheer in order to attain my freedom. Quindell was my gate-keeper, and this act was to be the bribe I paid so that I might secure my safe passage. That is the manner in which I viewed it, nothing more.

It was very late indeed by the time my new keeper was heaved into his coach. I was carefully placed on the seat opposite him, the prize he had won in a night of gaming. As the horses brought us to his house in St James's Square, Quindell lolled and sagged, muttering unintelligible drunken syllables as his chin bounced upon his chest. I watched him with folded arms, comforted by the knowledge that the unpleasant deed would not be committed upon that night.

Instead it was committed upon the following afternoon, as I waited patiently on a sofa. He came to me, clutching his sore head, his person still bearing the stink of port and brandy. For one who made so much of my 'sweet lips', and my 'longed-for kisses', hardly more than two or three were taken from me. He made no comment upon my beauty, offered no praise at his goddess's altar, but whimpered like a hound as he roughly pushed up my skirts and got himself inside me. I withstood the few thrusts he required with the fortitude of one who sits in a dentist's chair. Fortunately, after a moment or so, the entire ordeal was at an end and I rose up immediately to rid myself of his seed.

Earlier that morning, in the time that Quindell lay in a drunken doze, I had possessed the foresight to send out for a few necessities; several sponges, some strong vinegar, and lime water with which to wash my privy parts. Prior to that day, I had fretted a good deal about Quindell's potency, that he, unlike St John, was most likely to be in full command of his manhood. As you might imagine, now when I hovered at the very door to my escape, I wished more than ever to keep my womb free from any further burdens. Despite the burning of the lime water and vinegar, fear drove me to be fastidious in my rituals of douching. For those among you ladies who have never attempted it, the constant application of these solutions is grievously painful to the delicate area, especially when used with regularity, but I had little choice in the matter. In the short period that I was confined with him in his bedchamber, I was made to endure what seemed like an endless siege upon my woman-hood. Men possess such unquenchable fires when first they come to conquer us. It is forever the same. He pawed and panted and assailed me, just as did St John, but, dare I say, with greater success. I confess, after the first day, the soreness was so great as to force me to approach the maid for some lard to grease the passage. (This, you should know, is a useful measure and never fails to provide at least a small degree of relief to the injured parts.)

It is quite astonishing what a person is willing to withstand when she believes a reward for her suffering to be in sight. As I lay, as passive as a landed fish, in his bed, I congratulated myself that soon I would be away, and I would wash from my memory the trials of this mode of life, these abhorrent beds of other men; I would purge them utterly, never again to recall the sounds or scents of another. I fixed my eyes on the nearest window as Quindell huffed and puffed atop me.

'Philly,' I asked in a pretty voice upon the morning of the second day, 'when shall I have my own lodgings?'

'Hmm?' came his response as he lay expired upon me.

'My apartments, dear heart,' said I, with a false smile. I fear I now sounded quite impatient, for indeed I was.

328

'Tomorrow,' said he, slithering away on to his side.

'You see, I must send for my wearing apparel and jewels. I must send for Lucy, my maid. I do not trust St John; he will turn her out for sure. I must have my belongings, Philly,' said I, sitting up. 'I fear it is most urgent.'

But Quindell did not seem to be in a state of mind inclined to matters most urgent. He sighed.

'I shall arrange it today.'

Of course, I had been correct in my belief that St John would turn Lucy Johnson out. When I failed to return with him on the night of the Prince's gathering, it became clear to her that my plan had succeeded.

'If you do not mind my saying, madam, this made me a good deal pleased for you, but ever so fretful for my own situation,' she told me when she arrived at St James's Square, carrying her bundle beneath her arm. 'I did not know what would become of me. I feared you would depart for Paris directly!'

I hushed her frantically, and she clapped her hand across her mouth in shame, before continuing her tale in a lowered tone.

'Mr St John fell into such a state of melancholy. The household feared for him, what with all that hollering and moaning, as if he were sick and dying. That's what comes of the drink.' She nodded with a look of superiority.

She recounted to me that St John returned from Carlton House and confined himself to his rooms, much as he had done following the Roman feast at Mrs Windsor's. He seemed determined to sink his woes in wine and porter; so much so that when he at last emerged, the housemaids found nearly forty bottles from his cellar scattered about the floors and surfaces.

'Two days passed before he summoned me. I was sorely frightened, madam, for he looked to me like a demon! His face was whiter than I ever did see and his mouth was blue from the wine. It was then he showed me the door and said, "Go to that bitch, if you dare. I do not want you here no more." I said, "As you wish, sir," and then asked if it might convenience him if I was to pack your belongings, but he roared at me that he would see fit to do it himself.' She offered me a hesitant smile. 'It was a good thing I knew where you were to be found, madam.'

To be sure, her arrival on that, my final night under Quindell's roof, could not have pleased me more. 'I am ever so grateful that you came to me, Lucy,' I said in a whisper, pressing her hand. 'We have only to await my belongings to be sent, and then . . .' I could not keep the smile from my lips, '. . . we shall make our escape.'

And so it came to pass that early the following morning, Quindell escorted me to a house on Clarges Street, one of several in his possession. Indeed I was later to learn that his father had, many years ago, spun his sugar wealth into property and bought up a good many houses in the newly laid streets around the edges of Hyde Park. He had been a much wiser man than his son, whose only investments had been in whores and racehorses. I would even wager that Philip Quindell might have earned a name as the most reckless spendthrift of his generation had his life not come to an untimely end in 1793. He was only twenty-four. As I understand it, he and Major Hanger had been larking about with brandy and pistols at a race meeting.

The house in which he installed me could not have suited my purposes more perfectly. Philly took me by the hand, eager to show me all of its luxuries and to enumerate the expense of filling it.

'The silver, plate and books were acquired from the Duke of Chandos, when his lordship could not make good on his debts.' Quindell removed a yellow porcelain dish bearing a ducal crest from a sideboard, and waved it before me with a self-satisfied smirk. 'When he died, I had his collection of paintings from him too, but they are rather dull things.'

It was, to be sure, an exquisite townhouse. Its rooms were beautifully furnished *à la mode*, with elegant, thin-legged white chairs and pier tables. My bed, which was a grand feat of Mr Linnell's design, wore a stately crown of cobalt silk drapery. However, at the time, I had no mind for any of it. I wished only to rid myself of Quindell, to gain possession of my belongings and to make my departure. He pushed me down upon the coverlet, but I rolled away, complaining, as Miss Ponsonby often encouraged me to do, that I had 'begun to bleed, and would not wish to disgust him with it'. The ploy served me well, as he rose to his feet, sighed and made his excuses.

I waited until I heard him depart before I summoned Lucy. Alone in my private lodgings, I was so thrilled that I could hardly contain my excitement. I had already begun to calculate how many days might pass before all my jewels and the most expensive part of my apparel could be transformed into money, and thence into a passage to Paris.

I pulled on the bell rope once more, and then, in a fit of impatience stepped out upon the stairs and called for her.

'Madam!' She came charging up the steps. 'Your box has arrived.' Behind her strode one of my footmen with a trunk of my belongings. My face burst into a smile.

'Have them brought to my dressing room,' said I, fairly singing out my directions.

When Lucy reached the landing, I took her by the hands and squealed with joy. 'Oh my kind-hearted Lucy,' I exclaimed, 'our plan has been a success,' and with that, I flew to where the box had been placed upon my floor.

It struck me as odd that there was but one trunk: a coffer the size of a large tea chest. Lucy went to unlock it.

'And where might the others be?' I wondered aloud, merrily. 'Surely this must be the first of several.'

I peered into the coffer and saw only a small selection of my wardrobe. There was a pile of linens, stockings, caps, handkerchiefs, gloves, shawls, ribbons, night shifts and assorted necessaries. Beside these articles were the two pairs of shoes and two suits of clothing that I brought with me from Herberton: the riding habit and the gown of blue striped silk. I rummaged through the contents, growing all the more anxious. My casket of jewels, which I had expected to be returned to me, was nowhere to be found. Instead, I came across a note with St John's seal upon it.

I might have guessed as much; I, who had seen the man in his weakest moments, who understood his petty jealousies and his mean nature. Why had I not foreseen this? He had anticipated the day when I would fly from his control; why then had I allowed myself to be so trusting of him?

He wasted scant ink upon me, and that which had been used was mixed with bile. 'I have restored to you what is yours and, because I am not given to cruelty, have granted you some linens, etc. As for your gowns and jewels, these I have withheld for the occasion of your return to me. St John'.

I did not wish to believe it. My plan, which had been so expertly constructed, could not be toppled here. Not now, when I had endured so many perils, so much hardship and unpleasantness to free myself.

'Lucy,' I gasped, rising to my feet. 'Lucy ... Mr St John ... this is all ...'

My maid stared at me, her eyes opening wider as she followed my distress.

I began to pace. My head pounded with fury. 'How dare he!' I cried. 'How dare he clip my wings!'

I wished to write to him at once, to hurl all manner of insult at him, to inform him directly that I should never, so long as I breathed air, return to him, that I loathed and abhorred him, that I should rather sleep upon the street than in his bed. He was a monster! He was the devil himself! But I collected myself, I contained my passion and wrapped it in reason. I called upon my strength of mind, that quality which Allenham had so admired in me.

It would do me no good to spit venom at St John, so long as he had Georgie in his command.

Greatly shaken, I sat down upon a chair and stared blankly at the wall. 'What am I to do now?' I murmured after a time.

My faithful servant came quietly to my side and laid a gentle hand upon the back of my seat.

'Begin once more, madam,' she sighed.

Chapter 35

When I first compromised myself and threw my person upon the mercy of St John, I had made a firm resolution. I determined that I should not collapse into a fit of sobs at every perceived setback, for it never improved matters to do so. It is true that at times my perseverance wavered, but I believed I had finally conquered this weakness when I mustered the courage to quit Park Street. Unfortunately, I did not foresee such a blow to my fortitude as this.

All afternoon, fury boiled within me. I steamed with rage, as might a pudding in a pot. I clenched my fists; I chewed my lip till I drew blood. At last, exhausted and dizzy, I threw myself down upon the bed. 'I shall not weep, I shall not shed a single tear for that scoundrel of a man!' I scolded myself, while pinching my eyes shut. It was in this agitated state, writhing and grimacing like a colicky infant, that Quindell found me.

The Boy Barbadian was not the sort to idle patiently on the opposite side of a door. By Jove, if he wished to make his presence known, he would push right through into a room, without so much as a gentle rap. So, when he returned that evening, his purse loaded from a win at the *rouge et noir* tables, he would hear none of Lucy's excuses.

'Great Parnassus! Whatever is the matter, Henrietta?' he exclaimed, upon spying my contorted features.

I shook my head woefully. 'Oh Philly,' I peeped, before shamefully covering my face.

Quindell sat down at the side of the bed and stared at me. 'What has happened?'

It was then I felt my eyes begin to prickle and the anguish rise inside my breast. Unable to restrain my passion any longer, it burst forth from me like fire from a volcano.

'St John!' I cried out, in an explosion of bile and tears. 'That beast! That wretch has refused to send me my gowns and jewels!'

I was uncertain how my new keeper would take this information. Would he be angered that the man from whom he had acquired this prize mount had refused to send over its bridle and saddle? Would he champion me, as ought a true gallant defender?

'Have you nothing at all to wear?' he enquired, quite unmoved by my distress.

'Beside the gown I wore upon the night of the ball, I have but two modest gowns only . . . and some linens'.

He shrugged, as if this caused him no concern whatsoever, and slouched down upon his chair.

'I should not worry about it,' he muttered, studying the sheen of his fingernails.

I looked at him, aghast at his callousness.

'I had always intended to attire you to my taste. You do not think I would have you dressed in St John's rags?' He sighed. 'Now it seems the matter has become more pressing and we must set to it immediately.'

Why, I could scarcely believe my ears. Could it be that simple?

'Dry your tears, my goddess.' He smiled at me. 'Your wardrobe shall soon be the envy of all the muses and nymphs in London.'

And so, the following day, began in earnest Philip Quindell's campaign to convert me from the slightly awkward mistress of a timeworn man of forty-four into a courtesan worthy of high keeping. Once again, I was given over to the mantua-maker. I was plunged into the same scene of fussing and tacking, of examining pattern books and rolls of ribbon and lace, fur trims, heel shapes, felt and chiffon. However, on this occasion, it was not my inclinations or the cultivated judgement of the draper, mantua-maker, milliner or shoe-maker that dictated the cut of a bodice or the design of pattern, but rather Quindell's taste. 'No, no,' he would complain, 'that stripe is too narrow,' or 'the colour of that gauze is far too dull – no one shall see it, let alone admire it.'

I stood no better than a wax doll, upon which were pinned all his visions for the mistress of an *haute ton* gentleman. I had not the slightest say in how I was to be attired. No protest that I did not like this shade of green or that taffeta would be heard. My keeper simply brushed my thoughts aside. Upon the one occasion when I positively refused a trimming of gold fringe, he subjected me to a lecture.

'Come now, you think a gentleman cannot have a view on how he should like his mistress to appear? Why, I spied the Duchess of Devonshire wearing just such an adornment the other day. If you wish to cut a figure among the fashionable set, Henrietta, you must pay heed to such things.' He snapped, 'Appearance counts for everything.'

I could do little more than sigh and hold my tongue.

To be sure, my friends, I might have withstood the complete subversion of my choice of attire had Quindell's taste proved more refined – but, oh, to see what sartorial horrors this man imposed upon me! I had collars that lay upon my shoulders like flounced shawls, I had buttons as large and shining as new shillings, I had paper nosegays pushed into my décolletage, and high-crowned hats so decorated with rosettes and trailing ribbons that they appeared more like maypoles than works of millinery.

I recall him swelling with pride as he examined me in a creation of his own choosing, a violet watered silk, worn with a skirt of cerise and yellow stripes and a vast cloud-like buffon tucked into my bodice. '*C'est magnifique!*' he crowed. 'I had always thought you near enough to perfection and the handsomest piece in all of London. You merely required a few adjustments.'

'Adjustments?' I rejoined, not half offended by his opinion.

'Oh,' he attempted to mollify me, 'only in your dress, my goddess, for it was not so *à la mode* as it might have been . . . but I have improved upon that,' said he, approaching me with squeezes and kisses. After he had taken his fill of these, he stood back to admire me once more. A thought passed through his head and he crunched his brow. 'What fool attires his young mistress in the fabrics of nearly twenty years past?' he remarked and rolled his eyes. 'His Royal Highness thought it a positive cruelty of St John to have dressed you so. A man who permits his mistress to be the subject of ridicule should be pilloried alongside fraudsters and perjurers, I say.'

This revelation quite shamed me. I had no notion that my clothing had been the subject of such tattle.

'And that is all?' I asked, my voice quivering with poorly disguised annoyance. 'You do not think me meriting of any further *adjustments* than that of my mode of dress?'

Quindell hesitated. 'Perhaps there is one other.'

'And what might that be?' I enquired, now a good deal injured.

He stammered and struggled with his words. 'If you were . . . it might become you . . . to go upon the stage.' He then moved towards me and took my face into his hands. 'Dear little goddess, you have asked me what else, and this I must confess to you: it is my fondest wish to see you beneath the glare of the lights. Since I was old enough to feel the sensations of love melting in my breast, I hoped to capture the heart of an actress. I fear that Mrs Siddons rebuffed my advances, and Nancy Storace threw me over for another. I said to myself then, "Quindell, what you require is a beautiful creature, unknown to the world, whose name you would have the honour of making by putting her upon the stage." One day, I should like that creature to be you, my cherished one.' He sealed his declaration with a hard kiss upon my lips.

I am not sure which part of his revelation left me more speechless: the insulting frankness of his admission, or the exposure of his absurd vanity. I had no desire to go upon the stage. Brazen strutting was not in my nature. I harrumphed, I spluttered, I drew breath, but in the end I decided not to waste my spleen in protesting. None of this would matter one fig, as I planned to take my leave of Philip Quindell long before he could persuade me to memorize the lines of Shakespeare.

When he made his confession to me, I could not name with certainty the date of my departure, but I was determined that it would be soon. As Lucy had wisely counselled me, if I wished to flee to Paris, I had the dispiriting task of plotting my escape once more. I had to begin again, and amass a hoard of objects worthy of hawking for my freedom.

At first, this seemed to me a daunting undertaking. How might I possibly acquire so many things of value without turning thief? It might take months, if not years, I bemoaned. But, gentle reader, the answer lay before my very eyes, and initially, I had been too blind to see it.

Here, I fear my tale is about to take a turn that will not accord with many of your more delicate sensibilities. It would sadden me to think you believed me to be avaricious, or driven by base desires. Certainly, by now, you have read far enough in my narrative to know that I am not of that sort. I had not the grasping talons of Miss Greenhill or of others among my acquaintance. To be sure, I had lived so much of my life in a modest fashion that I had no experience of extravagance. My life at Melmouth was a humble one, and you have seen how innocent were my countrified pleasures at Orchard Cottage. Why, I believed St John to be as generous as Croesus. In fact, the truth of the matter was, I had never known genuine wealth until I met Philip Quindell.

I thought his gesture of outfitting me kind enough in itself. In truth, I did not hope for more. So you can imagine my bemusement when he began to present me with regular tokens of his affection.

In a given week, Quindell would stay in my bed on three, or perhaps four nights. On one of those mornings, without fail, he would produce a gift. The first of these arrived unexpectedly, after he had taken his pleasure with me. Quite without warning, he rolled on to his side, reached through my bed-hangings and pulled upon the bell rope. He waited a moment and then rang again, this time clambering to his feet and hollering for his valet in the most brutish fashion.

'Philly,' I scolded him, 'I am not fit to be seen by your man just now.'

'Sam!' he cried from the door, standing in his chemise for all to see. 'Bring up Miss Lightfoot's bauble directly!'

There were sounds of shuffling in my dressing room and then Quindell returned to me, carrying a small round object in his hand.

'I feared you would miss me when your bed was cold,' said he, handing me the item. 'So I have had Mr Cosway paint my portrait in miniature.'

I examined the item in my palm: a skilfully rendered likeness of Quindell in a burgundy coat, holding his head aloft like a gun dog. Surrounding it was the most exquisite frame of brilliants I had ever seen.

'They are true diamonds,' he remarked, as he tugged the bell rope once more, summoning his valet to dress him. 'I shall not insult you with paste, like that beggar St John.'

It was an extraordinary gift. I felt the weight of it in my hand and marvelled at the tiny squares of light as they gleamed and flashed. It was then that I allowed hope to re-emerge in my heart. I saw the first suggestions of a path opening before me.

There was, of course, more to come after this: a pair of bracelets, a pair of gold shoe buckles, a brooch of seed pearls, with earrings of the same, a set of enamelled redingote buttons inlaid with rubies, and a gold filigree necklace, like that which Quindell had spotted around the neck of the Duchess of Devonshire at Almack's. My stars, I could scarcely take it all in – all this treasure in little more than two months. At times it seemed I need only to hold out my hand and the Boy Barbadian would fill it with my passage to France. Indeed, on one occasion this was quite literally the case.

On an afternoon in early April, I returned to my house to find a parcel and a box awaiting me. They were gifts from Mr Quindell, I was told. Inside the round box lay an enormous black-plumed beaver hat with a small brim and a chin strap. In the parcel was to be found a scarlet riding cape, adorned with frogging, braiding and brass buttons. I could not for the life of me comprehend what this was about, so when Philly appeared that evening, I questioned him.

'Ah' said he with a smile. 'You are to wear those tomorrow with the blue redingote. We are off to a race meet in Hyde Park.'

'What? A race?' I questioned.

'You shall see, my goddess', he replied, and then added, 'I am afraid you must humour my little whim.'

The following day, Quindell's curricle, drawn by two sleek stallions, was brought round to Clarges Street. He and a groom assisted me into the high-sprung carriage, which then, after a jolt, set off quick as lightning down Piccadilly. Startled, I gripped the side of the carriage and placed one hand atop my beaver hat. Seeing this, Quindell threw back his head with a laugh, and reached into his waistcoat pocket for his flask of brandy.

338

He continued to drive us at breakneck speed into the park, where I soon spied in the distance a gathering of similar curricles, horses, men in tall boots and brightly coloured women. Quindell waved his hand and hallooed to them.

'Philly,' I asked with some concern, 'you do not mean me to race with you?'

He grinned as he pulled up his chariot beside Sir John and Lady Lade, who was dressed in a powder-pink habit and matching riding hat.

'No, my goddess,' said he, 'it is the ladies who are racing today.'

I sighed.

'You shall be riding with Lady Lade, in her curricle.'

'Philly!' I cried, now in quite a passion. 'This is too much! I shall not bear it!'

'Come, Hetty dear,' said my friend, extending her grey-gloved hand to me. 'There is nothing to fear. I am reckoned to be the best chariot driver in all of England. Not once have I overturned.'

I looked at my keeper, his lips curled wickedly in amusement.

'Come,' demanded Lady Lade. I had no choice but to do their bidding.

My sturdily built friend placed her arm around my waist, her cheeks already bright red from the cool springtime air. 'We are to race against Mrs Hodges today,' said she as we walked. She gestured with her whip to a slender young woman in green, sipping champagne and surrounded by admirers. 'The Prince has his eye on her, that Mrs Bumpity-Bump. They say she is certain to land in his bed, legs akimbo. But she's only just run off from her husband with Mr Wyndham, so they've plenty a fucks left before they tire of each other,' said she, with a throaty laugh.

I studied the figures surrounding the neatly tailored Mrs Hodges, and saw, all at once, my former companion, Mrs Mahon, in a gold-coloured cape and a feathered military hat, emerge from the throng.

Lady Lade saluted her with her whip, and Gertrude Mahon blew her kiss in return.

'My dear Letitia,' she called, before smiling hesitantly at me, 'and Miss Lightfoot.' She bowed her head.

My mouth quivered. I suppose I may have briefly smiled, but then looked away, rather awkwardly. I felt my heart tighten.

'I know you have a bone to pick with her, Hetty,' scolded Lady Lade, 'but can you not let it rest?'

I raised my eyes to her, chastened somewhat.

'It is not my place to meddle between friends, but I see no good will come of this.' She shook her head. 'You know she is to race in Mrs Hodges' curricle, against us? They contrived it that way, Quindell and that devil Wyndham. They know all about your rivalry and thought it amusing to put you in a pit together, to compete like a pair of fighting cocks.' She sneered. 'Aye, two cocks is what they are, but of the poxed sort!'

Lady Lade and I were then assisted into her chariot, tied with all manner of streaming coloured ribbons. She took the reins into her hands. 'I dare say you've never flown in one of these before, eh, chicken?'

'No,' I breathed, my eyes as wide as the wheels.

'Just you hold tight, then, and nothing ill shall befall us,' she announced as she flicked her whip towards the horses.

A rope had been tied to mark our starting line. We were to race a mile, to a distant cluster of trees, and then turn round and make our way back to the start. All sorts of wagers had exchanged hands. Shortly before the pistol was fired, I heard Colonel Tarleton shout, 'Twenty guineas that Lady Lade overturns and Miss Lightfoot is thrown.'

'Twenty guineas says you are incorrect, sir; that Lady Lade wins, and I thrash you with her whip,' fired back Quindell in my defence.

Then, quite suddenly, the shot went off.

Our team of horse bolted as if their very tails had caught alight. Gracious heavens, had Lady Lade not warned me to hold tight, I fear that impertinent man might have won his wager within the first few moments! I screamed in terror as we shot through the park like a bullet, my companion cackling beside me. I bounced and jumped with each jolt of the wheels. Trees and spectators soared past in a dizzy blur. For the better part of the race, we held the lead, Lady Lade whipping the horses into a positive frothing frenzy. Her face was set in an expression of intense fury, her brows arched, her mouth pinched. She appeared mannish in her determination, and suddenly I understood why no respectable lady would ever be seen to engage in such a competition.

'Heeeeee!' She whooped like a drunkard as we rounded the cluster of trees and began our way back. 'Hey-hooooo!' She waved her whip at the distant crowd.

By then, my heart was in my throat. My fingers and arms were nearly broken from their grip upon the carriage sides. The sight of the finish provided me with only the smallest relief, for while we had completed half of the race, we still had a further distance to ride before I knew for certain that I would be removed from the chariot alive. I spotted Quindell in his greatcoat and modishly tilted round hat from afar, and at that moment, I felt a true loathing for him; from his head to his top-boots. Indeed, my indignation was raised to such a pitch that for a fleeting instant I wished Lady Lade would charge our vehicle directly at him! Suffice to say, the mere thought of it brought an instant smile to my lips.

As we neared the finish line, Mrs Hodges' curricle suddenly broke from its position behind us. In a daredevil show of sportswomanship, she was nearly standing upright in her vehicle, whipping her horses with vixen-like ferocity. This prompted Lady Lade to charge her team even harder. My heart quite unexpectedly leaped with thrill, as my entire person reverberated to the frantic beat of hoofs. I shut my eyes and prayed that the wheels stayed firmly upon the ground, that the axle held in place, that the springs did not pop away from beneath the vehicle. When I opened them, I saw Gertrude Mahon.

Sophie Hodges' carriage was nearly flush with ours, and my friend was but two arm lengths from me. She seemed entirely unruffled. Her expression was calm, composed and slightly sad as she gazed upon me. I looked away, ashamed, as we crossed the finish line, a nose in front of them.

I was unaware that we had won until Lady Lade paid me a kiss and Quindell jumped up upon her gig. He pulled me down into his arms. 'You have won me more than £250 today, my little Venus!' He exclaimed, whirling me around. 'And I am to thrash Ban Tarleton with Lady Lade's whip for your victory!'

My keeper remained in high spirits for the entirety of that day, drinking and bounding about like the puppy he was. As for me, well, I required several hours to recover myself. Even by the time our party repaired to the Star Tavern for refreshment, my knees were still a-tremble.

As we sat in Quindell's curricle bound for the edge of the park at Knightsbridge, he nodded at me, 'You shall have a curricle of your own.'

'That is most kind of you, dear heart,' I began.

'When the Prince sees you attired in your hat and cape, His Royal Highness shall think you the most charming of all the equestriennes.'

I did not know quite how to put it to him, but I had no wish to drive a curricle. 'Philly, I would rather . . . I am not so much a sportswoman as Mrs Hodges or Lady Lade . . .'

I struggled with my words. He appeared so self-satisfied, so pleased at his plans. I recalled my fury upon seeing him, whooping at the finish line while I rode with Lady Lade, terrified out of my wits. He had observed me as if I were his prized stallion, his fighting dog, his silver-spurred cockerel. My aim had never been to be owned by him. Why, I was only here, under his protection, for a short stint, I reminded myself. It was at that moment that a sharp thought stuck in my head. It came upon me so rapidly that I stunned myself even by thinking it: I cared not for charging through Hyde Park in a bouncing two-wheeled carriage, but I did fancy dashing to Paris in a much sturdier vehicle. Might I be so bold as to ask for this? My pulse set off at a pace.

'You see, dear Philly, I am so slight of build, so small . . . all throughout the race I feared I would be thrown from the chariot. Why, I thought I might sail away in the breeze like a leaf.' I lowered my eyes. 'I . . . I am not made of the stuff of those heartier creatures. I require protection, my dear.'

He looked at me fondly, though not without a hint of irritation. He did not wish to have his notions challenged.

'Do you not think a vehicle of a stronger make might suit me . . . such as a town coach?'

He exhaled in exasperation. Then, taking one of my gloved hands in his, he examined my narrow wrist. 'Perhaps you are right, my little

Venus. You would do better in a chariot driven by doves.' A faint smile came upon him as he reconciled himself to this. 'A town coach you shall have,' he announced proudly. 'With a lining of deep blue silk to complement the cornflower of your eyes.'

Chapter 36

I had never before been to a coachmaker, so when Quindell suggested that we pay a visit to Messrs Roberts and Williams on Long Acre, I was most intrigued. We had hardly stepped through the door of their premises when it became apparent to me that Philly was a frequent visitor there. Mr Roberts, a dashing young gentleman, not much older than my keeper, was a racing acquaintance of his and owed him a fair sum of money. It also became apparent that our unexpected appearance at his shop caused him no end of uneasiness. He laughed falsely as he attempted to amuse me by spinning wheels and demonstrating the brightness of his mirrored coach lanterns. Suffice to say, Mr Roberts was eager to take a commission from Philip Quindell, at a generously discounted rate.

The thought of owning my own coach delighted me, for I knew it would provide me with more liberty than I had ever before enjoyed. It was my first genuine step upon the road to Paris. As the town coach's manufacture would take at least two months, Philly permitted me the use of one of his vehicles for my visits to Georgie. I had, until then, been relying upon the hire of post chaises to ferry me, three times a week, to Mrs Brown's cottage in Primrose Hill. As you might imagine, I was enormously grateful that St John had not deprived me of this pleasure. The thought of taking my little boy into my arms never failed to make my heart leap as I came over the hill, and glimpsed the copse of trees behind which the cottage stood. I would sit with him for several hours, feeling him upon my lap, admiring his gurgles and ever-changing expressions. Our time together seemed always to slip away, but after Quindell had promised me my own coach, I began to console myself with the promise of soon coming to claim him. I even permitted myself to imagine the day of my departure. I saw my shellacked carriage stacked with boxes. I savoured how it might feel to travel in complete comfort to Dover with Georgie cradled in my arms. I contemplated the day when I should roll through the narrow grove of trees, through the pasture where the cows grazed. I imagined that I should lift him from his cot where he blew bubbles, and gaze into the eyes he had borrowed from his father. I should hold him at my breast and bid farewell to Mrs Brown, pressing a fat purse into her hand for her troubles. That was how this chapter would end, and how my happy life would commence, I decided.

So think, then, how I felt when, later that month, Quindell's coach brought me to Mrs Brown's cottage and all appeared still. It was usual for the wet nurse or one of her ruddy-cheeked children to throw open the door as soon as they heard the approach of my wheels, but upon that day I was greeted only by the barks of a lone dog. I rapped upon the cottage door but there came no answer. Although it would have been most unusual, I began to wonder if the family had gone out. I knocked again, and this time was certain I heard the scamper of children's feet.

'Mrs Brown,' I called out, 'are you at home?'

I tipped my head and listened, but heard only quiet from within. The dog in the courtyard continued its infernal barking.

'Mrs Brown, it is Miss Lightfoot come to see Master St John,' I tried again.

Several beats of silence were followed by the shout of a young child. Unable to hide herself any longer, Mrs Brown unlatched the door, but ventured only to poke her nose through. Her face appeared drawn.

'Oh madam, how I have dreaded this day,' said she, her eyes wide with fear.

At those words, I do believe my heart stopped. Without so much as a thought, I threw my hands at the door and pushed against it with all my might.

'Oh dear God, Mrs Brown, is he dead? Is my boy dead?' I cried, but the nurse shook her head and reached through to grasp my arm and calm me.

'No, madam, no, he is quite well! He is in the best of health! Oh, I did not mean to alarm you so.'

At that, I fell back, my face still white as powder. 'Then I must see him!' I demanded.

'I am afraid you cannot, madam, for Mr St John has taken him away. He came last week and had him from me. He has taken the child to Wiltshire, to be raised in Lord Bolingbroke's nursery with his lordship's boys.'

Her words came upon me like a hail of arrows. 'He . . . took him away? I can no longer see him? My son, I can no longer see my son?'

She shut her eyes and gently wagged her head.

'I am so very sorry, madam,' said she, her own heart, the heart of a mother, ringing with my pain.

My eyes filled with tears.

'You must beg of Mr St John that privilege,' she said, but I fear she knew what little result that would yield.

It seemed always this way for me. Fortune handed me an advantage, from which Fate then drew a tax.

Lucy hurried to me as soon as she saw my faltering steps. Wailing and defeated, I collapsed into her arms. She bundled me into Quindell's coach, where I continued to sob uncontrollably against her. Dear God, how I cursed St John. When he threatened me on that night at Carlton House, I could not have fathomed what punishment he held in store for me. I had no right to Georgie, not when St John had acknowledged him as his own. In truth, I had always nurtured a fear that he might do with him as he pleased, and now that my boy was gone from me, there was nothing left in the world for me to do.

I did not wish to go home. I briefly considered instructing the coachman to take us to Park Street, to confront the villain who had stolen my child, but then came to my senses. We drove round and round the squares of St James's and Mayfair, until I called out our destination: number 12 Dover Street.

When I approached her door, I prayed that she would see me. I pressed my handkerchief to my face as I knocked, attempting to collect myself, but I knew it would be of no use.

Her butler showed me inside, before disappearing up the stairs to see if she would admit me. 'Please,' I beseeched Fortuna, 'if she turns me away I shall wish myself dead.' But she did not turn me from her door. Instead, the butler escorted me up to her drawing room. The mere sight of her landing, the familiar surrounds of her home, started my tears once more, so that by the time she saw my face and rose to greet me, I was quite beside myself.

She took me to the sofa and laid my head against her shoulder, hushing me as she had on the night I brought Georgie into the world. She stroked the fallen curls of my hair as I sobbed and blubbed like a child.

'Please forgive me,' I muttered between sobs. 'Please . . . please.'

Gertrude Mahon rocked me gently. 'Of course you are forgiven, dear girl. Of course.'

Once I had caught my breath, and my tears had slowed to a trickle, I recounted my tragic tale to her. She listened intently, continuing silently to smooth my hair.

'When you came to me, Hetty, I knew from the look upon your face what had come to pass.'

I shifted my head and glanced up at her. 'How do you mean?'

There was a faint smile on her lips. 'I knew it because this fate befalls us all at some time. Virtuous women too. We are destined to be parted from our children. It is the way of things.'

Her words brought back my silent flow of tears.

'You are most fortunate, my dear,' she continued in a soft voice. 'Little George is lively and healthy. That which took him from you was not death, but the promise of a life of privilege. You could not provide that for him, could you? You could not take him in with you, to live at Philly Quindell's expense. Few men are good enough to tolerate the burden of another man's child under their roof. Women of our sort depend entirely upon the charity of men who do not find children as diverting as do we. No, dear girl. Think instead on how your little son will lead his life.' She touched my cheek and smiled at me. 'He will be raised with his noble cousins in the country; he will enjoy the healthful benefits of Lord Bolingbroke's estate and have the education of a gentleman. St John will make him a settlement, and he will have all the connections he could ever want. When St John sought my counsel on sending George out to nurse, it was these matters I considered. I knew you would disagree, because you are young, my dear, and you know only love, not its consequences.'

I wiped my eyes. She was correct. She had been correct all along, but my heart ached too much at that moment to accept all she said.

'Why, consider your own dear mamma, Hetty. Did she not make a sacrifice similar to yours? Did she not give you up so you might be raised in a noble household, with good connections and an education?'

In the midst of my dilemma I had not reflected upon this uneasy truth. I had not thought for an instant on how entwined my fate had become with that of my mother. What sadness this gave to me, when I did.

'And look what has come of that,' I stated glumly. 'I am here, a gentleman's whore, my life no better than hers.'

This silenced my counsellor, though only briefly.

'It is different for boys. His life will not follow your course.' She then drew breath as if to speak, but stopped. This sudden pause caused me to turn and study her expression, which all at once seemed contemplative and distant.

'Pray,' I breathed, 'tell me your thoughts, Gertrude.'

She smiled. 'I have not told you this before now, but I knew your mamma – though not well, and only briefly.'

'You knew her? But why have you not spoken of this before?' I asked, intrigued.

'Because you are not at all alike,' she laughed. 'You have the wits she never did. She wished only to be amused, to be at the centre of all gaiety. She could be powerfully cruel to her companions, or any person who stood between her and what she desired. There were some among my acquaintance, Mrs Robinson, and Dally Elliot, who said that it was of her own doing that Mr Byram ended up a debtor in the Fleet. She ruined him, and all her friends had abandoned her by then – all but St John.' She turned her warm dark eyes on mine. 'So you see, *petit chaton*, your life is better than hers. You are loved. Your heart is a good one.'

I sighed and thought. 'Perhaps,' I uttered, after a spell. More than anyone in my life, and certainly more than Lady Stavourley, Gertrude Mahon had been like a mother to me. Until then, I had been too stubborn, too impetuous, too childish to appreciate her guidance, but at that moment I began to see its merit clearly, like a constellation among a scattering of stars.

'I am grateful to you, dear Gertrude. I know I have been a fool, on many occasions. I am much in need of advice, on most matters.'

She glowed with pleasure at my words. 'I should hope that, by now, you have acquired some wisdom from me, as well as from your other friends.'

'I have.'

'I should hate to think of you without confidantes when I am abroad.'

At that, I sat up suddenly.

'I have been meaning to tell you, dear, I am departing for Spa with Lord Beauchamp, who means to take the waters. Then, there is talk of Paris, if there is no more unrest.'

I did not know what I should say. I merely sat with my mouth agape.

'But when . . . when do you depart?'

'Tomorrow evening.'

'Oh no, dear madam, no! Not so soon as that . . .'

'Hetty.' She placed her hand upon mine, her tone somewhat chastening. 'I shall return within the year, perhaps within a few months. You need not fear, I am a most constant correspondent.'

Dear reader, I did not take her news well. Indeed, it produced in me such a surge of conflicting emotions that I very nearly did precisely that which my friend had forever warned me against: I all but blurted to her my plan to flee to Paris. I wanted to say that we might even be so fortunate as to meet in that city, should Fate permit it. But in keeping her counsel, in doing what she would have advised me to do, I held my tongue.

Were I to reveal to her my scheme, she would make further enquiries. I would be forced to disclose my history with Allenham, and then she, being most canny, would tie together the various ends of my tale and learn of Georgie's true parentage. From there, it would be merely a slip of the tongue away from Lord Beauchamp's ear, and a letter away from St John. That is how the machinery of gossip turns, and how lives are caught among its gears and torn to shreds. Considering this, I do not doubt she would have commended me for keeping my silence.

I remained with Gertrude Mahon for the better part of the day, knowing that when I quit her house, it was unlikely that we would meet again for some time, if ever. When at last that hour came, the time of our parting, she embraced me, as a friend of the dearest, truest sort.

'I wished to ask,' she began, as we descended her staircase, arm in arm, 'and I hope you do not think it impertinent of me . . .'

My eyes begged her to continue.

'Upon your childbed, you called out a name – Cathy.'

How strange it was to hear my friend speak of her. It caused a sudden shiver to pass through me. I was not quite certain what I should say, and I shrugged uncomfortably.

'She was my sister, Lord Stavourley's legitimate daughter.'

Mrs Mahon continued to regard me, hoping I should throw her further scraps of this story.

'She died on her childbed?'

'No. She died before I fled my father's home, of a fever.'

'Did you flee . . . on account of her death?' Gertrude Mahon could spy a truth in the heart of any tale, no matter how abridged or embellished.

I dropped my head in silence, and then gradually nodded.

'They . . . the servants blamed me, but I did . . . nothing,' I breathed. Even as I spoke of it, I felt the tugs of remorse within me, those terrible remembrances floating to the surface of my mind. I had not permitted myself to think of it for some time; those fears locked within me, the absurd notion that I had somehow willed her death. 'She haunts me,' I admitted, before adding, 'if only her memory.'

Gertrude Mahon touched my shoulder. 'Then remember her with fondness, as you will remember me.'

Chapter 37

To have lost my child and my dearest friend upon the same day was a bitter medicine to swallow. But, like most medicines, its effects were ultimately beneficial. Ah, but now you think me heartless. How is it possible, you may ask, for a mother to suffer her infant to be taken from her and believe it for the best? I confess, at first I struggled with this reversal of fortune. I mourned my son, thinking it unlikely that I would see my Georgie again, and fearing that if we should ever meet, he would not recognize me. How I ached at this notion: my own son a stranger to me. But then I reflected upon my friend's advice and, much like the first time Georgie was taken from me, soon came to see the advantages in this. I had no authority, no power of law or financial means of recovering my boy. Indeed, the only person who did was the child's rightful father, and the sooner I made haste to him, the greater the possibility that we three might one day be reunited.

If my resolve to quit London had in any way grown soft, then it was the departure of my friend and my son that once again stiffened it. In those two months, I became single-minded in my determination to amass the wealth required to fund my journey.

Unlike my previous attempt, this time I thought very closely upon the matter of my escape. Rashness would not do. Each step I took was contemplated with the utmost care, for I did not wish to misjudge Quindell's powers of observation. I knew not if he would notice the sudden absence of a patch box or an aigrette. Although he permitted me use of his credit at any shop in London, would his bankers not raise the alarm if they sighted irregularities? If I ran up too many jeweller's bills and had no new bracelets or earrings to show for it, would he not think it odd? You see, my friends, I had learned some discretion from my past follies.

Shortly after my final interview with Mrs Mahon, I began to keep a ledger of Quindell's gifts. On its pages I made a record of every article of attire, piece of porcelain or jewel I might pawn in order to gain my liberty. I sifted through my assortment of gowns, hats and shoes and decided which among these items I could part with. By summer, I reasoned, I would have no need for heavy cloaks, or for a broadcloth riding habit that clinked with brass and braid. The beaver riding hat might be sold, in addition to an enormous veiled creation, shaped like an upturned basket, which I had disliked from the very moment my keeper had chosen it. A swansdown muff and a tippet of the same would fetch a pretty price, thought I, adding these items to my book. By these means, I would know what I possessed, and then, once I had gathered the courage, I would have each item appraised for its value. When the appropriate time arrived, I would exchange them for ready money. This was a slow and steady strategy, to be sure, but one less likely to trip me up.

Before I launched my campaign, I made some careful enquiries among my acquaintances and learned where a lady might sell a few items without raising too many questions. Only then did I begin my programme of visits to pawn shops around the capital. I established a routine whereby I would undertake my errands in the morning and in the early afternoon return to Clarges Street to mark the quotes into my ledger. Goodness, I thought myself vastly clever, and at least as shrewd as half the merchants in the Royal Exchange.

Now confident that my scheme would succeed, my daring increased, and I began to carry a selection of my trinkets to various jewellers. A snuff box, a pearl bracelet, a gold watch on its chain with a key and fobs, were each assessed in their turn. I brought in for a valuation as well the diamond necklace and eardrops I had been wearing on the night I parted with St John. I had pinned a good deal of hope on achieving a sizeable price for these, but the jeweller, taking the sparkling collar from my fingers, held it to the light and tutted.

'Vauxhall glass and paste gems,' he said, 'but of a good make. One shilling and sixpence.'

I could hardly believe it! Sitting in the coach on my return home, a wry smile crept upon me. Indeed, I began to wonder if St John had not confiscated my jewels in an effort to spare his pride rather than to punish me.

Perhaps it was the disappointment of this discovery that encouraged me to increase my game, for by early May I had decided to sell a few of my trifles. These were merely small objects that would not be missed: a garnet-studded hairpin, a gold comb, a pearl buckle. If queried, I would simply claim I had lost them. I eagerly handed these over to the jeweller, but was dispirited by the small sums they produced. Travel was so dear, and I knew I required a great deal of money to make my way to Paris. I would have bills for my lodgings and meals, I knew not for how many weeks. There would be the hire of a coachman, perhaps a postillion as well, in addition to Lucy's wages. Gracious, until then I had never considered how costly were such matters. I was no house-keeper, I had no mind for economy. Nevertheless, as a result of my prudent little sales, I soon gained the satisfaction of feeling coins in my hand.

I confess, this secret occupation of mine eventually came to consume me. My quiet moments were given over to counting and cogitating. I felt myself turning magpie, forever admiring trinkets in shop windows and wondering at their prices. Without Georgie to possess my thoughts, this mercenary activity filled my days. Why, had I been a person of lesser morality, I might have been tempted to filch a number of the glittering objects which lay all about my home. Certainly this was the course of action recommended by Miss Ponsonby when she first called upon me at my new lodgings.

She and the Greenfinch had paid me a visit shortly after Quindell installed me at Clarges Street. As I led them through the rooms, Caroline Ponsonby gawped like a child at St Bartholomew's Fair. She sighed at the Duke of Chandos's Sèvres china and the fine Irish linen, and gasped at my modishly appointed drawing room, adorned with Roman style furnishings.

'Oh, he has done well by you, to be sure, Hetty,' she marvelled, with wide eyes.

Miss Greenhill said nothing, but silently took in the surroundings, her face perfectly stony.

'Have you not considered what riches are at your disposal?' remarked Miss Ponsonby.

'Well . . .' I stammered. 'No, I have not . . .'

'Oh, but look about you,' she enthused. 'Why, you might sell the vases and the silver alone and find yourself as rich as Croesus.'

'But why should she want to do that, Caroline?' spoke the Greenfinch at last. 'These are not *her* belongings, you goose. They belong to Mr Quindell, and Hetty could be hanged for thieving,' she sang out, her eyes fixed on me, as if daring me to attempt it. 'No, my dear, if Miss Lightfoot is in want of funds, then she must be sure to pawn only her keeper's gifts, and not be so foolish as you . . .'

Miss Ponsonby fell suddenly silent. A flush spread across her face, though I could not determine whether it arose from shame or indignation.

'Caroline was sent to the Fleet for her debts,' Miss Greenhill announced with a provocative arch of her brow.

'But only for a fortnight,' Miss Ponsonby protested.

'My dear,' began the Greenfinch with a haughty snort, 'to attempt to flee one's keeper in the broad light of day, when he has not yet settled your shopkeepers' bills, is the behaviour of a dunce.'

'I was but fifteen and he was a booby,' declared Miss Ponsonby.

'But not so much of a booby as to forget to set the bailiffs on you.'

Caroline Ponsonby glared angrily at her friend.

'No, Miss Lightfoot,' Mary Anne Greenhill continued with a coy simper, 'a woman of our sort must be clever with regard to all manner of things.' Her gaze wandered downward towards my middle. There, upon a blue silk ribbon, hung Quindell's miniature portrait, surrounded by diamonds. I noted her rapt expression. How dearly she wished to fondle that expensive bauble! Her fingers twitched in anticipation. I held it out to her, and from the instant she took it in her hand, a broad smile appeared upon her face. 'For example, should you find yourself in need, you might sell ... this ...' Her eyes twinkled as she admired the piece, then, in a sudden fit of girlish giggling, she looked away. 'He is most handsome, Mr Quindell.'

While I understood perfectly well that pawning the contents of Quindell's house was more likely to lead me to the gallows than to Paris, I confess there was one instance when I made an exception.

Friends, that which I am about to disclose to you may on first reading do nothing to improve your opinion of my character, but I ask you to consider all the circumstances before passing judgement.

As you well know, my home on Clarges Street belonged in every way to my keeper. Any say I had in its decoration or use was at his discretion. To all intents, he saw my abode merely as an extension of his own. He came and went at his leisure, most of the time unannounced. Furthermore, he possessed a habit of decamping to my quarters with an entire cortège of friends and strangers. Besides his usual associates, on any given night I might discover anyone from the Prince of Wales and the Duke of York to a jig dancer and a blind fiddler in my drawing room. Why, one evening I returned after dining with Sir John and Lady Lade to find Quindell slumped drunk in a chair, and Lord Barrymore lying upon my sofa with a tawdry young whore in frayed ribbons beneath him.

Naturally, I was required to act the hostess on these occasions: to dance and roister with them, to play a hand of cards, or, on less barbaric evenings, to host a supper. Sadly, all of my well-bred curtseying and simpering was lost on them, for they had no mind for politeness when making use of my home. To Philly Quindell, George Hanger, Ban Tarleton, the Barrymores and Lord Sefton, my lodgings were no better than a nursery stocked with diverting toys. They cared not for the fine china; their elbows regularly knocked plates and teacups from the polished tables. Wine glasses were thrown into the fire so they might watch the flames spit. An urn of flowers was set alight, and a hot poker pushed through the table linen. Not even the paintings were spared from ill-use. One night, Tarleton acted out some scene he had witnessed during the American War. He prowled about the dining room, a carving knife in his hand, and then, with the cry of a Mohawk warrior, plunged it through the breast of a portrait. The company roared with amusement, but I gasped in horror. In wielding his knife, he had not only cut out the heart of the matron within the frame, but scratched a small Dutch landscape beside it.

The following morning, overcome with sadness, I examined the scene of this atrocity. 'Dear Philly,' I complained to him, 'it shall not do to have a picture on my dining-room wall in such a bedraggled state. Might I have it mended?'

Quindell, who was suffering from the previous evening's merriment, merely groaned. 'Hideous things, those pictures. I do not mind what you have done with them.'

And so, at his command, I wrote directly to a Mr William Birch, artist, picture restorer and dealer in art, who possessed a shop on New Bond Street, and requested that he call upon me on a matter of business. This he did the following morning, whereupon I directed him to the dining room, the scene of the misadventure.

'Pray, Mr Birch,' I begged, 'is it beyond repair?'

Mr Birch folded his arms and studied the hole. He poked it and then stood back. 'I dare say not,' he concluded, after a spell. 'And what of the landscape?' he asked, approaching the canvas filled with sky, cloud and flat Flemish scenery. 'Should you like this repaired as well, madam?'

I had not considered the second picture. The scratch was discernible, but did not mar the placid beauty of the image.

'I . . . I . . .'

'If I may be so bold, madam, it is an exceptionally well-rendered piece,' he encouraged me. 'Jacob Van Ruisdael, I believe. A Dutch artist, very much in demand among connoisseurs.'

'It had not occurred to me . . .'

'Might you consider selling it, madam? Notwithstanding the scratch, I would pay you handsomely for it.'

I stared at him, not knowing what reply to make. Certainly, the painting was not mine to sell and I opened my mouth to tell him as much, when something prevented me.

'You say you would pay me handsomely?' I ventured, anxiously fingering the ribbon at my throat.

'Eighty-five pounds, shall we say? . . . No more than £90.'

Ninety pounds! I did all I could to prevent myself crying out. To think that I might acquire ready funds so instantaneously! Why, that amount was likely to account for all of my travelling expenses and still leave a surplus. It would enable me to make my escape as soon as my coach had been completed and delivered. I pressed my hand to my breast and turned from Mr Birch.

'I shall venture as high as £92, madam, but that is all I am able to make good on for the moment.'

Had Philly not instructed me to do as I would with the pictures? He loathed them. He had no eye for art. They were of no more interest to him than the wall upon which they hung. Would it not be better for someone to enjoy the scene? A connoisseur, who could admire the artist's skill, who would hang the painting proudly among similar treasures?

'Yes,' I responded, 'very well then. You may have it at that price.'

Mr Birch made me a humble bow. 'Then I shall have my boy collect both tomorrow and order my banker to write out a draft.'

My brazen deed left me a good deal shaken. I fretted that Quindell would miss the picture and, after an enquiry or two among my staff, learn the truth of my actions. But he never did. In fact, he never even noticed that the work had gone.

Dear friends, I know what you make of my deed, how dishonest you think it, but I urge you to withhold your censure. Think only that some gentle soul, some person of refined taste, now enjoys the beauty of that Dutch landscape. Think only of how I preserved this distinguished object from its likely ruin at the hands of one who saw no value in it. Why, think – perhaps this fine example of a painting is now a subject of study for young artists, who learn by Mr Van Ruisdael's skill. So you see, my action was not so base as you might think, for not only did it serve to benefit me, but others as well.

Two days' later, a banker's draft for the princely sum of £92 was handed over to me. Oh, that you might have seen me at that moment. I beamed with gratitude, my fingers grew hot, my face flushed with excitement. I could think of little else but what this slip of paper was to buy me, and carried it immediately to my dressing room. There, I went to my clothes press, unlocked a cabinet and a drawer, and pulled from beneath a pile of linens my small coffer of funds.

First ensuring that my dressing-room door was safely locked, I laid out all my money before me, much as I had on that day at the Stag when I was still an ingénue. I counted out my coins into piles, and with a racing heart tabulated the total. There before me was £112 2*s*. 4*d*. – a small fortune, to be sure, but this was only the half of it. In my ledger was an estimate for the value of my apparel, trinkets and jewels. By then, I had determined to sell only several select items of jewellery and preserve the rest, in case I should be in want of funds in Paris. These items would amount to a further £289 8*s*. 3*d*. – a vast sum indeed. My stomach turned over with excitement. *I would go to Paris!* I had only to await the arrival of my new coach.

On a mild morning during the first week of June, I was drawn to the window by loud shouts and brays from the street below. There, before the door to my house, was a perfectly shining, dark green and black coach, its wheels tipped with red paint. Harnessed to it was a team of two bay horses, their heads crowned with green feathers, and perched atop the matching hammer cloth was Quindell, driving them.

'Oh!' I cried in astonishment, and flew down the stairs. I could scarcely contain my high spirits. 'Lucy! Lucy!' I called out. 'My town coach! Mr Quindell has brought my town coach!'

Philly came to me wearing a broad smile. ' My Venus, you have now a chariot.' He bowed with a theatrical flourish.

The remainder of that day was spent driving through the town and parks at dangerous speeds. Quindell whooped with childish glee as he shook the reins and urged the team into a gallop. On another occasion, I might have screamed with terror as I was tossed from the leather seat against the blue-damask-lined cabin, but that day I was numb to every-thing but dreams of my future. I sat in a glassy-eyed reverie, still and contemplative.

That evening, I summoned Lucy to me. 'My dear,' I announced with a slight smile and a tremble, 'the time is upon us.'

Remembering Caroline Ponsonby's cautionary tale, I proposed that we take our leave on the night of the ninth of June, in precisely five days. Together we began to gather the gowns and winter apparel, shoes, hats and feathers I proposed to sell. All of these, along with various jewels, trinkets and an unwanted ivory snuff box given to me by Major Hanger in a secret bid for my affections, were to be exchanged within the next four days. I had also the task of acquiring the necessary documents for travel. I did not know if such a feat were possible, and, more to the point, if it might be accomplished within that short time.

'No one,' I breathed, 'not a soul alive should know of my plans.'

Lucy nodded vigorously.

Then, recognizing the sternness of my words, and knowing how true she had proven herself to me, I laid my hand upon her shoulder. 'But I trust in you completely,' I said, smiling.

Now imagine, dear reader, how difficult were the following days for me, with so much plotting and planning afoot. I slept no more than a few hours at a time and rose early every morning to begin my errands. My first task was to purchase the silence of my household. It pained me to distribute no less than £9 in bribes between the five servants. As Quindell had hired both a coachman and a postillion for me, I was not inclined to trust them. Not only was it necessary that I buy their confidence, but that I convince them to accompany me upon my journey to Paris. The coachman had a wife and family to feed, and so I found myself pressing a further £3 into his hand. And it did not end there. Any set of eyes that might observe the bustling to and fro from my address, any pair of ears that might overhear some detail of my plan, required payment: a shilling here, five pennies there. Let it not be said that maintaining a secret costs nothing, for my purse was lightened long before a single trunk was loaded upon my coach.

As I occupied myself with this matter, Lucy was sent out with my belongings, wrapped in parcels and hidden in boxes. Dutifully, she would return to me, like a labourer coming home from the harvest, the fruits of her endeavours jingling in a purse. My bounty grew larger; my head spun with numbers, my fingers became blackened from handling coins. Indeed, by the third day, I grew so distracted and desperate to depart that at times I found it difficult merely to sit still. The worst of it by far was the effort required to maintain my composure in the company of others.

I did not have the heart to turn my regular callers from the door. My dear companions, Lady Lade and Miss Ponsonby, and even the infuriating Miss Greenhill, arrived each in their turn and were shown into my parlour or dressing room. We sipped our tea as we had always done, while Spark darted through my apartments, growling at the maids. At the sight of such an ordinary scene, one might never have believed that a great change was on the way: that Lucy was, at that moment, selling my apparel; that, rather than listening to the Greenfinch boast about her new fur-edged cloak, I was dwelling on the matter of my impending sea crossing. Indeed, in those final days, I scarcely felt myself present anywhere but in my head.

On the day before I was due to depart, Lady Lade came with Mrs Cuyler and gossiped all morning about Mrs Robinson's quarrel with Ban Tarleton, while I sat with a blank face, fidgeting.

'Child,' Letitia Lade began as she rose to leave, 'your colour has gone off, for sure. You have not seemed at all yourself these past few days.' Her eyes then wandered down to my belly, before she raised a brow enquiringly at me.

'No.' I smiled, shaking my head.

'You mind that,' she warned, wagging a friendly finger.

As I watched her depart, I sighed. I was sorry that I could not bid any of my acquaintances farewell, those friends whose companionship I had come to value greatly, whose spirited good humour had raised me from misery on so many occasions. I know not how I would have endured my life with St John without their company, or tolerated Philly Quindell's antics, but to confess my plans to them would have been folly.

To be sure, it was far more difficult to keep my secret from my friends than to hide it from Quindell – he failed to notice any change in my demeanour whatsoever. Philly carried on as he had always, filling my ears with drunken prattle and nonsense, exclaiming over a bet he had lost at Almack's or recounting a tale he had heard of a lady who found a mouse in her nightcap. Then, when it came time to tumble me upon the bed, I turned my busy mind to thoughts of my beloved and

361

his welcoming arms. Only once my keeper was snoring soundly beside me did I dare to offer my usual prayer of gratitude that yet another day had passed without my plot being discovered.

On the fourth night – the eve of my departure – I was too pre-occupied to do even that. I had strategized my every movement like a general preparing for battle, and now the time had arrived to execute my plans.

My first concern was Quindell. It was necessary that he should be kept as far from Clarges Street as possible, so that the enormous under-taking of packing my belongings and loading my coach could be performed undetected. That afternoon, I had taken care to send him a note claiming that I was 'inconvenienced with a female complaint' and begged that he would not call upon me until the following afternoon. Once that had been dispatched, Lucy set to work, emptying my presses and drawers and filling my boxes for travel.

I had my windows shuttered and the drapery pulled as soon as darkness fell, but the candles continued to burn late into the night. I stood over Lucy, pacing and chattering anxiously. I had no wish to rest or even to stand still, and rebuffed the beckoning advances of my bed, whose coverlet I refused to touch.

I cannot say what time it was when I heard a loud commotion at the door downstairs. My belongings were packed and Lucy had just embarked upon sewing my most precious jewels into the hem of the riding habit I was to wear. The noise startled me, and I crept from my dressing room on to the darkened landing to listen. It was then I heard Quindell's unmistakable voice rise from below.

'Dear God!' I breathed to Lucy. 'Mr Quindell is here!'

Terror spread across her face like cracks upon a sheet of ice.

I took the key from the door and locked her in, and then went sail-ing down the stairs.

'Philly!' I cried to him as he gazed up at me from the hall. There was no need to feign illness, for my face was pallid from shock. 'Whatever is the matter?'

But Quindell's bright expression did not burn out upon meeting with my cold one.

'Hetty! Oh dearest Hetty!' he sang out. 'I have such thrilling news to relay, I could not bear to keep it from you for one moment longer!'

I stopped still where I stood, a false smile twitching upon my lips.

'What? What might that be, dear one?' I enquired, a sense of dread rising within me.

'Mr Sheridan has agreed for you to play Maria in *The School for Scandal*!'

I continued to regard him, unmoved. His words made no sense to me.

'Miss Bates was thrown from her horse this morning and Sheridan was all at sea as to what to do – until I proposed you as her replacement! I say, it was a stroke of genius on my part . . . I know not why it never occurred to me before to do such a thing . . . Why, I had him right beside me at the faro table. I turned to the devil and offered him £500 to engage you in the role, and by Jove, he agreed!'

I could do nothing but stare at Quindell. My ears had not yet conveyed to my mind all that he said, or the implications of it. My mouth parted, and somehow, I began to speak.

'I do not wish to go upon the stage,' I stated numbly.

Quindell then bounded up the steps and took hold of me.

'But *I* wish you to! Oh my dear Thalia, my muse of comedy, you shall be celebrated by all of London! They shall all hail the name of Quindell for having found you! You shall be another Mrs Farren, another Mrs Siddons! They shall cry your name as I escort you from the green room, they shall throw roses at your feet wherever we walk!'

'But—'

'Darling goddess,' he said, going down upon his knees. 'You, *you* are to play opposite Mrs Jordan, *the* indomitable Mrs Jordan as Lady Teazle, and the great Kemble himself as Sir Peter!' he exclaimed, dizzy with drink and high spirits. 'I have dreamed of this moment, when I should be the adoring swain of an actress who is fêted by all society! And, dear girl, you need not fret, for I shall be there beside you, to help you to learn your lines, to keep watch over Mr Kemble and his direction . . .'

He reached into his coat pocket and handed me a book. It bore the gilt words *The School for Scandal* upon it.

'Rehearsals have already begun, but I dare say you, my clever muse, shall require scarcely any time to commit Maria's part to memory,' he beamed. 'You begin tomorrow, dear goddess, and make your début next month. Oh, come, sweet morning! Tomorrow begins your triumph upon the stage! And I shall be there. I shall wake at your side and deliver you to Drury Lane myself, where I shall sit and observe my Thalia perform!'

Perhaps it was the exhaustion, or the thunderous shock of it all, but I sensed my lower lip begin to tremble. Then my chin followed suit, and my eyes grew sore and wet. Soon, fat tears were streaming across my cheeks. I could say nothing, I could do nothing, but stretch my mouth into an odd, fixed grin. It was, dear reader, my first attempt at acting.

Chapter 38

There are two things I recall most about that morning. The first is the rain, for it came in torrents. It hammered upon the roofs and streamed down from the eaves, until the streets flowed with mud. It coated the windows of Quindell's coach in a silty wash of taupe grey, a hue that matched the colour of the sky. As I sat within this viewless carriage, Philly pressing my hand, I felt as if I was travelling to the theatre in a tightly locked box. I remember, too, my thoughts: how I wished to tear at the door and flee, how I chanted to myself all the while, *I cannot stay, I cannot remain here. I shall take my leave tonight . . . or tomorrow. I need only an hour or so to make my escape.* My heart continued to urge me forward with the determination of a cavalry commander, but my head, I fear, was not entirely inclined to obey its orders. Doubt had begun to creep upon me and weigh me down, long before I had lifted my head from my pillow.

Philly had risen before me and ordered his valet to fetch his finest suit of deep-blue silk and his gold waistcoat from St James's Square, so he might be suitably dressed to accompany me to Drury Lane. To be sure, his mind was so preoccupied with his plan for me that even my packed boxes and the empty tables of my dressing room failed to arouse his notice. He was entirely blind to my reluctance, to my stooped shoulders and slow, heavy gait. Instead he fairly danced with joy and preened himself like a peacock in all the looking glasses.

Upon our arrival, we were shown along a network of stairs and corridors to the rooms of Mr John Philip Kemble, who was, as you might remember, not only a heralded presence upon the stage, second only to the late Mr Garrick, but, like the former, also the manager of the Drury Lane theatre. Before we had so much as approached this man's door, I had some idea of what I was to find behind it. There came from down the corridor such a blaze of high-pitched shrieking that I feared someone to be in distress. I looked with trepidation at Quindell and then at the theatre's liveried servant, who seemed completely unmoved by the sounds. He stopped and rapped at the door, whereupon the cries were suddenly silenced.

'Come!' instructed a deep voice.

The door opened to reveal a scene which at first I believed to be a rehearsal for a farce, for before me stood the great Kemble, his hands upon his hips, opposed by two ladies: one, the tiny Mrs Kemble, in hysterics, a sodden handkerchief in her hand; the other, the resplendent Mrs Jordan, her mane of curly brown locks crowning her proudly held head. Our arrival brought an abrupt end to their theatrical disagreement.

'Mr Quindell, sir . . .' announced the servant, 'and . . .'

'Yes, I know,' Kemble interrupted, his face taut with irritation. 'And this is the Maria thrust upon me by our dear proprietor. Dear, dear Mr Sheridan, so concerned about the fortunes of this theatre that for a price he will put the mistress of any man in London upon its stage.'

Mrs Kemble's swollen eyes fixed on me, unrelenting and furious. I could not imagine what I had done to so immediately raise this woman's ire, but I would soon learn.

'Your name, madam?' asked the manager.

'Miss Henrietta Lightfoot,' said Quindell with pride.

At that, Kemble's stormy features suddenly rearranged themselves.

'*Miss* Lightfoot?' he asked, intrigued. 'Miss?' Then he released a whirlwind of laughter.

His wife looked away with a smirk.

'Why, the last I read of you was in the *Morning Herald*. Mr John St John was parading you about London, holding you aloft like a Papist's Madonna for all the world to bear witness to your immaculate conception. You bore him a son, did you not? A bouncing addition to the house of St John?' He rolled his eyes and sighed. 'That man and his pen. He is a plague, I tell you. Not one word of worthy drama has ever dripped from it.' He turned to Quindell. 'She is yours now?'

'My devoted Thalia, yes,' he gushed, his eyes affixed on Mrs Jordan. Indeed, I, too, was dazzled to be standing so near to this celebrated player. Her very presence overawed me. Certainly, I could not possibly appear upon the stage beside this lady. Why, I possessed no talent for acting. I would be humiliated, to be sure. The very notion of this turned my stomach.

'Mr Quindell, sir, with all due respect to you, I cannot in good faith bill her as *Miss* Lightfoot.'

Quindell furrowed his brow. 'Why ever not?'

'Because, sir, due to the efforts of your predecessor, the entire world knows she is no *Miss*! I should be pelted in the street, laughed off the stage and lampooned in the engravers' shop windows – as should your fair Thalia, sir.' He drew an exasperated breath and lamented, 'Yet again I have been sent another Maria who is as much a virgin as Messalina.'

'Heaven forbid, another Mrs Jordan,' his wife simpered, examining her rival from the corner of her eye.

'No, sir, in my house she shall be billed as Mrs Lightfoot, to spare her blushes.'

And that, dear reader, is how, just shy of my nineteenth birthday, I acquired the name which has followed me ever since.

From that, the day of our meeting, I did not much care for Mr Kemble, and he, resentful at having a wealthy rake's mistress thrust upon him in the interests of Mr Sheridan's pocket, found me especially disagreeable. Indeed, within just a few days I came to dread him, to fear his dark, rumbling appearance, and the manner in which he charged at me with his sharp, lance-like scolds. With the wisdom of age, I have now found it in my heart to forgive the man. I cannot blame him for his frustrations, for I was a hopeless performer and entirely unsuited to appear in a work of comedy. Undoubtedly, Kemble sensed this from the outset. What promise of success could a young lady with a drooping head and a downturned mouth have offered him?

Nonetheless, as a manager he understood perfectly who paid his wages and, in truth, had no more say about my appearance in this production than did I. After a great deal of scowling and huffing, he dispatched me to the stage, along with Mrs Kemble, who was to play the part of Lady Sneerwell, the lanky Mr Preston, in the role of Snake, and several other members of the company, so we might read through the first act. Timidly, I crept behind the troop of experienced players as they jested and jigged their way backstage, knocking the wigs from one another's heads and laughing at each other's antics like schoolboys. Hesitantly creeping out upon the boards, I caught sight of Quindell in his fine laces and silks, perched like a monkey in his box, his face the only thing aglow in the empty house. It was as if this entire performance had been arranged for his delight alone, which, in a manner of speaking, I suppose it had been. He had paid £500 for the privilege.

And so, dear friends, I stood upon the stage at Drury Lane, that very place at which I had gazed countless times, surrounded by the illustrious personages whose talents I had so admired, and was so overcome with trembling that I could hardly hold my volume of *The School for Scandal.* Oh, so many would have exchanged places with me in a heartbeat! So many young ladies dream of such a début, and yet at that moment I would have bartered with the devil not to have been there, but upon the potholed road to Paris instead, or tossed upon the sea in a packet ship bound for France.

Carefully, I followed the reading, as Mrs Kemble, Mr Preston and Mr Fallon, in the role of Joseph Surface, volleyed their lines between them in a spirited fashion. Then came my turn. I attempted to swallow the lump lodged in my throat, but failed.

'"O there's that disagreeable lover of mine, Sir Benjamin Backbite, has just called at my guardian's, with his odious—"'

'Mrs Lightfoot! If you will speak up!' boomed Kemble from the left of me.

I stopped, too terrified even to offer a nod. I began once more.

'"O there's that disagreeable lover of mine, Sir Benjamin Backbite—"'

'Damn you, girl! I will have no mice upon my stage! Speak up!'

Mrs Kemble pricked me with her needle-like eyes before snorting with disgust.

Now I was truly beside myself, the distress upon my face plain for all the company to view. I drew a deep breath and belted my line: '". . . with his odious uncle, Crabtree, so I slipt out, and ran hither to avoid them."'

There was a pause as the actors and actresses awaited my further chastisement. None came, and so we continued.

With every turn of the page my terror renewed itself, as the name Maria appeared in bold, once, twice, thrice – so many lines! Each opening of my mouth brought further disapproval.

'Mrs Lightfoot, if you are to act in my theatre, you must use your lungs! Zounds, girl! Pretend for once that you are not reading at the bedside of your elderly aunt!'

'Are you made of wood, girl? Where is your sensibility, madam?'

So it proceeded, until all the company came to rolling their eyes, or sighing or sniggering at each of my attempts. When at last we arrived at the end, I thought I was certain to collapse from the strain of it. I had never known such mortification, and I nibbled at my lower lip in the thin hope that I should succeed in pressing back my tears.

Kemble threw up his arms and exhaled in that dramatic manner which actors are known to assume behind as well as in front of the curtain.

'We shall have scene two now,' he declared, whereupon a dresser arrived to escort me to my room backstage.

'Mrs Lightfoot,' he called after me, 'I dare say you should use your time wisely and impress upon your brain Maria's lines.' He then squinted into the darkness of the house and pointed his look at Quindell.

'I know not how I am to carve an actress from this block of wood, Mr Quindell, for she is by far the worst Sheridan has ever sent me. You tell him that, sir. Do enquire of him if he shall be pleased with his five hundred pounds when she causes the curtain to fall early on his celebrated masterpiece.'

Wishing to flee from the stage as quickly as I could, I hurriedly followed my dresser, clasping my book against my breast as if it might shield me from further blows. We had hardly moved behind the curtain when I was accosted by a sharp hiss. I jumped with fright and turned to find Mr Preston reclining beneath the cast of a wall sconce, smiling wickedly at the reaction he had caused.

'Take no notice of Kemble, pretty Mrs Lightfoot. He is in sore need of a fuck,' he purred. 'As am I.'

I regarded him, too rattled by events to respond as I ought to such an affront, and scurried on through the blackness.

'I dare say we shall have some business together,' he called out after me, 'pretty little whore.'

It is true, to some degree, what the moralists say about actors: many of them are of the lowest sort – lewd, depraved, foul of mouth and temper. On that first day, they seemed to me like overgrown children, who, having received no discipline in the nursery, retained their precocious, wild ways. They did as they pleased, said what they pleased and battled constantly among themselves over the most trifling of matters. The disagreement between Mrs Kemble and Mrs Jordan that my arrival at the manager's dressing room had ended had, I was later informed, been over the ownership of a silk handkerchief. Oh, dear reader, I was not formed for this sort of life. Remember how tender and genteel had been my upbringing? Although I had learned to contend with the whims of Lady Catherine, this, I feared, was an entire nest of vicious vipers and cats. I knew not how I would defend myself against their slurs, their jealousies and attacks. Their claws flew at me from all directions. 'Dear God,' thought I, as I followed my guide through this backstage Hades, 'I must flee this place – but *how*?'

We wove our way through an entire city wrapped in darkness, the like of which I could never have imagined existed, behind the mountainous set pieces upon the stage. Ropes and rigging hung like vines from above our heads, through which emerged an array of foreign faces and sounds: banging hammers, the blast of a French horn, a bellowing signora crying out some Italian curse. Two dancers – olive-faced girls with suspicious eyes – followed me as we passed between the curtains of their dressing room, their flounced costumes thrown over chests and looking glasses. Guttering candles offered only pinpricks of light along our course, through which I failed to spy so much as a single door or window that might lead me to the outside world. A baby cried somewhere out of sight and the scent of oil paint and beer permeated the air. Seamstresses and laundresses pushed by us with their baskets. I squinted hopelessly through the dim labyrinth, searching for whatever menace might come at me next, eager to find a possible passage to freedom. At last I arrived, like Orpheus led through the underworld, at a small corner surrounded by drapery. This was to be my place. A single light fluttered upon a dressing table, over which some thoughtful hand had written on a card, 'Maria'. My heart sank as I read it. Once the card might have borne the name 'Henrietta Ingerton', another time, 'Miss Lightfoot', but now this was the role I was expected to play, the next step in a continuous succession. Quindell had paid for me to dance to his desires, he wished me to leap at the crack of Kemble's whip. I was to perform like a puppet, like a slave girl in chains.

'I require nothing further.' I swallowed anxiously, knowing that as soon as the servant withdrew, I would be left alone and unguarded. As I watched her depart, my stomach suddenly lurched. 'Now! Flee now!' urged my heart, thudding wildly beneath the volume of *The School for Scandal* still clasped at my breast. My eyes began to dart this way and that, but my feet refused to follow.

It was doubt that caused my legs to hold fast. Over the hours, the few seeds of uncertainty that lay within me had swollen and grown. I thought of Lucy, who by now would have completed the unpacking of my boxes. I thought of Quindell pursuing me, discovering me at Clarges Street. I thought of how he might detain me, or restrain me. These pictures consumed me, confusing my spinning head with further hesitation and fear, until that brief moment in which I might have attempted an escape was lost.

'Dearest Thalia!' came an all-too-familiar voice. Quindell's sudden appearance caused me to leap with alarm and sent my book flying from my startled hands. In horror, I watched as the volume flung itself at my dressing table and fell upon the lit candle. Together, the pair tumbled to the floor in a fiery embrace.

Dear friends, you know well enough that I am not one to make kindling of books. On any other occasion I might have sprung to the aid of this imperilled tome, this unwanted gift from my keeper. In fact, I moved to snatch it from its certain death, but stopped. The volume lay at my feet, open at its frontispiece, whereupon a portrait of Richard Brinsley Sheridan glowered at me. I beheld his face, the face I had seen as a girl at Melmouth, the face of the man who now owned me. We stared at one another for but an instant before I saw the flames advance upon him, burning away his name, his cheeks, his mercenary eyes. I permitted the pages to blacken and smoulder, to dissolve into fire, for on this occasion, on this one instance, I could not find it in my heart to do otherwise.

Chapter 39

It was Quindell who burst forward and stamped upon the flames, crushing the smoking book beneath his diamond-buckled shoes. A replacement was ordered immediately. Scarcely had he caught his breath than he sent his manservant flying to the nearest bookseller.

'Jehu,' he sighed, 'what good fortune that I arrived to protect you from the conflagration.'

From that moment, I recognized how my life was to be ordered. Indeed, it was just as my doubting mind had feared: Philly would not let me be.

As you know, my keeper would not have his desires denied to him, and with his heartfelt wish so near fulfilment, he grew all the more eager to see it come to pass. In his eyes, I ceased to be a mere mistress, a charming and distracting possession. Instead, I became his chariot to glory.

He was loath to leave my side, and when he could not attend me personally, he sent his valet, Sam, to do so. It was, he explained, his sole intention to wait upon my every need.

'I shall be as a slave to you, my Thalia, the cup-bearer to a goddess,' he pledged as he escorted me back to Clarges Street. 'I shall be forever at your service. I vow to pass every night in your bed, to purchase for you the finest costume any Maria ever wore upon the stage. We shall recite your part together every day, until Sheridan's celebrated words are graven upon your heart. Be assured, dear muse, I shall see to it that you triumph,' said he, planting a kiss upon my forehead.

But to me, his promises sounded like a sentence of death.

All that evening, I could think of nothing but his decree. I knew that, under such conditions, the likelihood of an escape would continue to grow dimmer, until it expired altogether. I could not fathom how I would orchestrate such a move without my keeper's knowledge, how my belongings might be packed in secret, how I would prepare for departure away from his watchful gaze. And for those among you who wonder why I did not simply take hold of my heavy purse and bid Quindell adieu, I knew too well that brazenness would achieve nothing. Philly would have engaged every bailiff in London to impede my route to Dover and drag me back to Drury Lane by way of the debtors' sponging house. I dare say I knew better than to repeat the fateful errors made by Caroline Ponsonby, whose cautionary tale remained lodged in my mind. No, dear friends, by that night, I came to recognize my defeat. Doubt had conquered hope and trounced my resolve.

It was only as I lay in bed, staring up at the canopy, that I understood what had come to pass that day. This unfortunate turn of events was no accident – it was my sister's doing.

I had chosen to dismiss Lady Catherine's appearances in my dreams. My rational mind had convinced me that her visitations and hateful words were my imaginings. But they were not. She had cursed me.

Upon my childbed she had warned me that I should never keep my son – and indeed, my Georgie was taken from my arms, twice. Still, I did not care to heed her threats. She had promised me soured joys and blackened triumphs, she had vowed that I would never escape my prison. I was foolish enough to think she spoke of an earthly gaol, a dungeon with doors and locks, but now I saw what she intended for me. I had no means of escape from the life into which I had been thrown. This, I came to believe, was my rightful punishment for straying from duty and honour, for living by my heart, for wandering. I would not go to Paris. I would rot here instead.

Over the following weeks, I slipped into a sort of numbing melancholy. A lethargy attacked my limbs, and when Kemble did not require me to attend rehearsals, I lay in bed as if ill. My malaise was worsened by Quindell's tireless vigil. He devotedly upheld his promises to me, forever hovering, forever reciting from that wretched play – in his coach, at his table, in my bed – until, driven to despair, I would shut my eyes and feign sleep. At times it seemed that wherever I directed my gaze, he came into my line of sight, whether I stood upon the stage or in my apartments, whether I sat in the green room or at my dressing table. He became more than a shadow at my back: he became my puppet master, and I his marionette.

As you might imagine, my heart sank very low indeed. I ceased to receive callers at my home, for I no longer desired company or conversation. When Quindell demanded these of me, I could scarcely muster more than a pathetic smile to charm him. In public, I was but a hollow shell of myself. In truth, I wished for nothing more than to hide from society, but I found that impossible. If Quindell wished me to accompany him to Sadler's Wells, or to watch the races on the Sussex Downs, I obliged him, for it mattered not to me. My will had ebbed away. And it is here, dear friends, where I truly began to come undone.

To wear a sullen face amid a scene of gaiety is a difficult task indeed. Any party of revellers will look askance at one who abstains from merriment and dampens the tone. So, not wishing to draw attention to myself, I soon learned to feign enjoyment, an art I had never before practised. I would bend my expression into a lively one, moulding this mask of pleasure over my mouth and eyes, while continuing to gaze emptily from behind it. Thus disguised, I could then contend with the world, for in addition to covering my true expression, I also covered my heart. After a spell, I then found myself quite able to dance, to jest – even, dare I say, to flirt, for it was not me who reeled upon an assembly-room floor with Tarleton or Hanger, or who allowed Lord Craven to run his foot along my leg as we played a hand of whist. I no longer cared for the consequences of my actions. I took brandy, wine and port with as much abandon as my keeper. At taverns, I sipped sickly usquebaugh cordial along with common whores. I would giggle and sing and sway until I fell in an intoxicated swoon into the arms of my keeper or one of his lascivious friends.

It was when I was in this perilous state that Lady Lade saw fit to bend my ear. A party of us had been returning from a visit to Sackleigh Park, the Surrey estate which Quindell had recently purchased, when we stopped for refreshment at the Pack Horse tavern in Chiswick. It was a fine day in early summer. The gentlemen were well filled with drink and had plied me with it too, when Major Hanger lifted me from the table and insisted that he should push me on the swing. With a great whoop, Quindell and his companions followed us into the tavern's renowned pleasure garden and to the sturdy oak where hung the apparatus. To be sure, I was in no fit state for such an exercise and could scarcely hold my head straight. From behind me, I saw Lady Lade, never one to frown upon revelry, wearing an unusual expression of concern.

'Henrietta,' said she sternly, taking hold of me as the Major began to draw the swing back, 'this is no good, girl. This is no good.' But before she could finish, he let the swing fly. I had not even the wherewithal to hold on to the ropes and fell face first into the dirt, my skirts lifted for all the world to glimpse my thighs and rear.

As the company raged with laughter, Letitia Lade came to my rescue, sparing my modesty and raising me from the ground. I placed my arm about her neck, expecting a gentle reproach. Instead I received a hail of abuse.

'What the devil has come over you, Hetty? You know where a love of that damnable bottle ends? On the street, girl! You make yourself ridiculous! Rollicking like a poxed old bunter, like a tuppenny whore, for shame, girl! If you do not mend your ways, they will take you for one and treat you as such.' She narrowed her eyes. 'I know well enough of what I speak.'

Indeed, I am most grateful to her. From that day, she observed me closely, hovering beside me, forever snatching glasses from my determined grip and whispering sharp remonstrances. To some degree, I do believe her vigilance saved me, but, unlike Quindell, it was not in her power to follow me everywhere. With drink comes carelessness, which is why most women but the basest creatures make certain to shun its excesses. I soon learned my lesson. In my dizziness, I permitted all manner of liberties to be taken with my person. While Philly was sodden with port, Hanger stole kisses and caresses, and that scoundrel Barrymore at last had what he had wanted from me all along, in the cabin of a coach.

Lady Lade knew too well what came from such recklessness. Indeed, she was correct in guessing what had befallen me, for in my wretched state I had left off my diligent efforts with the sponge and vinegar.

One morning, while Quindell was out, she and Mary Anne Greenhill called upon me. I had yet to rise from my bed when they were shown into my dressing room by the attentive Sam. The pair greeted me with solemn looks and a small black bottle of Blatchford's elixir.

'Drink it down at once,' ordered Lady Lade.

I stared at her, my face void of expression.

'Do you wish to have another brat?' she shouted. 'I tell you now, that rascal Philly Quindell will not own it. You shall be finished!'

Her volley of words caused me to hang my head, for I recognized the truth in them. Indeed, there was some part of me that wished for my own ruin. I had released the reins of control, and now circumstance guided my actions. That I should be led to dishonour myself and commit deeds abhorrent to me was a punishment, to be sure, but I alone had engineered it. Dear reader, the very recognition of this caused my heart to fill with disgust and my eyes to pool with tears. Softly, I began to weep as my companions looked on in silence. Then, after a spell, the Greenfinch held out her kid-gloved hand.

'Hetty, you need not be afraid,' she whispered. Tilting her head beneath her heavy crimson hat, she showed me a gentle smile. 'We shall nurse you, dear.'

I sat on the edge of my bed, and with my companions standing over me, removed the cork from the bottle and swallowed back the inky mixture, which tasted of iron and soot and bitterness. Within the hour I began to shake. My body was racked by spasms, my arms and legs danced and shivered all through the day. Then came the terrible waves of sickness. My stomach convulsed, throwing out its contents, as Lucy held my chamber pot and Mary Anne Greenhill held my sweating, trembling head. I heaved many times over and long into the night, when my belly had nothing left to give. Indeed, there were moments when my suffering was acute. The pain, the twisting in my gut, the throbbing in my skull and limbs, was at times so intolerable as to cause me to cry out in agony.

'It shall pass soon enough, Hetty dear,' chirped Miss Greenhill, taking hold of my hand. 'I have taken the purgative twice since last year. Why, it was quite remarkable, for on both occasions, I scarcely felt any discomfort and recovered my health perfectly within hours.'

I gazed at her from my pillow, exhausted. For all of the Greenfinch's faults, it must be said that she was no dullard. She possessed the alertness of a wild creature and was keenly alive to the opinions of others, particularly where they related to her. Sensing my disbelief, her smile soon began to quiver and then, by degrees, to fall away. She sighed heavily and lowered her eyes. 'But I suppose you know that not to be the truth,' she admitted. For a moment, she sat perfectly still, her brow set in contemplation. 'I know not why I . . . am so ill-mannered at times, or why I boast or . . . fib. I suppose . . . I suppose it is because I fear you should disdain me otherwise,' she confessed, while staring into her lap. 'I have not half your beauty, nor your breeding. All my manners and graces, I acquired by aping my betters, whereas you . . .' She shrugged. 'When I first made your acquaintance, I was certain you would eclipse me . . . and then where would I be? Hetty, I am but the daughter of a poor, drunkard tailor. We had scarcely more than a crust to eat before I was taken into keeping . . . and now . . . well, I should sooner throw myself from a bridge than return to that life.'

Something of the Greenfinch's words, those of a frightened young woman who knew herself to be very much alone, touched me greatly. For all her frivolity and thoughtlessness, my plight was not so unlike hers.

'That shall not be your fate, dear Mary Anne,' I whispered, gripping her hand. 'Of that I am certain.'

She returned my words with a tender look and an honest, grateful smile.

At morning light, the seizures in my womb began. Shortly thereafter, the obstruction came away and I could feel once more that familiar wetness of thick blood running from me. As the rags between my thighs revealed, the dose of Blatchford's elixir had been a success.

By then, the Greenfinch, who had remained devotedly at my side throughout the night, had drifted off into sleep. She sat, leaning her cheek against her hand, her features arranged in a serene, child-like expression. After an evening of ordering Lucy about , and closely studying my progress, Lady Lade, too, had gone off to doze upon the sofa in my dressing room. On waking, she came quietly to my side.

The sickness that had torn through me like a storm in a cornfield had passed, and she found me lying grey, weak and still. Noticing Miss Greenhill resting soundly, she raised a finger to her lips. Then she began a close examination of my face with a stern but compassionate eye. Once satisfied that I had survived the ordeal, she stood back and paid me a nod.

I lifted my hand towards hers. She took it, warmly enfolding it within her own.

'Bless you, dear madam,' I whispered. 'Bless you.'

Chapter 40

I have often found that nothing straightens a wayward path more effectively than an illness or an accident. My day and night under the influence of Blatchford's elixir did just this. By the end of it, I had not only purged myself of possible offspring, but also of my foolishness. As I was rendered an invalid for several days, I had sufficient time to contemplate the error of my conduct, and to resolve that I should never again set out upon such a path of ruin.

Gradually, with the assistance of beef tea and small morsels of bread, the colour was restored to my face. So too did reason resume its natural place in my mind. My melancholia, unfortunately, would not be dispelled so easily, for its cause was ever-present. In spite of my nurses' efforts to keep it from me, it returned with the steady persistence of the tide.

'Thalia! Dear muse!' Quindell cried as he rushed into my bed-chamber on the following morning. 'Oh dear girl, you cannot imagine what dread, what misery your illness inspired in me.' He urgently pressed my feeble hand to his lips. 'I passed the entire night in the parlour below, fretting that you should require a physician. Oh how I feared for your début!' He then smiled with relief. 'But now that I see the blush returning to your cheeks, I am assured of your survival.' He sighed and took a seat beside me, removing a copy of *The School for Scandal* from his pocket. 'Shall I recite your lines?'

My return to Drury Lane did even less to lighten my depressed spirits. For nearly a week, my illness had preserved me from Kemble's tyranny, his wife's sneers and Preston's lewd remarks, but when faced again with these assaults, my heart instantly began to sink.

Now, friends, you know me to have been a diligent and scholarly child. Never in the past had I failed to commit to memory verses of poetry or passages from the Bible. Why, then, I struggled to remember Maria's lines remains a mystery to me. Neither my fear of Kemble nor of certain disgrace upon the stage encouraged me to learn my part. I possessed no valid excuse for my ignorance, especially as Philly had taken it upon himself to tutor me. But nevertheless, day after day, I gazed vacantly at the pages before me, sighing and sobbing in turns.

With a mere fortnight until our opening, I continued to carry my book and to read from it during rehearsals. Alas, Kemble grew so weary of my habit that he snatched it from me and threw it into the wings. Thereafter, I was forced to rely upon the prompter, who sang out my words to me like Cyrano de Bergerac. Worse still, my talent for performance had not improved, nor had the power of my voice, which remained no louder than the chirp of a sparrow. I appeared more mop than actress: part stiff, part limp, propped up but with a drooping head.

As you might imagine, my listlessness vexed Kemble no end. Even Quindell began to lose his patience, and eventually retreated backstage. There, with Sheridan's blessing and a further bribe of £150, he passed the time ingratiating himself with the actresses, playing dice with the actors, and making use of the theatre owner's rooms. It was only then, once my keeper was out of earshot, that the manager abandoned the last of his restraint and lunged at me with the fury of a guard dog

'What am I do to with this heap of wood today, hey?' he bellowed at me. 'Burn it, perhaps? Ha! I should get a more heated performance from you, madam, if I were to set you alight!'

I simply looked away in shame. He then strode up to me and put his face to mine. 'Do you not understand, you silly little bitch? Are you deaf as well as dumb? We shall open in a fortnight and you shall ruin us all!'

'I shall attempt my best not to, sir,' I whimpered.

'Attempt? Attempt? We are beyond attempting, girl. You must perform!'

Were this not mortification enough, Mrs Kemble also did her best to heighten my sense of shame. How I dreaded rehearsing our scenes together. When it came to disparaging me, she would take her cue from her husband, listening first to his insults and then adding her own. She would often begin with sighs and then advance to whispered curses before erupting into a stream of shouted torments.

'Fie, sir, how do you expect me to appear beside such a feckless little hussy as this? This is what comes of putting any man's whore upon the stage. You force me stand beside this harlot, to show myself in her company, as if I were no better than she. What humiliation you do me, husband, when I am a respectable wedded lady.'

Naturally, these outbursts would raise sniggers from the company, while I struggled to disguise my mortification and continue with my scene. Oh, what degradation I was made to suffer! Into what depths of despondency was my heart plunged!

When the Kembles had inflicted upon me the last of their pillorying, I would be dismissed to my dressing corner. There, broken and miserable, I would pass a few quiet moments, sitting in the darkness, staring morosely into the looking glass, before Quindell returned to harass me.

But on this occasion, as I made my way through the drapery, barrels and boxes backstage, something quite different awaited me.

Mrs Dorothy Jordan had, until now, paid me little more than passing nods and curtseys. In truth, her star shone so brightly that I feared to approach her. She was constantly surrounded by a mélange of servants, seamstresses, hairdressers, admiring actors or children, forever fawning or sobbing, bickering or pulling at her sleeve. She would appear upon the stage to deliver Lady Teazle's lines, then retreat once more to the sanctuary of her rooms. Indeed, not to stare at her required some degree of forbearance, for her very movements, even the simple delivery of one short sentence or the utterance of a witticism, were captivating. I had watched her so many times upon the stage, and admired her in *The Fair Penitent*, in *The Romp* and *Twelfth Night*, to name only a handful. What shame this caused me, for I understood that I had no right to appear beside her in this production! In our uncomfortable scenes together, I could hardly bring myself to look at her, and never failed to weep my eyes red afterwards.

For this reason, I was greatly surprised to behold the luminous form of Mrs Jordan, in her white muslin gown and with her flop of curls, standing before my dressing table. I stopped suddenly and, like a humbled fool, dropped into a deep curtsey.

'Mrs Lightfoot,' she began, in a soft but firm tone, 'please do excuse my intrusion, but I wished to speak with you.'

I sensed immediately that I was to receive a scolding and, in anticipation of this, hung my head.

'I have noticed you do not seem content with your role. You do not wish to play Maria. I suspect, Mrs Lightfoot, that it was never your desire to go upon the stage in the first place.'

At that, I lifted my chin and, while still avoiding her gaze, nodded. 'It was Mr Quindell. I would not wish it for myself, but he insisted.'

She sighed. 'That much is apparent.'

'Oh, Mrs Jordan, I never wanted to be an actress . . . I am no better than a Circassian slave girl.' I gazed up at her, hoping all the while that she would not berate me. Much to my surprise, her eyes did not hold contempt but, rather, sad empathy. Upon seeing this, my heart could hold back no longer and unleashed a torrent of emotion.

'I . . . I once foolishly believed . . . that I could exercise my own will, and, by that means, lead a life of happiness. Someone had impressed that notion upon me . . . But now I see how ridiculous I have been. Gentlemen might live by those rules, but our sex . . . it is not within our power to do so. I have always known that to be true, so why I chose to believe . . .' I ventured to look at her before continuing, and seeing that the kindness still remained in her expression, persisted.

'I fled my father's house to avoid making a disagreeable match. I had been encouraged to do so . . . by someone. At the time, I believed it to be the correct course, but now . . . now I see it was not, and I am no more at liberty to determine my own fate than I would have been had I married the man my father intended for me. I am owned, madam . . . and traded, and . . . and made use of for everyone's pleasure but my own. What hope of true happiness have I, when I am condemned to live no more freely than a prisoner? Oh madam, I despair,' said I, the tears falling fast down my cheeks.

Never had I related my story until now, and hearing my quivering voice deliver the words startled me. This was followed by sudden horror at what I had done: in a fit of passion, I had unburdened myself to none other than the redoubtable Mrs Jordan! But, curiously, her sweet expression remained unchanged. The great actress beheld me with a calm, angelic countenance, as I slowly recoiled in shame.

'You are incorrect, Mrs Lightfoot,' said she, after a moment.

I looked at her, puzzled by her comment.

'You think yourself condemned, but you are not.' She smiled. 'I was your age when I first played Maria. Every actress plays Maria at some point. Mrs Kemble did too, which is why I suspect she so dislikes you. You remind her that she is no longer young, and Maria is a role for a girl in the prime of her beauty,' said Mrs Jordan with a hint of wistfulness.

'I played her in Dublin, at the Crow Street Theatre, under the direction of Mr Daly, who was as much a tyrant as Mr Kemble, but worse; Kemble does not demand of the young actresses what Mr Daly asked.' She paused and allowed her eyes to wander over my dressing table, the mirror, the curtain. 'There are some people, men in particular, whom I believe can scent weakness, much in the way a hound can unearth a fox. Daly was one such villain and he used me ill when I was far too young to know better. Like you, I was also rehearsing the part of Maria.' She sighed. 'What occurred was a terrible misfortune. One day, he professed his love for me and claimed that he meant to have me for his mistress, but when I protested that I would not give myself to him, he laughed and explained that I had no choice in the matter. As he paid my wages, I was his to do what he liked with. Indeed, he was so persuasive, and I so cowed and foolish, that I knew not how to refuse him. He locked me in a room . . . and . . .' she paused and raised her brow '. . . so it was. Imagine then, dear Mrs Lightfoot, what I was to think when I found myself with child by him. When he learned of it, he would have nothing to do with me. I was sent packing. We had no means, my family. My mother had been an actress, my father an actor – they never married and he abandoned us. I was the bastard of a whore, who became a whore who bore a bastard. It is often the way.

'When I considered my disgrace, madam . . . well, you can imagine what were my thoughts. I had no hope in my heart, and as much stomach for playing Maria as you now possess. At the time, there seemed no possible redemption for me, no hope. I believed all my dreams to be entirely crushed, but I soon learned otherwise.'

'How?' I enquired, humbled by her tale.

'Persistence, Mrs Lightfoot, and a degree of patience. The tide often turns when we least expect it, and then opportunity arrives upon it,' said she with a nod. 'But you must keep your eyes on the horizon, and not down, sullenly staring at your feet.'

Ashamed, I lifted my gaze from the floor.

'I could not have foreseen what lay in my future. My mother took me to a relation in York and there I found work upon the stage and bore my daughter. It was only then that I learned my most important lesson: not to concern myself with how others judge me. I admit, that is a difficult lesson for our sex, for we are taught to care for nothing but our reputations. You see, they hissed me in York, those fine ladies, when they heard I had not a husband.' A wicked smirk then emerged upon her lips. 'I shall confess to you, dear Mrs Lightfoot, I still have no husband, and more children, but no one dares hiss me now. I get huzzahs instead, and the house is full every night.' Then, laying her hand upon my arm, she peered directly into my eyes.

'The world has kept a great secret from you, madam,' said she, leaning in and lowering her voice. 'When a lady loses her respectability, she gains all the liberty she might wish for. She is free to do as she pleases, to follow whatever mode of life amuses her. She may go upon the stage, or travel abroad, or choose a lover to suit her heart.' Then she narrowed her eyes and held her lips together in a playful manner. 'But think what mischief should come to our world if all governesses were to teach their young charges such things!' She giggled. I, too, smiled at this absurd notion. 'To speak frankly,' she continued, 'you are beholden to no one, much as a man might be. Perhaps this was the lesson your friend wished to impart to you when you eloped from your father's home?' she suggested, paying me a sideways glance.

I had not considered this before. Allenham had warned me not to pay heed to the censure of others. Perhaps she was correct. I studied Mrs Jordan, while contemplating her words.

'This whim of your keeper's, that you go upon the stage, it should not hold you – *he* should not hold you. Why, this caprice of his, it does not spell the end of your existence. You are young and exceptionally handsome, Mrs Lightfoot, and with some cleverness I am certain you will find a way to do and have what you wish.' Her gentle gaze lingered on mine until it teased from me a bashful smile. 'Now, shall we read through your lines together?'

I do not care to think what would have become of me had Mrs Jordan not intervened on that day. That peerless lady, the most gifted of actresses, took it upon herself to draw me back from the precipice. It was with her coaching and encouragement that I was at last able to commit my lines to memory. Much to Quindell's delight, we spent several days in her dressing room, where she guided me with her firm, instructive hand.

'When you address Sir Peter, turn your face thus . . .' she coaxed. 'Ah yes, like so! You have it. Now speak your line from your belly, puff it out as if your stomach were a pair of bellows . . .'

I listened and followed. I must say, I was as much under Mrs Jordan's spell as any of her adoring admirers. Of course, this was in the months before our King William fell captive to her charms. He was then Duke of Clarence and could not have predicted what Fate intended for him. While some moralists disdain their union to this day, it was undeniably a long and fruitful one, which brought them both no small degree of happiness while it lasted. What, then, I ask, is so reprehensible in that?

Suffice to say, I learned much from Dorothy Jordan, and Maria's scripted lines were not the only thing I committed to my memory. Truly, it is remarkable how the spirit can be revived by the kind words of admirable people. To win the regard of one so universally esteemed restored me. As if by magic, I felt myself shielded from the piercing darts of Mrs Kemble's looks, and the stinging contempt of her husband. To put it plainly, Mrs Jordan restored in me that which had been sorely lacking for weeks: courage.

And, dear friends, I wish you had been present to glimpse Kemble's expression when I first strode out upon the boards and rattled the chandelier with my voice! Why, his stormy features positively convulsed with disbelief. His eyes stared, his mouth gaped.

'Great God of Mercy!' he declared, putting his hand to his head with the flourish of a tragedian. 'Is that you, Mrs Lightfoot?'

'It is indeed, sir,' I responded with the strength of a commander of a man-of-war.

'Well . . .' he stuttered. 'Well . . . this is a transformation.'

And not a word more was said on the matter.

Chapter 41

To be sure, a great alteration had come about in my character. My courage had cleared the murkiness about me. No longer did obstacles appear as daunting as they had in the past, and hope unfurled its petals once more. Within a short time, I found myself contemplating my future. I even dared to entertain the possibility of mounting another escape, though how precisely I might plot and execute such a plan continued to vex me.

I dare say my mood had shifted to such a degree that even Quindell's constant presence irked me less. In truth, when he saw that I now stood ably upon my own feet, he did not hover as closely as he had once done, choosing instead to linger over his dice games and read through the prospective plays which were daily heaped upon Sheridan's desk.

But while I considered myself transformed, there were others who saw differently. To these hound-like creatures, I remained a cowering fox. They had caught the scent of my weakness a while earlier and had been sniffing and scratching at my den ever since.

On a morning shortly before our début, while Quindell sipped tea with Sheridan, I took myself to the green room. There, I determined I would rest upon a couch and read until summoned to rehearse a scene. The quiet and the warm daylight rendered the room so peaceful that I soon drifted into a shallow sleep. Never again shall I be so foolish as to slumber unguarded where my enemies circle.

I do not doubt that Mrs Kemble had a hand in what transpired. Unbeknown to me, I believe she spied me lying there on my back. It was she who plotted this vile trap for me. It was she who noted that Quindell was engaged with Sheridan and alerted Mr Preston to my defenceless position.

As I had not given myself over entirely to sleep, I was aware of sounds and movements from beneath my closed lids. I heard a light footfall and breathing and soon realized there was a presence beside me. No sooner had I opened my eyes than Preston struck, as swiftly as a cobra. He clapped his hand across my mouth and threw himself atop me.

'Hush! Hush!' he commanded, while glancing over his shoulder to make certain we were alone. 'Mrs Kemble said you had called for me, that you lay ready for love,' he panted, as he began to fumble with my skirts. I attempted to rise and scream all at once, but his weight and his hand prevented both. He scrabbled at my hem and then at my thighs as I twisted and groaned, my heart pounding with fear and fury. I could think of nothing but releasing myself. His attack raised in me such indignation that I began to rage with the violence of an animal. I gnashed my sharp teeth and curled my hands into claws. I bucked and kicked and howled, until my mouth came down with such vengeance upon his finger that for an instant I thought I might have succeeded in removing it.

With a yelp, he pulled back from me, gripping the finger into which my teeth had torn. His hand now ran with blood.

'Vicious bitch!' he cried, as I rolled to my feet. Gasping for breath, I backed away cautiously, not knowing what he was likely to try next. It was then I noticed what lay upon the table. A number of objects intended for use in our scenes were scattered in a jumble, and among them I spied the hilt of a sword.

Instantly, I dashed for it. I had never before wielded such a weapon, and although this was a mere dummy, I boldly pointed its blunt tip at my assailant. Preston, who was more concerned with his bloodied hand, took several steps backward.

'How dare you, sir?' I shouted, the sword shaking in my grip. 'You are a depraved monster!'

He locked his eyes on mine and sneered crookedly. 'And you, madam,

389

are a depraved actress.' Then, with an overblown bow and a dripping hand, he retreated from the room.

For several moments, I stood catching my breath and resting upon my rapier. I dare say I was as stunned as Preston at my actions. Never before had I defended myself with such vigour, or displayed such courage. I doubted he would be likely to attempt such a trick again.

As you might imagine, I was unusually pleased to see Quindell that afternoon, when he escorted me to dinner. Wishing to regale him with my tale of bravery, I held my tongue until we were sitting at his table. I could scarcely wait to boast of my conquest, to relate to him how I had wielded my sword like an Amazon against my attacker, but no sooner had I launched into my story than he leaped from his chair in a passion.

'How dare that scoundrel?' he exclaimed. 'I shall call him out!'

'Oh no,' I protested, for I had no wish to see this act avenged, when I had defended my honour well enough. 'Dear Philly, I should die if some harm came to you,' I pleaded, employing my acting skills.

With some gentle persuasion, I finally succeeded in cooling his hot temper, and by that evening I believed the matter all but forgotten. In fact, I thought nothing of it when, the following morning, he insisted on accompanying me to my dressing table, which he had not done for several days. But when he then moved left down the corridor, rather than right to my corner, I began to grow suspicious.

'Where is Preston?' he roared like a lion, once inside the labyrinth. 'I demand to see the rogue!' I placed a restraining hand upon his arm, but he shrugged it off angrily. 'Preston! Mr Preston!' he called out into the darkness. Players and servants backed away from him as he stamped through the forest of curtains and ropes. I chased after him, but he seemed intent on losing me.

'Who calls for me?' came the actor's voice from behind a set piece.

Quindell's nostrils flared. 'Preston, show thyself!'

The performer, with his hair in curling papers, had no sooner stepped from behind the wooden wall of Sir Peter Teazle's study than my protector flew at him. With one swift draw of his fist he pelted Preston across the face and I gasped in horror as his lanky, ribbon-like figure collapsed into a heap. Until I heard his groans, I feared for an instant that Quindell had murdered him.

'That, sir, is for the insult you paid Mrs Lightfoot.'

Preston moved upon the floor, his bandaged hand over his right eye.

'I shall consider honour served,' the Boy Barbadian concluded with a bow.

The actor snorted. 'I believe honour was served yesterday, sir. Your bitch nearly bit off my finger before attempting to run me through with a sword.' He then began to laugh wickedly. 'I would be damned if I ever tried her again.'

Quindell squared his shoulders. I am certain he did not hear Preston's comments, nor would he deign to respond to what he would have believed to be a patent lie. I, for my part, felt quiet pride in my actions: that I had managed to defend my own name, without the able assistance of my protector. I confess, my violent action was not the sort of behaviour appropriate for a woman who professes concern for her character. But here I remind you of Mrs Jordan's sentiments: that a woman must throw off the yoke of reputation before she is able to enjoy the spoils of liberty.

To be sure, that was an exceptional day, which ended with as much excitement as it had begun.

Backstage, all talk was of the contretemps between Preston and Quindell. Indeed, by the afternoon, the tale had spread to the adjoining Rose Tavern, and from there to the rest of Covent Garden. Soon I was hearing the entire story recounted as some great feat of heroism, where Quindell had dragged the actor by the hair from his dressing table, smashed in his face, and very near slashed his throat. All this for the love of a whore, it was said, though I am certain that that last embellishment came from Mrs Kemble.

To be sure, this entire incident caused me great uneasiness, for you know my dread of being made the object of gossip and speculation. So you might imagine my discomfiture when, shortly before we were to conclude this, our final rehearsal before our scheduled première in three days' time, a servant came to me with a message. I was told that a gentleman had appeared at the stage door and requested a word with me.

'I am afraid he would not give his name, madam, but he said it was a private matter of some urgency.'

'Oh goodness!' I exclaimed, casting an anxious glance at Philly, who sat in a far corner playing Hazard with the scene shifters. 'Is it the magistrate?' I whispered. My heart began to pound, for I feared that this incident of Quindell's was about to rebound upon me.

The servant claimed he did not know, so I asked that the mysterious visitor be shown into the green room.

As I made my way through the corridor to greet him, I fretted terribly. Had Preston made some accusation against me? Was I to be arrested? My terror increased with each step I took towards the green room. Gracious heavens, was I to be sent to Newgate? By the time I had placed my hand on the door, I could hardly draw breath.

But the gentleman whom I found standing before me appeared nothing like a Bow Street Runner. Attired entirely in buff silk and a waistcoat embroidered with a profusion of tiny pink and emerald flowers, he paid me a deep and courtly bow.

'Forgive me if I am incorrect, but you are, I believe, Miss Henrietta Ingerton?'

The name, which I had not used since I began my life with Allenham, caused the blood to stop within my veins. I took a step backward. I was, I must admit, too much in a state of shock to speak.

'But I have alarmed you,' my visitor began to apologize, his French accent now clearly apparent. 'That was not my intention, mademoiselle.' He bowed once more.

'Who wishes to know my name?' I enquired, still a-tremble.

'I am Charles Hercule Lancier de Laveret – *comte* de Laveret. I am a friend, mademoiselle.'

I continued to stare in puzzlement at the *comte*. He was a complete stranger to me.

'Miss Ingerton, I have not been long in your country and therefore I know little of what the English understand of the situation in France. Many of your politicians speak of liberty, but what transpires in my country . . .' He paused and turned his gaze to the window. Although de Laveret was a young man, his face was lined and troubled. 'Do you read the newspapers, Miss Ingerton? Do they report the recent events in France? That the King and Queen attempted to flee the country, but were captured by revolutionaries at Varennes?'

I nodded slowly, unsure why he should relate these details to me.

'Then you will know that they are now kept as prisoners in the Palais de Tuileries,' said he, lowering his solemn gaze to mine. 'There are some in my country who call for their death, the death of the King of France, mademoiselle.' He shook his head. 'Miss Ingerton, I am a man of education and I know what becomes of imprisoned kings, which is why, as a loyal servant of the King of France, I fled Paris. There are many among us – some have gone to London, others to Switzerland, or Brussels. I was en route to that city when I broke my journey at Calais. I believe it was Fate that brought me to Dessein's Hotel, for I met there an old acquaintance of mine, the Baron Allenham.'

He had no sooner spoken my love's name than a gasp escaped my lips. I pressed a hand to my mouth in surprise.

'It was he who persuaded me that London would prove a safer haven than Brussels and assisted me in securing the necessary papers. I am very much in his debt, mademoiselle. That is why I am here.' He studied me for a moment, attempting to read the emotion on my face: fear or hope, or some of both.

'It has taken me the better part of a week to find you. No one, it seemed, knew of a Miss Ingerton. But a Miss Henrietta Lightfoot, that was a different matter. He had not expected you to keep that name.' The comte smiled tenderly, in a manner that suggested he had been told a lengthy tale of love.

'Before I parted from Lord Allenham, he begged me to locate you in London, to see you with my own eyes, so that I could make certain of your well-being. He also wished that I should relay to you directly his words – that you remain his one true love. Married in the heart, before the hearth. I am afraid my English is poor. I am not certain I have translated that correctly.'

But the tears that pooled in my eyes confirmed that he had. I could do no more than nod my head.

'He said you alone would understand the meaning of that.'

My right hand had now joined my left in front of my mouth. I held them there, for I was certain that if I did not, I would wail with emotion.

'Mademoiselle, this news has distressed you,' he said, leading me to sit.

'Is he there, still?' The comte did not comprehend my question.

'Is he at Calais? Is he there now? At Dessein's Hotel?'

'I am afraid I do not know.'

'But that . . . that was not even a fortnight ago? I thought him in Paris . . .'

'There has been much upheaval, Miss Ingerton. I know not where he may be now . . .'

'He could be at Dessein's. He could be there now, at Dessein's in Calais.' I rose hastily from my chair, my face broad and beaming with this realization.

'I do not know, mademoiselle,' reiterated de Laveret, now looking as if he feared a madness might descend upon me. 'I would advise against your journeying to France at the present time. It is not safe. Calais is filled with your countrymen wishing to return home and my countrymen wishing to escape. I beg you, Miss Ingerton, do not hazard it. His lordship would not wish you to imperil yourself.'

But it was no use warning me. His news had entered me like a drug; drawing it out again would prove impossible. It coursed through me freely, overtaking all other thoughts. No matter how much de Laveret attempted to dissuade me, from that moment I resolved to go to Allenham – immediately.

I had hardly bid the comte adieu when, there in the green room, I summoned some writing paper and, with a shaking hand, scrawled as rapidly as I could the first thoughts that fell from my pen:

> My dearest, most beloved Allenham, I have just now received a
> visit from your friend the comte de Laveret, who has delivered to
> me the most propitious news of your presence at Calais. Oh my
> truest heart, my adored husband, knowledge of your

whereabouts has instantly rendered my life here intolerable. I intend to make for Calais within these few days, at my first convenience. I shall come to you at Deissen's Hotel, where I shall direct this letter. Oh my angel, my devoted Allenham, my hand trembles so violently that I sign myself with great difficulty, your eternally faithful and loving, H. Lightfoot.

In sealing that letter, I likewise sealed my promise to him – and to myself. I determined at that moment that my pledge to travel was fixed. I would no longer wear the chains of a captive, or permit obstacles to bar my path. And to be sure, nothing, dear friends, required more of my courage than to swear to that.

Chapter 42

I was now faced with a great number of pressing dilemmas. I suppose you have already guessed their nature.

Simply because I had received word of Allenham's location and resolved to take my leave instantly did not mean I had formulated a method of doing it! I assure you, I applied a good deal of thought to the matter, but still I could not fathom how I might distract Quindell and avoid discovery.

'Dear Lucy,' I despaired, after revealing to her my intentions, 'I know not how it can be done, for I have scarcely an hour when Mr Quindell or his valet are not at my side. You have seen how he is forever in my house or attending me at the theatre. He will uncover our plot, to be sure.'

Lucy smiled cheerfully, undaunted by the challenge. 'Not if I am secretive in my errands, madam. I promise to be as quiet and crafty as a mouse.'

'But I fear there is so much preparation – the horses, the documents, the packing, the expense of once more buying the silence of my household . . .' I shook my head and sighed.

'I am a swift worker,' said my maid with a gentle, encouraging tone. 'Why, I believe these tasks would require no more than two days to complete.'

'Two days,' I echoed in disbelief. 'Are you certain?'

Lucy nodded.

A mere two days. It seemed incredible. In two days I could find myself en route to my beloved. My expression suddenly brightened – and then, just as rapidly, fell. In two days' time, I was to be upon the stage, making my début as Maria.

'Oh, I am forever dogged by hindrances!' I cried in exasperation. 'How could I possibly take my leave on the very day when all eyes will be upon me? I shall not have a moment unguarded!'

Lucy had been observing me calmly as I paced and chewed at my fingers. 'Madam, if you will allow me, there is not a time better suited to making an escape than the night of your début.'

I furrowed my brow at her suggestion.

'I mean, directly after the play. That would seem a convenient moment. They shall not have their eyes upon you then.'

I halted my progress along the floorboards and considered her suggestion. She was, of course, correct. I could steal away after I had given my final curtsey. The afterpiece which followed *The School for Scandal* would form a perfect distraction. While Quindell sat in his box enjoying it, I would fly to Clarges Street to meet my waiting coach. Why, by the time he discovered my absence, I would be well on the road to Dover!

I could scarcely believe it, for this scheme seemed the very solution I had sought all along. Indeed, it appeared almost too simple.

I glanced at my maid. Lucy and her clever designs, thought I, as a mischievous smile began to slide across my lips. Upon catching my eye, she too began to simper, but turned quickly away.

Uplifted as I was at the prospect of finally making my departure, I also understood how treacherous would be the days leading to that event. Although I trusted Lucy and her discretion, I could not be certain that her preparations would go undiscovered. Was this matter not unsettling enough, I had yet another upheaval with which to contend.

Some of you, cherished readers, may recall that in the summer of 1791, His Majesty's Theatre at Drury Lane closed to undergo improvements. An arrangement had been struck whereby Mr Kemble's company was then to assume a short period of residency in the recently reconstructed Little Theatre at the Haymarket. I shall not bore you with how it came to pass, but suffice to say our production of *The School for Scandal* was to be the first among the season of summer entertainments there. You may imagine the confusion that resulted when all the set pieces and properties, the servants, musicians, dancers, singers, painters and carpenters, indeed the entire crew that sailed the Drury Lane ship, came to dock in this foreign port. What cries of woe were heard to echo from our captain Kemble when he found how dwarfed were our sets upon this spacious stage! What battles were renewed behind the curtain, when La Kemble and La Jordan examined each other's dressing rooms! And all this, upon the very day of our première!

To be sure, I was vastly anxious on that occasion, but not for the reasons cited above, and not even because I was due to make my first appearance upon a public stage, in one of England's best loved plays. It was not because I was to perform *The School for Scandal* in the presence of its author, Mr Sheridan; nor was it because I should be seen by all of society, including those who may have known me, however briefly, as Henrietta Ingerton. Indeed, I was so distracted by the prospect of my journey that the painful possibility of my father's presence, or that of Lady Stavourley or of the two young men whom I now understood to be my brothers, had only fleetingly entered my mind. When I claim I had room in my head only to contemplate my flight, you will under-stand how entirely consumed I was by the road that lay before me and he who awaited me at its end. On that day, I could not have cared less what Kemble or Quindell asked me to do upon the stage; if they wished me to walk a tightrope or sing a ballad or dance a jig, I would do it willingly, so long as I could flee when the curtain fell, so long as Lucy had prepared my boxes and my coach awaited.

As I arrived at the Haymarket theatre and crept through the curious dark unknown landscape backstage I was terribly uneasy, though not one nerve within me twitched in fear of my performance. As the singers prepared their voices and the musicians their instruments, as the cursing began and tempers rose, my heart beat in a constant, furious rhythm. As I was laced into the lavish rose and gold costume that Quindell had purchased for me, I shook. The dresser placed her hands upon my shoulders. 'It shall pass as soon as you step out upon the stage,' she attempted to reassure me. But I knew the quivering was unlikely to subside at all that night.

The *friseur* came and arranged the ribbons in my hair. A great jar of powder was blown upon me until my features disappeared beneath a storm of white. With the assistance of carmine, my lips and cheeks then re-emerged from my blank visage. Only Preston's face was more obscured. In an attempt to disguise the eye that bulged like a purple pincushion, he had painted on a good many layers of lead. Much to his dismay, he could not obscure the deformity from view, which greatly delighted the editor of the *Morning Herald*, who printed the entire story of the actor's defeat at the hands of 'the Brave Boy Barbadian'.

Mrs Kemble, too, came in for some scorn from that newspaper. In the confusion of the decampment to the Haymarket, it seemed that the trunk which contained Lady Sneerwell's costume had been mislaid. I must confess, to this day I fear I may have been to blame for this misfortune. You see, the box had been placed beside my dressing table and, upon recognizing that it was Mrs Kemble's, I ordered it to be removed at once. Of course, had I known what an inconvenience this was likely to cause, I would have delivered it myself to our manager's wife directly, and seen that she had received it, with good grace.

Poor Mrs Kemble. Three servants and a dresser were deployed in an attempt to locate the lost costume, but all failed. As time did not permit for another costume to be delivered from the Kembles' home, Mrs Kemble was forced to appear on stage in an ordinary muslin gown. The *Morning Herald* decried her choice of attire as 'Less Lady Sneerwell, and more Lady Wornwell'.

The great case clock in the corridor backstage ticked away the minutes of that evening. Each actor or servant who passed it counted the moments until the curtain rose, while I noted only the moments until its fall.

Eventually, from the back of the house came the sound of the bolts being removed from the doors, and soon after, the audience poured into the pit, roaring with laughter and cries. It was a hot, close night, and the arrival of so many bodies into the theatre acted like a shovel of coal upon an open fire. The heat intensified, causing the air to grow thicker and the stench broader. My chemise and petticoats were now wet through with sweat, and I quaked noticeably from nerves. Wishing to distract myself, I placed an eye to a parting in the curtain and surveyed the house. The chandelier hung, pendulum-like, above, like the great sword of Damocles.

As I stood in the wings, waiting for the poorly attired Mrs Kemble and the swollen-eyed Preston to assume their places for the first act, I felt a warm hand upon my shoulder. I looked up to see the tender expression of Mrs Jordan.

'You have nothing to fear, Mrs Lightfoot,' she said calmly, having noted the widening of my eyes. 'Courage,' she whispered into my ear, before placing a quick kiss upon my cheek. I returned her kindness with a look of adoring gratitude.

And then came my cue.

All at once I found myself striding upon the boards at the Little Theatre. Dear reader, that instant when I spoke my first line and heard my once meek voice reverberate like a church bell through the theatre – why, I can hardly describe it! With each word that flowed from my mouth, I seemed to captivate the attention of all of London. How extraordinary it felt! Six weeks earlier, I would not have believed myself capable of such a feat.

The glare from the lamps was much brighter than I had anticipated, but this did not render it entirely impossible to recognize faces through the blaze of illumination. I saw first Quindell among the middle right boxes, precisely where he had directed me to search for him. I knew him immediately, for he sat flush against the edge of the box, his hands gripping the edge of it, rapt with anticipation and delight. Around him, I could make out the forms of his companions, that boisterous brood of bucks and bloods, Hanger, Tarleton and Lord Barrymore, the most formidable collection of rogues I ever chanced to know. Although my dear companion Mrs Mahon was abroad, I was gratified to see my other friends, Miss Ponsonby, Lady Lade and Miss Greenhill, each wearing enormous feathers in their hair and fanning themselves against the heat.

I could not find St John amid the silhouettes. Perhaps I simply failed to spot him, or perhaps he could not bring himself to attend the performance. Perhaps he had quit London for the summer and gone to his nephew, Lord Bolingbroke, in Wiltshire, where he sat dandling Georgie upon his knee. The image made me grimace and I quickly pushed it from my mind. I shall never know if he saw me upon the stage that night, nor shall I know if any among my relations witnessed my début. For the sake of my father, I hope he did not.

The first act came and passed so rapidly that I could hardly believe it. I was more astonished still to observe how well I had acquitted myself, how ably I had played my role. As I retreated to the wings, I caught my breath and shut my eyes, but my heart was beating faster than ever.

I awaited my next cue, and with as much confidence as I had had before, executed my part to perfection. In fact, it seemed that one act rolled into the next with the smooth momentum of a wound mechanism. As the sets were moved and turned, and trap doors shut and opened, I felt this obligation of mine wheeling closer to its end.

It was as I awaited my scene with Kemble in Act Four that he saw fit to pass comment upon my performance. This was the part of Sheridan's play – Maria's interview with her guardian, Sir Peter – that had reduced me on so many occasions to fits of tears. As I stood stoically beside him, preparing to advance into the glow of the lamps, he examined me out of the corner of his eye.

'I hardly thought it possible, Mrs Lightfoot,' said he. 'This has come as a surprise. A pleasant one.'

It was, I believe, a compliment.

The curtain, it seemed, had no sooner lifted upon Act Four than it came down again. The scene shifters dashed out across the stage, and I, with a throbbing head and heart, sought a moment's calm in my dressing corner. As the backstage clock ticked away the final quarter-hour of *The School for Scandal*, the company prepared to celebrate a successful first performance. While others began to sigh with relief, my discomfort was now reaching a climax. I was nearly sick with anticipation.

I had been contemplating all night how rapidly I might be able to make my escape. Fortunately, Kemble refused to tolerate visitors backstage on performance nights. It was a rule upon which Sheridan insisted, and on this occasion, not even Quindell was exempt. This, I calculated, would ensure that I could throw off my cumbersome costume with its beaded, glittering petticoat, unhindered by the attendance of an undesired visitor. I would then have sufficient time to slip away while the three-act afterpiece was still being performed. Following the conclusion of the night's entertainment, I imagined that Quindell and his companions would sit in his coach, awaiting me. After a half-hour or so, he would grow impatient and make enquiries. Only then would the servant at the stage door explain that I had departed some time ago.

With the execution of this strategy heavy upon my mind, I found the final scene, in which Charles Surface announces our engagement, extremely difficult to perform. When Maria was declaring her affection for her suitor, I was imagining how soon I might wipe the powder from my face. By Jove, I could think of nothing but witnessing that curtain fall and wresting myself free of my costume!

But alas, the curtain call still remained.

They roared for Mrs Jordan and cheered for Kemble, and even for me there were cries of 'Brava! Brava, Mrs Lightfoot!' But while my fellow players wished to revel in this, the moment of their celebration, my feet itched to run.

When at last the curtain came down upon the first night of *The School for Scandal*, I tore away with such urgency that I very nearly tripped over the players, making their way to the stage for the afterpiece. I felt my path through the unfamiliar backstage geography of the theatre. Eagerly I pushed my way between set pieces and canvas, and passed through a variety of doors and rooms, until I spied before me that long network of curtains where I knew my dressing table to be. Striding determinedly towards my corner, I had just begun to unpin my hat and call for a dresser when I was brought to a sudden halt by the spectacle that greeted me.

There at my table sat Quindell, Tarleton, Hanger and Barrymore, with two bottles of champagne between them.

'My queen!' Quindell cried upon spying me. 'My triumphant Thalia, my muse of comedy! She hath arrived!'

I swear it, I could not move for the shock of this sight.

'I did not expect you here,' said I, flustered and angry. 'How is it that you are here?' I demanded loudly. It was the first time in my life that I had raised my voice at anyone. 'Kemble said he did not permit—'

'My dear Thalia!' He lifted his arms to me, paying no heed to my question, 'Oh, do look! Her charming face is all alight with passion! Come, darling nymph. Come here and sit upon my knee,' he slurred. 'I will be damned if I allow a mere manager, or that debtor Sheridan, to dictate how I, a gentleman, should come and go.'

'Philly. Gentlemen,' said I, maintaining my distance, 'if you would be so kind as to excuse me, my costume . . . it is late . . .'

'No, my darling Hetty,' interrupted my keeper, balancing a slipper of champagne in his hand, 'you have no need to dress for the occasion. I wish you to wear your costume all about town. We, your devoted slaves, shall parade you like the Queen of Sheba!' he declared with an unsteady flourish and bow.

'But I am most tired, sir,' I protested.

'Come with us, Mrs Lightfoot!' ordered Major Hanger. 'Come with us to Vauxhall, where you shall find all your friends and we shall raise toasts in your name!'

'Yes! Yes! To Vauxhall Gardens!' cried Tarleton.

'To Vauxhall', added Barrymore, momentarily distracted by the sight of a pretty dancer.

Try as I might, I could not convince them to set me free.

'Philly, no!' I commanded. 'I am in no mood . . .' but, encouraged by the cheers of his companions, my keeper pulled me into his arms and threw me like a sack of wool over his shoulder.

'No, Philly!' I cried again, in vain, as the entire party tumbled into his coach.

Through the steamed window, I watched in distress as the vehicle wheeled us down the Haymarket, south towards Pall Mall and further away from Clarges Street.

This could not be! This was not my plan!

'Philly . . .' I moaned in despair, but my protests only provoked the jests and laughter of his associates.

Into the night-darkened depths of Westminster we went, the lamps casting small pools of illumination along the streets. Across the bridge into the squalor of Southwark and then down into the fields of Lambeth, until the lights of Vauxhall Gardens could be seen shining against the moonlit waters of the Thames. Dear readers, at that moment the sight of this place held as much joy for me as might the gates of Hell.

In those days, those final years of the century now passed, there was no place in London so full as Vauxhall on a balmy summer's night. Everywhere bodies pushed here and there, infusing the air with fulsome stenches and heavy perfumes. Quindell led me by the hand through the crowd, his valet following three steps behind, portering a half-quaffed bottle of champagne. 'All hail Mrs Lightfoot!' he bellowed. 'Make way for the Queen of the Haymarket!'

Heads full of feathers and felt hats turned to observe the commotion, while I attempted in vain to hide my eyes.

'Ave Maria!' laughed Barrymore.

'Exalted lady of the Little Theatre!' whooped Banastre Tarleton.

Just then, Quindell reached for the arm of a passing fiddler and bade him to follow us with a merry song.

I was pulled deeper into the maddening heart of the carnival, with its swaying swags of paper lanterns, the singing, the cheering, the fiddler's chords screeching against the sounds of a nearby band of horns. With a champagne-addled Quindell at one arm and a dizzy George Hanger at the other, we moved unsteadily through the mêlée, treading upon ladies' trains and colliding with scowling gentlemen.

'Supper! A feast to celebrate my Thalia's triumph!' Quindell suddenly announced, directing his companions to the rows of painted supper boxes. By then our party had expanded to include two plump whores, cheeks smeared with rouge, and an Italian boy with a monkey on a ribbon.

Reader, I fear at this juncture I once again began to think as an animal might. I recalled once having observed a caged ferret twist and snap its jaws with such ferocity that it tore through the wicker that held it and escaped down a lane to freedom. I believed myself near to doing the same. With my arms restrained at either side, I felt my breath come in hard bursts. I shut my eyes and tightened my jaw. I would run, I told myself. I would fly as soon as Quindell loosened his grip.

But he did not.

We moved into the box, Quindell's arm still proudly interlaced with mine, and Hanger pinning me against him at the other side, his fingers toying with my thigh until I smacked them down. The two lardy whores sat at the end, entertaining Barrymore and Tarleton as the gentlemen hallooed and called out to their acquaintances.

'My gifted Mrs Lightfoot has made her début at the Haymarket tonight!' Quindell announced to all who would listen, and, sour-faced, I accepted their well wishes. My ability to raise a smile had long since left me.

They called for punch and more champagne. Liveried waiters hurried with bottles and glasses, elbowing their way through those who had stopped and gathered at our table. A bubbling slipper was placed in my hand.

'To Mrs Lightfoot,' they toasted. Quindell rose to his feet with difficulty. 'And good sirs, do not forget the gentleman who put her upon the stage with the great Jordan, with the venerable Kemble . . .'

'To Quindell!' the party cried.

He smirked and held his glass aloft. 'To you, gentlemen! To all the fair ladies who grace the stage! To Jordan, to Farren, to Siddons! To Lightfoot, whom I have placed among them! To my fair Thalia, who all the world will admire . . .'

I studied my keeper as he spoke his absurd panegyric, as if he believed he was some ancient orator. The words had begun to run into a long rambling stream.

'. . . I, dear friends, I shall be the envy of every man alive, so I shall . . . to have this celebrated queen of comedy upon my arm . . . They shall look longingly at my fair muse and desire her for their own . . . but, good sirs, she is mine . . . even His Royal Highness has displayed his desire for my Thalia, hey? What about that, Ban, is she not like your Perdita, hey? Desired by the Prince of Wales. Is she not as lovely, and much younger still than Mrs Robinson, who lies abed an invalid, hey?'

Ban Tarleton did not respond favourably to this thoughtless reference. It was well known that the once-fêted Mrs Robinson had suffered cruel treatment at his hand.

405

'That, sir, is enough!' he shouted, stabbing his finger at Quindell. Tarleton attempted to rise, but was now so laden with drink that he was incapable of pushing himself from the table.

I returned my gaze to Quindell, who had completed his speech but remained upon his feet, rocking where he stood. His mouth hung flaccid, while his eyes and thick brows seemed to sag at their corners. I stared at him for another moment, until a great realization struck me. How had I failed to appreciate this? As I watched him in all his unashamed stupidity, I soon came to understand that Quindell was desperately, perilously and irrevocably drunk.

Hanger's face, too, had slid into a delirious simper, while Barrymore and the two buxom Cyprians had strayed from the table.

It was then as if the dawn had broken. I could see my escape as plainly as day. I began to giggle and then to laugh harder until I positively shook with mirth.

'It is the champagne!' burbled Quindell

But it was not the champagne that caused me to laugh.

I had only to sit there, perhaps an hour longer. In that time it was remarkable how my spirits lifted. Why, I had changed from a huffy, dour madam to a lively spark, who called out constantly to the waiters, demanding that the gentlemen's glasses be refilled. 'Brandy!' I cried. 'And a bottle of Madeira!'

It worked like poison. Two more glasses, perhaps three for Hanger, before I had the pleasure of observing each of them slip like infants into sleep. After emptying the contents of his stomach at the side of the table, Quindell was the last to slump into a comfortable stupor, his chin still glistening with vomit.

I placed my hand lightly on his arm, but he did not stir.

'Farewell, dear Quindell,' I whispered.

Chapter 43

Lucy had waited up for me in the hall. She had drifted off to sleep in a chair, but sprang to her feet when she heard the door open.

'Oh madam,' she cried, blinking her tired eyes, 'I did begin to fear that something had befallen you!'

'I could not take my leave,' I explained.

She examined my attire with a puzzled look.

'You must assist me out of this. Immediately.'

We hurried to my apartments, where the familiar scene of packed boxes greeted me once again. By the light of a single candle, she pulled me free of my bodice and released me from the heavy cage of my costume. We changed my drenched chemise, stays, skirt and stockings for fresh ones before she placed me into my travelling attire: a tea-coloured riding habit, fit for the dusty summer roads. At last, my face was washed free of powder and paint and Maria's girlish ribbons were plucked from my coiffure. I paused for a moment after catching sight of myself in the looking glass. I could not help but recall the frightened Miss Ingerton, who had dressed herself in the early hours of the morning before throwing herself upon the mercy of the world. Even when free of the carmine and powder, the reflection that regarded me bore little resemblance to her.

My tardy return to Clarges Street signalled the start of a great scramble. A housemaid ran to fetch the coachman and the footman who would ride with us and offer a degree of male protection upon our journey. I was profoundly grateful that my household, though in

Quindell's pay, were complicit in aiding my plans, which was due, I believe, not only to the considerable bribes I had paid them, but to the fact that I had treated them with kindness, and done my best to fatten them with puddings, chickens and pies. Not one utterance of dissent was ever heard. They each understood perfectly that they were to say nothing to Quindell, only that I had left in the middle of the night with no indication of my destination.

While my coach was brought and my trunks and baskets loaded upon it, I had two parting tasks to complete. The first of these was to pen a brief note to my keeper. One vice of which I may never be accused is that of ingratitude. Before I took my leave of him for ever, I wished Quindell well, and expressed my pleasure in granting him, 'even for one night, the joys of seeing his mistress upon the stage'. Then, after sealing my note, I laid next to it the miniature portrait he had given to me, in its frame of shining brilliants.

It is worthy of mention that I heard, many months later, that the Boy Barbadian wasted scarcely a handful of days in mourning my departure. He immediately found a balm for his broken heart in Miss Mary Anne Greenhill, who, it was reported, made her unexpected theatrical début in the part of Maria on the night following my disappearance. *Bon Ton* magazine reported that 'The Greenfinch has indeed flown Lord S—n's nest and now soars about town with a diamond miniature of Mr Q—l at her proud breast.'

My final deed before quitting the house was to take from my pocket two keys I kept upon a ring. I had learned well the lessons from my past. I had come to understand that I must never trust anyone, no matter how intimate, with my most precious possessions. To this day, I maintain always on my person a small pouch in which is kept the little metal objects that unlock my prized items and my secrets. With the long key, I opened a small inner drawer within my linen press and removed from it a copper box in which was stored the purse containing funds enough for me to travel from London to Calais.

You see, I had become very clever. This purse, which I would carry in my pocket in the conventional manner, contained only a fraction of my recently accumulated wealth. I was not the fool I had been in earlier days, when I had counted my coins upon a tavern table and offered my entire purse for pillaging by the stagecoach driver. I would not be so blockheaded as to wear jewels that could be stolen from me, or embark upon a journey without some understanding that strangers rarely ever offered kindness for no return. No, I knew better now, which was why I had instructed Lucy to devise a hidden network of pockets to be sewn into two of my travelling gowns. Around the hem were open pouches into which my jewels had already been secreted, while the linings of my bodices contained slits into which my banknotes were placed. Why, it might even be said that Lucy's alterations had greatly increased the value of my travelling attire.

It was nearly three o'clock when I boarded my coach. The sun would be appearing in a few hours, but I knew very well that Quindell would not be stirring until the late afternoon. By the time he made his way to Clarges Street I would be in Dover, and far beyond his reach.

As my coachman flicked his whip, my heart leaped. I wore the broadest smile that I can heretofore remember. Through the window I bade farewell to my modest townhouse, to Piccadilly and the gates of Green Park. I allowed my eyes to linger on Arlington Street as we passed it and thought of the dear owner of number 5, with whom I would soon be reunited. It would be only a matter of days, I told myself, days which would become hours, which would reduce into minutes. Minutes before he would hold me. Only movements of a watch hand.

The coach rocked us through the London roads I had come to know, along Haymarket and past the Little Theatre, sleeping in darkness after its evening of entertainment. Once more that night, I crossed Westminster Bridge, but this time we continued east, rather than west, beyond the stinking tanneries, the breweries and dyers, the manufactories and lumber yards. I pulled my shade against the miseries that night drew out in this place: the scenes of destitution, the shadowy figures, limping and roving like demons. I thought of my bodice of banknotes and wrapped my arms around myself.

When I next lifted the shade we were in countryside and well upon our route to Dover. London was mere dust behind me and the sun's brightness was already beginning to warm the horizon.

Shortly after dawn, we stopped to breakfast and rest the horses before carrying on for several hours more down the Canterbury Road to Kent. As you might imagine, I was a good deal tired by then for I had enjoyed not a moment's rest, but, I confess, on that morning my appetite for sleep had entirely disappeared. I wished to remain alert for every moment I could endure, observing the sky mature into its daytime hue, listening to the summer birds call out within the trees, thinking all the while of my beloved, breaking the seal upon my letter at Dessien's Hotel, waiting every day for my appearance.

As you may know, it is near eighty miles from London to Dover, and in 1791, that was a considerable distance. Now the roads are greatly improved and with the invention of steam locomotives, anything seems possible, but in my day it required a good twelve hours or so of journeying. Eventually I gave up my vigil and was softly bounced into a slumber. I dare say this was quite fortunate, for the winding roads of Kent were to prove by far the gentlest leg of my travels and sleep would not again come so easily.

By the time we arrived in Dover it was late at night and I had no hope of boarding a ship. With the assistance of Lucy, who was as washed of life as her mistress, I procured lodgings at the Mermaid, a clean but weather-worn inn. I sent her early the next morning to purchase for us a crossing upon the first packet ship due to leave port, but much to my dismay I learned that this would not be until that evening. Oh readers, imagine: I felt myself so near and yet unable to speed my progress across the sea. Why, I could look out from the hills of the town and see the very shores of France!

Until we boarded the vessel, I spent the tedious day in a state of profound agitation, fretting constantly about our voyage. I had never been upon a ship, and this one did not appear so grand or sturdy as I had pictured. In addition to the sacks of post there were a great many passengers aboard it: fat Dutchmen speaking garrulously through their noses; Frenchmen with horse-like teeth; a collection of Jew bankers; and a large family of acrobats en route to Lille. Although I had seen many a dark face in London, and heard all manner of languages spoken, while in Dover I was dazzled by the spectacle of foreigners and shouting sailors, uniformed men and those in styles of dress I had never before seen. I looked all about me on this ship and saw not a single soul whom I might know as a friend. It was only then that the enormity of my undertaking came over me: I was departing England.

Fear sank into me, but it was too late to abandon my plan. I had paid my £8 4s. for the passages of my household and the additional £1 6s. expense entailed in the dismantling and shipping of my coach. I sat in my narrow, oak-panelled berth, listening to the sailors' footsteps on the deck above. I had no need to be frightened, I scolded myself, for Allenham was there; my beloved was in Calais. Without him, England held nothing for me.

We did not put to sea for some time, for, as the captain instructed me, there were strong winds in the Channel and storms that looked likely to impede our progress. Noting my concerned expression, he jested that I should make myself comfortable.

'Do you sleep well, madam?' he asked. When I responded that I was not known to, he drew in his breath: 'Then take no supper, only brandy to ease your way to sleep. And, if you will forgive my indelicacy, do keep your chamber pot near.'

Having never before embarked upon a journey such as this, I did not quite comprehend his advice, but after we had quit the smooth waters of the harbour, I immediately came to understand his meaning.

Since my departure from Melmouth, I never was made to feel more like a helpless child than I did during that night upon the seas. We sailed inside an inkpot of blackness, the waves pitching our frail packet this way and that, as if we were tumbling freely through nothingness. The walls of my berth rose and fell; my small wooden chair was thrown from one end to the next by some angry, unseen hand. To dispel the darkness I had lit the two lamps upon the walls, but soon grew so terrified that the candles would fall free and set my room alight that I extinguished them. Without their glow, I was left entirely to the terrors of the night and cruelty of the sea. I sat upright in my hard bed, weeping, as Nature sent her brutal forces to battle us: the lashing waters, the howling winds and relentless rain. Oh, and if this did not provide distress enough, I was soon afflicted by the most incapacitating sickness. The captain's words rang in my ears as I clung with one hand to my chamber pot and with the other to the wall beside my bed, fearing that the waves should break through at any moment and sweep me away. Soon all below deck were stricken equally, and the sounds and stench of their evacuations were unavoidable. I have never known a hell quite like the hull of a ship and, since that most wretched of experiences, have come always to dread sea crossings.

We were eight hours at the mercy of the Channel, which a fellow passenger informed me was not so bad as seventeen hours, which he had once had the misfortune to endure. By the break of morning, the worst of the storm had passed and the seas flattened, which permitted those on board to rest before the packet made its way towards the harbour of Calais. In spite of a weakness in my limbs, I wished to rise and dress as soon as I spied daylight for I knew us to be near. All at once I swore I could not tolerate my confinement a moment longer, or the suffocating dampness of the berth heavy with the stink of vomit.

'I am in need of air,' I complained, and with an impatience most uncharacteristic, I insisted on being dressed that very instant. Lucy was still attempting to affix my hat to my head when I pushed through the door and up the stairs to daylight.

There before me, against a marbled sky of grey, white and blue, could be seen the spires and scenery of the town, and just beyond it, a large fortress and a harbour tangled with sails and masts. The sight caught my heart unaware, but the wind whipped away my rapturous exclamations, carrying them, I imagined, into the port ahead of us. Oh, would that I could travel with the force of the breeze, thought I, and fly like a silk handkerchief to the shore.

I remained upon deck for the remainder of the journey, watching as the land grew before us, until I could see the figures, carts and horses, the streets and houses.

After weighing anchor, a small fleet of rowing boats approached the ship and the passengers were assisted down a rope ladder to a waiting skiff. This situation somewhat distressed me and the other members of the fair sex, for my shoes, though sturdy enough, were by no means suited to such an activity. How frightened I was to be taken under the arm of a sailor smelling of mouldy linen, who, with a clay pipe clenched between his teeth and my small form beneath one arm, portered me down to the rowing boat, laughing all the way at his good fortune.

Once the boat had been filled with its cargo of pale and dismayed passengers, we were rowed to the shore. I cannot convey to you, friends, my sensations upon reaching land, for my legs shook like those of a newborn colt and my head rattled as though full of water. My cloak and riding habit were soaked with sea spray, so much so that one might have guessed we had swum the final leagues to the shore. But our trials did not end once upon dry earth. Oh no, I was not free to speed away to Dessein's just yet, for there was all manner of business to tend to; the *passavant* to be issued, my presence to be registered in a large ledger – gracious heavens, it all proved too much to bear! These French officials took more liberties than any servant of His Majesty I had heretofore met with; they bowed and offered a good deal of politesse, before asking of me in rough Picardy accents the nature of my business, then sneering and leering at whatever answers I produced. The Customs men were no better; in fact, I was made to withstand even more shameful indignities. All of my trunks were opened and my belongings thrown about; my linens, stockings, gowns. No bandbox was safe from their grime-stained fingers. This disgraceful scene continued until they saw the look of distress upon my face and held out their paws for an appropriate 'tax'.

When at last they pronounced my examination to be at an end, I stood for a moment hardly able to grasp their words.

'*Merci, mademoiselle*,' said the unshaven deputy in his cockaded hat. 'To where do you repair now?'

So exhausted and manhandled had I been, so tossed about and sickened, that I could barely make sense of my surrounds. I looked at him and at last uttered the name I had been wishing to pronounce for a week: 'L'Hôtel de Dessein.'

With my belongings, my servants and my assembled coach to follow, I asked to be taken post-haste to the hotel on the rue Royale.

My breath was now coming so quickly that I feared I might expire as I stepped into the sedan chair. My stomach, though empty, churned with great force as the chairmen hurried me along the route. My beloved was now but minutes, but paces from me! I looked through the glass, searching for a chance glimpse of him as they turned towards the hotel, surrounded by its high yellow stone walls. Through the arches we came and into the courtyard of what looked to be a bustling country château. The chairmen deposited me at the foot of a double stair leading to the doors, whereupon I was greeted by a servant.

'Monsieur Dessein,' I breathed, all in a fluster, 'I must see him.'

Without delay, the servant showed me into the hall and went to fetch the proprietor.

No more than a minute passed before I was met by a short, round gentleman who strode towards me with the purposeful air of a butler. After introducing himself as Dessein, I inhaled and presented him with a nervous smile.

'I would like to see the Baron Allenham,' I stated, my voice trembling.

Dessein, ever accustomed to pleasing, turned his expression into a mirror of my own.

'Ah!' he exclaimed. 'Yes, I know the name.'

His words of recognition threw an instant clap of sunshine across my face. I beamed with hopeful anticipation.

'And who, if I may enquire, are you to him, mademoiselle?'

It was desperation that drove me directly into a lie. My lips were moving before my mind had completely formulated a response.

'I am Lady Allenham, the Baron's wife.'

Dessein's eyebrows raised into two happy arches, 'Ah,' he said again with an obsequious bow, 'do forgive me, my lady. I believe I have something here for you.' As my pulse galloped, the proprietor excused himself to retrieve this item, this sign which my beloved had left for me.

He returned with a polite smile and a letter in his hand.

'Now that you have arrived, I can commit this in your care, safe in the knowledge that your husband will receive it.'

Even before I took the small packet from him I recognized the writing, and upon spying it, all my joy, my certainty and anticipation melted away.

I had no doubt that my letter had arrived at Dessein's, for there, in my hand, was the proof, and proof also of that which I had refused to consider from the outset of this long, hazardous and tiring journey: proof that Allenham was not here.

Chapter 44

One cannot fault Monsieur Dessein. In his lifetime as a hotel proprietor, I do not doubt he had seen every charade, every trick, every expression of weakness to which the human soul is prone, but still he possessed enough understanding to recognize a case of true distress when it was laid before him. With my senses so shaken from my crossing and my body so weakened, I am afraid I was reduced to tears as I explained my story.

'My husband', I sniffed, 'had directed me to come to him in Calais. I received word from the comte de Laveret that he met with him in this hotel not a fortnight ago.'

'Ah,' said the proprietor, his face now moulded into an expression of deep sympathy, 'a fortnight you say? A fortnight? I fear there is no telling where he may be, my lady, and the fact that the good comte met with him at my hotel does not mean that your husband was resident here. Why, he may have been a patron of any hotel, though if he is an Englishman, I cannot think of any other house in Calais beyond mine where he might have resided, for all your countrymen stay at my establishment,' he concluded with a slightly insensitive, self-satisfied nod. 'But I shall consult my records and see if his lordship was ever among my guests.'

Dessein then offered me a modest set of rooms in his hotel, apologizing profusely that, due to the disturbance in Paris, he found himself 'near entirely full of your countrymen, and many of mine, wishing to make their passage to London or Brussels. Alas, I am besieged daily by these refugees, supporters of the King and those fearful of the mob. It is an uncertain time, my lady, but a good one in which to be an hotelier.' He gave a little laugh. 'Now, you must rest and take some nourishment.'

To this I agreed and soon after found myself alone in my small drawing room. Only then did I give in entirely to my despair.

It was not until the following morning that I emerged, dressed, composed and utterly firm in my determination to locate my beloved. I had reasoned with myself that the comte would not have taken such pains to discover me merely to relay a falsehood, and if Allenham had been at Calais, then certainly there should be some in this place who knew him and his whereabouts. Monsieur Dessein, however, came to me early with discouraging news.

'I am sorry to report, my lady, that I have been unable to find your husband's name among my books. He has neither resided here, nor hired a vehicle from me, nor exchanged money.'

The proprietor noted my look of disappointment.

'But this is not to say that he was not here, that he did not dine here, which may have been the circumstances in which he met with the comte de Laveret, whom I know to have been among my guests.'

'It is possible, then, that he resided elsewhere?'

Dessein's face appeared doubtful, but he smiled obligingly.

'Anything is possible, my lady.'

My thoughts now began to dance in many directions.

'Then I should like to know the names of the other establishments in Calais where his lordship may have lodged. I shall send enquiries to the proprietors of these places,' I resolved.

Dessein held his smile gracefully as he composed a list of his competitors in the town. After making his bows, I set about writing, in my best French, six letters of enquiry, which were later dispatched by a hotel waiter. After completing this task, I then took up my pen once more and, with the assistance of my agreeable host, composed further missives to the five of Dessein's guests who had been in residence at the time of Allenham's appearance. I was pleased to find that this produced an immediate response from a gentleman by the name of Townsend, who claimed to have knowledge of his lordship.

Fired by a sense of renewed hope, Dessein brought me to the salon of his hotel where I was introduced to Mr Townsend, a man who, the proprietor explained, lived permanently at his establishment, so as to evade his creditors in London. But my heart dropped when I laid eyes upon the aged fellow in an unfashionable bag wig and faded velvet coat, and it fell further still when he began to reminisce about his days in Turin, when he dined 'near every evening at the palazzo of the Minister Resident', which was, he admitted, 'in the year 1770, before your birth'.

It was following this unsuccessful encounter that I began to grow truly despondent. I simply could not stay where I was, wringing my hands, awaiting responses that I feared might not arrive. What if Allenham were lodged near by? What if he might be preparing to depart tomorrow, or even tonight? Such are the thoughts of the distressed. Reason soon gives way to panic.

I summoned Lucy to me and directed her to call at every hotel and place of resort in Calais, enquiring for his lordship.

I saw in her eye some hesitation as she curtseyed, but paid no heed to it. It would have been unseemly for a lady to undertake such an endeavour, traversing the streets and byways of an unknown port, visiting all manner of tavern and lodging in search of a gentleman whom she called her husband. Why, no one would have believed my story. But it was to this act that I feared I would be reduced when my maid returned to me late in the evening, bearing an expression stricken with distress.

'Oh madam,' she began, her face pursed so as to restrain the tears, 'I have called at all the hotels upon the lists and . . . and . . .' She began to quiver. 'I am afraid I speak no French.'

Poor dear Lucy. I had been wicked in causing her to suffer so.

I passed a second night at Dessein's Hotel having made no further progress in my quest. I rose from my bed and under the moonshine paced and wept as might a madwoman. 'What am I to do?' I cried. 'What am I to do now?' But I knew very well what I must do.

The next morning, I dressed, as might a modest but wealthy English wife, in a redingote. I wore no jewels, no ornamentation of any sort. I requested that Lucy accompany me on my foray into these foreign and most daunting streets. And so, having had no response from the correspondence that I had dispatched the day before, I set out on foot in what was my final hope of locating Allenham.

I had understood from the moment of my arrival in this place that I was no longer in England, for the houses, the churches, the very colour of the stone was of a sort I had not before seen. The manner of dress, the vast number of townsfolk without shoes, or who tripped about in clogs, astonished me. But I had viewed this carnival of oddities from within the privacy of a sedan chair, and now, well now, dear friends, I found myself amongst it, carried within this vast stream of peculiarities and unknown menaces. For all that I had learned of France and all that I had read of its literature and its philosophies, this was not how I had imagined it. The great words of Voltaire and Montesquieu had come from this place of squalidness, where monks walked about in sackcloth and thin mongrel dogs ranged freely. This was the land on which Rousseau had roamed. It was sights such as these that had surrounded him and coloured his views of life.

Lucy kept so near to me that, on several occasions, I felt her hand brush against mine. I do not know what she had seen and encountered when I had so thoughtlessly sent her off into the night, but whatever it might have been, it had caused her to become powerfully suspicious of this place.

Carts and carriages, the design of which I had never seen, jostled us. Mules were taken through the streets. Songs were sung that I had never heard before.

With so many distractions, it proved vastly difficult to locate the first of my intended destinations, the Lyon d'Argent, a hotel only slightly smaller in size than Dessein's. Upon approaching the place, I was met by the proprietor, to whom I made my enquiry. Having admitted to receiving my letter, he rubbed his head and made his apologies, for to his knowledge, he had not played host to any gentleman known as the Baron Allenham.

It may come as little surprise to you that I was to encounter this response, or one not dissimilar, upon every further enquiry I made. Sometimes the proprietor would be kind enough to ask for news of my beloved among his guests of rank, of whom there seemed to be a good many. From behind closed doors would emerge liveried footmen instructed to deliver messages to their masters or mistresses, who had been living awkwardly from a handful of rooms as they awaited their passages north. None among these people of quality, or even among the well-to-do merchants, or tradesmen travelling with their families from Paris, had heard the name Allenham.

Certainly, I urged myself, unwilling to let the last strings of hope slide from me, he would appear at the next door; some person would know him at the French Horn, or if not there then at the Golden Arms; but at each inn I met with doubtful looks and shakes of the head. '*Je suis désolé*,' was forever the response.

'Perhaps he resided with some local family of, note, for there are many châteaux near to Calais, are there not?' I suggested to one.

'Madame, were an English gentleman of title to come within sight of Calais, there is but one man who would know of it: Monsieur Dessein,' came the disheartening response.

When at last that fateful moment arrived, when I had been turned from the Prince of Orange, the final establishment upon my list, without having acquired knowledge of my beloved, I had no choice but to accept the certainty of my failure. This was not a truth I wished to apprehend, but there it lay before me, so hideous that I refused to open my eyes to it. I chose instead to feel and see nothing. I stepped out on to the cobbles, slick with straw and muck, and simply stood. After several moments, Lucy lightly laid her fingers upon my arm.

'Madam,' she whispered, 'what will you do?'

I could not provide her with an answer. I felt my heart beating steadily within my ribs, my breast rising and falling with the air, but my head, my once determined mind, had ceased to move. My ears took in the sounds of fishermen calling out in their guttural rural French, the scream of gulls, the clack of clogs upon the road. My eyes filled with shop signs I did not know and faces that looked dark and alien.

'What am I to do?' I asked beneath my breath. 'What . . . what . . .' My chest now began to heave and pant.

I called out to a man in a blue woollen coat, wearing a tricolore cockade in his hat. He seemed to me to be some town authority.

'Monsieur,' I breathed in desperation. 'Monsieur, I am searching for an English gentleman, my husband . . . my husband, the Baron Allenham . . . he was here and I cannot find him.'

Although I addressed him in his own language, he recoiled from me and looked at Lucy, who bore a frightened expression.

'I am afraid I cannot help you, madame, but you may take your complaint to the police or the Governor,' he replied, touching his hat and backing away.

Now I felt I could not breathe. I grabbed my head as the street swirled about me. I began to walk swiftly, madly.

'Madam!' cried Lucy, chasing after me. 'Madam!'

But I would not hear her and strode on ahead, though to where I could not say. I searched this way and that, surveying every foreign feature of this landscape: the girls in their striped skirts; the long skeins of sausage and dried fish hanging from the windows; the gabled roofs; the painted shutters; the men in *bonnets rouges*.

'He must be here! He must be! Oh my dear love, you could not have abandoned me!' I muttered in a frenzy.

I rested my hand upon the cold grey stone of a wall, before turning my gaze upward. It was a church. As I had never before, I wished at that moment to enter it, to feel the comfort of its embrace.

Lucy found me upon its steps.

'Leave me!' I cried in despair. 'Let me be!'

I stumbled into its darkened fold; its air still hung with the richness of frankincense. This was the first time I had ever entered a preserve of Popery. 'Havens of superstition,' I had heard my father once call them.

I recall how very quiet it was, and how this stillness seemed to seep into me. A handful of candles fluttered beside the altar, which lay bathed in a rainbow of colours flooding from the window above.

There was in this sacred place all the imagery one associates with the Roman Church: the paintings of weeping Magdalenes and bleeding saints, the suffering of martyrs, the unhappiness, the sorrow.

Oh, how the tears flowed from me; and there, before the altar, I fell to my knees in despair.

For a great spell of time, I bowed my head and wept. As I did so, I plundered my memory and drew forth questionable decisions I had made. No sooner had I permitted my mind to begin to stray, to pick over regrettable incidents, to admonish myself for my follies, than my sister's image assembled itself once more from the darkness. Her face took shape suddenly and startled me. I gasped and opened my eyes, but still my head was filled with her. 'No,' I commanded. 'No!' I did not wish to believe in her. I knew her to be a figment of my mind. I had convinced myself absolutely of it. 'You are not real,' I insisted. 'You cannot haunt me.' At that moment, something I cannot rightly explain caused me to raise my head.

I had not noticed her when I entered the church, not even when I fell to my knees before the altar. She sat in an alcove to my right: a pretty statue of the Madonna; her hair was the colour of straw, her eyes two close-set blue gems. The resemblance to Lady Catherine was uncanny. A chill gripped me, but began to subside the longer I beheld her kind and placid features. There in her face lived no fury, no jealousy nor anger, only benevolence and forgiveness. I shut my eyes and thought of Gertrude Mahon's parting words: 'I remember you with fondness,' I said, my voice resonating through the cold church. 'I remember you with love.' The echo reverberated from wall to wall, and then, like the ghost that had plagued me, faded away for ever.

I warned you that there would be much in this tale of mine that would not be to your liking. Here you must prepare yourself to read one more such thing.

Ah, I see you now, shaking your head and tutting, 'So here she repents, so here she renounces her sins.' You think, 'Ah, so it is true, she gave herself over to the Catholics.' I can confirm, dear reader, I did nothing of the sort. While I may have harboured some regrets, I had nothing of which to repent.

No, my friends, instead I shut my eyes and prayed, just as I had on that day at St Mary's Melmouth, when I was not quite nine years old.

I prayed for that which I had prayed for as a girl: I prayed for love. I prayed that I might know it again.

I cannot say how long I remained there. The light that fell through the window had begun to dim. The toll of bells calling worshippers to evening Mass rang out. That was when I rose to my feet and departed.

The sky had filled with cloud and a summer storm had blown in from the sea. As I walked solemnly back to Dessein's Hotel, my head hung down like that of a penitent monk. My face stung with grief.

My rooms lay in shadow when I entered them. Though Lucy was not to be found, there was evidence that she had returned. My disordered belongings had been straightened and a gown had been brushed down. It was then that I noticed something peculiar: a book left open upon a pier table at the far side of the room. It lay on its front with its spine to the air. I would not have been so careless, and so I approached it, piqued with curiosity. But once I saw its title I stopped quite abruptly. My skin prickled. In gold letters I read the name 'Goethe' embossed upon it. Cautiously, I turned it over, my hands trembling.

'*The Sorrows of Young Werther*,' I breathed.

Then a warm, rich voice came from behind me and cited the very passage which lay open before me.

'"Once more I am a wanderer, a pilgrim, through the world. But what else are you?"'

For a moment I stood entirely still, incapable of making any motion at all. My eyes remained locked upon the sentence before me. I could scarcely draw breath. That which I had heard, I dared not believe. For all my attempts to flee that had come to nothing, for my struggle to free myself from Quindell, for the hardships endured during my crossing, for the disappointments I had met with upon arriving in Calais – tell me, dear friends, what human breast could suffer such defeats and live to hope once more? I could not bring myself to turn, to confirm with my own eyes that he was indeed real, for I feared too much that he would not be.

I remained there, composed, my quaking hands steadied upon the open pages of Goethe's work. I felt the smooth, dry leaves of paper – *these were real*. The stiffness of the binding below them, resting against

423

the table . . . *this too was real*, affirmed my rational mind. This was no dream, no projection from my head. I was finished with fantastical imaginings, I had laid the last of those to rest. I pressed my palm firmly against the page. *No, it was real – so he must be.*

Gently, cautiously, I began to turn, still doubting, still fearing all the while that I should find myself mistaken, that he should prove nothing but another shadow.

'George . . .' I murmured.

I could not look at him, even when he stepped towards me. I could not lift my head. Even when he drew me into an embrace, even when I inhaled the warm familiarity of him, the faint scents of lavender and citron, the heat of his person, glowing through his silk waistcoat and his linen shirt. Even when I felt him against me, solid and strong. Even withstanding these indisputable proofs, I dared not gaze at him.

He moved his cheek upon mine, and when at last our lips met, my eyes had already been closed for some time.

Oh reader, I blush to recall those kisses, their honesty and urgency. How we embraced and caressed – as if they were the first kisses, as if we were in the closet at Herberton, amid the gems and treasures. It was only after that, when I understood this to be no dream, that I opened my lids and beheld him.

His luminescent eyes, bright azure and rimmed with tears, gazed back at me.

'I did not think it possible . . .' he whispered against my temple, my cheeks now streaming with tears of delight. 'I did not at first believe it when I heard the news: my wife had arrived at Dessein's?' he said, in mocking disbelief. Then, all at once, he collapsed into laughter. It came as a roar of pure joy, a cry of the fullest relief. Within an instant, I too was overcome with mirth. We laughed and wept and kissed, and tumbled upon the sofa, until his kisses were replaced by soft strokes of my face, and his laughter faded into solemnity.

We lay together in silence for some time. His face was a picture of adoration, and mine a mirror of his. Speech had left us, for neither of us understood what might be said, nor how to pose the questions we wished to ask, for fear of tainting our reunion. There were demons I could not bear to release into this happy scene.

'That you should come here . . .' he began uneasily. 'The comte de Lavert, he revealed to you my whereabouts . . .'

'I could not have remained in London when I learned . . .'

'Yes, yes, my love,' said he with an anguished smile, 'it is because you are brave . . . so very courageous, and because you know not what . . .' He sighed and looked away. 'It is far too dangerous here and I have taken a great risk in coming to you – in so much as sending de Lavert to find you, I have imperilled myself . . .' he said in a low voice.

'I do not understand.'

'There is no need to understand. There are many things I cannot reveal to you at present,' Allenham whispered. 'Understand only that I did not choose to quit England or to be apart from you. It was not my choice. It would never have been my choice.'

'But who . . . but why, then . . .'

He hushed me and then stopped my mouth with kisses. 'I do what I am required to do – for the greater good. For England as well as for France.'

My eyes narrowed in question. At that moment I could not entirely comprehend his meaning; I was too overwhelmed by his presence to consider the subtleties of what he was disclosing to me, but with time it came to make perfect sense.

'But you're here now . . . you're *here*!' He beamed.

'Yes.' I nodded and smiled proudly. 'I willed it to be. I made it so. You bade me to survive, to live for our reunion, you wrote as much in your letter . . . and so I did. I lived as you directed me, my beloved . . .' I paused, for even saying that much brought to mind the compromises I had made to ensure the arrival of this day. It drew from me the memory of those deceits, those actions in which I had engaged, deeds of which he would not have believed me capable. 'But I care not for censure,' I whispered.

He took my face into his hands and fixed his eyes on mine. 'No,' he said resolutely. 'Nor do I. I care not for scorn, nor remorse, nor regret, nor pain . . .'

'Nor errors, transgressions, deceptions, shame . . .' I added.

'Nor those either.' He smiled as he smoothed my ruffled hair. 'I care not for those things . . . and never shall. I care only for you, my dearest, truest love.'

'And I am eternally yours,' I pledged.

'And I yours, as no institution of man can ever bind us.'

'And we shall wander together . . .'

'And live by our hearts, and think not of what tomorrow brings,' said he.

'Nor of yesterday.'

'Nor of any other matter, my love,' he muttered as he kissed me. 'Not until morning. Not until then.'

Author's Note:
Historical Fact vs. Historical Fiction

What we don't know about the past is sometimes as intriguing as what we do know, especially for the historian who is given free rein to write fiction. Being allowed to speculate and invent has been wonderfully liberating, but my exercise in creating historical 'faction' is bound to raise a few questions among readers.

Henrietta and her entire family, including the Earl of Stavourley, are products of my imagination, as are Lord Allenham and Philip Quindell. Their characters are drawn from the real-life experiences of a composite of historical figures – fallen women, aristocratic Whigs, wealthy colonials, and young noblemen swept up in the fervour of the Romantic era. Their personalities and views of the world grew out of the many eighteenth-century diaries, memoirs, letters and auto-biographies I have read over the years.

Then there is everyone else. The majority of the other characters featured in *Mistress of My Fate*, including John St John, Kitty Kennedy, Lady Lade, Gertrude Mahon, and all the 'Avians', Lord Barrymore and his cohort, George Selwyn, Mrs Jordan, John Philip Kemble and his wife, and Richard Brinsley Sheridan, are real. Some of these people we know a great deal about, while others are more mysterious, but in this book they've all been subjected to a bit of artistic licence.

The places and most of the events referred to are also real, as are a number of the shops, inns, and eighteenth-century products mentioned. Hooper's Female Pills were advertised widely in the news-papers for their abilities to 'remove obstructions from the womb, and bring on the menses'. Blatchford's elixir is invented, but based on similar 'purgative' tonics available to women for the purposes of inducing abortion.

And finally, a word about *The Sorrows of Young Werther*. Hetty and Allenham were not the only young people to succumb to 'Werther fever'. Goethe's novel quite literally rocked Europe. In the late eighteenth century, it became a cultural phenomenon and jettisoned its author to fame. Plays, operas, firework displays, porcelain ware, fans, clothing, even fragrances were created to commemorate his book, which was also rumoured to be responsible for a number of copy-cat suicides. Where literary sensations are concerned, some things never change.

Acknowledgements

I have a number of people to thank for their considerable input, advice, support and faith. My agent, Claire Paterson at Janklow and Nesbit, has been exceptionally helpful, as has her counterpart in New York, Tina Bennett. Similarly, I owe a great debt to my editor, Jane Lawson, for sustaining me with her enthusiasm and wisdom. In fact, the same could be said about the entire team at Transworld, who have been unflagging in their optimism and hard work throughout – especially Marianne Velmans, Claire Ward, Kate Samano and Polly Osborn.

I would not have maintained my sanity while writing this book were it not for the London Library, their helpful staff and the wonderful community of fellow authors who work there, hidden away in the stacks. On odd days, I've also had the benefit of working in the Soho Theatre's writer's room, and for this I have Alix Thorpe to thank.

And finally, none of this would have been possible without the love and encouragement of my husband, friends and family. It is to you that I owe the biggest expression of gratitude.

Hallie Rubenhold is an historian and broadcaster and an authority on British eighteenth-century social history. She has written two works of non-fiction to critical acclaim: *The Covent Garden Ladies* and *Lady Worsley's Whim: An Eighteenth-century Tale of Sex, Scandal and Divorce*. *Mistress of my Fate* is the first in the series *The Confessions of Henrietta Lightfoot*. Hallie lives in London with her husband.

Visit her website: www.Hallierubenhold.com